MW01137223

The Mask Revealed

The Jacobite Chronicles, Book Two

Julia Brannan

DISCLAIMER

To Jason Gardiner and Alyson Cairns, who taught me that I didn't have to choose between love and freedom, but that both are possible. I love you dearly.

ACKNOWLEDGEMENTS

First of all, I would like to thank my good friend Mary Brady, who painstakingly read and reread every chapter as I wrote, spending hours on the phone with me, giving me encouragement, and valuable suggestions as to how to improve the book. I owe her an enormous debt of gratitude.

I also want to thank my wonderful partner Jason Gardiner, who put up with me living in the eighteenth century for over two years while I wrote the first four books in the series.

Thanks also to all the friends who read my books and encouraged me to publish them, including Alyson Cairns and Mandy Condon, who has already determined the cast list for the film of the books, and also to everyone who has read Mask of Duplicity, has given me their valuable feedback. I hope you enjoy book two as much as you've enjoyed book one!

Thank you to the other successful authors who have so generously given me their time, advice and encouragement, especially Kym Grosso and Victoria Danann.

Thanks also have to go to the long-suffering staff of Ystradgynlais library, who hunted down obscure research books for me, and put up with my endless requests for strange information.

If I've forgotten anyone, please remind me and I will grovel and apologise profusely, and include you in the acknowledgements in my next book!

HISTORICAL BACKGROUND NOTE

Although this series starts in 1742 and deals with the Jacobite Rebellion of 1745, the events that culminated in this uprising started a long time before, in 1685, in fact. This was when King Charles II died without leaving an heir, and the throne passed to his Roman Catholic younger brother James, who then became James II of England and Wales, and VII of Scotland. His attempts to promote toleration of Roman Catholics and Presbyterians did not meet with approval from the Anglican establishment, but he was generally tolerated because he was in his 50s, and his daughters, who would succeed him, were committed Protestants. But in 1688 James' second wife gave birth to a son, also named James, who was christened Roman Catholic. It now seemed certain that Catholics would return to the throne long-term, which was anathema to Protestants.

Consequently James' daughter Mary and her husband William of Orange were invited to jointly rule in James' place, and James was deposed, finally leaving for France in 1689. However, many Catholics, Episcopalians and Tory royalists still considered James to be the legitimate monarch.

The first Jacobite rebellion, led by Viscount Dundee in April 1689, routed King William's force at the Battle of Killikrankie, but unfortunately Dundee himself was killed, leaving the Jacobite forces leaderless, and in May 1690 they suffered a heavy defeat. King William offered all the Highland clans a pardon if they would take an oath of allegiance in front of a magistrate before 1st January 1692. Due to the weather and a general reluctance, some clans failed to make it to the places appointed for the oath to be taken, resulting in the infamous Glencoe Massacre of Clan MacDonald in February 1692. By spring all the clans had taken the oath, and it seemed that the Stuart cause was dead.

However, a series of economic and political disasters by William and his government left many people dissatisfied with his reign, and a number of these flocked to the Jacobite cause. In 1707, the Act of Union between Scotland and England, one of the intentions of which was to put an end to hopes of a Stuart restoration to the throne, was deeply unpopular with most Scots, as it delivered no benefits to the majority of the Scottish population.

Following the deaths of William and Mary, Mary's sister Anne became Queen, dying without leaving an heir in 1714, after which George I of Hanover took the throne. This raised the question of the succession again, and in 1715 a number of Scottish nobles and Tories took up arms against the Hanoverian monarch.

The rebellion was led by the Earl of Mar, but he was not a great military leader and the Jacobite army suffered a series of defeats, finally disbanding completely when six thousand Dutch troops landed in support of Hanover. Following this, the Highlands of Scotland were garrisoned and hundreds of miles of new roads were built, in an attempt to thwart any further risings in favour of the Stuarts.

By the early 1740s, this operation was scaled back when it seemed unlikely that the aging James Stuart, 'the Old Pretender,' would spearhead another attempt to take the throne. However, the hopes of those who wanted to dissolve the Union and return the Stuarts to their rightful place were centring not on James, but on his young, handsome and charismatic son Charles Edward Stuart, as yet something of an unknown quantity.

I would strongly recommend that you read Mask Of Duplicity before starting this one! However, if you are determined not to, here's a summary to help you enjoy Book Two...

The Story So Far

Book One - Mask of Duplicity

Following the death of their father, Elizabeth (Beth) Cunningham and her older half-brother Richard, a dragoon sergeant, are reunited after a thirteen year separation, when he comes home to Manchester to claim his inheritance. He soon discovers that while their father's will left her a large dowry, the investments which he has inherited will not be sufficient for him to further his military ambitions. He decides therefore to persuade his sister to renew the acquaintance with her aristocratic cousins, in the hope that her looks and dowry will attract a wealthy husband willing to purchase him a commission in the army. Beth refuses, partly because she is happy living an unrestricted lifestyle, and partly because the family rejected her father following his second marriage to her mother, a Scottish seamstress.

Richard, who has few scruples, then embarks on an increasingly vicious campaign to get her to comply with his wishes, threatening her beloved servants and herself. Finally, following a particularly brutal attack, she agrees to comply with his wishes, on the condition that once she is married, he will remove himself from her life entirely.

Her cousin, the pompous Lord Edward and his downtrodden sisters accept Richard and Beth back into the family, where she meets the interesting and gossipy, but very foppish Sir Anthony Peters. After a few weeks of living their monotonous lifestyle, Beth becomes extremely bored and sneaks off to town for a day, where she is followed by a footpad. Taking refuge in a disused room, she inadvertently comes upon a gang of Jacobite plotters, one of whom takes great pains to hide his face, although she notices a scar on his hand. They are impressed by her bravery and instead of killing her, escort her home. A secret Jacobite herself, she doesn't tell her Hanoverian family what has happened, and soon repairs with them to London for the season.

Once there, she meets many new people and attracts a great number of suitors, but is not interested in any of them until she falls in love with Daniel, the Earl of Highbury's son. The relationship progresses until she discovers that his main motivation for marrying her is to use her dowry to clear his gambling debts. She rejects him, but becomes increasingly depressed.

In the meantime, the Jacobite gang, the chief members of whom are Alex MacGregor (the scarred man) and his brothers Angus and Duncan, are operating in the London area, smuggling weapons, collecting information, visiting brothels etc.

Sir Anthony, now a regular visitor to the house, becomes a friend of sorts, and introduces her to his wide circle of acquaintance, including the King, the Duke of Cumberland and Edwin Harlow MP and his wife Caroline. Beth does not trust the painted Sir Anthony and thinks him physically repulsive, but finds him amusing. Following an ultimatum from her brother that if she keeps rejecting suitors he will find her a husband himself, she accepts a marriage proposal from Sir Anthony, partly because he seems kind, but chiefly because he has discovered a rosary belonging to her, and she is afraid he will denounce her as a Catholic, which would result in her rejection from society and her brother's vengeance.

The night before her wedding, Beth is abducted by Daniel, who, in a desperate attempt to avoid being imprisoned for debt, attempts to marry her by force. Beth's maid, Sarah, alerts the Cunninghams and Sir Anthony to Beth's plight, and she is rescued by her fiancé. He then gives her the option to call off the wedding, but thinking that being married to him is the best of the limited options she has available to her, she agrees to go ahead as planned.

STUART/HANOVER FAMILY TREE

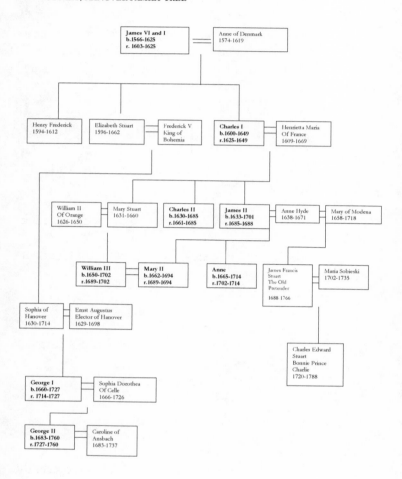

LIST OF CHARACTERS

Sir Anthony Peters, Baronet
Lady Elizabeth (Beth) Peters, wife to Sir Anthony

Sergeant Richard Cunningham, a Dragoon and brother to
Beth
Sarah Brown, formerly lady's maid to Beth.

Lord Edward Cunningham, cousin to Richard and Beth
Isabella Cunningham, his eldest sister
Clarissa Cunningham, his middle sister
Charlotte Stanhope, his youngest sister, widow of Frederick

King George II, King of Great Britain, Elector of Hanover
Edwin Harlow, MP
Caroline Harlow, his wife
Lord Bartholomew Winter
Lady Wilhelmina Winter, his wife
Anne Maynard, impoverished great-niece of Lord Winter
Lydia Fortesque, his daughter
Jeremiah Johnson, a Puritan gentleman
Thomas Pelham, Duke of Newcastle

Gabriel Foley, leader of a smuggling gang

Alexander (Alex) MacGregor, Highland Chieftain, currently
living in England
Duncan MacGregor, brother to Alex
Angus MacGregor, brother to Alex

Iain Gordon, liegeman of Alex
Margaret (Maggie) Gordon, his wife

William (MacGregor) Drummond of Balhaldie, a gentleman

Graeme Elliott, formerly Beth's gardener
Thomas Fletcher, her former steward
Jane Fletcher, wife to Thomas
Mary Swale, a scullerymaid
Ben, a boy servant

James Stuart, (the Pretender), exiled King of Britain
Charles Edward Stuart, his eldest son
John Murray of Broughton, a Jacobite gentleman
Katerina, maid to an Italian Countess
Sir Horace Mann, British envoy in Florence
Nathaniel and Philip, his clerks
Sir Thomas Sheridan, tutor to Charles Stuart
Father Antonio Montefiori, a priest

Louis XV, King of France
Marguerite, his mistress
Henri Monselle, servant to the King

PROLOGUE

August 1743

Once he'd divested himself of his shoes and his coat, he sank back into the chair, which was positioned in front of the hearth in his bedroom. As always, when he found himself alone at last, he sighed with relief. He enjoyed this nightly routine, needed it even. His days were so busy, so full of activity, that during them he couldn't take even a moment for himself. He had to be constantly on the alert, and although physically he exerted himself less now than he had ever done, by the end of each day he was usually mentally exhausted.

No matter how tired he was, before undressing and getting into bed, he would always sit for a few minutes and try to relax, to forget the worries of the day and let tomorrow take care of itself.

He attempted to do the same tonight. He stretched his arms above his head and his feet out towards the hearth, in which a small fire burned merrily. He felt his muscles and tendons lengthen, and the tension in them melt away. Then he stared into the fire and waited for his mind to become hypnotised by the flames, to calm.

After a few minutes, he sat back and sighed. There would be no peace for him tonight. He had been a fool to think there could be. He looked across at the bed, knowing he really should climb into it, and try to get some sleep. Tomorrow would be a long and arduous day, but that would be nothing compared to the days to come after that.

1

He sighed again, and looked longingly at the crystal decanter of amber liquid that sat invitingly within arm's reach on a small table at the side of his chair. No. He had had enough to drink this evening, and anyway, the only way he could calm his mind tonight would be to drink himself into a stupor, and he could not do that. He had to be sharp tomorrow; he wanted to be sharp tomorrow.

He could only hope he was doing the right thing. He was not accustomed to taking stupid chances. Chances, yes; they were an almost daily occurrence, but they were all taken with the bigger picture in view. This, though, was a chance he could not justify in terms of the cause that had dominated his whole life for the past years. This was personal.

He did not mind the risk to himself; but in what he was about to do, he risked his men, his family. He knew they thought his decision to be a wrong one, yet they would follow him nonetheless, and die for him and with him, without a word of censure, if it came to it. It was up to him to make sure it did not come to that.

In that moment, as the fire burned lower and the candle in its holder on the table guttered, he was suddenly seized with the certainty that he was wrong. His instincts, which usually served him so well, had failed him, and he and those whose lives he held so dear, would pay for his recklessness with their blood.

Somewhere in the distance a dog howled mournfully, twice. He shivered suddenly, although the room was not cold, crossing himself instinctively as protection against the *Cù Sìth,* in case there should come a third howl, and then just as instinctively glanced around to make sure he had not been seen. Which was ridiculous, because he was alone in his room.

He laughed out loud at this, and the black mood which had possessed him for a moment dissipated. He stood, moving away from the fire, and began to prepare himself for bed. His decision had been made. It was too late to go back now, and if he were being honest, he would not go back if he could. It would work out, as everything he'd done until now had worked out, in the end.

He would make it so.

CHAPTER ONE

Beth had felt somewhat reassured by the actions of her fiancé on the eve of their wedding, sufficiently so that, against all her expectations, she had actually managed to sleep for a few hours. Impressive though it had been, it was not his rescuing her from the imminent prospect of a forced marriage to the impecunious and desperate Lord Daniel that had reassured her; it was his offer to release her from her promise in the carriage on the way home that had made her feel more comfortable about marrying him.

She had no idea why he had made such an offer. After all, he had coerced her into agreeing to marry him by his unspoken threat to expose her as a Catholic and, by implication, a Jacobite. It was clear to her that whatever his real reasons for wishing to marry her, he had been willing to resort to blackmail to secure her reluctant agreement to his proposal. So why he had, at the last moment, given her the chance to back out, she had no idea. Maybe he had just acted on impulse, although it was becoming increasingly obvious to her that Sir Anthony Peters was not an impulsive man.

But whatever his reasons, the fact that at the last moment he had truly allowed her the choice, had given her a sense of freedom, a feeling that to some extent she had control of her own destiny, something she had not felt since her father had died and Richard had returned home. And for that, at least, she was grateful to him.

By the evening of the following day, however, all the camaraderie Beth had felt with Sir Anthony the night before had evaporated, replaced by renewed doubts as to whether she was doing the right thing.

Whether she was or not, it was too late to worry about it now, she reflected, as she sank down wearily into her chair at the dinner table. In actual fact there were several tables; the head one at which Beth, Sir Anthony and all the Cunningham family were seated, and the rest adjacent to it, at which all the other guests were accommodated, nearly two hundred in total.

It was a great relief to be able to sit down at last, and once settled, she slipped her feet unobtrusively out of her shoes and wriggled her crushed toes ecstatically, reflecting on the day's events so far. To her satisfaction, she had managed to drag the cumbersome weight of her shimmering gown down the stairs and up the improvised aisle in the drawing room with surprising dignity, although the effort had left her momentarily breathless and flushed, which had merely enhanced her ethereal beauty, causing not only the bridegroom but also most of the guests to catch their breath. It was generally assumed that the blushing bride was overcome with the emotion of the occasion, and everybody expected her to swoon delicately away at any moment.

They were disappointed. Beth gave her vows in a clear, confident voice. Sir Anthony, dressed tastefully for once in silver-embroidered cream silk, also made his responses unwaveringly, but as she raised her hand to his for him to place the ring on her finger, she noticed with surprise that his hands, gloved as always, were trembling as he placed the plain gold band on her ring finger. The trembling was slight, but not an affectation, Beth was sure of it. Until now she had avoided meeting his eyes, but once the ring was safely in place, she glanced up at him, surprising a look of such tenderness that she had looked away, momentarily confused by the rush of sympathy she felt for him.

By the end of the ceremony though, Sir Anthony had himself firmly under control, and any sympathy or warm feelings Beth may have felt for him had been well and truly annihilated by having to stand at his side and endure an hour and a half of his simpering, unctuous and fluttery responses to the endless parade of guests giving their congratulations. Although, she had to grudgingly admit, he was very good at it. He had managed to give a different response to everyone, and enquire after their health and families. Sir Anthony was so enraptured by all the attention he was receiving that Beth thought the wedding banquet would never be served. Her stomach was grumbling rudely by the time the summons came to go in to dinner.

Sir Anthony had disappeared to 'refresh myself a little, quite overcome, you understand, dear wife', leaving Beth to make her way into the dining room on the arm of her brother, with whom she had agreed an armed truce, reassured by the fact that he would be returning to his barracks next week, and hopefully leaving her life forever.

Her husband now returned and plopped himself into the vacant seat next to hers. He waited for a time, until the meal was under way and any comment would be covered by the chatting of guests and the clattering of cutlery and crystal, then he leaned over to her.

"You look tired, my dear. Are you well?"

"Yes," she answered curtly. "I did not sleep well last night." Which was hardly surprising, under the circumstances.

"Don't worry, you look perfectly ravishing. No one else would notice, I assure you. I have absolute sympathy, nay, may I say empathy with you. I also hardly closed my eyes yester eve. I am afraid, however, that the minimum we can do for politeness sake is to stay for the meal and at least an hour of the dancing, before we may retire to bed without appearing rude. Do you think you can endure that long?"

Beth had been attacking her salmon with gusto, but at these reassuring words her appetite suddenly vanished, replaced by a dull, leaden dread in the pit of her stomach. She was married now, for good or ill. What the distant future held for her she would face when it came. But the immediate future held the consummation of her marriage to this man who she found physically utterly repulsive. The fact that he had ridden gallantly to her rescue last night did not change the fact that she was dreading the moment of their physical union more than anything. She put down her knife and fork and turned to him.

"Not only can I endure that long, Sir Anthony," she replied with false brightness, "but I am looking forward to it immensely. One is only married once, you know, and must cherish every moment of the bridal feast." She gave a brittle smile that did not disperse the terror in her eyes.

He raised one eyebrow and smiled warmly back.

"I am delighted to hear it, my dear Beth, for as you know, I do love excellent and exalted company. And there is so much of it here! I would like nothing better than to converse and dance until the small hours, as it seems you are also inclined to do so. But please, I would ask you, as we are now husband and wife I do not think it necessary that you remind me of my title every time you address me. Anthony will do perfectly well."

He patted her hand affectionately then turned away from her to his left, engaging himself instead in conversation with Lord Edward, and managing not to bait him or say anything deliberately contentious for the whole of the meal.

Beth was left to ponder whether her rash decision to put off the dread moment for as long as possible had in fact been wise. She realised that she had now condemned herself to several hours of purgatory, with the dreaded bedding ceremony still to be faced at the end of it all, when she would no doubt be almost comatose with fatigue and far less able to cope. Perhaps it would have been better after all to get it over with early, when there would still be plenty of the night hours left to sleep in.

She picked moodily at the rest of the meal, managing to rouse herself with some effort to respond to Isabella's enraptured comments on the success of the day, and tried to shake off her dread and make the most of the evening ahead. *I'm free,* she told herself, looking across at her brother who was seated next to Isabella on her right. He was smiling as he ate, and to her surprise she realised that he was quite handsome now that his habitual scowl had been smoothed away by his imminent officer's commission and return to barracks. Society life suited him no better than it did her, Beth realised. He was a soldier by nature, and she reflected that given a different upbringing they could possibly have been friends, instead of the deadly enemies they were.

She had just started to reflect on the sort of childhood that would result in a Sir Anthony, realising that she knew frighteningly little about the man she had just irrevocably linked her life to, when the signal came for the diners to leave the table and repair to the drawing room for liqueurs, while the ballroom was cleared of tables and prepared for dancing. She felt around under the table with her toes for her shoes, locating one, and managing to push her foot into it. The other appeared to have disappeared, however, and she hunted for it in vain.

"What is wrong, my dear?" her spouse whispered. "Everyone is expecting us to lead the withdrawal to the drawing room. Are you in pain?"

"No," she hissed. "I slipped my shoes off earlier and cannot find one of them. It must have rolled away somewhere." She stretched her foot out, sliding down in her seat, to no avail. "Damn it!" she muttered under her breath.

Sir Anthony stood up, and for a moment she thought he was going to insist she accompany him with only one shoe on. Then his napkin fluttered from his knee to the ground and with the assistance of his foot, disappeared under the table. Before the hovering footman could bend down to retrieve it, the baronet had vanished under the table. Beth felt the wayward shoe push against her toes, and slid her foot gratefully into it. A second later a hand circled her foot and her husband's lips delicately caressed her ankle. She jerked instinctively, and if he had not been holding her she would have kicked him in the face. Before she could draw breath, he had regained his feet and was standing smiling down at her, offering his hand. She accepted it, blushing furiously with a mixture of anger at his presumption and shock that she had been surprised rather than repelled by his action.

He is not being presumptuous, she reminded herself, as she accompanied him from the room to the applause of the guests. *I belong to him now. He can do whatever he wants.* Which unpleasant thought did not reassure her through the hours of dancing and conversation that followed, during which she learned many things about Europe and the places that one simply must see or avoid at all costs, how to avoid being seduced by the superficial glitter of the Catholic faith when in France or Italy, and which members of the aristocracy at this moment abroad, would be amenable to a visit from the happy couple. But the most important things she learned were that it is not wise to slip uncomfortable shoes off swollen feet, when you will have to put them on again and wear them for several hours afterwards; and that you should never tell a social butterfly that you do not wish to miss a moment of an evening unless you mean it.

By the time her husband trotted over, fresh as a daisy, and suggested it was time they retire from the company, Beth's feet were throbbing with agony, her face was aching from smiling so much, and her brain had come to the end of its fund of courteous platitudes hours ago. She had now gone beyond tiredness, and while her body craved rest, she knew that she was beyond sleep for now. Nevertheless, accompanied by a few select female attendants, she left the room gratefully, in spite of the dreaded ordeal to follow.

CHAPTER TWO

When the door opened on the bridal chamber, Beth could not stop herself from gasping with shock. Charlotte had gone to town on the room. The bed was huge, a four-poster hung with a heavy royal blue velvet canopy and curtains. The bedding was turned back, and the sheets liberally sprinkled with rose petals. Candles blazed on every conceivable surface, making the room almost as bright as day, and adding a considerable amount of warmth to that given out by the fire which burned in the hearth. There was a table laden with a tray of small fancies, and a decanter of wine accompanied by two crystal glasses. Somewhere in the midst of the blazing light a small lamp burned a heavily spiced fragrant oil, which, clashing with the scent of the rose petals, filled the room with an overpowering cloying smell. Beth looked at Charlotte's eager face and summoned all her acting skills.

"Oh, it's amazing!" she said truthfully, clapping her hands in a gesture she hoped would denote joy. "You have worked so hard, Charlotte. How can I thank you? How can I thank all of you?" She looked around at her beaming female cousins, carefully avoiding the faces of the other ladies who had accompanied them. If she caught Caroline's or Sarah's gaze, she would burst out laughing, she knew it. Instead she concentrated on the rapt faces of the Cunningham sisters. They really were such good people. Beth fervently wished she could truly like them; they deserved it. She felt herself unworthy, knowing how she scorned them secretly for their ignorance and vapidity, and resolved to try harder to show her appreciation of the festivities planned for tomorrow.

They now helped her to undress, chatting excitedly all the time, the married women offering pieces of useful advice.

"It will probably hurt a lot the first time," Lady Winter said tactlessly. "But it does get a lot better after that, and can even be enjoyable at times," she added hurriedly.

"The important thing is to find out what he likes, and then to make sure he's satisfied in bed. If you can do that, you'll find it easier to persuade him to give you what you want outside the bedchamber. Men are all the same, please them in bed and they're your slaves," Sarah advised practically.

The other women looked at her in shock. Sarah was single. A single woman should not know of such matters, and if she did, should certainly not speak of them. But of course, she was only a maid. Lady Winter sniffed disdainfully and moved forward, preparing to give Beth the benefit of her years of legitimately gained sexual experience.

"What do you suggest I do then, Sarah?" said Beth, forestalling the older woman. She needed all the useful advice she could get, and knew Sarah must have slept with many men she found abhorrent. She cursed herself for not asking before, but she had not wanted to think about the dreaded consummation, and now it was upon her she realised that she had no idea what to expect, or what to do.

Sarah smiled brazenly at Lady Winter, who had been about to speak but who now closed her mouth and subsided huffily onto a chair.

"Well, this first night, I would suggest you let him take the lead," the maid advised thoughtfully. "After all, he will expect you to be innocent, as you are, of course, and he will be highly suspicious if you show any imagination. But try to be responsive, pretend that you enjoy it a little. Comments on his masculine prowess, the size of his member and amazing strength tend to go down well."

Caroline laughed merrily into the shocked silence that followed this honest comment. She eyed Sarah with interest. Not only was there more to Beth than met the eye, her maid was something different as well. She would certainly be visiting the girl's beauty emporium as soon as it opened.

The silence lengthened as everyone tried to imagine the effeminate Sir Anthony showing any signs of masculine prowess at all.

"Well," continued Sarah after a minute, unfazed by the waves of hostility emanating from Lady Winter and the Cunninghams, her mind bent only on helping her mistress. "You must make the best of what you've been given. Take your cue from him. It can be a blessing to have a man who is not overly interested in the opposite sex, as long as he can give you a few children to quell any unsavoury rumours, of course." There was a gasp of horror from the company at the forthrightness of the speaker, and Sarah reddened, remembering suddenly her position. She tended to forget this when alone with Beth, who treated her as a friend rather than a servant.

Beth heartily wished that Sarah had been a close relative, rather than a soon-to-be ex maid who she was unlikely to see much more of. She laughed.

"Right now, I would appreciate that. I hardly slept last night."

"Oh, I'm sure you'll get plenty of sleep tonight." Caroline smiled, remembering her own wedding night. "If he isn't too drunk by now to do anything at all, he'll be so eager the first time, it'll probably all be over in seconds."

"Caroline!" Isabella protested in a shocked voice. "This is Elizabeth's wedding night. We should be encouraging her, allaying any fears she may have regarding the imminent loss of her virginity." The sisters looked tragic at the unromantic nature of the conversation.

Caroline was about to say that as far as she was concerned, she *was* being positive and encouraging, but Beth broke in to soothe her cousins' feelings.

"I am sure it will be a most memorable night, Isabella. How could it fail to be, when the surroundings are so beautiful and conducive to romance?"

She brushed her hair out carefully in front of the mirror, not seeing the women's envious looks as the shining white-gold waves tumbled down her back to her hips. Then she made her way to the bed and climbed in, pulling the sheets up to her neck, although the voluminous nightgown she wore covered her from throat to ankle.

She was just in time. Outside could be heard the sound of several masculine voices in various states of intoxication. The door burst open and Sir Anthony was propelled in, accompanied by Lord Edward and three of his cronies. At least Richard wasn't there, Beth observed gratefully. She had expected the whole company to come upstairs, although the ones who were here made up for their lack of numbers with noise and ribaldry. The women shrank back into the corner, making way for the men.

The men squinted at the blaze of heat and light that greeted them.

"Well, here he is then! I hope you're ready for him!" said Lord Edward. "At least you'll be able to see what you're getting, Anthony."

"Indeed," Sir Anthony replied, swaying slightly. "If I don't set fire to the room in the process." He took off his coat with a flourish, narrowly missing knocking over several candles.

"Well, of course, you can extinguish some of the lights before you go to bed, Sir Anthony," Charlotte's disappointed voice came from the corner. "I just wanted to create the right mood."

"And you have," the groom replied. "It is most delightful.

And such an interesting scent!" He removed his waistcoat and bent down to take off his shoes, staggering slightly as he did so. His voice was a little thick. Beth's hopes rose.

"Oh, do you like it?" Charlotte cried. "I mixed the oils myself!"

"It's making me feel sick," said her brother brutally.

Good, thought Beth nastily. *Maybe you'll leave quickly.*

"It's wonderful, Charlotte," she said loudly from the depths of the bed. She glared at Lord Edward, willing him to go away, but he showed no signs of doing so, plopping down on the edge of the bed instead.

"As long as you get a good fire going in the bed, Anthony, that's all that matters, eh?" he slurred, looking across at the younger man, who was standing by the mirror eyeing himself admiringly. Up to now he had not even glanced her way. Beth realised with relief that Sarah was probably right. It didn't look as though there would even be a spark in the bed tonight, drunk or not.

Sir Anthony was now in shirt, breeches and stockings, and apparently had no intention of undressing further until the others had vacated the room.

"Come on, man, disrobe yourself. The lady wants to see what she is getting, don't you, Elizabeth?" Lord Edward roared.

Not particularly, no, Beth thought.

"I am sure Sir Anthony will join me in his own time," she replied primly. He looked as though he was as attracted to her as she was to him. It seemed that the rumours about his sexual preferences were true. The baronet sat down at the dressing table and leaned forward to peer at his face in the mirror. He reached up to remove the crescent-shaped patch from his cheek.

"What say we revive an old custom?" James, a florid-faced paunchy friend of Lord Edward's suggested, eyeing Beth

15

lasciviously. "In my great-grandfather's time the woman used to be displayed before all the company, to make sure that everything was intact, if you get my meaning." He swayed over the bed, leering. "What do you say to that, sweetheart?" His podgy hand moved crab-like towards the sheet. He was very drunk, Beth realised, seeing his bloodshot eyes. Sir Anthony had stopped halfway through peeling his patch and was preternaturally still, observing the scene behind him through the mirror.

"I'll tell you what I say to that, sir," Beth replied icily. "Anyone who tries to revive that jolly custom will certainly find that if he is fully intact now, he will not remain so for long."

James moved abruptly back from the bed, and Sir Anthony finished removing his patch, placing it on the table.

"You look tired," Lord Edward said from his position by her side. "If you need a little sleep, take it now. I'm sure it will take your husband a good half hour to remove his paint. You won't get much sleep after that, eh?" he chortled.

"The sooner you leave, the sooner we can proceed with whatever we intend to do this night," Sir Anthony said pointedly. The ladies took the hint and moved towards the door.

Lord Edward settled himself more comfortably on the bed.

"Of course, if you should find that you cannot rouse him enough to pleasure you, my room is just down the hall. I'll be happy to oblige," he said, eyeing his cousin through a lustful drunken haze. God, she was a desirable little filly! His wig was slightly askew, and his breath smelt unpleasantly of cigars and brandy. He belched softly.

"How considerate of you, cousin." Beth lips curled upwards in a sketch of a smile. "Allow him half an hour to remove his powder, and I'll send him directly to you. I'm sure you'll have more success than I in pleasuring him. And more enjoyment too, I don't doubt."

***

"Well, that seemed to have the requisite effect," Sir Anthony observed dryly thirty seconds later, as the door closed, leaving the bride and groom alone. He was still sitting at the dressing table, and Beth observed him apprehensively. His voice betrayed no emotion, although he was trembling slightly, she noticed. In spite of his effeminate ways, he was a large man, and Beth knew she had gone too far. She had never seen him intoxicated, had no idea if alcohol made him aggressive, as it did many men.

"I'm sorry," she said sincerely. "I had no right to say what I did."

He stood suddenly and turned towards her, and she shrank back instinctively.

"Don't worry, my dear Beth, I'm not angry with you. Quite the opposite, in fact."

She looked up at him in surprise and saw that he was trembling not with rage, but in an effort to control the laughter that now spilled out. It was rich and infectious, far removed from the affected titters she had heard him utter previously, and in a moment she was laughing with him.

"I have never seen that buffoon move so fast," he said in a strangled voice, after a time. "I knew you were a match for him, but you excelled yourself tonight, my love." He sank down on the bed, in the spot the previous occupant had so hurriedly vacated.

"Yes, but even so, I had no right to insult you as well and I'm sorry for that."

Sir Anthony waved his hand airily about in that familiar irritating gesture.

17

"Oh, my dear, I am neither blind, deaf nor stupid. I know what is said about me behind my back, and I couldn't care less about it. But I see I shall have to prove to my wife at least that the rumours are unjustified. It will be a most pleasurable task, I hope." He looked at her, and the tension crackled between them. He showed no sign of being drunk at all now they were alone. It had all been an act, she realised, dismayed. She huddled instinctively deeper under the bedclothes.

He reached out one gloved hand and gently stroked her cheek.

"Do not be afraid, my dear," he said softly. "I intend it to be a pleasurable experience for both of us. I will do my utmost to make it so." Then he stood, and the bed creaked a little.

"Now, if you don't mind I will get rid of this nauseating oil and blow out some of the candles before we do indeed cause an inferno."

He took the lamp and moving to the window opened the shutters and threw its contents into the garden below. The sudden draught of fresh air that blew in saved him the job of extinguishing several of the candles, and he moved silently around the room, blowing out the others, until only one remained. He took this to the dressing table and commenced removing his make-up, leaving the window open until he had finished to allow the heavy cloying scent to escape.

The fire had died down to a few embers by now and Sir Anthony had his back to her. Beth could see nothing of his face as he scrubbed at the powder and paint that adorned it. She was curious to know what he looked like, but once he had completed his ablutions, he leaned across and snuffed out the remaining candle, plunging the room into darkness. She could hear the soft rustling sounds as he removed the rest of his clothes and his wig, and then the tiny amount of starlight coming through the window was blocked out by his bulk as he closed the shutters.

She didn't hear him cross the room, and jumped as the bed suddenly gave beneath his weight. He lay down beside her, keeping a small distance between them, although she could feel the heat emanating from his naked body as she lay there in the pitch black. His hand reached out and clasped hers, then he lay quietly. She stiffened, expecting his fingers to creep up her arm, or for him to suddenly leap on her. Or something. He didn't move. Just when she was wondering if he had fallen asleep, he stroked the palm of her hand gently with his thumb.

"Would you like to talk for a while?" he asked softly. "Tell me what you were expecting from tonight?"

"I don't know what to expect," Beth said candidly, too tired and tense to prevaricate. "The general consensus of opinion is that it will hurt a lot, but be over in seconds."

Sir Anthony let out a whoop of laughter.

"Oh God, I asked for that," he said, giggling. She felt him move, and his voice when he spoke a moment later came from above her.

"Let us prove the general consensus of opinion wrong," he said. His mouth moved down to touch hers, gently. "On both counts."

His lips were butterfly-soft on hers, not harsh and invasive she had imagined. They lingered for a moment, then moved to brush her eyelids, the tip of her nose, her hair. The room was so dark that when she strained to see him, curious to know what he looked like without his paint, she could see no more than a vague pale shape, and when he raised his head a few inches away from her, she could see nothing at all. She had not known such darkness since she had moved from Manchester. In London there were always lights burning somewhere nearby.

There were advantages to this utter blackness, she realised.

When Sir Anthony commenced the inevitable invasion of her body, she would be able to see not the patched and painted foppish face of her husband, but anyone she cared to conjure in her imagination. The problem being that there was no one to whom she wanted to surrender herself, no one she trusted to care for her. She did not want this, and even though last night she had agreed freely to marry him, knowing that what was about to happen was part of the package, still she resented it deeply. This was a high price to pay for freedom from her brother.

Lost in unpleasant thoughts, she had barely noticed her husband's caresses, and where they had now led him. His lips had made a trail of feather-light kisses down her throat and over the thin silk of her nightgown, and now he gently brushed his mouth across her breast, lingering on the softness of her nipple, which sprang suddenly to life of its own accord, jerking her from her reverie as an unfamiliar, electric tingling coursed through her, coalescing in the pit of her stomach. He murmured something, an incomprehensible endearment. His lips were warm and soft through the fine silk. One hand caressed her hair. Every move was delicate, unbearably tender. She felt her muscles slacken and her limbs start to melt, and deep inside, the slight rush of moisture as her body prepared itself automatically to receive him.

A sudden vision filled her mind, of Richard's lust-crazed features leaning over her, smiling as he reached up to grab for her breasts, and the melting tingling was gone, instantly replaced by blind panic.

"No!" she cried, reaching up to push him violently backwards and throwing herself away from him. She misjudged the distance, landing heavily on the floor at the side of the bed, bruising her knees in the process.

There was silence for a moment, broken only by the sound of Beth's ragged breathing as she fought to control her panic.

"Have you hurt yourself?" Sir Anthony asked. She had expected him to be angry, but his tone held only concern. Tears rushed to her eyes, and she thanked God for the darkness of the room.

"No," she answered in a choked voice. She sniffed, and swallowed. "I'm sorry. I didn't mean to...I..."

"You are very beautiful. I was too hasty," he said, although in fact it had taken a great deal to restrain himself as he had. He wanted her, more than he had ever wanted anyone, and his body trembled with the effort of holding himself back.

"You did nothing wrong," she replied honestly, her voice steadier now. She got to her feet, and when she spoke again, her voice came from further away. "If you will give me a moment to compose myself, we can try again." Soft sounds came from the corner of the room.

"What are you doing?" he asked.

"I thought to light a candle," she said. "It is so dark in here, I cannot see anything."

"It is better that way," he replied, and his voice had an edge to it which stopped her hand from striking flint to tinder as she had been about to do. She knew with sudden certainty that he must be horribly disfigured, and that he did not want her to see him tonight without his mask of paint. It was the least she could do for him after the way she had just behaved. She replaced the tinder box on the table and hovered, uncertain as to what to do next.

"Come back to bed," he said softly. She hesitated. "I will not touch you, unless you wish it. Come."

He sensed rather than heard her move closer to the bed, until she was a faint blur of white hovering over him, unmoving. He backed off across the mattress, leaving her space to climb back into bed without having to touch him. He waited. Nothing happened.

Julia Brannan

"If I wished to ravish you, I could," he said finally. "I am your husband. No one would come to your rescue. The law says that you are mine, to do with as it pleases me. It will only please me to have you when you are ready and willing for me to do so, however long that may take. I swear I will not do anything until that time, however much I may wish to. Now, come to bed. You must be growing cold."

She came, and they lay there for a while in silence, a small distance between them as there had been earlier. She shivered slightly and he resisted the urge to embrace her and share with her the heat from his body.

"Thank you," she whispered. She could not bring herself to tell him why she had reacted so violently to his caresses, but she owed him an explanation of some sort. "I did not act as I did because you repulse me, Si…Anthony," she said. "Although you are not the sort of man I thought to marry, I am not sorry that I have done so."

"I am pleased to hear it, my dear," he replied, amused by her forthrightness. "That is a more promising start than some marriages have."

"I have had an…unpleasant experience in the past, and was reminded of it. I am sorry. It was my fault, not yours, that I reacted as I did."

"I see. Do you wish to tell me who was responsible for this unpleasant experience?" His voice was calm, gentle, but she was not fooled. She had revised her opinion of him since the previous night. Effeminate and foppish he might be. Afraid to shed blood he was not.

"No. Not now," she replied. To her own surprise her hand reached across the gap between them, touching his tentatively. The long fingers curled around hers, comforting, protective. "I am still virgin," she said. "He did not…it…" her voice faltered away into silence. They lay, the tentative link between them maintained.

He had not expected her to speak of it again, and when she did he jumped slightly, not only at the sound, but at the tone of her voice, which was suddenly cold and hard.

"I defended myself," she said. "It will not happen again."

His whole body stiffened at these words as a horrible suspicion formed in his mind, and it took all his willpower to force it to relax, to soften the rigid muscles, to lie as though at rest.

"No," he said softly. "It will not. I will defend you from others now, and you have no need to defend yourself from me. I wish to be your friend, at least, but I cannot be that while you are afraid of me."

Was she afraid of him? She had not thought of it like that before. She did not see how anyone could be afraid of Sir Anthony Peters! Yet Daniel had feared him yesterday. And she had not leapt from the bed earlier in anger, but in terror of what he might do to her against her will. She *had* been afraid of him, she realised.

"I am not afraid of you," she said tightly, and realised as she said it that at this moment it was true. He was a gentleman. He had sworn not to touch her until she wished it, and she trusted that he would keep his word. Her hand relaxed in his, and he smiled in the darkness.

"Good. Then let us sleep, and tomorrow we will see if we can start to be friends."

He let go of her hand then. She thought he meant to turn away from her, and perversely, felt strangely bereft. Then she felt his arm slide under her, lifting the heavy mass of her hair and pillowing her head in the crook of his arm. She rested there, and after a time, when he showed no sign of making any further move toward her, she relaxed and closed her eyes.

It took her a long time to go to sleep, but he knew when she finally succumbed, because she turned then instinctively into his comforting warmth, throwing a slender arm across his chest, murmuring softly as she snuggled in to him. He settled her closer to him, his arm cradling her, her head resting on his shoulder, and inhaled the sweet perfume of her hair. Then he lay sleepless, staring unseeing at the canopy of the bed and feeling the soft warmth of her breath against his neck as she slept.

He realised that his first instinct regarding the identity of her assailant could not be correct. *It is not possible,* he thought. She had told him that her hatred for Richard stemmed from his regarding her as a commodity. She had been besieged by potential suitors in the past months. Any one of them might have pressed his attentions a little too hard and passed beyond the bounds of propriety. He would believe her, he decided, both in her reasons for hating her brother and in her assertion that whatever damage her assailant had done, he had not deflowered her. Until she trusted him enough to confide in him, which he doubted she ever would, he could not act. He tried to empty his mind unsuccessfully for a time, then, realising that sleep would be a stranger to him tonight, he arose carefully so as not to disturb his bride, and opening the shutters, stood for a long time in silence, staring out into the darkness, listening to the muffled wheels of the night-soil cart as it went about its business in the dead hours, the subdued voices of the men doing nothing to allay his solitary mood as they went about their unenviable task.

* * *

When Beth awoke some three hours later, a thin grey early morning light filled the room. Sir Anthony was sitting at the dressing table, already clad in shirt and yellow breeches, his stockings gartered, his wig freshly powdered. As she stirred he turned towards her, and any hopes she had entertained that today she would awaken to finally see the face of the man she had married were dashed. He had obviously been awake for some time. His usual mask of white paint was in place, two spots of rouge sitting high on his cheekbones. A star-shaped patch adorned the corner of his mouth, and one eyebrow was pencilled in a high black arch, giving him a slightly startled look.

"Good morning, dearest wife!" he trilled. "I trust I did not wake you whilst performing my ablutions? I did endeavour to dress myself in silence."

For a moment she wondered if somehow Sir Anthony, after blowing out the candle last night, had stealthily left the room, allowing another, kind, considerate, masculine man to take his place in her bed, only returning when the first cock crowed. When she was a child, her mother had told her stories of handsome princes laid under enchantments, who only appeared in their real form at night, transforming back into frogs or misshapen beasts by day. She smiled to herself, and her husband, attributing her happiness no doubt to her newly married state, beamed back at her.

"What time is it?" she asked, stretching drowsily. She had not slept until about two a.m., and was still very tired.

"Not yet six of the clock," he replied. "If you allow me a moment to finish dressing, I will leave you in peace to sleep a little longer if you wish. I would advise it. Your cousins have a day and evening packed full of amusements planned for us. If you are to show the requisite enthusiasm their labours deserve, I would suggest that you try to snatch a few hours more repose. I will send Sarah up to attend you at nine."

He turned back to the mirror, and picking up a small pot and a fine stick, proceeded to pencil in his other eyebrow. She watched him from the bed. *No, he is no enchanted prince,* she thought. Although she had not had a great deal of contact with him last night, the hand enfolding hers had been large and strong and the arm beneath her head had been no slender twig; she had felt his bicep flex as she had pillowed her head on his arm. She looked at him now as if for the first time, as he sat at the table, and saw the powerful set of his shoulders, tapering down to a slender waist and long, strong legs. His posing, fluttery affectation, ridiculous clothes and make-up, combined with his high-pitched voice and flowery speech, all detracted from the fact that he was really a tall, well-built young man. Young? Was he?

His make-up completed to his satisfaction, the object of her attention now stood and put on his waistcoat of primrose silk and his coat of rich burgundy velvet, fussily pulling the lace out of the cuffs and arranging it carefully over his wrists.

"There!" he said, pirouetting daintily on one toe before looking expectantly down at her. "What do you think?" His coat skirt flared around him before settling into perfect folds. At least the tailoring of his hideous outfits was excellent. He smiled, his eyes betraying a tenderness that caught suddenly at her heart.

"Exquisite," she said, smiling back at him with genuine warmth. His smile widened and he bent over her, planting a kiss on her forehead. Then he turned to leave. She watched him as he minced across the room.

"How old are you?" she asked impulsively. He hesitated, his hand on the door handle.

"The eldest, and in fact only son of Sir John Peters and his wife Anna made his first entrance into the world in 1713, my dear," he replied verbosely. "Why do you ask?"

Thirty, then. Or twenty-nine, if his birthday was late in the year.

"I have realised, we are married, and I know so little about you. I know only your public face," she said. "I want to know more about you."

He cocked his head slightly to one side and surveyed her for a moment, his eyes suddenly serious.

"Let us endure this day, my dear. I have already told Isabella that we will not sleep here tonight, in spite of her protestations. I intend for us to spend a few days together at my house before we embark for Europe, so that we can get to know each other better. I will tell you anything you wish to know then. Does that satisfy you?"

"Will you even show me your face, unpainted?" she asked, then blushed. If he was disfigured by smallpox, as she was certain he was, it was up to him, not her, to choose the moment when he felt he could reveal his scarring. He had not pressured her to reveal the name of her assailant last night. She had no right to pressure him to reveal that which he wished to conceal. She opened her mouth to apologise, but he spoke before she could.

"Yes, I will even show you my face, unpainted. I think, as we are to spend some considerable time together, that would be inevitable in any case," he said. He did not seem distressed or offended. If anything, her words seemed to amuse him. "Now, sleep. I will see you later."

In spite of the sense of his suggestion, Beth could not go back to sleep. Instead, when Sarah entered at nine o' clock, her arms full of a breakfast tray and her mouth full of questions about the wedding night, Beth, rather than tell Sarah every detail as she had intended to do, found herself saying only that Sir Anthony had been a gentle and caring lover, feeling that to reveal any more than this would somehow be a betrayal of him.

CHAPTER THREE

Sir Anthony was right. She did need all her energies to survive this day showing enthusiasm. By early afternoon she was flagging badly. She had survived breakfast for thirty-five seemingly close friends, who sniggered and made suggestive comments or smiling enquiries as to the state of her health and how she had slept, in a thinly disguised attempt to discover the answer to the question no one would ask directly, now they were no longer possessed of alcohol-induced confidence. She deflected them all good-humouredly, but it was hard work, made harder by the fact that she had no assistance from her husband, who was engaged in conversation at the far end of the table, and who did not join her as she had half-expected.

In the afternoon the breakfast guests were joined by yet more 'friends' for a card party, many of whom Beth had met for the first time only yesterday. At least Edwin and Caroline now put in an appearance, and Beth spent as much time as possible with them. She had expected her husband to stay by her side for most of the day, in tribute to the romantic mood Isabella and Charlotte had tried so hard to create, but in fact she hardly saw him. He seemed to be avoiding her, and she wondered if he was, after all, angry with her, or perhaps even regretting his decision to marry her.

At dinner he couldn't escape being with her, as they were seated together. He did ask her briefly how she was bearing up under the strain, but she had barely replied that she was coping although feeling the lack of sleep, before he had become engaged in conversation with Edwin, who was seated on his right. He was at his most gregarious, keeping the table in uproar with jolly anecdotes, and she felt obliged to keep up with him, chatting gaily with everyone in the vicinity, blushing prettily at the compliments her mint-green satin dress attracted, and generally being her vapid and trivial best. It was exhausting.

After dinner the company all decamped en masse to another room, which Isabella had designated 'the music-room', although none of the family were particularly accomplished in any instrument, apart from Clarissa, who was only technically proficient, and whose harpsichord had been dusted off and moved to the improvised stage for the use of the visiting musicians. As Lord Edward was not particularly interested in listening to music in any form, it was seldom heard in the house. That his three sisters felt very differently was obvious by their excessive excitement at the thought of listening to an hour or so of Handel, Corelli etc., played by an ensemble of professional musicians. The combination of the prospect of good music and the fact that their dear cousin was so newly married to such a fine man as Sir Anthony Peters had rendered the three ladies almost hysterical with excitement, and the smelling-bottle was resorted to on several occasions.

If they were disappointed that the new bride herself showed no signs of joyful delirium, and that her husband seemed to be virtually ignoring her, they were too well bred to comment on it. Caroline, however, cared enough for her friends to ignore propriety, and approached Beth as they entered the room, where rows of seats had been placed for the audience.

"Is everything all right between you and Anthony?" she asked without prevarication. She knew she would have only moments alone with Beth before they were interrupted.

Beth's instant blush gave her the answer to her question.

"I am tired, that is all," she replied. "And he is making the most of the attention, I think. You know how he adores being at the centre of things."

Caroline was weighing whether to accept this evasive reply or to pursue the topic, when Charlotte came bustling up and swooped Beth off to show her to her seat. Instead she exchanged glances with Edwin, who was eyeing Sir Anthony with a similar expression of concern on his face.

Beth, although she loved music, was devoutly praying for the evening to come to an end, so that she could escape this situation which was becoming intolerable to her. If Sir Anthony had chosen to fuel rumours that their marriage was on the rocks before it had even begun, he could not be doing a better job than he was with the way he was behaving towards her. In spite of his consideration last night, she was starting to feel humiliated, and annoyed with him. Surely he could at least pretend *some* affection towards her, just for a few hours? She was also puzzled by his attitude. His words to her on leaving the bedchamber this morning had suggested that they would endure the day together, as companions and friends, when in fact she had rarely felt more lonely than she did at this moment, thanks to him.

Lord Edward threw himself down into the seat next to her. He was also in a bad mood, but for different reasons. He resented the amount of money his silly sisters had spent on this wedding, and resented even more the fact that he was required to be present at every tedious entertainment, when he could have been out hunting, or at his club. Still, once he had suffered this ridiculous musical soiree, he would have the joy of waving goodbye to his ill-bred, rebellious cousin, hopefully for a very long time. At least she was no longer his responsibility, and judging by her husband's behaviour, the baronet was already regretting his choice of wife. Still, too late now! Edward smiled smugly, and glancing round to make sure no one was listening, he leaned over towards Beth, who was fanning herself vigorously in an attempt to stay awake.

"Glad to see that you were able to entertain Anthony without my help last night," he said. Beth stopped fanning herself, but didn't reply to his comment, hoping he would take the hint and find another seat. "And glad that in spite of your ill-breeding you were able to hold on to your virginity until your wedding night. Congratulations."

Beth was aghast. Surely Richard would not have told him... She looked up at her cousin, her face aflame. Misreading her expression as one of puzzlement rather than shock and incipient rage, he ventured an explanation.

"Inspected the sheets myself. Only right, you know. It's tradition. Normally the father's job, but as the eldest male relative..." He smiled, relishing her discomfort. "So whatever is amiss between you both, at least I can be assured that it is not that your husband is angry because I have sold him soiled goods."

He stood before she could summon up a reply, and vanished into the crowd. She sat for a moment, staring at her painted lace fan and trying to master her rage, before abandoning the effort. Mouth set in a tight line, she gathered her skirts together and was just about to go after her cousin when Sir Anthony, appearing from nowhere, took the seat that Edward had just vacated.

"So, dear wife, how are you enjoying your day?" he began, laying a hand on her arm. She moved to shake it off impatiently, but his fingers closed around her upper arm in a restraining gesture that no doubt appeared affectionate to onlookers, but which told Beth that he had no intention of allowing her to march off and confront Lord Edward. Thwarted, she turned her temper on him instead.

"I would be enjoying it a lot more if my dear husband

thought fit to speak to me occasionally!" she hissed. "And what is all this about inspecting the sheets?"

"I am sorry if you feel neglected, my dear," he replied calmly. "I have had so many calls on my attention today, but I will endeavour to make it up to you." Retaining his grip on her arm, he leaned over to whisper in her ear. "As for the sheet, surely you know that when a woman…ah…beds with a man for the first time, she bleeds a little. It is customary for the bridal sheets to be inspected the next morning to ensure that the bride was indeed a virgin on her wedding night, and that the man has been able to consummate the marriage. Did you not know that?"

She stared at him, her face crimson with embarrassment. One or two bystanders tittered, sure that Sir Anthony was making lewd suggestions to his wife.

"No, I didn't," she finally managed to say. "But we didn't…"

"Quite so," he replied before she could go any further. "So I gave myself a small scratch and…arranged matters, in order that neither of us would be humiliated. Do not be embarrassed, my dear. In times past, the bridal sheet was hung on the wall for all to see. At least we do not have to suffer that. Smile, Isabella approaches."

Before she had registered his last words, the lady in question was upon them.

"As the musicians have only just arrived," she flustered, "Mr Johnson has kindly agreed to give a recitation of poetry, until they are ready. Does that meet with your approval?" Her eyes pleaded with them to say yes.

"Excellent!" Sir Anthony enthused. "I do so love an ode or two. You have excelled yourself today, dearest Isabella. The entertainment has been incomparable."

She blushed at the apparent compliment, and reassured, moved off to ask Mr Johnson to take the stage. He did, standing silently and forbiddingly until all chatter had ceased. He cleared his throat loudly.

"A Hymn to Virtue!" he declaimed solemnly, frowning down on his audience as though he knew them all to be guilty of the most heinous sins. Beth remembered him now as the puritanical gentleman who had sat next to her on the day she had thrown the wine in Edward's face.

> "'Hail, heav'n-born virtue! Hail, supremely fair!
> Best-loved, and noblest object of my care!
> Inspire with wisdom, in the tempting hour,
> To spurn at pleasure and confess thy power;...."'

A light spattering of applause greeted the end of this poem, which was some eight stanzas long. A vague sound as of musicians unpacking their instruments came from the adjoining room, and more than one eye turned hopefully to the door. Jeremiah Johnson smiled condescendingly at his audience.

Beth sighed drowsily and settled into her seat. It was going to be a very long evening.

"And now, a few stanzas from an ode occasioned by the recent happy success of His Majesty's troops in Europe:

> 'But how, blest sov'reign! shall th' unpractis'd muse
> These recent honours of thy reign rehearse!
> How to thy virtues turn her dazzled views,
> Or consecrate thy deeds in equal verse?'"

"How indeed?" cried Sir Anthony, springing from his seat and rousing Beth, who had been falling into a doze. "Why then make the effort? Being but recently wed, I have a fancy for a love poem. Do you have such a verse in your repertoire, my dear Mr Johnson? If so, please indulge my dear wife and I by performing it without further ado." He smiled up at the disgruntled countenance of the performer, who was not at all inclined to indulge the ignorant fop with the sort of trivial nonsense he would no doubt appreciate.

"I am sorry to disappoint you, sir," he replied. "But I have not the facility to commit to memory verses of a superficial nature."

"Come, sir, one can hardly dismiss love as superficial!" came the rejoinder. "Was not Anthony undone by his love for Cleopatra? Were not Romeo and Juliet driven to the most desperate act of suicide by their passion? Was not King Arthur's Camelot laid to waste because of…"

"Yes, yes," said Mr Johnson, thoroughly discomfited by the combination of Sir Anthony's flowery outpourings, the titters of the company, and the general expressions of relief that his oration had been interrupted. "Perhaps you are right. Nevertheless, I do not recall any poems of love. If I may continue…"

"Then perhaps I may be so bold as to recite a small verse, if the audience and my dear wife will indulge me?"

The audience made it clear they would, and Beth, who thought she would rather hear anything than forty stanzas on the military prowess of King George, also nodded assent.

"Very well, then," said the baronet, placing one lace-covered hand on his hip and striking a tragic pose. "The poem is entitled *The Constant Lover.*" He bestowed a smile on his wife and began.

> "'Out upon it, I have loved
> Three whole days together!
> And am like to love three more,
> If it hold fair weather.

Time shall moult away his wings
Ere he shall discover
In the whole wide world again
Such a constant lover.'"

Sir Anthony paused to bend and place a kiss on his stunned bride's forehead, before continuing;

"' But a pox upon't, no praise
There is due at all to me:
Love with me had made no stay,
Had it been any but she.

Had it any been but she,
And that very, very face,
There had been at least ere this
A dozen dozen in her place.'"

He bowed to the assembled company, seemingly oblivious of the shocked silence that greeted his performance.

"Em, I believe the musicians are ready, Isabella," said Lord Edward in an uncharacteristic forced tone of joviality. He never would have believed that he could feel pity for his cousin, but at this moment he did. From his seat three rows behind her he could not see her face, but the back of her neck was burning with shame and probably, he thought with a shudder, rage. Anxious to prevent an outburst of violence from her, he stood and almost ran to admit the musicians, who now took their places.

He need not have worried. Beth had no intention of losing her temper, of giving her husband the satisfaction of knowing how he had wounded her. She now knew with absolute clarity what manner of man he was. No, he was not violent. But he was cruel, and he was showing her now how he intended to subdue her; not with blows, but using far subtler methods, lulling her into a false sense of security by his private acts of kindness and consideration, before plunging the knife of contempt and disdain into her in public. She would *not* react! By an enormous effort of will, she turned and smiled at him.

"That was most illuminating, Anthony," she said. "It must have taken you days to compose."

"Me, compose? Oh no, my dear. I have no facility for such invention. The poem was penned by Sir John Suckling. It was merely the only thing I could remember at a pinch. Not very good, I own. But anything was better than an endless catalogue of our monarch's triumphs, do you not think?"

No, she didn't. He was too clever not to know how his words would be taken by the company, and how that would reflect on their fledgling marriage. *Well,* she thought, as the musicians struck up their first piece, Vivaldi's Concerto for two mandolins, *I will not allow him to destroy me in this way, make me an object of pity and contempt.*

Beth loved music, especially when played by such skilled musicians as these were, but the evocative beauty of the mandolins and the rapt silence of the audience barely registered with her as she sat, outwardly composed, a vacuous smile pasted on her face, while she fought the utter despair that weaved its web around her heart, telling her that she had merely escaped one prison for another, that she would have done better to hold out somehow until she was thirty and could claim her dowry for herself. But the deed was done. She could not undo it, especially as, thanks to Sir Anthony's trick with the sheets, no one would believe that the marriage was unconsummated, rendering an annulment impossible. No, her dowry was lost, irretrievably so, but she would lose nothing else to this hateful, manipulative man.

Vivaldi gave place to Albinoni, and then to Handel, and Beth clapped politely between pieces. By the interval she had come to her decision. She would not give him the 'fair weather' to 'love three more' days. Tomorrow she would rise early, no matter how tired she was, and at the first opportunity she would make use of the leaving present her friends in Didsbury had given her, slip out of his house, and ride post back to them. She could not bear to be alone any more, and the loss of Sarah's company was the final straw. She knew how close she had come to the edge in the past weeks; she would break down completely if she had to continue living in this way. Despite his words, Sir Anthony had no intention of being her friend. He had made that very clear during the course of the day.

As soon as the musicians stood to make their bows, she rose and moved as far away from Sir Anthony as she could, ignoring Richard, who was smiling broadly, overjoyed by the fact that although he no longer had any power over his sister, Sir Anthony looked set on taming her by more subtle means. He hardly seemed to be aware that his wife had left his side, and turned immediately to his neighbour to exchange views on the performance so far.

Many members of the audience got up to stretch their legs, accepting glasses of wine from hovering footmen with trays, and then congregating into groups to discuss the performance so far. Sir Anthony remained where he was. Beth wanted nothing more than to go to bed and sleep. She was deathly tired, and aware that she would need a good night's sleep if she were to be able to carry out her plan effectively. She would endure the second hour of music, she decided, and then plead fatigue as an excuse to leave. Once alone with Sir Anthony, she would speak to him as little as possible, and hope he would keep his promise not to touch her until she wished it. This time tomorrow she would be on her way home, and that was some comfort.

She took a glass of wine, and moved to hover at the edge of a group who were comparing tonight's performance with a musical evening they had attended some weeks ago. She drank automatically, and realised suddenly that her glass was empty. She looked round for a waiter, and as if on cue, one appeared. She placed her glass on the tray and took another. As she raised it to her lips, a slender white hand descended on her shoulder.

"May I be so bold as to caution you against drinking too quickly?" Lady Winter said. Beth took a small sip of wine rather than the huge gulp she had intended, and turned to meet the concerned gaze of the lady and her husband. Charlotte hovered in the background.

"I see you are nervous, my dear child, as indeed was I when I was newly married to the inestimable Lord Winter." The inestimable Lord Winter smiled smugly as his wife continued. "It is the most exciting time for any young woman, when she has found her perfect partner and is about to embark on a lifetime of bliss. But it is also a time when it is too easy to become intoxicated by imbibing too much in an attempt to allay one's nerves." Lady Winter glared at Beth's glass as though it contained a demon, and Beth resolutely took another sip, to let the lady know that although she would take the advice on board, she was not about to relinquish her drink altogether.

"Lord Winter and I would like to take this opportunity to wish you the greatest of happiness in your marriage." She forbore from saying that she felt Beth would need more than good wishes if she were to make a success of this union. "Will you be joining us for the dancing when the music has ended?" The poor girl looked exhausted, although Lady Winter was too well bred to comment on this.

"I would rather not, unless my husband wishes it," replied Beth submissively. "I must confess to being a little weary. We are to spend tonight at his house, where we will stay for a few days until we sail for France."

"An excellent plan! It will give you the opportunity to become better acquainted in a tranquil environment before the distractions of the voyage take your attention from each other a little. Lord Winter and I did exactly the same thing, and it formed a solid foundation for the happy life we have since enjoyed together."

Beth wondered vaguely if she would have been expected to call her husband 'Sir Anthony' in public for the next twenty years. It was irrelevant now, in any case.

"Yes, I think that is my husband's intention." She took another sip of wine and attempted to move away, intending to find Caroline and Edwin. It had struck her suddenly that if she were to leave London tomorrow, she would be unlikely to see them for a long time, if ever, depending on the view they took of her desertion of Sir Anthony. The realisation came like a blow to her, and she felt a need to at least exchange a few words with them, even if she could not divulge her plans.

"Of course," fluttered Charlotte, moving forward to unintentionally block Beth's escape route. "Sir Anthony is the most delightful man. He reminds me greatly of my own dear Frederick…oh, I am sorry…" Her voice faltered, and she raised a scrap of lace to her eyes, swaying slightly as she remembered the lost bliss of her own short marriage.

Beth was aware of a sudden commotion around her husband, who was now standing by the open door, taking a little fresh air and making desultory conversation with Thomas Fortesque, father of the beautiful Lydia.

"Oh, you clumsy fool!" Sir Anthony's voice shrilled petulantly, and she looked across, as did several other people in the vicinity. She saw that the remark had been addressed to an unfortunate servant, who had managed somehow to spill claret over Sir Anthony's hand whilst attempting to serve him. The poor man blushed scarlet and attempted ineffectually to mop at the stain with a napkin.

"Oh, don't be ridiculous, man! My glove is ruined, quite ruined!"

Beth raised her eyes to heaven and turned her attention back to Charlotte, who had gone quite pale, and was being assisted to a seat by Lord Winter. She realised that she couldn't walk away from Charlotte without the poor woman thinking she had mortally offended her cousin, and as she had no desire to return to her husband's side to listen to him bewail the catastrophic ruination of a glove, she stayed where she was, waving her fan over the unhappy widow and listening with half an ear to the commotion.

Lord Edward had now joined Sir Anthony.

"Would you like me to dismiss the fool, sir?" he asked coldly. The waiter's complexion changed from scarlet to white in an instant, and Beth raised her head. She would intervene if necessary; she would not have a man's life ruined over a trivial accident.

"No, no, of course not! You over react, my lord," said Sir Anthony, apparently failing to see the irony in his comment. "It was an accident. I dare say I am partly to blame. But even so…if you would be so good as to fetch me another pair of gloves from my room, I daresay we can forget the incident." The servant disappeared as if shot from a cannon, leaving Sir Anthony holding his hand away from his body to stop the stain contaminating the rest of his outfit, and regarding his stained glove with a despairing eye. Beth wondered vaguely why he didn't remove the glove and throw it away, but then Charlotte started to revive and she was too busy assuring the woman that she was not at all offended by her cousin's swoon and that she did indeed hope to have such a happy relationship with Sir Anthony as Charlotte had had with dear Frederick.

By the time she looked up again many of the company had retaken their seats in anticipation of the music continuing, although her husband still waited by the door, presumably for the servant to return, Beth assumed. She supposed she should go over and show some concern for his distress. She was newly married, and would be expected to have *some* feelings for the over-dramatic idiot. And the less resentment she showed of his cavalier attitude towards her, the easier it would probably be to leave his house without arousing suspicion in the morning. She would search out Edwin and Caroline once the music had finished.

She moved towards him just as the servant appeared and handed Sir Anthony a fresh pair of gloves. Now he removed the stained glove and wiped at his right hand to remove any trace of liquid which had soaked through, before putting on the fresh one. She had expected his hands to be white and soft, but they were not. Beth looked at the strong brown hand of her husband, seen for the first time, mesmerised by the scar that snaked across the back of it from the wrist to his fingers. It bisected the knuckles of the middle and index fingers, and was disturbingly familiar.

Sir Anthony pulled on the new gloves and then looked round, suddenly aware of her proximity. Her brow was furrowed in puzzlement and she was still staring at his hands. He looked down himself, wondering what was engaging her attention, and in doing so he missed the sudden look of comprehension that crossed her features as she remembered where she had seen the scar before. All the emotional turmoil of the day was transformed immediately into an incandescent uncontrollable rage, and whilst he was still examining his hands, she crossed the space between them and hit him in

41

the face with her closed fist, putting all her force into the blow.

"You bastard!" she cried, causing half the room to look in her direction. There was a sickening wet crunch and blood exploded from Sir Anthony's nose.

Even as the blow landed, Beth's common sense was telling her that she had made a mistake. Unlikely as it was that two such different men would have exactly the same scar, that had to be the case. It was impossible that her dandified husband could also be the Scotsman who had threatened her with a knife in a back-alley room in Manchester. Behind her in the room, several people started to get to their feet. She opened her mouth to apologise, half expecting him to faint at her feet.

That was undoubtedly what the court fop would do, but in this circumstance he dared not react as Sir Anthony would. She knew, and how she knew he had no idea, but if he did not shut her up now, his life would be worth nothing. Thanking God that he was by the door, he staggered towards her as though about to collapse, then, seizing her arm in a grip so tight that any incriminating words she had been about to utter became a cry of pain instead, he swung her out into the hall. Before she could react he pushed her back against the wall, pinning her against it with his weight.

"I am sorry, my love," he murmured, then brought the heel of his hand up sharply under her jaw. The wall behind her stopped her neck from snapping back and being broken by the force of his blow, and added to the concussive effect. She became instantly limp, and he stood back a little to allow her to slide down the wall, before slumping against it himself, his handkerchief pressed to his nose.

Several people now appeared in the hall, curious as to what had transpired.

"Oh, oh, what can I say? I am so ashamed!" Sir Anthony

cried out in a voice somewhat muffled by linen. Someone produced a chair for him to sit on, and he sank down gratefully, whilst several women bent over the prostrate form of his wife. One of them produced a smelling-bottle, and he prayed he had hit her hard enough for it to have no effect in rousing her.

"What on earth happened, sir?" Lord Edward spluttered, clearly upset that such an undignified scene had taken place in his house, while secretly enjoying the diversion. Alone of the company, he was not enjoying the musical performance.

"I have not the faintest notion," Sir Anthony whined. "I was waiting for the servant to bring my gloves, as you know, when a most attractive maid passed by. I merely waved and smiled at her. I had no idea my wife was in the immediate vicinity, or that she would react in such an extreme manner. I do believe she has broken my nose!" He did indeed believe she had; the pain was intense, and the blood soaking into the fine linen showed no signs of abating.

"What did you do to her?" Richard asked admiringly. His voice showed no concern for his sister. Clearly he was amazed that this dandy would have the courage to hit her back, although it seemed that was what he had done.

"I, sir!" Sir Anthony screeched indignantly, wincing as the pain knifed through his ruined nose. "I did nothing. She merely looked at the blood and fainted. I must confess, I feel a little faint myself." Richard's expression changed from admiration to contempt. It seemed that after all, this effeminate rag was still in danger of allowing Elizabeth to bully him into an early grave. It was pitiful. That it was unlikely his hoyden of a sister would faint at the sight of blood did not cross his mind.

"Maybe you should send for a doctor, Lord Edward," suggested Lady Winter, looking up from her unsuccessful attempts to revive Beth. "I did warn her earlier against

43

imbibing too much alcohol, afraid that she would become embarrassingly drunk."

"No, no, I would not hear of it. I am so ashamed. We have quite ruined your evening, and all because of a careless gesture on my part. I am sure my wife will be mortified if she awakes to discover what a scene she has caused by her jealousy and intoxication. No, no, my carriage is ready. We must leave immediately."

There were many cries of protest at this, but Sir Anthony was adamant. His wife would come to herself far better in a quiet environment, and would be more likely to accept his profound apologies for his thoughtless flirting if she were not reminded of her actions by being surrounded by well-meaning people who would only unintentionally add to her humiliation.

"If we leave now, I am sure I can persuade her that nobody noticed the scene she caused, and that we left quietly, with your permission of course, Lord Edward? That will ensure that she is not too embarrassed to enter into your company when we return from our sojourn overseas."

Lord Edward couldn't wait to get rid of the annoying couple. With a bit of luck their departure would signal the break-up of the party and he could head off to his club all the quicker. Even the ladies realised the wisdom of this suggestion, although they were a little concerned at Beth's continued lifelessness.

Sir Anthony promised to send for a doctor the moment they reached his house, which was only a short distance away, and within moments the coach driver had scooped up the still senseless Lady Peters and spirited her away.

Lord Edward accompanied Sir Anthony to the door, offering him a new handkerchief to replace the blood-soaked one he now held. He could not resist offering a last piece of advice.

"This is what comes, sir, of marrying beneath yourself."
Sir Anthony looked up, and Lord Edward held up a hand.

"I do not mean you, sir. Elizabeth is after all, my cousin,
and is well-born enough. But her father married beneath
him, a *seamstress,*" this last word was delivered in scathing
tones, "and a Scot, at that. You will have to be firm if you are
to curb the bad blood she has inherited from her mother. I
advise you of this as a friend. She must be chastised for her
drunken behaviour this evening. What man does not eye a
pretty wench, eh?" Lord Edward winked conspiratorially.

Sir Anthony eyed him with an expression of utter disgust,
which Lord Edward would have recognised had not the
former's face been almost completely obscured by red-
stained linen.

"I think I may own that I was also in the wrong to behave
so inconsiderately so soon after my wedding. I will deal with
my wife according to my fashion, my lord," he replied curtly.

Lord Edward watched the carriage clatter out of the drive
with satisfaction and scorn. It would be a long time before
they were invited back into his house, whatever his sisters
might say. His cousin would be an unbearable shrew and her
husband a doormat within weeks. Not at all an example to
show to the females of his household, who knew their place.

* * *

Beth recovered consciousness in the coach, roused by the
bumping of the wheels along the uneven road. Her head
ached terribly, and her mouth was dry. When she tried to
moisten her lips with her tongue, a dart of pain shot through
her jaw. She lay still for a while until she felt less disorientated,
taking stock of the situation.

She was half lying on the bench seat, her head on her
husband's lap. His arm lay across her chest lightly, stopping

her from moving too much as the carriage bounced its way along. She opened her eyes slightly and looked up at him. He was sitting upright by the window, a cloth still pressed to his nose. Even in the dim light of the coach's lantern she could see the dark stain on the front of his yellow waistcoat, and remembered what she had done. Feeling a little better, she tried to sit up, but his arm tightened, holding her in place. He dipped his head to look down at her, and his eyes were dark slits in the pallor of his face. She opened her mouth, and he laid a finger warningly on her lips.

"Be quiet," he said softly. "We will have plenty of time for explanations when we arrive home. I trust my people implicitly, but not the coachman."

"But what..?" started Beth. The warning finger became a large hand, which covered her mouth, smothering whatever she'd been about to say and sending shards of pain from her bruised jaw shooting up the side of her face.

"If you insist on speaking," he said, "then I will have to render you unconscious again. I don't want to do that, but I will if necessary. Do you understand?" The voice was Sir Anthony's, but the tone was not. It was hard and cold. She froze.

"I said, do you understand?" he repeated softly. She nodded slightly. "Good. And do you promise to remain silent until we reach our lodging? If you do, I in return will promise not to hurt you, and to answer all your questions once we arrive."

She had no choice in the matter, and they both knew it. She nodded again, and the hand withdrew from her mouth. He lifted her gently into a sitting position, but did not relinquish his hold on her. She leaned back against his chest, having no alternative, and they travelled on in silence.

Was he after all the man who had threatened her in the derelict room, as she had thought at first sight of the scar?

It wasn't possible, surely? The scar was the same, exactly; she would never forget that, it was engraved on her mind as the only means she had of identifying him. She had thought from his careful concealment of his features that night that she must know him, but that this dandified, quintessential courtly Englishman could be the menacing, Gaelic-speaking Scot of the Manchester alleyways was incomprehensible.

Yet whoever the man who was now holding her might be, he was not any version of the Sir Anthony Peters she had seen before. His reaction to her blow and his behaviour now told her that. She shifted experimentally, hoping he would let her move away from him. She found the close contact with him disturbing; she didn't know him at all, and wanted to put a distance between them so that she could marshal her thoughts in preparation for what looked like being a very unpleasant confrontation at his house. His arm tightened again warningly; presumably he thought she might try to leap from the carriage if he let her go. She stayed where she was, her head against his chest, listening to his heartbeat, strong and steady as they travelled through the night.

Unbelievably, she must have fallen asleep. She struggled back to wakefulness as the carriage stopped. The door opened and the coachman appeared to assist her out. For a moment she wondered whether she should declare that she was being kidnapped and throw herself on his mercy, but when she looked in his face she saw the closed, indifferent expression of the servant who will do what he is paid to do, no more and no less, and knew that the chances of him risking his job to aid what he probably thought was an hysterical female were virtually non-existent.

She looked at Sir Anthony, who had also stepped down from the carriage and now took her elbow in a firm grip.

"If you would be so kind as to bring in our luggage," he said to the man, who turned immediately to do his bidding.

Then her husband propelled her firmly away, up the steps of the house, whose door had been opened by a servant, across the hall and into a lamplit sitting room, where he assisted her into a seat and with a firm command to her to stay there, disappeared.

She sat for a moment where he had placed her, before realising with alarm that if he could trust his people, as he had said, she could expect no aid from them, and no one else would hear if she were to call out for help. She stood, suddenly panicked, and looked around frantically for a means of escape. She made a move toward the window, just as Sir Anthony re-entered the room, closing the door quietly behind him. He had a tray in his hands which he placed on the table.

"I thought you might like some refreshment. You did not eat much at dinner," he said conversationally. "Or would you prefer to go straight to bed? To sleep, I mean," he added. "I know you're very tired."

Beth was flabbergasted. He was talking to her as though they had just returned from a pleasant evening at the opera. The whole situation took on an unreal aspect, and she wondered vaguely if she would suddenly awaken in her own bed to find this whole day had been nothing more than a bad dream. She looked at the man she had thought of until now as Sir Anthony Peters. He had removed his wig, and she saw for the first time that his natural hair was long and dark. The lamplight picked out chestnut highlights in its thick glossy waves. His face was still white, but in places the tan of his natural skin was showing through and his nose was red and swollen at the bridge. It *was* broken, she thought with satisfaction. His star-shaped patch had disappeared, presumably washed away by the flow of gore, and his face was smeared, although his nose was no longer bleeding. His accent was still unmistakably English, and Beth was confused absolutely.

"Who are you?" she said.

He sighed, and sat down. He looked unutterably weary suddenly, and she was reminded of her own fatigue. Only the sense of the danger she was in was keeping her alert, but she could feel the tiredness creeping in at the edge of her consciousness, dulling her senses. She had had less than five hours sleep in three days, and he looked as though he had enjoyed about the same amount of rest.

"I thought you had guessed who I was," he said. "Although how, I don't know."

"Your scar..." she said. Her eyes flickered towards his right hand automatically, and he looked down, seeing the ridged white line that marred the tanned flesh of his hand.

"Ah," he breathed, as realisation dawned. He never thought of it, he'd had it for so long, since he was a youth. Clearly he was growing careless, he thought with alarm. Or complacent at his easy success so far. It was small lapses like that that could lead him and others to the gallows.

"You're very observant," he said wryly, relaxing into the chair and stretching his legs toward the fire. "And you have a good memory."

"I find fear clarifies the memory like nothing else," Beth said.

"And you were very afraid that night, I remember. I'm sorry for that, but I had no choice." He spoke matter-of-factly. "I suppose you remember exactly what all the others look like too, down to the last eyelash."

"I think I would recognise some of them again, yes," Beth said, consciously speaking slowly to still the shake of her voice so that he would not be able to tell that she was afraid tonight, as well. "But you were different."

"In what way?" He was interested. Small things could be important.

"You were obviously the leader. And from the great pains you took to hide your face, I thought that we may have met before, and that you were afraid I might recognise you. So I tried to memorise as much as I could about you, so that if I saw you again in another guise, I would know you."

"And presumably denounce me to the authorities. Although you didn't denounce the others, did you? You could have gained great favour from your brother if you'd delivered up a nest of Jacobite traitors to him, you know," he said. He looked across at her, a foolish-looking flawed clown with his streaked make-up, the rouge still forming two perfect circles on his cheeks, and she wondered how he could look so ridiculous and yet be so intimidating. He was tired as well, she thought; maybe if she could keep him talking, she could edge past him to the door and make a run for it. It was worth a try. Was there anyone else in the house? Her mind raced. One servant had opened the door for them. Maybe that was it. It was late, the others would surely be in bed.

"I had no wish to gain the favour of my brother," she replied with sincerity, "least of all by betraying a lot of men who…." She stopped, deciding against what she had been about to say. "I don't know what I would have done," she continued after a pause. "I just wanted to know who you were if I met you again. I hadn't thought beyond that."

His eyes were closing, the warmth of the fire lulling him, but he still caught her sudden movement as she took her opportunity and made to run for it. His hand shot out like lightning, grasping her wrist as she moved past and stopping her in her tracks.

"Don't," he said quietly, almost wearily. "Even if you were to escape me, which you won't, you won't be allowed to leave the house until I say so. I can't let you go just yet, you surely understand that?" He held her gaze with his own. She expected a threatening glare, but his eyes held apology, a plea for understanding, although the grip on her wrist was relentless. She tugged experimentally, to no effect.

"You were lucky that night," he continued. "If I'd known you understood Gaelic then, I could not have let you live, do you know that?"

She blanched. Was he trying to tell her that he was about to finish the job now? Was that why he'd married her, to give him an excuse to get her on her own so he could silence her? She pulled against his grip more frantically, trying to prise his fingers open with her free hand.

"I didn't want to hurt you then, and I don't now, although I will if you give me no alternative," he said, leaning across to capture her other hand. "I didn't intend for all this to happen."

"How long were you going to keep pretending?" she cried. "Were you going to wait until I was asleep before you murdered me? Or were you going to do it in Italy or France, where no one knows us?"

He looked at her in shock for a moment then laughed, but there was no humour in the sound. When he spoke again, his voice was softer.

"I hoped to bring you here tonight as Sir Anthony's wife, and tomorrow, when we were both refreshed, I was going to tell you the truth about myself, in private, giving you time to come to terms with it before discussing the various options open to you. Your premature recognition of me spoilt things a little." He yawned and stood, retaining his grip on her wrists. "Let me make a suggestion. Let us go to bed and get some sleep. You can have your own room. I will not disturb you. In the morning we will both be more refreshed, and we can talk then. I have a lot to tell you, and I'm sure you have a lot to ask me."

"How do you expect me to sleep?" Beth retorted, as he started to lead her towards the door.

"If you are as tired as I am, long and deeply, the moment your head touches the pillow."

He led her upstairs, opening the door to a room on the first floor.

"Your bedroom," he said, pushing her gently inside. "As I said, I will not disturb you. I have never murdered anyone in their sleep yet, and I am not about to start now. I'll see you in the morning." He left, closing the door behind him. She heard the key turn softly in the lock, and she was left alone in the dark with no alternative but to undress and lie down, where, in spite of all her belief to the contrary, she did indeed fall asleep the moment her head made contact with the soft feather pillows.

CHAPTER FOUR

When Beth awoke in the morning, the sunlight was slanting in through the pale green curtains, bathing the room in a light so reminiscent of her bedroom in Didsbury that for a moment, in her pleasantly semi-slumberous state, she thought she was at home, and half expected Jane or Grace to knock lightly on the door at any moment to announce that breakfast was ready.

Then the last vestiges of sleep cleared from her mind and she remembered with a sickening lurch to her stomach that Jane and Grace were far away, and the chances of her riding to join them today were non-existent. Instead she was a prisoner in this house, in the custody of a man who...

Who what? Who he was and what he intended to do with her, she had no idea. She sat up in bed and examined her surroundings in an attempt to calm herself. They were elegant and tasteful. The oak bed she lay in was solid and well made, as was the rest of the furniture in the room, a large wardrobe and dressing table, and a chest for the storage of bedding. The room was wallpapered in a pale green stripe, with matching window curtains, whilst the large carpet on the floor was a darker, sage green. Sir Anthony, as she still thought of him, must indeed be reasonably wealthy then, to be able to afford to rent such an elegant house and clothe himself in such an ostentatious manner. Her eye came to rest on a large leather-bound chest which had been placed at the foot of her bed. During the night, someone must have brought her trunk into the room and closed the curtains, which she now recalled had been open when she had fallen into bed the night before.

If he intended to dispose of her, surely he would have done it whilst she was asleep and utterly helpless? It was some consolation, although not much, to realise that her life seemed to be in no immediate danger. It was more consolation, she noted as she slid from the bed and peeped between the curtains, that although the sun had risen, it was still very early. The window was painted shut and had clearly not been opened for some years. Even if she were able to prise it open without alerting the household, her room was at the back of the house and looked out onto the garden, beyond which fields stretched away into the distance. There was no chance of anyone hearing her if she cried for help from this room.

Moving silently across to the door, she tried the handle, in the hope that whoever had brought her trunk to the room had forgotten to re-lock the door. To her surprise, this was indeed the case, and she eased the door open a fraction, listening carefully. Silence. Quickly she went to her trunk, and dressing as speedily as possible in her least cumbersome gown, a dark blue linen day dress, she quickly searched through the rest of the trunk for the carefully wrapped package containing the three things she possessed that held value for her; her knife, her rosary and the six sovereigns that would guarantee her passage home if she succeeded in leaving the house unobserved.

She strongly suspected that the man who called himself Sir Anthony Peters was a spy. There was no other satisfactory explanation for the fact that he moved in both Hanoverian and Jacobite circles under at least two different identities. Whether he was in the pay of the Jacobites or the Hanoverians she had no idea, and although she was curious as to which was the case, as well as about many other things concerning the man she had married, she was not curious enough to miss the chance to escape if possible.

She soon realised, to her dismay, that her trunk had been carefully searched and her knife was missing, although the rosary and the sovereigns were still there. She pocketed them quickly, and then picking up a heavy cloak she edged her way out of the door on to the empty landing. The stairs curved in a semicircle down to the hall below, and she descended them cautiously, stepping carefully at the edges of each tread so as to avoid any creaking steps.

It was with a sinking heart that she saw the young man as soon as she turned the bend of the stairs. He was sitting between her and the front door, in the very chair where she had herself sat some four months before when she had come to apologise to Sir Anthony. Abandoning her attempt at stealth, she continued resignedly down to the hall, and he stood politely as she approached, bowing deeply.

"Good morning to you, *mo phiuthar-chèile*," he said, a mischievous gleam in his blue eyes. "Your name is Beth, is it not?"

Beth betrayed no emotion at his greeting, instead looking the young man in the eye with a calmness she was far from feeling.

"You have the advantage of me, sir," she said coolly. "You did not oblige me by revealing your name when you escorted me home from Manchester."

"Aye, that's true, but circumstances were somewhat different then," he replied. He bowed again. "Angus MacGregor at your service, madam," he announced formally. "Although I generally go by the surname Drummond, you understand."

No, she didn't understand, but she was not about to demonstrate her ignorance by asking him to elaborate.

"Shall I take your cloak?" Angus asked. "Ye'll not have

need of it for the present, I'm thinking, and I can hang it here." He pointed to the coat rack by the side of the door, then glanced back at her, intercepting such a look of longing as she gazed past him to the front door, to a freedom so near and yet unattainable, that his heart was moved to pity. "You need have no fear, lassie," he said softly.

The longing was instantly veiled, and she briskly handed him her cloak, as though that had been her express purpose in coming downstairs.

"He's in the dining room, having breakfast," Angus continued as he carefully hung the garment on a peg. "He wants you to join him, if ye've a mind to." He waved in the direction of a white-painted door that led off the hall.

Gathering her wits and her skirts together, she nodded her thanks to Angus and strode to the door, opening it with a flourish and entering the room as though marching to war.

The dining room was dominated by a long table lined with high-backed dining chairs. Places were currently set for two people. Along a side wall of the room was another table with a series of platters containing various foodstuffs. Her husband was making his choice of breakfast and had his back to her, but as he heard her enter he turned round, stopping her dead in her tracks.

She stared at him, completely nonplussed. Her first thought was that this was some sort of joke. The handsome young man standing facing her could not possibly be Sir Anthony Peters. He was taller, for a start, and seemed broader as well. He was dressed very casually, technically speaking only half-dressed, in a fine linen shirt and black silk breeches. He was barefoot and wore no stockings, and his legs were powerful, his calves heavily muscled. His shirt sleeves were rolled up revealing the brawny forearms she remembered from Manchester. He did not speak or move, but allowed her to observe him at her leisure.

His face was tanned through years of exposure to the elements, and, she noted with surprise, there was no sign that he had ever suffered from smallpox. His skin was clear, his features strong and regular. His hair was, as she had seen last night, a rich dark shade of chestnut brown, now brushed and tied back with a blue ribbon. Only his eyes were the same as those of the Sir Anthony she had known for over eight months; slate-blue, long-lashed and beautiful. And anxious, she realised with a start which brought her back to herself. He seemed as nervous as she was about this meeting, although she had no idea why he should be, when he had her so completely at his mercy.

Determined to make a fight of it, she straightened and walked a few more paces towards him.

"Good morning, Mr MacGregor," she said. "Or is it Mr Drummond today?"

His eyes widened in shock, she noted with satisfaction.

"How did…?" he began, then stopped. "I assume, then, ye've met Angus already this morning," he continued, with a slight smile. His voice was deep and rich, with a soft Scottish burr.

"Indeed. I met him just now, and as he called me sister-in-law before he introduced himself, I assume you are brothers and therefore have the same surname, although whether I should assume anything about you, I don't know, as everything I thought I knew up to now appears to be false."

He had the grace to look ashamed.

"Aye, well, as I explained last night, I had intended to tell ye the truth about myself under slightly less strained circumstances. I'm sorry." He ventured a smile, which she answered with a stony look. "Why don't you help yourself to some breakfast, sit down and I'll answer your questions while we eat. It'll be a wee bit more congenial than standing here as though we're about to fight a duel," he finished.

That was exactly how she did feel. She hesitated for a moment.

"Can ye eat?" he asked, suddenly concerned. "Is your mouth paining ye? I didna mean tae hit you too hard."

"It is sore. Very," she replied, casting him a withering glance. Her stomach rumbled loudly, and she reddened slightly. "But I think I can eat a little." She bustled about, choosing some bread rolls, butter, cheese, cold meat, while she marshalled her thoughts.

They ate in silence for a few minutes at the dining table, and she glanced surreptitiously across at him whilst he was eating, noting the swelling at the bridge of his nose and the dark bruising under his eyes. It would be churlish not to say something about her assault on him, especially as he had expressed concern about her injury. After all, she had attacked him first.

"Can you breathe?" she paraphrased his words. "I'm afraid I did mean to hit you hard. I think that makes us even."

Amused by the honesty of her words, he smiled.

"I had no choice. I couldna risk you exposing me in your temper."

"Was Lord Edward very angry?" she said, sounding completely unconcerned as to whether he was or not.

"I think ye could say he was happy to see the back of you, aye. I may as well tell ye now, I had to give some reason for you striking me, so I told everyone you'd caught me flirting wi' a maid, and after hitting me, had fainted at the sight of the blood. There was a guid deal of it," he finished ruefully, gingerly touching his nose.

"Thanks," she replied tartly. "So now, as well as being an ill-bred harridan, I'm also violently jealous. My cousin will never admit me into his rarefied society again."

"I'm sorry, but it's the best I could come up wi' at such short notice, ye ken. If ye'd warned me in advance that you were going to break my nose, I'd have maybe been able to think of something that met with your approval." There was more than a hint of sarcasm in his tone, although he didn't sound angry.

The silence resumed, broken only by the clatter of cutlery and china, and the crackling of the fire in the hearth.

She was aware that he was politely allowing her to take the initiative in the conversation, and tried to work out how to turn it to her advantage.

"So," she commenced. "You said last night that you'd answer all my questions." He nodded, his mouth full. "What I want to know is, will you answer them all honestly? Do you actually know what the word means?" Her tone was belligerent, and he stopped eating and looked her straight in the eye. They locked gazes.

"Aye, I ken well what honesty is," he said softly. "I'll answer all your questions truthfully, or not at all. What are ye wanting to know?"

To her annoyance she was the first to look away, angry and ashamed that she had tried to provoke him, and failed.

"Your name would be a good start," she said icily.

"My full name is Alexander Iain MacGregor," he replied. "I'm the eldest son of my parents. For my sins, I have Angus for my youngest brother, and there's another between us, Duncan, although he's away hame at the minute. Ye'll meet him at a later date."

"I assume by 'away hame' you mean in Scotland," she said. He nodded.

Well that was a relief at any rate. If he intended her to meet his brother, he clearly did not mean to do her any harm in the near future. She thought for a moment, wanting every question to count, occupying herself by spreading butter on a roll, while her mind raced.

Whether friend or foe, he was truly remarkable, she

thought with reluctant admiration. Not just his physical appearance, but everything about him was different from Sir Anthony; his stance, his voice, accent, manner. Which observation brought her neatly to her next question, for her the most important one in determining their future relationship, if there was to be one.

"Are you a spy for the Hanoverians or the Jacobites?" she asked bluntly, watching him carefully in the hope that his eyes would betray the true answer to her query, whatever his lips might say. But apart from a brief flicker of shock at the unexpected question his expression was unreadable. Of course, he had no doubt had years of practice at veiling his true feelings, she thought sourly.

"I thought I'd made it as clear as I could where my sympathies lie," he replied earnestly. "Why else would I give ye back your rosary when I proposed to you, unless it was to let ye know that I was Catholic, like yourself? Why would I suggest that we visit King James and Charles in Europe, unless I was a Jacobite?"

Why indeed? Oh God.

He watched with interest and curiosity as the colour flooded her cheeks. She bit her lip.

"Emm...I...ah...think I may have misunderstood those gestures," she said in a low voice. "Is that really what you were trying to tell me?"

"Of course. What else would I be trying to say?"

"That you knew I was Catholic, that you had heard the argument between me and Richard and were warning me that if I refused to marry you, you would tell everyone, causing me to be ostracised from society. And when you talked about visiting the king, I thought you meant George and the duke of Cumberland, and that you were just reminding me that I was trapped, were rubbing salt in the wound." She had no idea how he would respond to her confession, and looked up at him nervously. Whilst she had some idea how Sir Anthony might react, this man was a completely unknown quantity. His face was blank, unreadable. "I was so sure you were Hanoverian, in spite of the fact that you claimed to have no allegiance. You're a friend of George's, and you've said many times that the Jacobite cause is a lost one," she cried defensively. "How was I to know?"

He leaned forward, placing one elbow on the table, and rested his forehead on his hand for a moment, before looking across the table at her. His eyes were soft, gentle, not at all angry. When she would have looked away, he reached across and placed his hand under her chin, turning her head back towards him.

"I see now that there have been many misunderstandings between us. I'm sorry, but I couldna be more open with ye then. I think perhaps I should tell you a wee bit about myself, so you can judge me better." He removed his hand from her face and sat back in his seat.

His touch had been disconcerting, and for a few moments after he had removed his hand, she could still feel its warmth against her skin. She had an irrational urge to stroke the place where his fingers had been, and mastered it with difficulty. He was very attractive, this man, compelling even, and she marvelled at the transformation a layer of paint and a few affectations could make. She covered her confusion by pouring herself a cup of chocolate, and waited for him to begin.

"To answer your question, first, I am without any doubt whatsoever, a supporter of the Stuart king, and yes, I am a spy, had been for just over a year before we met," he said. "Sir Anthony has several functions. The first is to convince George and his son that James, and more particularly his son Charles Edward, present no threat to them, that the Jacobites have grown too complacent to rise in any force, to reassure him that the French will no' give military support to the Stuart cause and generally, to lead him and his sycophantic followers into a false sense of security so that they will be unprepared when the invasion comes. He does this by letting slip useful pieces of information that he claims to have gleaned from his many acquaintance in all walks of society."

"Does this mean then that the Earl of Derwentwater has not in fact lost heart in the cause?" Beth asked.

Alex laughed.

"I see that has been worrying you for a long time. Ye mentioned the matter once before, I remember. No, I can reassure ye now, the Earl Charles is as fervent as ever. And far from the earl thinking Prince Charles Edward incapable of finding a whore in a brothel, as I seem to recall telling your cousin, in fact he is actively fighting to secure funds and support in France for an invasion. Christ, his brother was executed. A man doesna forget that easily."

"Go on," Beth said, fascinated. "What are your other functions?"

"I'm sure ye've noticed, think yourself, in fact, that Sir Anthony may be educated, but is nevertheless a superficial fool, who doesna fully understand the import of what he's saying, or what is said tae him?"

She nodded.

"Well, that gives him the chance to let slip all kinds of information to the Hanover crowd, all unaware, of course. And it also puts them off guard. They are less worried about talking of important matters within his hearing, because they think he's too stupid to realise the import of what they've said. That's why he's friendly with everyone, and claims allegiance to none."

"Does that not also mean that some people are wary of talking to you because you may let all sorts of things slip to the Jacobites – all unaware, of course?" Beth asked.

"Aye, you canna have everything. But if Sir Anthony devoted himself to the cause of Hanover, then he'd have no reason to hear things from other quarters, and wouldna be able to divulge information without people growing suspicious as to how it was he'd come by it. There are others who do that. It doesna fit with Sir Anthony's character. But it does mean that while he is chatting merrily away about the merits o' this or that silk, he can be listening to a conversation nearby about the military capacity of Fort William, or whatever, without anyone being any the wiser. In short, he is generally treated like a woman by many men. He's there, he's human, just, but of no great relevance. No one would dream of confiding military secrets to him directly, but they have no qualms about discussing such matters within a few feet of him when he is apparently deeply involved in a trivial conversation with others. Ye must have heard all kinds of useful information because the men havena even registered your presence as an intelligent being in the room?"

He smiled at her, and she smiled warmly back, her fear of him temporarily forgotten.

"He behaved differently with George," she commented, unconsciously falling into the habit of referring to Sir Anthony in the third person, as Alex did. She had no difficulty in doing this. In her mind, Sir Anthony Peters and Alexander MacGregor were so unlike it was easier to envisage them as two different people than as two aspects of the same man.

"Aye, he did. But no' so different as to cause comment. He just tones down the more outrageous aspects of Sir Anthony. George is lonely, in many ways. Until his recent victory at Dettingen he's been living in the past, retelling over and over again the stories of his glorious achievements in Oudenarde in 1708. No one wants to listen to him. People call at St James's at the start of the season because it would be improper not to, stay for as little time as possible, then leave. George bores them. He isna what they expect from a king. He's dull, ignorant and boring. So of course he appreciates greatly the company of an Englishman who is not only willing to listen to endless repetitions of his past exploits with rapture, but to whom he can also speak his native language."

"And while he is talking about the past, he also lets slip his plans for the future," Beth said.

"Precisely."

"Do you feel sorry for him?" she asked. "You paint him as quite a pathetic figure."

"No, I dinna feel sorry for the man. He holds my people in contempt. In fact, he holds the English in contempt too, if they could only see it. He drones on about religious tolerance whilst exacting punitive measures towards Catholics and other non-conformists just because they choose to worship differently. He hasna any interest in being king of Britain, except in that it benefits his beloved Hanover. He would far rather live there than in London. He is unpopular and unfit tae be king, and I would admire him greatly if he had the courage to abdicate. I think he probably would if William Augustus were his eldest son instead of Frederick, whom he hates."

Beth shuddered at the thought of the duke of Cumberland ever taking the throne.

"Do you think it possible that William will ever be king?" she asked.

"Aye, but only if Frederick and his bairns die, or are done away with. If that were to happen, I think I'd seriously consider regicide. William is arrogant and brutal, and what is worse, intelligent too. What angers me is that we have a king here who is not only unfit but doesna even want the throne, whilst in Rome is a man who would make a fine king, and who is eager to do it, as well as having the hereditary right."

"Although there are those who argue James is too weak to rule, and lacks charisma," Beth said, engrossed in the conversation.

"I'm no' speaking of James Stuart," replied Alex. "I'm talking of his son, Charles Edward. But I'm supposed tae be telling you about Sir Anthony, no' blethering on about the usurper and his family. We can discuss them at any time. I think it more important we sort out what's between us, do ye no' agree?"

She nodded and nibbled at a roll, her appetite suddenly diminishing as she remembered her present circumstances. He was disarming, this man. With his relaxed and pleasant attitude, he had succeeded in getting her to completely forget that she was his prisoner, and that she still had no idea what he intended to do with her.

"Well, then, those are the main functions of Sir Anthony, in England, in any case." Alex continued after a moment. "In the meantime, my men are raising money from English Jacobites, trying to persuade them tae get off their apathetic ars…posteriors and fight, when the time comes, and of course, we are smuggling weapons into the country, as I assume ye ken already, if ye'd been listening at the door for a while that night."

She flushed a little, remembering last Christmas Eve, and reflecting that she was in only a little less danger now, however friendly her jailer might appear to be. Honesty had worked for her then; would it also suffice now? Alexander MacGregor appeared to be being truthful with her. She would repay in the same coin; it was the easiest way, in any case.

"Yes," she said, "I did hear something about swords, and a problem with storing them, but not as much as you seem to think. My mother taught me the Gaelic, but it's years since I heard it or spoke it. In fact that's why I stayed long enough to be caught," she admitted. "I couldn't resist it. I was listening to the tone more than the words, really. It reminded me of my mother. When I was discovered, I was sure that I was dead." She remembered his words of the previous evening, then, and the colour left her face in a rush.

"I was tired last night. I shouldna have said what I did," Alex said, clearly sharing Sir Anthony's facility for reading her mind.

"You meant it, though," she said in a soft voice.

"Aye, I did," he admitted. "We'd been discussing a good many things that night, any of which would have sent us and others to the gallows, had they been reported. Ye're lucky that we didna expect anyone south of the border tae speak our barbaric gibberish, as the Gaelic's called by the English. If I'd kent ye did, I couldna have taken the chance of trusting you. Many of the men thought I'd run daft that I didna kill you anyway. But I already had a liking for ye, and was willing to take the chance that ye'd no' tell. We didna use that room again in any case, and I knew that, myself excepted, the chance of you meeting any of the others again was slim. I thought I'd hidden myself well enough." He flexed his hand, glancing down ruefully at the scar that had betrayed him.

"And now?" she asked, meeting his eye. "What do you intend now?"

"I dinna intend to kill you, if that's what you're feart of," he said.

It was. The relief was so obvious on her face that he closed his eyes momentarily, ashamed that he had frightened her so, when his only intention in marrying her was to release her from fear.

"Why did you marry me?" she said, finally asking the question he'd expected to be her first.

"I told you why I wanted to marry you when I proposed to you," he said, gathering his breakfast dishes together and placing them on a tray.

"No," she replied. "Sir Anthony told me why he wanted to marry me. Alexander MacGregor did not."

"Alex," he corrected, standing, and moving across to the fireplace. In spite of the fact that it was August, the large room was chilly, and the fire gave out a pleasant heat "True. But in this case, we were one and the same. We do overlap on occasion."

"So, then," she replied. "Rather than being murdered in my bed, I can expect to travel widely, have adventures, and meet exciting and intelligent people, once we have consummated the marriage, that is?" A strange frisson ran through her at her last words, and she realised that she was actually attracted to Alex, in a way she never had been to his alter ego.

"We *have* consummated the marriage, as far as society is concerned, which is what matters in this case," he replied impassively. "As for the rest, that is up to you. Once matters are clear between us, ye can do as ye will."

His indifferent tone stung her and she replied without taking the time to think about what she was saying.

"And what if I want to denounce you? What's to stop me doing that? I would gain great favour with King George if I did. I would be the toast of society." These were hardly the words to guarantee her safe passage, and she regretted them the moment they were out of her mouth.

"Aye, ye would," he replied consideringly. "For a wee while. Everyone would love you. You'd be invited to every party in London. But then you'd rapidly become an embarrassment to King Geordie. Every time your name was mentioned, he'd be reminded of what a fool he'd been, that he'd been cozened by a Jacobite, and a barbaric, savage Highlander at that. Give it three months, at best, and no one would want to know ye. But there are other reasons why ye'd no' even consider betraying me for a moment."

"Such as?" she asked, annoyed by his assumption that he knew her so well.

"Ye're a Jacobite, for one, and the daughter of a MacDonald, for another. And the MacDonalds are loyal to the cause. And if that's no' enough, which I think it is, there's the small consideration that ye're married to Sir Anthony Peters, not Alex MacGregor. If you denounce me, ye'll be in the unenviable position of being single again, without your dowry, at the mercy of the brother I'm trying to save ye from, and, as far as the world is concerned, deflowered by a traitor. I wouldna give much for your marriage prospects or your life, for that matter, if your brother's as ruthless as I suspect he is."

He smiled coolly at her and sat down in a chair by the fire, beckoning her to take the seat opposite him. He forbore from telling her that if she were to betray him, she wouldn't live long enough to either enjoy or regret the fruits of it, as every one of the fifty or so clansmen who called him their chief would make it their life's work to kill her.

Beth stayed where she was, reasoning that the further away from this disturbing man she was, the more clearly she would be able to think.

"So," she continued after a moment, "do I assume rightly then that the only reason you married me was to give me my freedom, and to obtain twenty thousand pounds, which, judging from your circumstances," she took in the opulent room with a glance, "you have no need of?"

"No," Alex replied. "When I proposed to you, I told you that my marriage would stop eager parents of prospective brides looking in depth into my background, which you'll now appreciate is risky for me. As for your dowry, you're wrong on both counts. I do have need of your twenty thousand pounds. What you see, and Sir Anthony's fine clothes, carriage, everything, dinna belong to me, but to my sponsor. Having said that, I have no intention of using it."

Beth was flabbergasted.

"What *do* you then intend?" she asked, finally coming to the crux of the matter.

"I intend for us to separate, immediately," he said, matter-of-factly. "That's why I behaved so badly towards you yesterday, ignoring you, reciting hurtful poetry, and although I didna intend it, giving ye a nasty-looking bruise on your jaw, which you can say I inflicted on you whilst I was beating you terribly after we arrived home. Ye can then retire to set up house in the country, or wherever ye choose. Even after Richard's commission is paid for, you'll still be able to live verra comfortably on what remains of your dowry. No one will dispute the validity of the marriage, and no one will look into Sir Anthony's dubious background again, as he's no longer an eligible bachelor. That is what I intend. Sir Anthony meantime, will proceed with his tour of Europe, in an attempt to restore his shattered nerves. He has business there."

She stared at him from her place at the dining table.

"I don't believe you," she said flatly. "If there's one thing I've learnt since I've been in London, it's that no one does anything for nothing, or for such little gain. What other reason did you have for marrying me?"

This time he was the first to break eye contact, under the pretence of leaning over to throw another log on the fire, but in that moment she had seen his gaze shift, and knew he was hiding something from her.

There was a perfunctory tap on the door, after which it opened, and Angus's face appeared.

"I've come tae fetch the dishes, if it's all right," he said, smiling at his brother and then at Beth. He had the same blue eyes as Alex, she noted, but whereas his were currently bubbling with merriment and not a little curiosity as to how matters were going, his brother's were carefully shielded, revealing nothing. Without waiting for an answer, Angus moved to the table, and began piling the dishes. Alex continued talking as though he wasn't there.

"It's of great gain to me that I know Sir Anthony's identity is safe," he said.

"I'm sure it is," she retorted, following her husband's example with regard to Angus. "But there's another reason, isn't there? You said you would answer my questions truthfully. What are you hiding?"

"What I said," Alex reminded her, his voice testy, "was that I would answer ye truthfully, or not at all. Any other reasons I have for marrying ye are none of your concern."

The arrogance of his tone left her speechless for a moment, and she felt the familiar tingle of her temper rising.

"Dh'innis thu dhomh gu bheil gaol agad oirre," Angus put in cheerfully from the corner of the room. *"Nach do dh'innis thu dhi?"*

Alex's sudden stillness told Angus immediately that he'd made a terrible mistake. In a split second he registered the fact that Beth had somehow understood his words, and that Alex was about to explode. Knowing his brother well, and being possessed of a strong survival instinct, he abandoned the dishes and ran.

He was almost through the door, twisting his body sideways to make himself less of a target, when the chunk of wood flew past him, catching his arm as it went, and causing him to lose his balance and stagger forwards for a few steps before landing on his knees in the hall. Thanking God that Alex had had no more lethal weapon to hand than a piece of wood, he scrambled to his feet and disappeared.

Beth looked at her husband with astonishment. The transformation from calm and peaceful to enraged and violent had been instantaneous. The man standing by the

70

hearth, fists clenched and clearly torn between staying in an attempt to explain what his brother had unwittingly revealed, and going after him to tear him limb from limb, was as far removed from Sir Anthony as it was possible to be. Here was the formidable Highland warrior her mother had told her about on dark winter nights, quick to anger and to violence. As she debated what to do, he took a step in the direction of the door.

Hoping her mother had also been right when she'd said that the Highlander's temper subsided as quickly as it flared, and that they generally abhorred hitting women, Beth also stood, the movement drawing Alex's attention.

"I assume by your reaction that your brother spoke true?" she said.

He stared at her unseeing for a moment, then he scrubbed his hand violently through his hair and the coiled spring of tension relaxed a little. He did not make any further move to follow Angus.

"He had no right tae say that," Alex growled through his teeth.

"He didn't know I would understand him though, did he?" Beth reasoned.

"No, I havena told him that ye ken the Gaelic." He rubbed his hand through his hair again, but less violently this time. Beth relaxed a little. The crisis seemed past.

"But you have told him that you love me, which it seems to me is indeed of concern to me, in spite of what you might think. Is that then the other reason why you married me?"

There was a silence, during which Beth wondered whether he would explode again to avoid having to admit it, or would come up with some plausible reason why he'd told his brother such a falsehood.

In the end, he did neither, instead keeping his promise to tell her the truth.

"Aye, it is," he said. He threw himself down in the chair again, and this time Beth came and sat opposite him. "But it's no' the sort of thing a man would want everyone to know."

"But I'm not everyone," she pointed out. "I'm your wife. This changes everything."

"You're Sir Anthony's wife," Alex replied logically. "And whatever I may feel for you, it doesna change the fact that you and I are going to separate, and you are going to go off and live in the country somewhere, while I go to Europe."

For a moment she contemplated what would happen if she fell in with his plans. She could retire to the country, live a quiet life, bring Graeme, Jane, Thomas and Grace to live with her. She was free of her brother, she could be free of the endless stultifying society round, could ride her horse bareback whenever she wanted, could…could what? What meaning would her life have? As appealing as the idea of an eventless existence seemed at this moment, she knew herself well enough to be certain that in time she would find it as stultifying as the London life. She couldn't marry again and have children, as long as Alex/Sir Anthony lived, and interesting adventures are hard to come by in country villages, as are tall handsome men who love you, even if they are reluctant to admit it, and a bit frightening into the bargain.

"No, I'm not," she said. "You promised me that if I married you you'd give me adventure, and I'm going to hold you to it. I'm coming to Europe with you."

CHAPTER FIVE

"No. Absolutely not," Alex replied, his tone brooking no argument.

"I've never been to Europe. Never been anywhere, for that matter, apart from Manchester and London, of course. It would be wonderful to travel," said Beth, pointedly ignoring both his declaration and the tone it was delivered in.

"I'm no' stopping ye from travelling. If you want to go travelling, that's fine by me. I'm giving ye your freedom."

"Good," Beth replied. "So where are we going first?"

"*I*," said Alex, with great emphasis on the singular pronoun, "am going to Calais, and then to Rome as quickly as possible. *You* can go wherever you wish, but no' with me."

"But why not?" Beth asked. "Surely I'd be safer travelling in company with my husband than alone? I believe Europe can be very dangerous."

"I certainly wouldna advise ye to go alone. But I'm sure you can find other people who'd be willing to go with you. Isabella for one, or Clarissa, perhaps."

Beth shot him a withering look.

"I hardly think I'm likely to get the adventure you promised me, or to meet intelligent and interesting people, as you also promised, if Clarissa and Isabella accompany me," she said scathingly. "I assume you're off to Rome to meet King James. Well, now I know which king you were referring to, I *do* want to meet him. And I can't do *that* with Isabella or Clarissa. No, I'm coming with you." She sat back, her face determined.

Alex held on to his temper with difficulty. He should have foreseen this, knowing how spirited she was. But he had thought her first wish on discovering who he was would be to get as far away from him as possible. For his peace of mind, he *needed* her as far away from him as possible.

"Beth," he said, slowly and reasonably. "I married ye to free ye from danger. From the danger of being forced into a marriage against your will by your brother. From the danger of his violence if you refused to do as he wished. If I agree to you coming with me, I will be putting you in greater danger than you could ever be from your family, d'ye no' understand that? If we separate now, and I am later caught or betrayed, ye can claim that ye had no idea I was anyone other than Sir Anthony Peters, court fop extraordinaire. It would be a whole different matter if we were to stay together. No one would then believe you were innocent. I can trust you to act the part of surprised estranged wife, to ensure your own safety. It's a completely different thing to act a part day in and day out, aware all the time that one wrong move could betray ye. Now do you see why it's impossible for you to come with me? Ye'd endanger not only yourself, but me as well."

"You're not giving me a chance," she replied hotly. "I've been acting a part for the last eight months."

"Aye, and look how many mistakes ye've made in that time," he responded, his voice rising a little. "The rosary, the outburst at the table, to say nothing of telling your brother your intention to declare for the Pretender and kill George. If your family and their friends were no' so arrogant as to believe it impossible that anyone of their acquaintance could favour the Stuarts, they'd have known ye for a Jacobite long since!"

"That was different. I've changed since then," she said, leaning forward in her seat.

"In what way? Your circumstances have changed, that's

74

all."

"You're wrong," she said. "Yesterday I had nothing to live for. I was living a life I hated, with no prospect of it ever ending. I had no true friends here, no one who cared for me as I really am. I couldn't care less whether I was found out for a Jacobite or not. More than once I've contemplated taking my own life, especially because I knew if I did, my brother would not get my dowry. I married you because I hoped that you were kind, that at some point you would allow me to retire from society, to return to Manchester and free my servants from their dependence on Richard."

He looked at her incredulously.

"Well, what's the problem, then? I *am* kind, and I *am* allowing you to retire from society."

"Yes, but I now know that you married me not to get your hands on my dowry, or my body for that matter, but purely because you loved me. Loved me enough, in fact, to throw away twenty thousand pounds that you have need of, and to take the risk that I might betray you anyway. *That's* what changes everything, what changes me, not my freedom! Can't you see that?" Unbidden, her eyes filled with tears, and she looked away from him, searching in her pocket for a handkerchief.

He stared at her, frozen. He wanted to strangle her. He wanted to throw her down on the hearthrug and take her now, brutally. He wanted to cradle her on his lap and kiss away the tears she was trying so manfully to swallow back, not wanting him to pity her. He could not do any of those things. Instead, in desperation, he did the only thing he could do, without giving in to her.

"Christ, woman, have ye gone daft?" he shouted, losing his temper. "It's no' a game I'm playing. If I'm caught, I'll be tortured until I betray my friends. Then I'll suffer a traitor's death. D'ye ken what that is, lassie?" Before she could open her mouth to answer, he continued, scrubbing his hand viciously through his hair. "First I'll be paraded through the streets on a hurdle, for people to spit and throw shit and stones at me. Then I'll be allowed to make a brave speech for the entertainment of the crowd, while I try to hold on to my bowels so as no' to disgrace myself. For I'll be terrified, knowing what's going tae happen next, and knowing there'll be no escape from it. Then I'll be hung, not long enough tae die, ye ken, just long enough to suffer, badly. After that I'll be cut down and have my private parts cut off, before being disembowelled slowly, and my heart thrown on the fire. And I'll be alive and feeling for every endless minute of it. That's what I'm risking. And I can expect no mercy, because I'll hae made a fool o' the king, and of half the aristocracy of the country. And by Christ, they'll make sure I suffer for it!" He glared at her. Her eyes were huge in her white face. He had frightened her. Good. He stood up, towering over her, and passed his hand through his hair again.

"And as for yersel'," he continued, his Scottish accent more pronounced in his passion. "If ye do as I tell ye, and leave me now, and then I'm discovered, you'll be cast out of society, which I ken ye dinna care a fig for. If ye insist on coming wi' me and having romantic and glamorous 'adventures', as ye seem tae think they'll be, and we're caught, then ye can at least be assured that women dinna suffer quartering. Ye'll merely be burnt alive, or if you're really lucky, hung until dead, which can take up to an hour, depending on the skill of the hangman. Have ye ever seen a hanging?"

"No," she replied quietly, "But..."

"Well, then," he interrupted. "I have, many times. It's no' a pretty sight, I can tell ye that, certainly no adventure, and in all the hangings I've seen, no one has ever come riding in on a white horse at the last minute tae rescue the damsel, as they do in all the best poems and novels. Before they burn or hang ye, however, ye'll be kept in a filthy, cold prison cell for weeks, in between being 'questioned', which, as ye're no a lady o' quality, but a mere barbarian Scot's wife, will consist of a damn sight more than polite requests for you tae reveal your accomplices. Whatever 'unpleasant experience' ye suffered that made ye so feared of my advances the other night was nothing compared to what you'll suffer if you get a brutal questioner. Which you will, because you'll be the wife o' the man who made a fool o' the king and all society!"

Her face flushed scarlet at his last words, and he knew he had hit below the belt. But he didn't care. He had to make her realise the seriousness of the situation. He turned away, pacing the room, and scrubbed his fingers through his hair again, as he always did when deeply disturbed. When he turned back, she was looking at him, not terrified, as he had hoped, or angry, as he had expected, but laughingly.

"I saw a picture of a porcupine once, in a book," she said.

"What?" he said, utterly perplexed.

"That's what you remind me of now," she answered calmly. "A large, red porcupine."

He felt the top of his head, realised that his hair was standing up all over the place, the blue ribbon dangling precariously on his shoulder. The rage vanished, and he felt foolish suddenly, and not a little ashamed of some of the things he had said to her. He made an attempt to smooth down the wayward locks, and sat down again.

"Aye, well, I'll admit, I am feeling a wee bit prickly at the moment," he admitted. "I'm sorry if I frightened you. But I'm no' sorry for what I said. It's true, Beth, every word of it. It isna a game, no' something I'll have you involved in, an ye dinna know what the consequences will be if things go wrong."

"You didn't frighten me," she replied. "But you're right. I hadn't thought properly about the consequences. I can see I need to give it a lot more thought."

"Good," Alex said, deeply relieved. "I knew ye'd see reason, understand that it isna possible for you to come with me."

She looked across at him, surprised.

"Oh no," she said resolutely. "I'm still coming with you. I just need to think about the sort of wife people will expect me to be to Sir Anthony, that's all, and how I can play that role convincingly and to our best advantage."

Alex dropped his head into his hands in despair.

* * *

The three men and one woman sat in the kitchen. Between them on the table burned a single candle, which supplemented the light from the fire, and a bottle, which was regularly passed from one hand to the next.

"She does have a point," Angus ventured, after receiving the bottle from Iain, and taking a deep draught of the spirit within.

"No, she doesna," retorted Alex. "I never had any intention of her getting involved in all this. And why I'm even speaking to you at all is beyond me. I never thought my own brother would give my enemy such a weapon, knowing how well she'd wield it against me."

"Och, be fair, man," put in the representative female, Maggie, who, as well as being Iain's wife, also doubled as cook and general maid. "Ye didna tell any of us as she had the Gaelic. How was Angus tae ken? You've only yersel' to blame."

"And even then, how was I to ken she'd use how you felt for her against ye?" Angus added.

"Christ, man, have ye learnt nothing about women in nineteen years? Dinna ever tell a woman you love her unless you're wanting to be led around by the nose for the rest of your life."

"I often tell women I love them," Angus protested.

"Aye, but ye dinna mean it, as they well know. It's a different matter entirely."

"What are ye going tae do?" said Iain, interrupting the dialogue before it got too heated.

"I'm going to make her decide that she doesna want to come with me, that's what I'm going to do," Alex replied determinedly.

"Why do ye no' just forbid her to come? You're her husband, after all," Iain said. His wife snorted derisively as she reached for the whisky bottle. "And you're her chieftain too," he added hurriedly before Maggie could point out that she rarely took any notice of her husband, unless it suited her to do so.

"Aye, well, that's the other thing she doesna understand, having been brought up a Sasannach an' all. She'll no' obey me just because I'm her husband, in spite o' the marriage vows she took two days ago. She's too much spirit for that. And I've no' the time tae teach her about clan rules. If I forbid her outright, like as not she'll wait till I've sailed and book passage on the next boat to follow me. No, she's got to decide for herself that it's too dangerous. And I think I ken how to do it." Alex upended the bottle, draining the last dregs, and plonked it down on the table. "And you're going to make amends, by helping me," he finished, turning to his brother.

* * *

Even as Alex outlined his plan to his compatriots, Beth lay in bed, watching the single candle on the dresser cast enormous shadows round the room as it wavered in the draught which succeeded with effort in forcing its way through the window.

Her mind was full of the same topic. How was she going to convince Alex that she would be an asset rather than a hindrance to him if she were to accompany him to Europe? He was a very good actor, she had to admit that. Never in a million years would she have suspected that Sir Anthony Peters was a Jacobite Scottish Highlander. Now she had to convince him that she could act a part as well as he, if she put her mind to it.

She had spoken honestly to him. The fact that he loved her *did* make all the difference. She did not love him, but she liked him, and admired him immensely. And desired him too, although of course she was not about to tell him that, not yet, not until she was sure she wouldn't freeze in terror if he touched her. She had to convince him that not only was she capable of acting whatever part was necessary, but that she would not be as reckless with his safety and reputation as she had been with her own in recent months. How she could do that whilst cooped up in this house, however, she had no idea. She sighed, and blowing out the candle, settled down in an attempt to get some sleep.

* * *

The following morning she dressed more carefully, no longer feeling a desire to escape from the house. She doubted that Alex would be influenced by her appearance, but it couldn't do any harm to look pretty, and it would boost her confidence as well. She sensed that it was going to be a long and difficult day.

Having fought with her hair and a variety of clips and pins for a while, and bemoaned the lack of Sarah, she gave up the attempt at an elaborate hairstyle. Instead she contented herself with simply braiding it, tying the end with a pale blue ribbon which matched her dress. Not exactly a hairstyle to be seen by society in, but she expected to encounter no one other than her husband, and possibly his brother.

She was just about to turn the bend in the stairs, when the doorbell rang. She stopped where she was, crouching down to minimise the chance that she would be seen by whoever came to answer the summons. After a moment she heard footsteps in the hall, and then the door opened. There was a murmur of polite voices, one male, who she recognised as Angus, the other female, but at first too indistinct for her to identify its owner. When she did, her heart leapt, and, quick-minded as she was, she realised that here was a chance to prove to Alex that she was indeed worthy to play an active role in his affairs.

She swept down the rest of the stairs, afraid she would lose her nerve if she hesitated, and presented herself at the door before Angus could do anything to stop her.

"Isabella!" she cried, walking out on to the step to embrace her startled cousin, who had just been assured that, regretfully, Sir Anthony and his wife were indisposed to receive visitors. "And Clarissa!" Beth continued, seeing her hovering uncertainly in the background. "What a delightful surprise! Please, come in."

"Only if it is convenient." Isabella fluttered. "We were merely taking the air in the vicinity, and called in the hopes that you would be at home. We were sure you would forgive the intrusion. But your footman here said that you were not seeing visitors."

"It is true, Sir Anthony and I do not wish to encourage a flood of visitors, as we want to spend the time before we leave for Dover in becoming more closely acquainted. But of course we will make an exception in the case of yourselves," Beth enthused, ushering her cousins into the hall. "After all, without your kindness and generosity towards myself and

Richard, I would not have met my husband in the first place!"

She turned to Angus.

"Ah…"

"Jim," he supplied, his expression servile, his blue eyes dancing with mischief. He knew exactly what she was about, Beth realised, and did not disapprove.

"Jim," she confirmed. "Could you arrange for refreshments to be served in the library, please?"

He opened his mouth as if to say something, then seemingly thought better of it, instead making a slight bow, and turning to close the door.

Beth led her visitors, who were observing their surroundings with some curiosity, to one of the several doors which led off the hall, and opening it, turned back to address her company.

"I am afraid Sir Anthony is still asleep, having had a most restless night," she began, and then was arrested by Isabella's gasp of shock. She turned round to see what had caused her cousin's consternation, and was confronted by the sight of her husband lounging on a sofa reading a book, dressed as yesterday, in only breeches and shirt. When he was not playing Sir Anthony, he took every opportunity to dress as casually as possible. On seeing the shocked countenance of Isabella, he dropped the book and leapt to his feet. For a split second, Beth froze. She had expected Alex to be in the dining room as he had been the day before.

"Abernathy," came the helpful voice from the hall behind her.

"Well," she declared, walking into the room. "I can see that my husband has permitted his servants to take the most appalling advantage of his generous nature, but I can assure you, Abernathy, that I will permit no such laxity. You will repair to your room immediately, and dress yourself as befits a servant in the employ of a baronet. And if I see you taking such liberties again as I have now discovered you to be doing, you will be dismissed on the spot without a character. Do you understand?"

The man in front of her became instantly the picture of a servant caught in the wrong, red-faced and ashamed, resentful of the way he was being spoken to, but determined to conceal it in order to keep his very lucrative employment. He made a deep bow to his mistress and hurried from the room. God, he was good, she thought admiringly.

"I am most terribly sorry," Beth said, after the door had closed. Her heart was banging in her chest, and she thanked God that her nervous pallor could be attributed to the shock of encountering a half-naked footman. "Please, sit down. Are you all right, Isabella? You look most dreadfully pale."

"No, I am fine, I assure you," replied her cousin, who was too well bred to admit to her shock.

The two sisters took their places side by side on the sofa Alex had so hurriedly vacated. Beth wondered whether the cousins would comment on the remarkable coincidence that the servant Abernathy appeared to have a broken nose, just like Sir Anthony.

"We came to see you because we were a little concerned about your state of health," explained Clarissa. Beth looked at her, somewhat puzzled. "We wished to assure ourselves that you had not suffered any lasting harm from your indisposition."

For a moment Beth had no idea what Clarissa was talking about. She was still pondering whether she should volunteer a comment on Abernathy's bruising, which would draw attention to it, or wait until they said something.

"Oh, of course," she said after a moment. "What can I say? I am so bitterly ashamed of my behaviour. I am afraid I must admit that I had drunk a little more wine than was strictly prudent, and when I saw Sir Anthony flirting with that hussy…."

Iain was sitting comfortably at the table, watching his wife peel vegetables for the dinner, when Angus came speeding through the kitchen.

"What's wrong?" he said, automatically reaching for his swordbelt, which was lying beside him on the bench seat.

"Nothing," Angus called behind him as he shot through the door into the yard. "I'm just away out to take the air."

The couple had done no more than exchange a resigned glance before Alex pounded into the room.

"Where is he? I'll skelp the wee bastard when I catch him."

"He's gone to take the air. He'll be halfway to Oxford before ye catch up wi' him. Ye ken how fast he is. And he's wearing shoes," Maggie said calmly, looking at Alex's bare feet.

They both looked at him with interest, awaiting an explanation as to what mischief Angus had caused now.

"Tea," their chieftain announced enigmatically. "For three. Formal, on a tray, wi' cakes and such. I'll be back in five minutes."

"…Of course I wanted to come immediately and apologise to you, but Sir Anthony thought it better that I wait for a day or two. I never dreamed that you would be worried about me. Really, you are kindness itself." Beth leaned across and patted Isabella's hand, wondering if she was overdoing it a little. At least the colour had now returned to the sisters' faces, and they seemed more at ease.

There was a polite and hesitant knock at the door.

"Come in!" she called. "This will be the tea."

The footman entered, his arms filled by a huge tray, on which resided an exquisitely decorated teapot, sugar bowl, three delicate cups and a plate of biscuits. He placed the tray deferentially on the table, and stood back.

"Cook sends her apologies, my lady," he said in a rich west country accent. "She had no cakes, but hoped that these biscuits would suffice. They're freshly made this morning."

"Thank you, Abernathy," Beth said. "You may go."

"Shall I make up the fire first, my lady?" he asked. Clearly he was still fearful of losing his post, and was anxious to make amends.

"Yes, that would be lovely," she replied. "As I was saying," she continued, offering the plate of biscuits to her cousins and taking the opportunity to shift position so that she couldn't see Alex as he busied himself by the hearth. "Sir Anthony and I are now fully reconciled. He has apologised for his behaviour to me, and I to him, and we are looking forward greatly to seeing the sights of Italy and France. We talk of nothing else."

"Oh, it is so exciting!" cried Isabella. "Which cities will you be visiting?"

Oh, damn, thought Beth, cursing her last words.

"That is the most infuriating thing, Isabella," she replied without missing a beat. "Although my husband has expounded endlessly on the delights of Paris, the Alps, Venice and Florence, I still know no more than that we are sailing from Dover to Calais. He wishes the itinerary to be a surprise, and as he is so well travelled, and I have been so sheltered until now, I am content to let him do so. Although I confess, I hope that a visit to Rome will be included on the tour. I have heard much about the delights of Rome from Mr Fortesque, who of course spent several months there in his youth." She shot a furtive glance in the direction of the fireplace. The fire now replenished, Alex stood, and with a bow, vacated the room, closing the door quietly behind him and leaving the ladies to their conversation.

"Verra clever," came the voice from behind her as Beth stood at the door, having merrily waved her cousins off, promising to write to them from every place of note. She jumped. "And if you try a trick like that again, I'll tan your arse for ye."

She flew round to face him. Alex was standing directly behind her, and stepped back only far enough to allow her to close the door before moving forward again, so that she could not run past him, if she had a mind to. She didn't.

"What did you expect me to do?" she said hotly, glaring up at him. "I had to prove to you somehow that I could play a part as well as you." He looked at her, one eyebrow raised in a distinctly Sir Anthony gesture. "Well, maybe not as well as you," she admitted, still impressed by his instantaneous transformation from relaxed master of the house to guilty menial, "but you must admit I did well. Their visit was a God-given opportunity. I had to take it."

"You didna, as it happens," he replied. "I'd already decided to give you a chance to see what it'll be like if you insist on staying with me as you wish. This afternoon Sir Anthony is going on an excursion, and his wife is invited to join him. His footman will also accompany us, if I can keep my hands off the wee gomerel until then."

Beth was so delighted at this apparent change of mind that she jumped up on tiptoe and impulsively kissed him on the nose. In spite of his sour mood, the corners of his mouth turned up slightly.

"Where are we going?" she asked, her eyes sparkling.

"You'll find out when we get there," her husband replied. "It's a surprise."

Although Iain was acting as coachman, and Angus as the footman, Alex advised Beth before they left the house that it was better she treat him as Sir Anthony from the moment they stepped out of the door, so that by the time they arrived at a place where there were other people, she would be well into the role.

"I can slip in and out of the part as I need to," he said, checking his make-up in a looking glass hanging in the hall. "But it takes practice."

Beth did feel a little foolish, sitting in the coach under the amused gaze of Angus, making trivial conversation with the man she'd been at loggerheads with for the last two days, and who she now saw in a completely different light, in spite of the fact that the man sitting opposite her was indisputably Sir Anthony, from the heavy make-up and nauseating dark violet costume to the star-shaped patch which she now knew covered a disarming dimple which appeared whenever he smiled.

But this was a test, she knew that. He was clearly having no problems playing his role, even though all those present knew his true identity. She could at least attempt to do the same. She hunted for a topic of conversation as Sir Anthony fussed with the lace at his throat and cuffs.

"Abernathy is a most unusual name," she said after a moment. "Is it a traditional Dorset name? I assume the man is from that part of the world, judging by his accent."

Angus compressed his lips together in a tight line, and stared out of the window.

"Indeed, I believe not," her husband replied in a disinterested tone. "He was apparently named by a relative of his, in a fit of mischief, he told me. He has yet to exact his revenge upon that relative."

"He appears to be a most insolent fellow," Beth continued. "Although after I had chastised him, he was very deferential."

"Don't be fooled by that, my lady," Angus put in, unable to resist. "He's a man of most unpredictable temper, devoid of humour at times and liable to become violent at the slightest provocation, venting his anger on any innocent person who happens to be in his way at the time. I live in mortal fear of the man myself."

"Do you really, dear boy?" Sir Anthony said. "In that case, on my return home I will dismiss him immediately, and would strongly suggest that his name not be mentioned again, under any circumstances whatsoever."

It was obvious there was some private joke going on here, and Beth was curious. But she was curious about a lot of things she had not yet had time to ask. Why did Angus go by the name of Drummond? What had made Alex decide to be a spy? What had possessed him to take on the role of Sir Anthony? And at the moment, where on earth were they going? She had expected them to head for an afternoon entertainment at the house of one of Sir Anthony's many acquaintances, but instead of going east into the city, they were heading west along the Oxford road. The streets did seem very crowded, with great numbers of people walking briskly along, clearly eager to get to their destination. A fair, perhaps? The mood certainly seemed festive.

After a while the press of people grew too much for the carriage to proceed and it lurched to a halt.

"I am afraid we shall have to walk from here, my dear," Sir Anthony said. "It is not far, but do beware of pickpockets. I suggest you walk between myself and Jim, in order that your safety is assured."

The moment she alighted from the coach and looked in the direction the pedestrians were heading, her question was answered, as she saw the unmistakable triangular structure of the Tyburn gallows in the distance. She looked up at her husband, who smiled gaily down at her shocked face.

"You told me yesterday, my dear, that you had never had the privilege of witnessing a hanging. Imagine my delight when upon making enquiries, I discovered there was to be a hanging…three hangings in fact, this very day!" He took hold of her elbow, and began to lead her along the road. "Of course, it would no doubt be possible to witness an execution in France or Italy, but I thought it better that you see how our own dear nation deals with malefactors before we sail for France."

Her shock now gave way to first anger, and then resignation. She could see why he was doing this. The idea was that she would be so horrified by witnessing her possible fate, that she would head for the countryside with the greatest of alacrity.

I can do this, she thought, determined not just to watch the execution, but to appear unmoved by it. At any rate, judging by the density of the crowd, they would not be able to get close enough to see very much of the proceedings. Sir Anthony led her to an official, a tall, burly man dressed in a blue uniform and armed with a cudgel. As they approached, the baronet produced a paper from his coat pocket, which he presented to the officer with a flourish. After perusing it for a moment, the man nodded, and turning, began to clear a path through the crowd.

Within moments, Beth was taking her seat between her husband and his brother in the gallery erected for the privileged, mere feet from the scaffold. At this moment she hated him, all the more so because she was trapped. If she expressed a desire to leave, he would have won, and she would no longer be able to insist on accompanying him to Europe. She had no choice but to face this nightmare. She looked up at him as he arranged his coat skirts around him prettily, and their eyes met in a clash of wills.

"You cannot imagine, my dear, how prohibitively expensive it was to obtain these choice seats at such short notice!" he trilled. "But I will consider it worth every penny, my darling, if it provides you with a memorable experience."

"I am sure it will, Anthony, and I am most grateful," she

replied, leaning forward as if eager to witness the spectacle.

A shout went up from the crowd, who until now had been busily chatting and buying food, ballad sheets and souvenirs of the day from the numerous hawkers who were plying their wares.

"Here they come now," Angus said, reaching across Beth to accept a handful of cherries from his master. Beth also popped one in her mouth, although she had no appetite.

"There are certainly a lot of people," she commented, looking at the roaring crowd, which was now making way for two horse-drawn carts, flanked by constables carrying staves. A hail of rotten fruit and jeers rained down on the occupants as they approached the gallows.

"Oh, this is a very small crowd," Sir Anthony commented. "No one of note is being hanged today. The two men are highwaymen, but had not the time to become famous, being apprehended whilst engaged in their first crime. And the woman is accused of theft. Now when someone notorious is hanged, say, for example a highwayman who has captured the hearts of the public with his exploits, a murderer, or someone convicted of high treason," he paused to scrutinise her face, and she returned his look with equanimity. "Then you will see maybe four times the number of people assembled today. People have been known to be suffocated in the crush, and the whole thing can become very unruly and dangerous"

The carts had now arrived at the scaffold, and Beth noticed with a start that the prisoners were standing on their own coffins. The black-clothed minister now began to intone prayers, which the two men joined in, whilst the woman remained resolutely silent, which occasioned disapproving comments from the onlookers, who expected the prisoners to be suitably cowed by the thought that they were about to meet their maker.

"I thought they would be dirty and ragged," Beth

commented, remembering Alex's assertion yesterday that prisoners were kept in filthy cells for weeks before being hung.

"No, for most of these poor souls, it's their moment of glory," Angus explained, spitting out a cherry stone. "It's the only chance they'll ever get to be something. They wear their best clothes, and some of them give fine speeches too, although I doubt these will. They seem a sorry lot."

They did. The two men, although dressed in clothes that Sir Anthony might have worn, were white-faced and trembling, and looked on the point of collapse. The remaining prisoner, on the other hand, though dressed neatly, was not ostentatious, and as Beth watched her, fascinated in spite of herself, the young woman suddenly stamped her feet hard on the wooden floor of the cart. The minister stopped momentarily at the interruption, then continued in a monotonous drone.

"What's she doing?" Beth asked.

"She's trying to stop the trembling of her legs becoming too noticeable. I've seen it before. She has courage, that's certain," Sir Anthony replied, his voice soft, admiring.

The minister now finished, and the three criminals were given the chance to say a few words. The two men declined, clearly beyond speech. They looked utterly terrified, and Beth felt a sharp pang of pity for them, although the crowd, thus deprived of part of their expected entertainment, jeered. More missiles were hurled at the cart. Beth looked away momentarily to compose herself, then, aware of her husband's scrutiny, raised her eyes again. The hangman was busily tying the hands and ankles of the men, when the woman suddenly stepped forward. The jeers of the crowd quietened.

"I am innocent," she began, her voice faltering.

"That is what they all say," Sir Anthony murmured in

91

Beth's ear.

The woman swallowed and took a couple of deep breaths.

"I am innocent," she said again, and her voice rang out this time, across the heads of the crowd. She was greeted with a series of cat-calls, and waited until the noise died down before she continued. "I did not commit the crime for which I am to hang today. But I did commit another crime, which is far more serious than the theft of a diamond ring," she cried.

The crowd became quiet now, listening intently. The only sound was the mournful bell of St. Sepulchre's church, tolling for the imminent deaths.

"I committed the crime of not allowing Lord Eastwood to take my virginity when his wife was away from home. I committed the crime of telling him that I found him the most repulsive and disgusting man in the country. And I did not wish to catch the French pox from him, which I know for certain he must have, dealing as he does with whores of the lowest sort, which are the only ones who will service him!"

There was a roar of approval and applause from the onlookers this time, and to Beth's surprise, several tomatoes, apples and even a cabbage came flying over her head, one barely missing her as it soared into the wealthy spectators behind her. She looked round, her eyes falling on a richly-dressed stout middle-aged man, who, by the apoplectic look on his purple face, had to be Lord Eastwood, just as the white-faced lady sitting by his side was most certainly his wife.

Beth turned back to the animated features of the girl on the cart, her head flung back, her eyes fixed on her accuser, oblivious to the approval of the crowd. Her heart filled with admiration at the defiance the young woman was showing, who now raised her arm to point at Lord Eastwood. Beth noticed her wrist was raw and infected, chafed by the manacles she must have worn for weeks in Newgate prison.

"But know this," the girl said, speaking directly to her accuser. "I will die today, and you will live for many years yet. But when you die, your line dies with you. Your son will perish before you, and your daughter and her baby in childbirth. And you will live to regret what you have done this day."

"Holy Mother of God, she has the sight," Angus whispered in awe, his right hand automatically moving to his forehead to make the sign of the cross. Sir Anthony leaned across hurriedly to prevent him completing the gesture before anyone noticed. The sudden silence of the crowd was ominous, and the hangman, recognising this, moved forward, hurriedly tying the girl's hands behind her and throwing the noose over her neck. Without any further ado the horses were lashed and the cart moved off, leaving the three occupants suddenly swinging in space.

The mood was broken, and the crowd roared again, pushing forward to get the best view of the writhing, tormented trio. The girl's ankles had not been tied and her legs jerked wildly in a horrible parody of a dance. Beth's stomach heaved, and she felt the acid bile burning the back of her throat. She looked away, tears scalding her eyes.

"Watch!" came the fierce whisper in her ear. "See what you could come to if you persist in your desire to accompany me."

She made a valiant attempt to swallow down the bitter liquid, and raised her head to the rapidly blackening faces of the still jerking bodies. She hardly noticed the men; all her attention became focussed on the girl, so lovely and defiant but a moment ago, now reduced to a disjointed puppet thrashing in an instinctive, futile battle for survival.

After what seemed an eternity, during which the victims' struggles grew only slightly feebler, Sir Anthony spoke again.

"This is the point, my dear, at which those who are to be disembowelled are cut down," he said pleasantly. "As you can see, they are all still conscious, and aware. Their agony is clear to see on their features."

It was, but she hated him for reminding her of it. This was worse than she could ever have imagined. She had thought that there would be a drop when the cart rolled off, ensuring that the prisoners' necks were broken, and that they only suffered for a few moments. But the bodies had only fallen a very short distance, and were being strangled as slowly as possible. A dark stain spread slowly down the silk-clad legs of the men, and the pungent smell of urine wafted towards the aristocratic spectators in the gallery.

Bright lights flickered at the edge of her vision, and, recognising the signs, Beth immediately bent over, pushing her head between her knees, regardless of decorum, determined only not to give her husband the satisfaction of seeing her faint. After a few moments the giddiness passed, and she forced herself to straighten up again. A light tap came on her shoulder, and she looked round. A portly lady dressed in taupe silk was watching her with some concern, her kind brown eyes sympathetic.

"Are you all right?" she asked.

"It is my wife's first execution," Sir Anthony explained. "She has not been in the capital for very long."

"No," Beth said, "I was brought up in the countryside, and have much to learn of the ways of the world." Her voice seemed to come from a long way away, and she was aware that the danger of fainting had not yet passed.

The lady bustled about in her reticule, eventually producing a small paper.

"Here, my dear," she said kindly. "I find a honey sweet settles the nerves remarkably." She held out her hand

How Beth refrained from depositing her breakfast in the

lap of the friendly woman at sight of the sticky sweetmeat, she had no idea. Instead she managed to politely decline the offer, and turned round to see with desperation that the three figures were still twitching and jerking, their necks hideously distorted, their faces now completely black, eyes wide open and protruding.

"How long will this go on?" she asked despairingly.

"Normally they kick for about twenty minutes or so before they become limp," her husband replied matter-of-factly. "Of course that does not mean they are dead, only that they have become too weak to struggle any more. They are usually left for an hour before being cut down. There are several incidences of people surviving even that long. Or longer, in fact. I recall hearing of a lady in Scotland some years ago, who after being cut down, was placed in her coffin and taken for burial by her friends. Luckily they stopped for refreshment on the way, and it was there that they noticed the coffin lid moving! Imagine their surprise when the dead woman sat up! The story has a happy ending, as the lady was revived and lived in perfect health for many more years."

"Thank God for that," said Beth. In all the horror she was witnessing, it was good to hear something positive.

"That was in Scotland, though," Angus pointed out cheerfully. "In England she would have been taken and hung again. The laws are different here."

"Ah," said Beth weakly.

On the way home she was silent. Angus had decided to ride on top of the coach with Iain, the weather being fine, and Sir Anthony didn't speak, sitting instead in a moody silence more suited to his alter ego. Beth realised that he was allowing time for the dreadful spectacle she had seen today to sink in, to allow the full horror to become indelibly imprinted on her mind.

As she had watched the bodies slowly cease twitching and become limp, she had at first agreed with him. She could not bear to die like that, in such agony, in front of a howling crowd. She had been shocked at how quickly the mood of the mob had changed, from derision to approval, to hatred and fear when they had believed the woman to be a witch. It was horrible and barbaric, and she had to admit her husband was right; it was impossible to comprehend the true agony and degradation of such a death without witnessing it first-hand.

And yet to have the chance to be part of a movement to restore a rightful and worthy king to the throne! To be able to worship freely as she wished, without having to skulk down back alleys to abandoned buildings. In short, to have the same freedom of worship as the Anglicans, who were forever spouting about the religious intolerance of Rome, whilst practising the very intolerance they supposedly abhorred. To meet King James, and his son, and to know that you had done something worthwhile with your life, had fought for a cause you believed in, instead of skulking like a coward in the country!

They arrived home, and Beth ascended the steps, her mind in turmoil, hardly noticing as Sir Anthony leapt nimbly up the stairs to transform himself back into Alex, whilst Angus gently relieved her of her cloak before leading her to the salon, where she sank down into a chair. He left her then, and went down to the kitchen, where he spooned tea into a pot, whilst telling Maggie and Iain of his certainty that Alex's plan had worked, and Beth would not be going to Europe.

"The puir wee lassie's in shock," he said. "It's a shame to see her so. I've come to really like her. I thought she had the makings of one of us. But maybe it's for the best."

"Aye," replied Iain. "It's different for us, after all. We've really got nothing to lose, and a great deal to gain. Whereas she's got the chance to live a nice quiet life."

"I wouldna want a nice quiet life," said Angus. "It seems attractive sometimes, but it'd be awfu' tedious, I'm thinking."

"That's because ye've never had a quiet day in your life," Maggie said, pouring hot water onto the tealeaves. "And are not likely to either, while your name's MacGregor. There's a lot to be said for a peaceful existence, I'm sure. Now sit ye down, laddie, and I'll take the tea up."

"You're looking a wee bit pale yourself," Iain commented when Maggie had left the room. "Did the hanging upset you too?"

"Christ, no. What d'ye take me for?" Angus retorted. "No, it wasna the hangings as such. One of them was a lassie, though, and she had the sight." He crossed himself, no longer restricted by being in public view and commenced to tell Iain about the woman's prophecies, which being a Highlander, he found far more disturbing than any number of brutal deaths.

"Well, I'm assuming ye've now had time to think again, lassie." Alex's soft voice was the first thing to greet Maggie as she silently opened the salon door. She hadn't expected him to have changed so quickly and had thought Beth would still be alone. His voice was so full of concern and tenderness that she felt as though she was intruding on a very private moment. She hesitated on the threshold, undecided.

"Yes, I have. You were right. I hadn't thought things through properly," Beth replied.

Alex sat down next to her on the sofa.

"I hope you're no' angry with me," he said gently. "I ken it was a dreadful experience for ye. I didna mean to be cruel, but I thought it for the best."

"I'm not angry with you, Alex," she said, speaking his name for the first time. "I understand entirely why you took me to the hangings. It was the right thing to do. I can see everything clearly now. I was far too blasé about the whole situation before."

Alex took a deep, relieved breath.

"You canna know how pleased I am to hear that," he said, taking her hand in his.

"Yes," she replied. "I realise now that if I am to play my part convincingly, I cannot work out what kind of a wife I should be to Sir Anthony by myself. We need to discuss it together in depth, and I need you to help me practice my role as well. And as we only have three days before we leave for Dover, we had better start straight away."

Maggie edged quietly out of the door, taking care not to make any noise, and stole back to the kitchen.

Iain and Angus looked up as she entered, puzzled by the fact that she still carried the tea tray.

"What's amiss?" Iain asked.

"I think," said Maggie, dumping the tray on the table with a clatter, "that Alexander MacGregor has just met his match."

CHAPTER SIX

Once Alex had realised that his pig-headed and determined wife was not going to be dissuaded from accompanying him to Europe, no matter what he did, he resigned himself to the situation without further objection, and the next three days were set aside as Beth had suggested, to prepare her for the role she was to play.

"The best way to approach this is to think about what our acquaintances will expect our marriage to be like, and then to give them what they want. That will arouse the least suspicion," Alex said from his supine position on the library sofa. Decorated in warm shades of red and gold, this was the most comfortable room in the house, and as it was quite small, the owner not possessing a great predilection for books, the warmest too. It was the ideal place for them to closet themselves in order to discuss matters.

"I think my family are expecting the marriage to be a disaster," Beth replied. "Although now I'm off their hands, I don't think Edward and Richard could care less whether we're blissfully happy or at each other's throats from the first day."

"*They* may not care, but the rest of society will. Their whole lives revolve around gossip and little else, the women especially, and they'll be avidly watching us to see how we fare. Especially after our performance the other night."

"Yes, but we're going to be in Europe for the next few weeks. We could easily have become madly infatuated with each other by the time we return, if we wanted. And I did tell

Isabella and Clarissa that we were reconciled."

Alex stretched his long legs, laced his fingers behind his head and contemplated the ceiling for a minute, deep in thought.

"No, it wouldna work," he said finally. "We're too different. We couldna suddenly become a loving couple. No one would believe it. People would become curious, trying to find out what we were hiding, and that's just what we dinna want. We should give people what they're expecting, and if they think we're no' hiding anything, they'll no' look beneath the surface."

Beth could not dispute the logic of this.

"Very well, then, what sort of wife do you suggest I be?" she asked.

Alex unlaced his hands and sat up.

"When you thought you were married to Sir Anthony, how did ye think the marriage would turn out?" he said.

"Not very well," she admitted. "I couldn't stand your posturing and irritating gestures. I thought you could be malicious and superficial, and I found you physically repulsive." She stopped suddenly, embarrassed. The last words had slipped out without her thinking.

"Is that why ye recoiled so badly from me on our wedding night?" Alex asked softly. He didn't seem offended by her words.

"No. I told you, I've had an unpleasant experience. I wouldn't lie about that. But it didn't help that I thought the man I was in bed with was hideously disfigured by smallpox."

Alex laughed.

"So ye really believed that?" He grinned.

"Everyone believes that," Beth retorted defensively. "Why else would you wear such a heavy layer of paint?"

"Why indeed? I was hoping that's what people would think, but I wasna sure they did. Excellent!" He smiled warmly at her, and her heart turned a little somersault. She was certain he wanted their public marriage to be a disaster, and she was not sure she could carry this off, becoming, as she was, more attracted to him by the minute.

His next words confirmed her worst fears.

"I'm thinking that the only convincing way we can do this is for Sir Anthony to carry on as he is — he has to, really - and for you to start by trying to make the best of the situation, as you did when you first moved to London, and then quite quickly to become bored and contemptuous of the feeble excuse for a man you're wedded to." His eyes were distant now, as he contemplated their future relationship. "Aye, that could work out well. We'll be able to move in different circles, too, which will give us the chance to pick up more information. Yet we'll also have to do things together to try to prove that our marriage is working." His eyes refocused on the present, and he looked across at her. "I didna anticipate you coming with me, ye ken, but I think it can work. We can always improvise as we go along. It's the nature of relationships to change with time."

It certainly was. On her wedding day Beth would never have believed that two days later she would be trying to figure out ways of enticing her husband into her bed instead of banishing him from it.

"Will you be able to book another passage on the Dover packet?" Beth asked, hoping he wouldn't notice the sudden healthy glow to her face as she observed the athletic body draped casually across the sofa. The fact that he was dressed only in thin silk breeches and a shirt, which, open at the neck, exposed the strong column of his throat and not a little of his chest, did nothing to restore her equilibrium

"Your passage was booked three weeks ago," Alex said.

"But you said you had no intention of me coming with you."

"I didna, but Sir Anthony did. He had to book a place for you. He couldna possibly have known ye were going to argue so badly the night after your wedding. In fact, *I* couldna have possibly known that, either. Details," he said, suddenly serious. "It's often the details, Beth, that betray men. They spend too much time looking at the whole picture, what role they need to play, what information they need to obtain, and in doing so they overlook a wee detail that sends them to the gallows."

"Like a scar on your hand," Beth said.

"Aye, like that. Sir Anthony wears gloves all the time, to hide the scar, as well as the fact that his hands are no' as white and smooth as his lifestyle suggests they should be. But that night in Manchester I wasna Sir Anthony, but Alex. He doesna need tae hide his scar, and it slipped my mind that you might notice and remember it. It can happen to the best of us."

"And are you the best?" Beth asked, half seriously.

"No, I'm no' the best. But I'm damn good. And you'll have to be, too. Are ye still sure ye want to do this?"

She nodded.

"I'm sure. But I'm not sure I'll think of all the details."

"Dinna fash yourself about that," Alex reassured her. "I'll see to details. What you've got to do is play the role of Sir Anthony's beautiful and bored wife to perfection. D'ye think you can do that?"

"Yes, if you'll help me," Beth replied, sounding far more confident than she felt.

"Oh, I'll help ye, lassie. My life depends on it, after all."

* * *

This sobering statement stayed in Beth's mind over the next two days, whilst Alex put her through her paces. He was more exacting than the most finicky stage director, and picked her up on the slightest gesture or expression that seemed unrealistic. It was more gruelling than she could have imagined, and she fell into bed alone the first night, all amorous thoughts banished by exhaustion, wondering if she had bitten off more than she could chew.

"No!" he shouted at her on the afternoon of the last day, when she was practising for the tenth time a scenario in which she was supposed to be exasperated by the facetiousness of Sir Anthony. "You're no' on the bluidy stage! Ye've no need to make such dramatic gestures! Christ, woman, ye look as though you're about tae have a fit!"

He was wearing a bright scarlet outfit, powdered wig and full make-up to help her, and the sudden emergence of Alex's voice from the rouged lips of Sir Anthony threw her completely. She had actually, after a day and a half of finding it impossible to do so, finally forgotten that he *was* Alex, and was therefore all the more bewildered by his outburst.

"But you said it was like acting a part on stage! You're the one who told me to think of David Garrick's *King Lear,* and how convincingly he plays it!" she shouted back at him.

This was true, and Alex's anger subsided immediately.

"Aye, you're right, I did. I'm sorry," he said. "But Garrick *has* to make enormous overblown gestures, so that those at the back of the theatre as well as the front will be able to understand the emotions he's trying to convey. Whereas you'll be in a drawing room, mostly. You need to be more subtle than he is. It *is* like acting a part. You have to play the wife of Sir Anthony, and believe that's what you are. Your gestures have to be normal. Just be yourself, behave as you would if married to this ridiculous dandy." He raised a hand instinctively towards his hair, then remembering just in time that he was wearing a wig, let it fall back to his side. They sighed in unison, then laughed.

"We're both tired. Let's take a wee rest," he suggested.

They were in the drawing room, and Alex sat down at one of the card tables, picked up a pack of cards, and started toying with them absentmindedly. She took a seat opposite him, and putting her elbows on the table, cupped her chin in her hands, watching him as he shuffled the deck, glad of the temporary respite. He laid the cards out face down on the table, each one overlapping its neighbour, then, turning the first card, ran one finger lightly across the top of the deck so that all the cards were now lying face up.

"D'ye remember Isabella and Charlotte showing you how to play Quadrille?" he asked thoughtfully, gathering the cards together and starting to build a little house with them.

"Yes. Why?" Beth was watching his large long-fingered hands, mesmerised by their dexterity and grace as the precarious house took shape, each card balanced with perfect precision against its neighbour.

"Ye already kent how to play, did ye no'?"

"Yes," she answered. "I thought you suspected as much at the time."

"Aye, I did. But it's my business to be observant. The point is that nobody else guessed. You played the part of a novice card player perfectly. How did ye do it?"

Beth cast her mind back to the excruciating hours when she had sat with a puzzled expression on her face as Isabella painstakingly explained a rule she was already familiar with, of the stupid mistakes she had deliberately made in her first games.

"I did two things," she said. "Firstly I tried to remember how I'd behaved when I had really been learning the game, and play as I had then, but at the same time I tried to forget that I'd ever known how to play at all. That was difficult. But I treated the deception like a joke, a challenge, if you like."

"Right. Good. That's how ye need to think of this. Remember how you behaved when you were with Sir Anthony before ye found out who he really was. And forget that you ever did find that out. In some ways it is a joke, and it's most definitely a challenge."

"But that's the problem!" cried Beth. She raised her head from her hands, and the table shifted slightly, demolishing the delicately balanced card structure. "It's not a joke! I've got to get this right, or not come with you at all. And I do want to come with you, more than you know. I don't want to be buried in the country somewhere and grow old without having ever done anything worthwhile with my life! But this isn't like playing cards at all. If I'd made a mistake over that and Isabella had found out I knew how to play all along, she'd have been hurt. But I wouldn't have sent a man to hang because of it!"

Alex realised now his mistake. By taking her to the hanging he hadn't succeeded in his aim of deterring her from accompanying him. He had badly underestimated how important it was to her to be actively involved in the Jacobite cause. But he *had* frightened her enough for her to be trying too hard to get things right, terrified that he would refuse to allow her to come with him if she didn't, or that she would condemn him if she made one tiny error.

"Beth," he said, abandoning the cards and reaching across to capture her hand instead, "you're trying too hard. You dinna need to convince me that you can do this. You proved that on Tuesday when your cousins called. Ye played the part perfectly, and adapted quickly too, when you found me in the library. If I thought the risk too great, I wouldna let ye come to Europe, no matter what I had to do to stop you. I've frightened you too much, blethering on about torture and hangings and suchlike. It *is* a serious business, I'm no' denying that. But sometimes ye have to treat it like a joke, take chances. You have to relax. If you're tense all the time, ye canna be convincing. Many mistakes can be covered up. It was a mistake to come into the library with Isabella and Clarissa. You covered it up, and I helped ye by falling in with what ye decided to do."

"Angus helped there as well," Beth admitted. She was enjoying the feel of his warm hand enfolding hers, comforting, sensual. "If he hadn't spoken, I think I'd still be standing there now, frozen."

"Aye, well, now there's an example of someone treating the whole thing as a joke and getting away wi' it. He kent I was in the library all along."

"What?" said Beth. "Why didn't he tell me, or steer me to another room?"

"Because he wanted to give ye a chance to prove your acting abilities. And because he thought it'd be amusing to embarrass his older brother. It's no' the first time he's done something of the sort, and it'll no' be the last time either, unfortunately. I'm no' suggesting you approach this in the way Angus does. He can be a wee bit too flippant at times, to say the least, but in general he does well, because he doesna take himself too seriously, and can behave naturally because of that. That's what ye need to do. And ye're no' alone, remember. I'll be there to help you, and so will Angus for that matter. He's coming along as my personal servant."

She felt the tension dissipating, partly because of his reassuring words, but also due to the pleasant languor that was slowly permeating her body as he lazily stroked her hand.

"We can have another try at that scene, if you like," she said half-heartedly. "I feel a lot more relaxed now."

His eyes met hers and held her gaze, then he smiled slowly, knowingly, the dimple in his cheek clearly visible even through the layer of paint. He hadn't applied his usual patch to cover it, she noted absently.

"No, not yet," he said. "I dinna think you're ready to think of me as Sir Anthony just now. I'll go and get us something to eat."

He relinquished her hand, placing it on the table, and standing, left the room. Beth felt as though she'd been doused in cold water. She sat looking at her hand resting on the polished walnut surface where he had left it. She had been certain he had been going to lean across the table and kiss her. She had needed it, yearned for it, had seen her desire mirrored in his eyes.

She must have read the signals wrongly. She was hardly an expert in matters of love, she reflected ruefully. She had certainly read Lord Daniel badly.

By the time Alex returned from the kitchen with wine, freshly baked bread and cold beef, Beth was sitting calmly on the sofa, her composure seemingly restored. They ate in companionable silence for a few minutes. Alex had temporarily removed his wig, saying it was making his head itch, and the copper strands in his tousled hair caught fire in the late afternoon sunlight.

"So how did you get to become Sir Anthony?" Beth asked. Having now seen a considerable amount of Alex, she could not think of anyone further removed from him than the flouncing, effeminate baronet.

Alex emptied his mouth and took a deep draught of wine.

"Aye, well, that was partly my own fault. When we were bairns my father taught us all at home, when it was practical, that was. He was an educated man himself, and didna want us to grow up knowing nothing other than fighting. However, it came to the point where he'd taught me all he could, and so I was sent off tae university to learn more. He couldna really afford it, our circumstances being a wee bit difficult at the time, but he thought that if I got a good education, I could teach Duncan and Angus too, and he'd get three for the price of one. So by one means or another, he raised the money, and off I went."

"Is that where you acquired Sir Anthony's English accent, at Oxford?"

Alex smiled at her with amusement.

"Christ, no, *a ghràidh,* ye're forgetting that Catholics are no' allowed to go tae British universities. I went to Paris instead. That's where I learnt French, among other things."

Alex finished his roll, then left his chair and moved across to the fireplace, throwing a log on and manoeuvring it with the poker until it started to burn merrily. Beth watched him from her place on the sofa, her bare feet curled up under her, thoroughly relaxed now.

"It was in the cheap student taverns that Sir Anthony was discovered," he said, replacing the poker in its stand.

"I can't imagine Sir Anthony drinking in a cheap Parisian tavern," Beth said. "Didn't he complain about the poor quality of the wine and the bad service, not to mention the appalling roughness of the chairs, which pull the threads in one's clothes so abominably?"

"Not in those days, he didna," replied Alex, straightening up from the fire, laughing. "He wasna so privileged then. He wore plain homespun breeches, woollen shirts, and second-hand coats. He had very little money, ye ken. But what he *did* have was a remarkable talent for mimicking people, from unpopular professors to Walpole and even the king himself. No one was safe from his lampooning. It was just a wee bit of fun, and it paid for my wine. Until the E…until the man who was to be my sponsor saw one of my performances. It wasna the sort of place a man of quality would normally frequent, but he'd arrived in Paris late at night, in pouring rain, having broken down along the way. We'll no doubt experience the same thing ourselves when we're abroad. He took a room at the first inn he came to, and arrived in time to see me standing on the table, finishing off a portrayal of a French macaroni who had just been splashed by a dung-cart, before launching into a creditable and pretty unflattering imitation of our glorious King George discussing the philosophy of farting with Aristotle, German accent an' all, to great applause. The next morning I was called into the chancellor's office." He smiled as he remembered how terrified he'd been when he'd been told who the expensively dressed man in the chancellor's office was, and that he'd witnessed Alex's parody of the monarch.

"I nearly pissed my breeches, I was that feart," he said, smiling "I thought I was going to be expelled at the least, and knew my father'd kill me if I was."

But instead, after the chancellor had made the introductions and invited the shaking student to take a seat, he had left the room, leaving the young Scot and the man who was to be his sponsor to become better acquainted.

"When he told me what he wanted me to do, I refused at first," Alex said. "I told him I didna want to skulk around in mansions and palaces, that I didna ken anything of the society life, that what I kent was how tae use a sword and an axe, and that I'd already proved I wasna afraid to kill, if I needed to."

Alex's tone made it clear to Beth, as it had to his sponsor then, that he had killed a man already, maybe several men. He looked up at her, intercepted her look.

"That was seven years ago, Beth. I've killt a good many more men since then. Does that disgust ye?"

"No," she said sincerely. She would have probably killed the Scot in Manchester, if his reactions had not been so fast. "But you were very young, only twenty-three, was it?"

Twenty-three. The same age she was now.

"Twenty-one," Alex corrected her. "I'm twenty-eight now. Two years younger than Sir Anthony. Angus is nineteen, and he's killed, as well. It's a necessary part of life, if you're a MacGregor."

Was it? Why? She wanted to ask, but she also wanted to find out about Sir Anthony.

"Who is your sponsor?" she asked.

He hesitated, but only for a moment.

"Better you dinna know that," he said. "Dinna think I mistrust you, but if anything does go amiss, the less you ken about such things, the better. He's rich, very rich, and he's a Jacobite. And if I'm caught as a spy, I'll no' betray him, and he'll no' lift a finger to help me. It's part of our agreement, and I accept it. No one else knows his identity, no' even Duncan or Angus."

She wouldn't push him to reveal the name. It would do no good anyway.

"So, how did he persuade you to change your mind?" she asked instead.

"By wearing me down slowly, telling me that lots of men could fight, but not many had the skills I had. It was over a year before I agreed. The students used to put on plays and such, just for the other members of the university, and in one of them I played a character called Lord Foppington. He came to see the play, and Sir Anthony was born. Well, no' the name Sir Anthony, that came later, but the character. After that I left university and went to Germany, so that I could learn to speak the language, while my sponsor worked out a suitable identity for me."

"And it took him six years to invent Sir Anthony?" Beth asked. She knew the flouncy baronet had only appeared in London society just over a year ago.

"No," Alex replied. "My circumstances changed. My father died, suddenly, and I had to go back to Scotland."

"Oh, I'm sorry," Beth said. "Did you have to take over the family business?" That was what the eldest son normally did when his father died. Alex's mouth twisted in a wry smile.

"Aye, in a manner o' speaking," he answered, eyes dancing.

"What *is* the family business?" Beth asked, suspicious now.

"Cattle reiving, mainly. And trying to avoid being killed by the Campbells, or anyone else who's a mind to. My father was the chieftain. I succeeded him."

"The Campbells," Beth whispered. They were the bogeymen of her childhood, the demons from hell her mother had told her of, the men who had slaughtered her grandfather and many other MacDonalds in cold blood fifty years before, burning their houses and leaving Beth's grandmother and mother, then aged only two, to fend for themselves in the February snows and sub-zero temperatures.

"I remember now," she said softly, as Alex fixed her with a look which was a mixture of curiosity and concern. She glanced over at him. Dusk was falling, and the light from the fire glowed warmly in the room. In a short while they would have to light candles. "My mother always told me that no matter what the Campbells had done to us, it was nothing compared to what they'd done to the MacGregors."

"Aye, that's right," he agreed. "The MacGregors are proscribed."

At least the MacDonalds of Glencoe had received some reparation and had been allowed to return to their ruined homes after the massacre of many of their clan. But the Campbells had not only stolen the MacGregors' lands, but because of their allegiance to the English crown, they'd also succeeded in obtaining an Act of Proscription against Clan Gregor. Proscription meant they could not use their own names, were not allowed to carry a knife with a point, could not meet in numbers greater than four. Now she could see why Alex and Angus had no fear of danger, and were willing to take insane risks in an attempt to restore the Stuarts to the throne and get the Act repealed. Their very existence as a clan depended on it. It also explained why they used the name Drummond.

She looked at him with new understanding, and he looked at her likewise. He had not known she was of the Glencoe branch of the MacDonalds. They smiled at each other. They were not united merely by religion and the Stuart cause, strong though that was. They had just discovered a new bond, a personal and justified hatred of Clan Campbell. And in that moment they both knew that whatever else happened in the future, however successful or disastrous their marriage turned out to be, that bond would remain, at least.

It was a good start.

* * *

At Alex's insistence they abandoned all thought of rehearsing any more that day.

"We can practice some more on the way to Dover," he pointed out. "Iain's driving us there, so we'll be safe from eavesdroppers. Once we're in France, we'll have to be more careful, as I'll be hiring a postillion."

Instead Alex bounded off upstairs to take off his paint and get out of the ridiculous red outfit, reappearing in the kitchen ten minutes later in time for a huge bowl of mutton stew, after which the household repaired to the library to play a chess tournament, armed with a bowl of plums and several bottles of wine.

Alex played Maggie, and Iain took on Beth, while Angus, who claimed to have no interest in playing tonight, hovered behind his brother, making helpful suggestions. In spite of his sibling's assistance, Alex succeeded in beating Maggie, while Iain demolished Beth with insulting ease, before going on to thrash her husband in the final.

"I used to be footman to an old laird in Edinburgh," he explained later over a bottle of burgundy. "He was a wee bit infirm, didna get out a lot, but he was awfu' fond of the chess, and we used to play together of an evening. He taught me all I ken about the game."

"Aye, he taught ye all ye ken about drinking and idling too. Fine figure of a man Iain Gordon was when I married him," Maggie he winked at Beth. "Two years at yon lairdie's, and he's an idle sot."

"I'm no' idle!" he retorted. He didn't deny the accusation of being a sot, Beth noticed.

"Glad to hear it," his wife replied, so quickly that it was obvious her insult had been bait of some sort, and he had taken it. She was sitting on the floor near his feet, her elbows resting on his knees, her luxuriant red hair, which was her only claim to beauty and of which she was justly proud, hanging loose on her shoulders. "Ye'll have no objections, then, to chopping those logs for the fire in the morning, and fixing the snib on the privy door you've been saying you'll get round to for weeks."

"I've got to drive to Dover tomorrow!" he protested, wriggling feebly on the hook.

"Ye'll no' set off before ten, at the earliest," his wife pointed out. "Plenty of time to chop a few wee logs."

Iain groaned, remembering the enormous pile of wood in the yard. He glowered at Angus, who was grinning hugely.

"Aye, laugh while ye can," he said with mock rancour. "You'll be married one day, then you'll ken what it's like, and you'll be sorry."

"Not me," said Angus, with the supreme confidence of youth. "The lassie I marry will be sweet-natured and biddable."

"They're all sweet-natured and biddable when ye marry them. It's no' till after you've made your vows that they become shrews," he advised, glaring at Maggie.

His wife reached lazily back with one arm, and he ducked too late to avoid the deftly aimed ebony pawn which bounced off the top of his head and disappeared into the shadows in the corner of the room. He rubbed the sore spot with a bony finger and eased his angular body into a position more suitable for defence or retaliation.

"Any woman who has the misfortune to marry a Scotsman *has* to become a shrew, if she wants a decent roof over her head," Maggie countered. "Otherwise she an' her bairns'd freeze to death in their broken down huts while the men were out indulging in the national pastime of fighting. And when they're no' killing each other, they're sitting idle, drinking and telling tall tales, and waiting for the next brawl."

This was so accurate a picture of the traditional Highlander's way of life, that none of the men present could contradict it. "I'm warning ye, Beth," she finished. "Get out now before ye fall in love wi' the wee gomerel. There's no hope for ye after that."

Everyone looked at Alex and Beth, who were seated, wine glasses in hand, side by side on the sofa. There was a small, careful space between the couple, all the more noticeable because the MacGregors were normally a very tactile family. Maggie observed it with a slight frown, and snuggled closer to Iain, who reached down to lift one of his wife's fiery curls and wind it round his finger. He glanced back at the sofa. Next to her tall, well-built husband, Beth looked tiny, delicate. She felt relaxed, perfectly at home with her new family. Her cheeks glowed rosily with wine and happiness. She showed no signs of taking Maggie's advice and running for the hills.

"Aye, she may look the picture of innocence and beauty now, but gie her a few weeks and she'll be a tyrant, like all the rest of her sex," Iain remarked sourly.

"Less than that, I hope," said Alex. "I'm giving her three

days, at the most."

* * *

"They love each other, don't they?" Beth said, as they climbed the stairs. Alex had offered to see Beth to her room, as he was tired too. They left Iain, Maggie and Angus in the library to finish off the wine.

"Aye. Verra much," Alex replied. "That's one reason why I'm taking Angus instead of Iain as my servant. Iain'll no' be parted from Maggie for so long, and she doesna like to travel. England's as much as she's willing to endure, and she's no' really happy here. Iain would be a better choice to take, really. There's no family resemblance between us, although what wi' the make-up and the fact that people dinna look at servants closely, that shouldna be a problem. But Iain's older, and more level headed too. And he's worked as a personal servant before, which Angus hasna."

"What are the other reasons?" she asked.

"Angus is good at talking to people, at firing them with enthusiasm. He's persuasive too, and he can speak French, which Iain canna. And I'd prefer him where I can keep an eye on him."

They'd arrived at the door of her room.

"I'll wish ye a good night's sleep," he said, taking her gently by the shoulders, and kissing her on the forehead. It was a friendly gesture, the sort you might make to a younger sister, perhaps. He turned away.

"Alex," she began. He turned back, waiting politely for her request. What time is breakfast? Can I have another candle?

"Would you like to sleep with me tonight?" she blurted, then flushed instantly crimson. "Only it's the last night we can be sure of being alone together, and undisturbed, for weeks, and I thought…ah…it doesn't matter." She turned away, fumbling blindly for the doorknob. She had interpreted his hesitation as reluctance, he realised.

He placed his hand over hers, gently prising her fingers off the handle.

"I would love to spend this night with ye," he said softly. "But no' if you're only asking me because it's the last chance we'll have for weeks. I said I'd no' touch you until you wanted me to, and I can wait weeks, months if necessary, until you're ready."

Could he? *She is so beautiful. God, give me strength,* he prayed.

"I'm ready," she said. He closed his eyes, opened them again. She was standing there, still flushed, the pulse at her throat beating wildly. But her voice had held no doubt, and nor did her face. Shyness, vulnerability, but no doubt.

She turned from him, lowered the handle and went in, leaving the door open for him to follow. He did, standing just inside the threshold hesitantly, like a virgin schoolboy. His prayer did not change.

She busied herself lighting candles, tending the fire, turning down the bed. Then, when there was nothing left to do, she turned and looked at him helplessly. He had to take command of the situation, had to be gentle, careful. He was fully aware that if their marriage was to have any true chance of success then he had to erase the terrible experience she had had and replace it with something beautiful, although he did not know precisely what form that horror had taken, and therefore had no idea of what would recall that event to her mind, and what would not. He could not ask her. If he failed...

He would not fail.

He moved into the room, sat on the bed and patted the space at his side. She came and sat next to him, folding her hands demurely in her lap. He took one in his.

"You're very tense. What are ye expecting of this night?"

he asked. "Is it that it will hurt a lot and be over in seconds, as you said before?"

The corners of her mouth turned up slightly.

"No," she said. "I don't know what to expect, but I hope it will be something like I feel when you hold my hand, sort of warm and melting, only much more so."

Her honesty was disarming. Her innocence was devastating. Accustomed only to whores and experienced women, Alex felt as nervous as his wife. He realised in that moment that although he had had sex with many women, he had never truly made love to one before. The realisation that he was about to do so was exhilarating. Terrifying.

He placed one arm around her shoulders, bent his head, and kissed her on the lips, gently at first, until he felt her yield to him. Then he deepened the kiss, parting her lips, and placing his free arm under her knees, he lifted her smoothly on to his lap in a soft rustle of silk. Her lips tasted sweetly of wine, and she wrapped her arms around his back, clinging to him. When the kiss ended they were both slightly breathless.

"I think we should undress now," she said, surprising him; he had been wondering how to suggest that without frightening her.

He moved over to the far side of the bed to undress, turning his back to her in order to give her a little privacy. As he was only wearing shirt and breeches, disrobing would take seconds. He decided to take his time, lingering over every button, so that she could be undressed and decently covered by the sheets before he had finished.

He was just about to remove his shirt, when it occurred to him that she was wearing stays, and would need assistance with the laces. He turned round to ask her if she required any help and froze with his mouth open ready to frame the unnecessary question. She had known she would have no maid for a few days, and had anticipated the difficulty by buying some front-lacing stays, so that she would have no difficulties in dressing.

Or undressing. Alex was greeted by the totally unexpected sight of a perfectly formed naked young woman, her glorious hair cascading over one breast to her hips. He inhaled sharply through his mouth and turned away quickly.

"Don't I please you?" she said in a small voice, hating herself.

He turned round again.

"Don't you please me?" he whispered. "Ah, *mo bhean bhrèagha,* you are the most lovely thing I've ever seen."

My beautiful wife. The words were like a benediction, and although she blushed, she also smiled as his gaze lingered on her, on the perfect breasts, the slender waist, the soft roundness of her hips, the…

"Your turn," she said, and he realised he was still fully dressed.

He pulled his shirt roughly over his head, unbuttoned his breeches and slipped them off, giving her a momentary but gratifying view of his broad muscular back and taut buttocks. Then he slid into bed and pulled the sheet up to his waist. He didn't want to frighten her with his erection, which was fierce, demanding. He determinedly ignored it, and smiled reassuringly at her. He leaned over to blow out the candle by the bedside.

"No," she said. "Leave it."

He hesitated, lips pursed, surprised. He had thought, being a little shy tonight, she would prefer the darkness.

"I want to see you," she explained. "I want to know it is you with me. The dark can lead to…imaginings."

Ah. He cursed silently to himself. But the dark had been imperative that night, when he had had to hide himself from her.

"Come," he said. "Join me."

They lay together in the bed, as they had lain to sleep on their wedding night, her head pillowed on his arm. It was relaxing, peaceful, non-erotic, he told himself forcefully. His erection did not subside

"One of the things your friends told you about the wedding night was true," he said after a short silence.

"Which one?"

"It may hurt, but only a very little if we are careful, when I…"

"When you take my virginity," she finished for him.

He nodded.

"Thank God for that," she said. "I can take that. I thought you were going to say it would be over in seconds. I'm not sure I could bear that, after spending two days working out how to get you in bed with me."

A snort of laughter burst from him. This woman never ceased to amaze him. He hoped she never would.

"No," he said, leaning up on one elbow and smiling broadly at her. "It will not be over in seconds. Of that I can assure ye."

He bent down to her, kissing her again, and this time her lips parted eagerly to receive him, and she wound her arms around his neck. After a long minute he broke the kiss, then, as he had on their wedding night, he delicately kissed her, forehead, eyelids, nose, then down her throat, her collarbone, leaving a slow trail of burning kisses. She shivered suddenly, though the room was warm, but showed no signs of leaping from the bed.

Just to be sure, he avoided touching her breasts, instinctively aware that part of her unpleasant experience had involved them. Instead his lips moved between her breasts, only his unbound hair trailing softly across her nipples, which hardened in response. She smelled very faintly of the jasmine soap she used, and beneath that… he inhaled, drinking in the exclusive, sweet female scent of her. He nuzzled gently at the pale, translucent skin. Her fingers tightened involuntarily on his back, and she gasped.

When he reached her stomach he paused, and placing his hands round her waist, slid her effortlessly higher up the bed, before moving his body over hers, spreading her legs gently so he was lying between them, his head level with her stomach, his burnished hair falling forward over her hips, hiding his face. He moved slightly, infinitesimally lower, and she flinched. Dizzy with need, he halted his progress and looked up at her.

"I can stop, if you want me to, at any time," he said huskily. *Oh, God.* "You dinna have to feel obliged because you invited me…"

She reached down, and placed one finger on his lips. Her eyes were smoky, the pupils dilated.

"Don't stop," she whispered breathlessly. "Do anything, but don't stop. Please."

He didn't. His strong fingers stroked gently down the side of her ribs, which were frail as a kitten's, and his lips continued their downward progress, over the soft pale thistledown of hair and onward. His tongue teased out gently between her legs, and he tasted the sweet, musk scent of her. He sighed, deeply, contentedly, and bent to his task.

She made a deep guttural sound then, in the back of her throat, and arched convulsively away from him, but his hands were firm on her waist, holding her in place, and he made no further offer to stop, because the movement was a reaction to almost unbearable pleasure, and he knew it. Her fingers tightened in his hair, pulling his head towards her even as her body arched away, and she trembled from head to toe. His lips curved in a smile against her tender flesh. It was torture, what he was doing to her, and he felt her abandon herself to it, willingly, utterly.

This time the slight rush of moisture as her body prepared itself to receive him went unnoticed by her, although not by him. She was ready for him, breathless, flushed, almost, but not quite, at her climax.

As for himself, he was more than ready, and his body shook with the effort of restraining himself as he slid smoothly up the bed, taking his weight on his elbows so as not to crush her beneath him. Their bodies were joined from breastbone to thigh, and his arousal pushed eagerly against her. The urge to plunge himself inside her was almost overwhelming. Almost. With any other woman he would have given in to it.

He shifted position and eased himself slightly, a fraction of an inch, into her. He felt the tautness as her unaccustomed flesh closed around him, and he swallowed, hard. She raised her knees instinctively, opening herself to him, and he slid into her, one inch, two. It was unbearable. Sweat beaded on his forehead, and his muscles strained with the effort of holding himself back. Her head was thrown back on the pillow, her eyes unfocused, her breathing, harsh and ragged, matching his.

Then suddenly, unexpectedly, she lifted her legs and wrapping them around him, pulled him deep into her with one violent movement that lifted her off the bed. He felt the delicate membrane tear, heard her gasp of pain, and for a second her eyes looked straight into his, perfectly focused and perfectly happy. Then he was moving inside her, slowly at first, and then with increasing speed as her nails dug into his back and her hips intuitively kept rhythm with his, and his fragile control shattered, hurtling them both into sensual oblivion.

Afterwards they lay together for a short while, her head pillowed on his arm, as they had on their wedding night, but apart from their position in the bed, everything else had, irrevocably, changed. Long after her pulse had returned to normal, her breathing had slowed to the soft, regular sound that told him she had slipped into sleep, and the candle had guttered and died, he lay awake, smiling in the dark.

I've beaten you, you bastard, he shouted in silent triumph to his unknown adversary. *She's mine now, and will never belong to another, while I live. And God help you if I ever find out who you are.*

This surge of fierce possessiveness took him by surprise, accustomed as he was to relieving only his physical need with a woman, before departing cheerfully and forgetfully into the night. The responsibility felt good. It felt terrifying. He curled his arm around her, and she made a small inarticulate sound, before relaxing back into sleep. He would not press her to tell him who the man was. She would, when she was ready. And then he would find him, and kill him.

She woke in the morning to the dull thud of an axe rhythmically striking wood in the yard below. Voices engaged in friendly banter drifted up, the words muffled by the closed window, the tone unmistakably amicable. Beth smiled lazily, truly happy for the first time in months.

Alex was still asleep, lying on his side, one arm stretched out across the pillow under her head. Her back was curled into his chest. His other arm rested heavily on her waist. She lifted it gently and turned onto her back, then lowered it back onto her stomach. Turning her head, she watched him for a while as he slept, his face relaxed, mouth curved in a half-smile, long lashes sweeping his cheeks. Asleep he looked younger, and the resemblance to Angus was more pronounced. They had the same eyes, the same high cheekbones, and the same disarming smile.

She thought again about last night, and smiled. This wonderful, gentle man had laid her worst memories to rest. She would never be haunted by Richard again. If she dreamed of strong hands against her naked flesh in future, the hands would be Alex's, and the dream would not cause her to wake sweating and shaking with horror as in countless nights before, but at peace and relaxed, as she was now.

And sore. She had hardly noticed the tearing of her tender flesh the night before, but she did now. And she was thirsty. And it was late; the angle of the sun slanting through the half-open curtains told her that. She shifted position, wincing, and then, turning, started to slide carefully out of bed, so as not to wake him. His arm trailed limply across her stomach for a moment as she moved across the bed, then suddenly wrapped round her waist, halting her progress, and pulling her firmly back against him.

"Where are you going?" he said, his voice clear, alert. If she resisted, he might let her go. Hmm. She snuggled back into him.

"I thought you were asleep," she said. How long had he been awake, aware of her watching him, smiling to herself like an idiot?

"I was," he said. "You woke me when you moved."

"It's late," she said. "We have to get up."

"In a minute," he murmured, his voice drowsy now he knew there was no danger. He always woke clear-headed, ready for instant action if necessary. It was essential for survival. "Five minutes will make no difference. Are ye all right? After last night?"

"Yes," she replied. "A bit sore. But you warned me about that. And I daresay it won't hurt at all in the future."

"No' in the way of last night, no," he agreed. "But I canna guarantee I'll always be able to be so gentle as I was last night. I'll try, mind. But you are verra lovely, *mo chridhe*, and I'll confess I nearly lost control more than once."

She flipped over to face him.

"Can I take that as a compliment?" she said, kissing him on the tip of his nose. Something stirred ominously against her thigh. She smiled, delighted that he found her so desirable.

"Aye, ye can," he growled. "I've changed my mind. Let's get up. Now. Otherwise we'll be verra late and you'll no' be able to sit down tae breakfast, let alone endure the ride to Dover."

He had no wish to turn her slight soreness into a burning agony, which he would not be able to resist doing if she stayed pressed against him any longer. He swung his legs out of bed and got up. Contrary to what she believed, there would be plenty of private moments during the trip to Europe.

He would make damn certain there were.

CHAPTER SEVEN

Nice, October 1743

Dear Friends,

At last I have found the time to write a letter to you, and I am determined I will not allow myself to be distracted until I have told you all my news! I meant to write to you before this, but have really not had a chance. This is because Anthony was most anxious to reach the south of France before the weather becomes too difficult to attempt the sea or alpine crossing to Italy. His intention was to travel with all possible speed to Italy, which we could then explore at some leisure, and to see the sights of France on our return journey. When I pointed out to him that our projected tour is not to exceed some three months or so, in which case a winter crossing of the Alps would be inevitable, returning from Italy to France, he merely stated that one such crossing would be bearable; two would be beyond the ability of mortal man to endure.

What he had actually said was that traversing the Alps in December would give Beth a taste of winter life in the Highlands of Scotland, as, although the alpine mountains were higher than those of Scotland, the horrendous weather was comparable. Added to that was the fact that the Spanish were currently at war with the Duchy of Savoy, and were occupying the main pass between France and Italy, which ran over Mount Cenis. When Beth asked if a meeting with the Spanish army would give her a taste of Highland warfare, Alex had replied that nothing on earth would prepare her for that, as the Highland charge was both a glorious and unique sight to see.

The joyous gleam in Alex's eyes as he had revealed this rendered Beth both curious and apprehensive. She had seen that gleam in both his and his brother's eyes several times in the weeks they had spent travelling the length of France, usually when they were laughingly describing some highly dangerous and illegal raid they had participated in around the shores of Loch Lomond, in the days before he had become Sir Anthony.

From what she gathered, the chief purpose of the brother Duncan's current sojourn in Scotland was to spearhead as many such raids as possible, in order to provide the clan with sufficient food to keep the wolf from the door until spring. The fact that neither Alex nor Angus seemed unduly concerned about their brother's welfare led her to believe that he was very capable in his profession. Neither would they divulge any details about Duncan's appearance, saying only that she would see him soon enough for herself. She wondered if he was deformed in some way, although if he was, his infirmity presumably didn't stop him careering madly round the hills and glens.

As you will no doubt have gathered from the date of this letter, things have not exactly gone according to plan. The journey to Dover was uneventful, although the quality of the inns along the way gave me a good foretaste of what I was to encounter in France (more of this later). We took the packet to Calais, which Anthony assured me would take between three and five hours to reach, whereas in actual fact we were on ship for over ten hours, tossed about most alarmingly on rough seas. Both Anthony and myself felt a little queasy, but our poor servant Jim was violently sick from the moment he stepped on board, and has vowed that he will either swim back to England or remain in France for the rest of his life, rather than endure such an experience again. We were all most relieved to see the coast of France come into view, but then discovered that due to the rough seas, the ship could not enter the harbour, and we had to be rowed ashore in tiny rowing boats by sailors who charged the exorbitant price of two guineas for doing so. When Anthony engaged in vigorous negotiations to try to reduce this sum, Jim, whose yearly wage is only four times this amount, interrupted to say that he would willingly pay ten guineas if only they would get him ashore without any further delay. He was somewhat impertinent, but Anthony desisted from rebuking him, due to the pity aroused by his sickly green pallor.

Beth paused for a minute, smiling at the 'impertinence' which had taken the form of Angus hissing into his brother's ear that if he did not stop penny-pinching and get them on dry land within ten minutes, he would personally, and with the maximum of pain and blood make a eunuch of the baronet forthwith. The baronet in question, incapable of restraining his merriment at his servant's plight, had laughed out loud, remembering just in time to affect the high trill of Sir Anthony, at which Angus, hand on knife, had prepared quite seriously to carry out his threat.

Interposing herself hastily between them, Beth had shrewishly demanded, in a voice that carried across half the ship, to be put ashore *now*, as she was extremely hungry, and wanted nothing more than to sit down to a good meal of eggs and bacon fried in butter. As she had hoped, this mention of food sent Angus retching weakly over the side of the ship, during which respite from hostilities she rapidly brought the negotiations to a close and was assisted into the rowing boat by her husband before Angus could transfer his murderous intentions to her. That she hated fried eggs was well known to him.

She imagined the laughter that would resound around the kitchen in Didsbury, were she able to include this anecdote in her letter, and sighed. Whilst she had no qualms about deceiving the English aristocracy as to the identity of her husband, she was far less happy about lying to her friends, although she understood the necessity for it.

We then had all our baggage searched by the customs men, who would not release our goods until they were in possession of half a crown each. Luckily, Anthony has been in France before, and knew to have our trunks marked with a lead stamp, so that we would not have a similar experience at every garrison town between there and Paris. This did not, however, ensure us a speedy passage through France, as Anthony had hoped.

We have brought our own carriage, and decided to go by the post-route, in the hopes that there would be ample fresh horses, and that the roads would be good. We were wrong on both counts; due to the ongoing war, couriers have first claim on the post horses. On several occasions we were delayed by the fact that there were no horses to be had at any price. Add to that that the French roads are in general in no better a state of repair than English ones, coupled with the fact that the French postillion we hired seemed to think it his duty that our carriage achieve a speed of no more than four miles an hour and you will understand why it has taken us a full month to reach Nice! Anthony was beside himself at times, but all his threats and entreaties carried no weight with the postillion, who slouched over the horse in his enormous boots and greasy hat and continued resolutely at walking pace.

This really had been a problem. On previous trips to the continent, her husband had always travelled as Alex MacGregor, haring across the countryside on the fastest horses he could obtain, sleeping under hedges when necessary, and eating as he rode. The average journey time for Alex from Dover to Paris was three days or less. It had taken Sir Anthony Peters over a week to cover the same distance, and a further three weeks to reach Marseilles. He had to keep up his image, feigning exhaustion at the rigours of travel and accepting invitations to dine with various of his acquaintance along the way, staying sometimes for a couple of days. They had announced to all their intention to bypass Paris and visit it on their return, which was eccentric enough; they could not avoid all the sights along the way without causing comment. So in public Sir Anthony, his wife and footman had pursued their leisurely, powdered, flouncy way through France, and in the uncertain privacy of their rooms in various inns Alex had railed quietly but intensely at the fact that they would not reach Rome before Christmas, at this rate.

When Beth had asked him what the great hurry was, he had said that he was under an obligation to visit Rome and the Stuarts, and report back to Sir Horace Mann on his findings, but was reluctant to be away from his various enterprises in England for too long. Intercepting her questioning look, he had hurriedly taken her off for an evening stroll through the ancient town of Amiens, pointing out the beauties of the Gothic cathedral, and warning her in his piping voice to be careful that the glories of the churches in France did not mislead her as to the iniquities of the Catholic faith practised within. This, as intended, had elicited approving smiles from the group of English tourists they had been passing at the time, and Sir Anthony had continued his pompous expounding all the way down to the banks of the River Somme, where they had managed to find a private spot where there was no danger of them being overheard.

He had then acquainted her with his visit to the duke of Newcastle and his new role as double agent. Beth had at first been appalled at the added danger this would entail, but Alex, with many disarming smiles and a very persuasive turn of phrase had managed to convince her that it would be lunacy to turn down the God-given opportunity of seriously misleading the rabid anti-Jacobite Mann as to the intentions of the Stuarts. Besides, he found it very amusing that the

Hanoverians were covering much of the cost of the trip, and were therefore unknowingly paying for a Jacobite spy to report to his monarch.

She was well aware that her husband's powers of persuasion, coupled with her growing affection for him and her inclusion into the bantering, loving relationship he enjoyed with his brother, was clouding her judgement. She was in danger of being persuaded into any venture, because she now felt as relaxed and happy in the company of the MacGregor brothers as she did with the people she was attempting to write to.

Turning back to her task, she determined not to be distracted again. She must finish this long overdue letter tonight.

The countryside between Calais and Amiens consists mainly of open country, with many cornfields and some woodland, but further south there are vineyards and occasionally noblemen's chateaux to be seen, with landscaped gardens. Graeme would not enjoy working here; the French seem inordinately fond of topiary and very rigid neatly trimmed borders and paths. He would be clipping the whole day! At Chantilly we visited the Palace of Condé, where the gardens contrive to be more natural, with woods, fountains and canals. But it is still too formal for my taste.

We did not spend any time in Paris, and pressed straight on to Chalon, where we took a two day trip down the Saône to Lyons in a large boat holding about fifty people, and towed by two horses. Jim was very apprehensive about leaving dry land, but admitted later that he had not felt the slightest qualm, and indeed, by the amount of mutton he ate at dinner, I have no reason to doubt his assertion. It was a great relief to be away from the jolting of the carriage, and the views as we approached Lyons were breathtaking, mountains covered with chateaux and gardens, and the town itself very grand, with a huge square dominated by a statue of Louis XIV on his horse. We stayed a few days here, as

Anthony met yet another friend, Sir William Craddock. My husband has friends everywhere, and it seems that most of them are touring France at the moment! We visited a silk factory, where we watched as some patterned silk cloth was woven. The women seem to merely tangle a pile of coloured threads indiscriminately on a loom, which then moves back and forth, and transforms itself into an intricate pattern. They are very talented. It was really interesting, and Anthony was beside himself with joy, insisting on ordering some lengths of bright purple silk covered with crimson butterflies, which he intends to have made up into a suit at the earliest opportunity.

It was some relief to discover that Anthony does not intend to battle either with the Alps or the Spanish, and has opted for the safer option of sailing from Nice to Genoa. Yesterday we crossed into Savoy, arriving in Nice at lunchtime, and hoped to take a felucca immediately to Genoa, as the weather seemed to us quite mild, and the sea relatively calm. However, the sailors have informed us that the weather is far too dangerous to attempt a sailing, to the annoyance of my husband, and the great joy of Jim.

We have now taken an apartment, as the weather has freshened, and it seems we may be here for some days. The rooms are clean and comfortable; a refreshing change from some of the filthy, vermin-infested hovels we have stayed in en route. After I had been eaten alive for five days, getting no more than an hour of sleep a night, and too busy scratching by day to enjoy the scenery, Anthony purchased some travel mattresses, which you can roll up and secure to the carriage, and I bought a large quantity of lavender oil, with which I douse the beds each night to deter visitors, and we have slept peacefully ever since. Anthony has also abandoned his horrible violet cologne, thank God, as he says he smells so strongly of lavender from the bed, he has no need to go to the expense of wearing additional perfume.

Beth paused, setting down her pen and flexing her fingers to ease the incipient writer's cramp. She stretched her arms, and looked around the green and gold room. Clean and comfortable were hardly fit adjectives to describe her opulent surroundings. They had taken a suite of rooms with fine views across the countryside, with its groves of orange and lemon trees, to the olive-shrouded hills beyond. The apartment consisted of a large sitting room in which Beth, in a loose dressing gown, was now writing, and two bedrooms, the smaller of which Angus had appropriated. Having eased her muscles, and carefully loosened a strand of hair which was pulling at her scalp from the pins which held her elaborate confection of a hairstyle in place, she dipped her pen again. Lord Basingstoke, who had taken a house in Nice for the summer, had invited them to a ball that evening. They had to leave in less than an hour, and she wanted to finish this letter and dress before then.

The rooms are all green and gold. In fact, there is a little too much gold for my liking. It does look pleasant now as I sit here at dusk writing by candlelight, which mutes the glare of the gold. In daylight, with the sun streaming in at the windows, it can be dazzling, to say the least! As we arrived only yesterday, and spent today visiting several of Anthony's friends, we have as yet had no time to explore the town and I will have to describe that in my next letter. However, from the ramparts the streets appear narrow, and the buildings are of stone, many of the windows fitted with waxed paper instead of glass. As I write to you, Anthony is standing on the balcony, watching night descend over the mountains. The sea air is very clean and refreshing.

As if on cue, a cool salt breeze drifted through the open doors which led out onto the balcony, bringing with it the sounds of laughter, distant music from the town, and her husband.

"Would you be terribly disappointed, my dear, if we did not attend the ball this evening?" Sir Anthony asked. "Only I find that I am so dreadfully exhausted from the travel of the past few days, and simply do not think I can stay awake for much longer, no matter how tempting the party may be." The balcony doors were still open; there was a chance they could be heard from below.

"No, I don't mind," Beth replied. "It will at least give me a chance to finish my letter. But will we not be missed?"

"I hardly think so. There will be at least two hundred guests present. I doubt that the lack of our presence, scintillating as it is, will cast a shadow over the evening." The red lips curved up in a smile.

Sir Anthony closed the balcony doors, and then the curtains. The laughter and music were muted. He moved over to the dressing table, removing his wig as he went and placing it on its stand. Then, sitting, he began to take off his make-up. Beth turned her attention back to her letter, relieved at not having to make light-hearted conversation all evening. Maybe she could write to her cousins as well; she had promised them a letter from every place of note, and so far had not written a word.

I will write now of more practical, and indeed, more important matters. I am sure that by now Mr Cox will have been in contact with you to tell you of my husband's agreement that five hundred pounds be released to each of you. Indeed, by the time this letter arrives at its destination, it is most likely that you will already be in receipt of these funds. I want to assure you that Anthony imposed no conditions regarding this endowment; I am making no sacrifices in order for you to receive this money. You can use it as you wish, whether you wish to set up house together,

She had reached the bottom of the page, and taking another sheet of paper, dipped her pen again and continued.

…or go your separate ways. But please write to me as soon as you

have decided what to do. You need no longer write to Mr and Mrs Harlow's address. Anthony will not open any letter addressed to me.

You will have realised that my husband is as far from being like Richard or my cousins as it is possible to be. I am now sure that I did the right thing in marrying Sir Anthony Peters. In spite of the fact that he is still undoubtedly a 'purple popinjay', in private he is quite a different person. In fact, over the past weeks that we have been travelling together, I have come to l...

"Eeek!" she screeched, her hand jerking wildly across the paper. A large blot of ink appeared on the page, next to the letter 'l'.

"I'm sorry," said Alex, lifting his hand from her shoulder. "I didna mean to frighten you."

She looked down at the ruined paper and sighed. He replaced his hand on her shoulder and peered over the top of her head, surveying the damage

"Come to what?" he asked, bending down to kiss her slender neck, so beautifully revealed by the upswept hairstyle. He nuzzled softly at the sensitive spot just behind her ear. She shivered. "Live with his irritating habits? Like, just a wee bit?" One hand still resting warmly on her shoulder, he reached up with the other and expertly released her hair from its pins, watching appreciatively as it slid in a silken silver waterfall down her back. He bent over again, nibbling gently at her earlobe. "Lust after?" he murmured hopefully.

Beth leaned away from him, detaching her ear from his disturbing attentions and screwing the offending piece of paper into a ball.

"Loathe absolutely," she said firmly and untruthfully, picking up another sheet of paper and laying it flat on the baize surface of the desk. "I thought you were exhausted from travelling," she added.

"Sir Anthony is exhausted from travelling," he pointed

out, unfazed by his wife's professed hatred for him. One arm slid smoothly round her waist. His lips returned to her neck. "Alex is in quite another frame of mind."

"Well, Alex will have to wait," Beth said. "I want to finish this letter. And write to Isabella, too. I should have done this weeks ago."

"Tomorrow," he suggested, burying his face in her hair. "Mmmm."

"No. Tonight," said Beth, summoning the last of her resistance and reaching for a new quill from the pot.

The arm round her waist tightened suddenly and then he straightened up, lifting her off the stool and overturning it in the process. The pot toppled over, scattering quills across the desk and on to the floor.

"Alex, put me down. Someone might come in," she said desperately, wriggling and pulling at his arm in a half-hearted and futile attempt to free herself. Her feet dangled in space several inches from the ground.

"The door's locked," he said softly into her ear, before kissing it. "Only Angus has the key. He's out, and willna return till the morning. He thinks we're going to the ball, and he'll no' be needed tonight." He reached up with his free hand, brushing his fingertips lightly across her breasts. Her nipples rose eagerly through the thin silk of her dressing gown and she moaned softly, giving the lie to her protests. He chuckled quietly to himself and made his way to the bedroom, clutching his prize firmly to his chest.

* * *

From being a small child, he had learned to notice anything out of the ordinary in his surroundings. The slightest disturbance could signal the presence of a hidden enemy, a deadly danger. So the first thing Angus noticed when he opened the door of the apartment was the overturned stool and quill pot. The lamp was still burning, and candles too, on the dressing table and writing desk.

They would not go out and leave lights burning.

Motioning to his companion to stay outside, he drew his sword and advanced cautiously into the room. He paused at the desk and inhaled, his nostrils flaring delicately; jasmine soap, lavender, a hint of Sir Anthony's violet cologne, the pervading ozone tang of the sea. Nothing alien.

"*Cosa c'è?*" his companion whispered from the doorway. He waved his sword impatiently at her, hoping she would realise he was not threatening her, but telling her to stay there, then he tiptoed to the closed door at the far end of the room.

He pushed the latch down carefully and opened the door, preparing to slam it against the wall in case anyone was hiding behind it. He did not have to inhale this time. The unmistakable scent of sexual arousal, coupled with the brief glimpse he had of the bed before he backed out rapidly, closing the door as silently as he had opened it, told him there was nothing amiss. Quite the opposite, in fact.

Angus left the apartment, blowing out the candles and turning down the lamp on his way. The place could burn to the ground and his brother and sister-in-law wouldn't notice. He locked the door behind him, cursing silently under his breath in Gaelic, his own amorous intentions thwarted.

"*Mi dispiace,*" he said to his companion in slow, halting Italian. "*Non è possibile. Mio padrone...*" He let the sentence trail off, not knowing the words to explain any further, but hoping she would understand that they couldn't stay here tonight.

They stood for a moment in the corridor, the tall blond man and the slender brunette woman, pondering the situation.

136

"*Quanti soldi hai?*" she said after a moment.

What had she said? Something about money? He turned out his pockets, revealing several French louis d'or, and a few sous, and shook his head sadly. He had not had time to get any Italian currency, and hadn't thought he would need it tonight, having intended only to go for a walk around town, listen to some music perhaps, observe the sights that were cost-free. But then he had caught the eye of this beautiful dark-eyed girl dressed in a sunny yellow striped gown, and by dint of many hand signals, his pigeon Italian, and the irresistible MacGregor charm, had persuaded the girl, Katerina, to join him for the night. By going back to the apartment, he had hoped to treat her to an opulent evening for free. A bottle of wine, beautiful surroundings, anything was…no longer possible. Damn Alex!

The girl had taken the money from his hand and was counting it in rapid Italian under her breath. She was the personal maid to an Italian noblewoman, he had gathered from the few words he had understood of her chatter as she had walked beside him to the hotel. He would not tumble her in a back alley, even if she'd allow him to, which he doubted. She was no whore, and he was a gentleman. Damn Alex to hell! Why hadn't they gone out?

It was obvious why they hadn't gone out, and in one way Angus was glad. Over the course of the last few weeks, their relationship had gone from strength to strength. Angus had noticed the small gestures, the sudden smile when his brother came into the room, the trivial reasons Beth invented to lay her hand on his arm, the light in her eyes when Alex appeared from the mask of Sir Anthony and she could abandon the pretence of being bored with her effeminate husband, which she now, after a few initial hiccups, played to perfection. Angus would have known perfectly well what the unfinished 'l' word in Beth's letter was, even if his older brother was too dense to.

Katerina seemed to suddenly come to a decision, and handed his money back to him.

"*Vieni,*" she said, and taking his arm, began to tow him unresisting down the corridor.

* * *

Beth was surprised by the amount of noise Angus made when he entered the apartment the following morning. He was normally very quiet, but the loud scraping of the key in the lock was no doubt due to the fact that he was trying to balance a large silver breakfast tray on one arm while opening the door, although he brought breakfast to them most mornings without making such a racket.

Although the day was fine, they had decided not to eat on the balcony, as that would necessitate Alex donning all the trimmings of Sir Anthony, which he had no intention of doing until Beth had finished her letters and they had to go out. Instead they had set the table in the room, and Angus placed the tray carefully in the middle of it, before sitting down. He was a little dishevelled, Beth noticed. His hair had clearly been hastily combed with his fingers before being tied back, and his shirt was crumpled.

Not that either her or Alex could claim any pretensions to neatness, but at least they had washed, and brushed their hair. She eyed the table, to see what was for breakfast, and gave a sudden gasp of pleasure. In the middle of the tray, surrounded by a coffee pot, cups, a dish of grapes, slices of polenta and Parmesan cheese, was a slender glass vase containing a single perfect cream flower.

"Oh, where did you get this?" she exclaimed, never having seen a bloom like it before. "It's beautiful!" She picked up the delicate vase, and sniffed at the flower. The petals were thick and waxy and a faint pink blush tinted their underside.

Angus beamed.

"D'ye like it? It doesna have a scent, but it's awfu' pretty, is it no'?"

"What's it called?" she asked, smiling up at him.

"It's called an apology," Alex put in, lifting the coffee pot off the tray and pouring the steaming brown liquid into the three cups.

Beth looked between the two, confused. Angus had reddened slightly. He sat down.

"What do you need to apologise for?" she asked.

"Nothing," said Angus hastily, glaring at his brother. He should have known Alex would have registered his appearance in the room, brief though it was. He never missed anything.

"Angus came home early last night, and decided to kindly check on us and see if we needed him to sing a lullaby or tell a wee story tae send us to sleep," Alex continued nonchalantly.

"I...ah...thought there was something wrong," Angus said, blushing furiously and casting murderous looks at his brother, who smiled serenely back. "The stool had been turned over, and all the lights were burning..."

To the men's surprise, Beth did not redden with embarrassment. Nor did she lay into Angus for strolling into her bedroom in the middle of the night. Instead she turned on Alex.

"I *told* you someone might come in on us, didn't I?" she said. "But you wouldn't listen. And you could have burnt the place down and killed us both, not to mention all the hotel's other occupants! Men! Once they get amorous, they lose every ounce of common sense."

Alex stared at her, shocked by the unfair accusation. Beth had not thought about the fire hazard either at the time, and while Alex might have indeed carried her resisting to bed, she had neither mentioned the candles herself nor shown

139

anything other than a very energetic enthusiasm for what had followed once they had got there. He opened his mouth to protest, then shut it again, knowing it was pointless.

"You owe me four louis," Angus inserted into the pause, his composure restored now that his brother was in trouble.

"No, I dinna," said Alex firmly. "Ye had no right to be bringing lassies back here anyway. I'm no' paying for your whoring. An' if ye can afford to squander money on expensive flowers, you dinna need any from me."

"She waited outside, and didna see a thing." Angus anticipated Beth's next question. "And I didna pay anything for the flower. It's an orchid, by the way," he said to Beth, before turning back to Alex. "And she wasna a whore, but a maid to the Countess of somewhere or other in Naples, I think." He laughed suddenly, merrily, his blue eyes dancing as he remembered the previous night. "After we left here, I had to make it up to her. She suggested we go for supper. I didna know they take French money in Savoy. Anyway, she was a wee bit disappointed at no' being able to spend the night here, so we had oysters and champagne an' suchlike. Then she suggested we go back to the Count's summer residence, as he'd be at the ball you were supposed tae be out at. We went to his hothouse. No one goes there except the Count, ye ken, so she was sure we wouldna be disturbed."

"Which is where you got the orchid from," Beth said, sipping her coffee.

"Aye." Angus smiled. He fished in his pockets. "I got these, too." He laid three dark blood oranges on the table.

"Do you no' think the Count might notice that someone's been raiding his exotic fruit and flowers?" Alex asked.

Angus waved a hand dismissively.

"Christ, man, I could ha' brought a whole basket of stuff. The place is enormous. Anyway, when he goes in to water his plants today, he'll have a lot more to occupy him than a few missing oranges. There were pineapples, too, or I think that's what Katerina called them. A*nanasso*, that's pineapple in Italian, is it no'? Big things wi' prickly leaves. Too big tae fit in my pocket though," he said regretfully. "They dinna look anything like apples."

"Well, in spite of your disappointment at no' tasting pineapple, I'm still no' paying ye four louis," Alex said. "It sounds tae me that you got what you wanted anyway, even if it wasna in our bedroom." He winked at Beth, who fought not to give him the satisfaction of blushing, and succeeded in going only faintly pink.

"Believe me, *mo bhrathair*,' Angus stated confidently. 'It'll be worth four louis to you to know what happened next, and why the Count'll no' be counting his oranges the day."

"Aye, maybe you're right," Alex replied, leaning back in his chair and stretching lazily. "But it'll be cheaper still tae thrash ye till ye tell me. The result'll be the same, and it'll be more pleasurable than giving you money."

Angus put down his cup and shifted his chair backwards, smiling, eyes alert in anticipation of his brother's playful assault. Beth drained her cup and stood, going over to the desk, where the blank piece of paper still awaited her. She opened one of the drawers and there was a faint clinking sound from within.

"There," she said, throwing four gold coins on the table. Angus's hand shot out with lightning speed and the money disappeared. "We've failed to get thrown out of the hotel for burning it down. I don't want to be thrown out for brawling either. What happened next?"

Angus looked at his brother, then, satisfied that curiosity held precedence over the need for release of pent-up energy, he pulled his chair back under the table.

"Well, as I said, after the meal, we chatted as well as we could for a time, given that she doesna speak English or

French, and my Italian's no' up to much, and then she took me to the hothouse, where we made ourselves a wee nest in a lovely pile of straw at the back. It's used for mulching the plants, ye ken," he explained to Beth. "Anyway, it was while we were…er…embracing, that I heard a noise."

The first emotion Angus had felt when he heard the door open was frustration. It seemed that the gods were conspiring to thwart his amorous intentions at every move. The second emotion was anxiety. Not for himself; he was confident that he could either talk or fight his way out if discovered. But the girl would be at the least turned out of a job, and at worst accused of trespass or burglary. Alerted by Angus's sudden stillness, Katerina also heard the unmistakable sound of someone entering their haven, and the pair crouched down into the shadows. Angus quickly threw a few scoops of straw over them, hoping that it would be enough to conceal them, at least from a cursory inspection. The hothouse was enormous: if they remained still and quiet, they would not be discovered by accident.

Any thought that another couple might have had the same idea as them was dismissed by the intruder's first words, which came from a point closer to their hiding place than Angus liked.

"Now, we will not be disturbed here, and you can say whatever it is that you seem to think will interest me in complete privacy. You have five minutes." The man spoke in rapid and fluent French, and had the arrogant tone of someone who was used to being obeyed.

"When you hear what I have to say, my lord Henri, you will give me more than five minutes. My information is worth a lot of money." The second man's voice was more servile, but held the assurance that the information he had put him in a position of temporary power.

"I will be the judge of that. Tell me what you know."

"Very well. I will tell you a little, and then if you wish to know more, perhaps we can come to an arrangement. The king of France is planning to invade England."

The lord Henri laughed derisively.

"Is this the news you kept me from the opera to tell me?" he said. "Louis has been talking of invading England for twenty years, and will no doubt still be talking of it on his deathbed many years from now. You waste my time, sir." There was a rustling sound, as the lord turned to leave.

"He is doing a good deal more than talking, my lord," the other man put in hurriedly. "In August he sent his horsemaster James Butler to England, to find out the level of support for the Stuarts. He has now returned, and it seems there is a great deal of support for a French-led invasion. The king has now started planning. I assume you know that he is holding regular meetings with Amelot and Maurepas?"

Henri had stopped and turned back. Angus slid his arm reassuringly around the girl's shoulder, praying she would realise from the tone of the voices that this was no light-hearted assignation, and would remain silent.

"Yes," said Henri. "Regarding the war in Germany and Austria."

"That is what Louis would have everyone believe. But in reality, he is planning to invade England in the spring. He has already started to assemble his forces."

"These are serious assertions," the lord replied. "Do you have proof?"

"Of course. I can tell you where the troops will be massing, how many ships will sail, their destination in England, and the names of the leaders of the Jacobites in England who will assist them. It is most secret information, my lord. Even the royal favourite Noailly does not know of it. Nor does Cardinal Tencin, or Orry." The man paused.

"How is it, then, that you know?" asked his companion.

"I have my ways. Walls have ears, as you might say, and I am skilled at passing unnoticed. It doesn't matter. The fact is, I speak the truth."

"Yes, go on then," said Henri impatiently.

"I think this information is worth at least, oh, a thousand louis, my lord," the man replied. "Do you have the money?"

"A thousand louis?!" said Henri, incredulously. "Are you mad? Your news would make interesting after-dinner conversation, but is hardly worth a hundred louis, let alone a thousand."

"Do you not think, then, that the English would pay at least double that to know the full invasion plans of the French army?"

"Maybe they would," said Henri casually. "Is that what you then intend? To go to England with your information?"

"No, my lord. I am a servant, low-born. I could not get anywhere near King George, nor would I be believed if I did. Even if I was, I would receive little reward. Fifty pounds or so, perhaps, as befits my station. You, on the other hand, would receive a good deal more."

"I am a trusted employee of King Louis," replied Henri. "Do you not think it more likely that I will denounce you to the authorities as a blackmailer and a traitor, than go running to the enemy?"

"No, I do not, my lord," his companion asserted, confident now. "Because as well as knowing Louis' invasion plans, I also know that you are a spy in the pay of the Hanoverian king."

"A spy?" interrupted Alex. "Did ye get a good look at the man?"

"No," Angus admitted. "It was dark, and I didna dare to move in case we were spotted. I thought it more important that I heard all the conversation. But I think Henri was his

144

real name. After all, they thought they were alone. Why would they use false names?"

"Do you know him, Alex?" Beth asked.

"No," said Alex, considering. "But I havena been to Louis' Court for a good few years, and Henri is a very common name."

"I'd know the man again, in any case," Angus said. "Whenever he spoke the letter 's', he hissed through his teeth, just a wee bit, but enough to be distinctive."

"What happened next?" Beth asked, enthralled.

"Henri appeared defeated, promised the man money, or even gave some to him, if he had any with him," Alex answered.

"How do you know that?" Beth asked.

"Because it's what I would have done. Go on," he said to his brother.

"Aye, you're right. There was a sort of chinking sound, and Henri said that it was something on account, and he'd draw the rest from his banker, if the information was good. The other man assured him that it was, and that if he didna pay up, he would let it be known that Henri was no' all he appeared to be."

"So, did he reveal the plans?" Alex said.

"Aye," replied Angus. "They're a wee bit uncertain at the moment, still in the early stages of planning. But it seems the duke of Beaufort, Lord Orrery, Lord Barrymore and Sir Watkin Williams Wynne, to name but a few, have all agreed to actively support an invasion, and help the troops to land at Essex. Louis is collecting information as to the number of troops and ships that can be mustered. It certainly seems serious, Alex. Henri seemed to believe him." His eyes sparkled

"I wonder if Prince Charles knows about this?" Alex said.

"No, the informer said that Louis doesna want the Stuarts to know yet, because the prince is watched and if he leaves

Rome for France, it'll alert the British that something's afoot."

"Aye, well, Louis might not want Charles to know, but if he doesna know yet, he will do soon enough. He should. After all, no one in Britain, Jacobite or otherwise, will support a French invasion unless it's to restore James Stuart to the throne."

"He may not have heard yet," said Beth. "Isn't Rome virtually cut off from the outside world by the plague scare?"

Angus looked at his brother and laughed.

"So much for no' worrying the lassie," he said.

"How did ye know about the plague?" Alex said. "Why did you no' say anything?"

"I read the newspapers," responded Beth tartly. "And everything else I can get my hands on. And contrary to what everyone believes, I do occasionally listen to drawing room chatter too. There's plague in the Mediterranean, but in Italy it seems to have been contained at Calabria. But there's still quarantine in force everywhere, fifteen days in Genoa, I believe. I didn't say anything, because I knew you were trying to stop me worrying, which is rather sweet, although I'd prefer it if you didn't."

Alex looked not a little embarrassed, both at being called sweet in front of his brother, who would no doubt store this for future use, and at the fact that Beth had known about the plague all along.

"There isna any danger of contagion. I was going tae tell you," he muttered.

"You'd have had to, soon enough," she replied. "We'll be in Genoa in a few days, weather permitting. I'd much rather you told me everything, you know, good or bad. You're still underestimating me. I'm not the sort of woman who has the vapours at the slightest problem. You should know that by now."

Intellectually he did, but he still had difficulty reconciling

146

the fragile beauty of his wife with the indomitable spirit it concealed. Even though he had fallen in love with her wild and independent nature, she still aroused his protective instincts. He would talk to her about it, but not in front of Angus.

"What happened next, after the idiot had given all his information to Henri?" he asked.

What had happened next was that Angus had heard the unmistakable liquid gargling of a man choking on his own blood, and the sounds of a very brief scuffle, and then the blackmailer had crashed through some young banana trees and landed with a dull thud no more than a few feet from where they lay. The wire that Henri had used to garrotte the man had cut deeply into his throat, and a dark stain started to slowly spread across the floor towards their hiding place.

Angus still had his arm around Katerina's shoulder, and feeling her tense, had clapped his hand firmly over her mouth to stifle any scream, pulling her head into his shoulder so that she couldn't break his hold if she struggled. She stiffened for a moment, her eyes wide with threatened hysteria, then she relaxed into him. He drew his knife silently, praying that Henri would want to leave the scene of the crime as quickly as possible. The man was obviously dead, but if his killer wished to be sure, and came to examine his victim, there was a possibility that he would see the couple hiding in the straw. To his relief, Henri bent only to pick up the purse of money the man had dropped in his death throes, before leaving the room hurriedly.

"If I hadna been with the girl, I'd have killed him anyway," Angus said. "But she knows I'm Sir Anthony's footman. She's been here. She'd be bound to tell someone, and I couldna bring myself to kill her too. I'm sorry, Alex."

Alex rubbed his hands through his hair.

"Dinna be sorry, Angus. But it's a shame you were no' alone. We have to find out if the information about the invasion is true."

"Is it likely to be?" Beth asked.

"Aye, it's possible," Alex replied. "It would be a good time to invade, with most of the British troops fighting abroad. Although they'll be going into winter quarters soon, and a lot of them will be in Bruges and Ostend, from where they can return to England quickly, if they need to. So if Louis does plan to invade, he needs to keep it secret for as long as possible. If the French make a surprise attack, they could be in London before the troops could be recalled, and Charles could take the crown for his father. Once that happens, even his most circumspect supporters will declare for him."

The three Jacobites sat in silence for a moment, contemplating this wonderful possibility.

"We need to do something about this Henri, if we can find him," Alex continued, frowning. "We *have* to find him, I think. I'd like to double back to Paris, but I canna do that without arousing suspicion. Mann is expecting me to go to Rome, so I'll have to, but I think that now we should get there as fast as the quarantine will allow, and find out what Charles knows. We dinna ken why Henri is in Nice, of course. He may be enroute to Italy as well, for all we know. We'll keep a look out for him on the way. Aye, it may have been better if ye'd killed him while you had the chance, Angus, but there's no help for it now."

"Is that what you would have done?" Beth asked. The unasked question was written on her face. *Would you have been willing to kill an innocent young girl in cold blood?*

"I'm no' certain," Alex said candidly. "But on consideration, aye, I probably would have done. If the information is true, then we're standing on the edge of the best chance the Stuarts will ever have to be restored to the throne. And this man Henri now has the information to stop it, if he is working for the British." He looked intently at Beth, his eyes hard. "I will do whatever I have to to restore the Stuarts, Beth. It's our only chance for freedom. It's no' always possible to protect the innocent, although where I can, I will, and I dinna blame you for being human, Angus. Part of me would have thought less of you if ye'd been able to kill her."

Angus had laid his hands on the table, and was examining them, avoiding his brother's gaze.

"Like ye said once before," Alex said softly to him, "there's a big difference between killing a man when you're blood's up, and killing one in cold blood. You were willing to do that last night. Killing a woman at all, let alone one ye've just been tumbling, is another thing entirely. I wasna being kind when I said I'm no' certain what I'd have done, I meant it. I wasna there, I havena seen the girl, although I mean to."

Angus looked up. Alex's eyes were warm, affectionate, held no sign that he thought his younger brother was weak. Quite the opposite, in fact. Angus smiled, quickly, and then was serious again.

"I'm seeing her again tonight," he said. "She's verra bonny. But why do you need to see her? I took her to an expensive inn afterwards and managed to calm her. She's sensible. She'll no' say anything, I'm sure of that. If she did, she'd risk this man coming after her. She was terrified of him, that much I could tell in any language."

"You said the men spoke in French. Are ye sure she doesna understand the language at all?" Alex asked.

"Of course I am!" Angus replied. "I wouldna be spending half my time inventing hand signs, and wishing I'd learnt more than basic Italian, if she could speak French!"

"There's a difference between understanding a language and speaking it, though, is there no'?" Alex said. "Humour me. Bring her here tonight, just for a few minutes, and we'll make sure."

What Alex intended to do if it was discovered that Katerina did understand French, he was not willing to reveal.

They were going out that night, to a card party, and Alex took especial care over his appearance. Once dressed, in royal blue velvet edged with Brussels lace, her hair beautifully dressed by her husband, who was reasonably expert in such matters, being able to curl and powder his own wigs, Beth sat at the writing desk to put the finishing touches to her letter to Isabella. Angus had departed some time before, promising to bring Katerina for a brief visit at eight o' clock. He seemed as nervous as Beth about Alex meeting the girl, which, as he knew a lot more about the violent side of his brother than she did, made Beth even more anxious.

After some time, the bedroom door opened, and Sir Anthony appeared. Although Beth had seen the transformation many times, it still never ceased to amaze her. The tall, burly, indisputably masculine Alex MacGregor would disappear into a bedroom, and within half an hour, would metamorphose into the effeminate, affected baronet. Occasionally she had watched as he rose from his seat at the dressing table, having just applied the paint, rouge and patches. He would stand erect at first, still imposing, still Alex, in spite of the paint, and then he would slump his shoulders, loosen his joints, and compress his spine, shaving a couple of inches off his height in the process. After that he always gave a small sigh, before taking on the rest of Sir Anthony's mannerisms. The strong stride would shorten, become mincing, the muscular arms and wrists become almost boneless, the hands fluttering languidly. The compelling MacGregor charisma was still there, but subdued by the frivolous, superficial personality of the fop. It was remarkable.

Tonight it took longer than half an hour to effect the transformation, and when her husband finally made his appearance, even Beth, accustomed as she was to Sir Anthony's flamboyant dress sense, was taken aback.

"I am not going out with you, looking like that," she said, firmly. "What are you thinking of?"

He was dressed in magenta silk breeches, and a bright orange waistcoat of silk brocade, embroidered with yellow marigolds. His coat was of brightest scarlet, and above it, his cherry-red mouth beamed at her. It was impossible to envisage a more hideous combination of colours. He seemed to have had an accident with his rouge as well, which covered a far larger amount of his cheeks than normal. He looked hideous. Even for Sir Anthony he looked hideous. He cocked his head, and a cloud of powder puffed lightly from his wig. He coughed, delicately.

"Oh my dear Elizabeth, do you not like my choice of attire?" he simpered.

"Like it?" she said. "Have you looked in the mirror? No. I do not like it. That's an understatement. I detest it."

"Well then, I will change, just for you," he said petulantly, as a light tap came on the door. He backed away into the bedroom, leaving Beth to greet the visitors.

Angus had been advised to tell Katerina that his employer wished to meet her, that he was very severe, and that she must be on her best behaviour, for Sir Anthony was very unpredictable and could take offence at the slightest thing. That Angus had done his job well was obvious from the moment the couple entered the room. Katerina was trembling slightly, and her eyes were downcast. Angus loomed behind her, towering over her diminutive figure.

"Come in," Beth said, attempting to sound reassuring. Why Alex had wanted to make the girl terrified of meeting him she had no idea, but one look at her told Beth why Angus had been unable to contemplate harming her last night. She was lovely. Small, smaller even than Beth, but more voluptuous, she bobbed a curtsey, and raised her head to observe Beth with a pair of long-lashed, anxious soft brown eyes, set in a perfect heart-shaped face, framed by masses of dark brown hair, pulled up into a simple chignon. Beth's heart went out to her, and she wondered how she could make the girl feel at ease.

"*Buona sera. Piacere di conoscerla*," she said, exhausting almost all her Italian with her friendly greeting. She motioned for the pair to sit down, which they did, side by side on the sofa. Beth noticed the girl put her hands in her lap and clasp them tightly in an attempt to stop their trembling being noticeable. Whatever Angus had told her about Sir Anthony, it had worked. She looked as though she were about to meet the Devil himself. Angus looked around the room for his brother.

"My husband…ah… *mio marito*…is dressing," Beth said, pantomiming someone putting on a coat. Katerina smiled, uncertainly.

"On the contrary, my dear Elizabeth, I am already dressed, and cannot wait to make the acquaintance of this delightful young lady!" Sir Anthony cried from behind them.

Both Angus and Katerina sprang to their feet, and turned to the apparition that had appeared from the bedroom. Beth frowned. She thought he had gone to change, but it seemed, by the stench of violets that announced his entrance, that he had only gone to douse himself in the scent Beth had hoped he'd renounced for good.

Angus's eyes widened slightly, but otherwise he showed no reaction to the rainbow figure. Katerina gave a snort of laughter, before flushing bright red and dropping into a deep curtsey. Sir Anthony moved forward and took her hand, raising it to his lips and gallantly kissing it. She stood, and looked cautiously at him, struggling not to laugh, her eyes dancing. Her free hand came up over her mouth and she covered up the second giggle that escaped with a cough.

"*Bonsoir, mademoiselle*," he trilled. "*Vous êtes tres belle.*"

Angus opened his mouth to translate, but Katerina put her tiny hand on his arm.

"*Yo capisco*," she said, smiling. "*Merci beaucoup, Monsieur le Comte,*" she replied in heavily accented French. Beth and Angus exchanged twin glances of apprehension. If she understood that, what more did she comprehend? Then Sir Anthony was motioning the pair to sit down again. He did not disabuse the girl of her notion that he was a Count, Beth noticed.

"So," he continued in French. "Jim here tells me you are maid to a countess on her way to Paris. Have you been to France before?"

The girl looked expectantly at her companion, who translated slowly, in halting Italian.

"No," she replied, in the same language. "But I am very much looking forward to it."

Once again, Angus translated, slowly. Sir Anthony showed no sign that he could, in fact, speak Italian quite well, certainly a lot better than the young man struggling to translate. Beth stood back, observing as the conversation continued for a few minutes in Sir Anthony's flawless French, and Katerina's beautiful Italian, punctuated by 'Jim's' painful attempts at translation. The girl showed no sign of understanding any more French than his first compliment to her beauty, which she had undoubtedly heard from every Frenchman she had ever met in Italy. How long would her husband continue this charade? Beth felt more sorry for Angus than Katerina now. She had recovered from her first sight of Sir Anthony, although her eyes were moist with the effort of not laughing.

Angus's command of Italian was being tested beyond its limits, however, and he was clearly becoming irritated.

The weather and the delights of Paris now being exhausted, the conversation finally drew to a close, and the young couple rose from their seats to take their leave. Sir Anthony took Katerina's hand and once again lifted it to his lips.

"Your mother was a whore and your father fucks pigs," he said pleasantly, still in French, smiling warmly at her.

Beth inhaled strongly, through her nose.

Katerina glanced up at Angus, awaiting the translation. Angus blinked once, then looked calmly at his brother, and smiled. He turned to Katerina, then pointed at Sir Anthony and Beth, before walking his fingers through the air in the direction of the door.

"My master and mistress are going out," he said carefully. He pointed now at himself, and her, before making a sweeping gesture which took in the whole room. "They have said we can stay here this evening. After our meal," Angus rapidly wielded a knife and fork upon a generous helping of air, then raised an imaginary glass in toast to Sir Anthony. "Which he will pay for," he finished, miming his master paying a large sum of money to an invisible waiter. He smiled and bowed his gratitude to Sir Anthony, and it was Beth's turn to choke back a laugh.

"Oh, *Grazie mille, Segnore!*" Katerina cried, curtseying deeply, her eyes sparkling.

"Cleverly managed, Jim," said Sir Anthony in French, throwing his purse at his footman, who caught it deftly. "But you'll need to go out while I change into something a little less garish. I suggest you find an eating house. There's an expensive one by the harbour, which should empty that purse somewhat, and ensure you a successful night. We will return at dawn. Be gone by then."

"Are you going to explain?" Beth asked, as Alex rubbed the excess rouge off his cheeks, and selected a new outfit in the comparatively sober colours of mulberry red and lemon.

"Do I need to?" he asked. "Were you offended?"

"By your comment? No. If she was pretending not to understand your normal conversation for some reason, she would nevertheless have shown some reaction to your appalling insult. She didn't. Are you satisfied now that she didn't understand Henri?"

"Yes," said her husband, unbuttoning the garish orange waistcoat. "But not just because of her lack of reaction to my comment. Tell me something. If you understood French, but knew that your life depended on people not knowing that, would you react if I called your mother a whore and your father a seducer of animals?"

"No," said Beth, "I wouldn't."

"But on the same basis, if you knew that the man you were about to meet for the first time was not only a man of title and power, but who also became very violent at the slightest provocation, would you laugh at him if he turned out to look like a circus clown and smell like a brothel?"

Understanding dawned.

"No, I wouldn't," she said. "But she did, and had difficulty controlling herself for some time. So you knew then that she was not adept at concealing her emotions."

"Precisely," said her husband, still in the tones of Sir Anthony, which he would now maintain for the rest of the evening. "The girl is delightful, and quite ingenuous. She displays her emotions for all to see. She is quite taken with Angus. And in answer to your next question, no I wouldn't."

"No you wouldn't what?" said Beth, unaware that she had had another question to ask.

"Have been able to kill her, if I had been tumbling her in the hothouse last night."

Beth heard with relief the answer to the question she had not known she wanted to ask, and realised how well her husband knew her. It was warming, disconcerting.

"I'm very glad you weren't," she replied after a minute. He had shrugged on his coat, blown out the candle, and moved towards the door. He paused, his fingers on the handle.

"You're very glad I wasn't what?" he asked, smiling down at her.

"Tumbling Katerina in the hothouse, or any other woman, anywhere. Because if you were, and I found out, I would be quite capable of killing you. Although my blood would be far from cold at the time."

He turned back, and reaching, cupped her face with his hands. The skin of his gloves was soft, warm against her cheeks.

"I am yours, until I die," he said, startling her with his sudden seriousness. "If you ever have cause to kill me, it will not be due to my unfaithfulness. I will love you, and only you, and will take no other, not even in play, while you live." In spite of the make-up and clothes, it was not Sir Anthony, but Alex who leaned forward, and kissed her, gently, on the mouth. His lips were warm and dry. "One day, when you are ready," he said, "I hope you will say the same to me. But I do not demand it. I know why you married me."

She looked at him, unblinking. The soft touch of his strong hands on her skin, the scent of the suede, the intensity of his dark blue gaze burned themselves into her memory, and she knew she would never forget this moment, however long she lived.

"I am ready," she said.

CHAPTER EIGHT

The young couple walked along the second-floor gallery of the Palazzo Muti, the clicking of their shoes on the polished wooden floor echoing dully from the walls and high ceiling. Portraits of long-dead women wearing ruffs and holding flowers, or men in full armour and outmoded wigs, hands on hips, stared down at them as they made their way to the door at the end of the gallery, which was guarded casually by two men with sheathed swords.

Beth, both nervous and excited by the meeting to come, had dressed modestly, although elegantly, hoping to minimise her beauty, and therefore observe rather than be observed. She had never expected to meet the man behind the door, and had no idea what to expect, as her husband, although acquainted with him, would divulge nothing, telling her only that he wished her to make up her own mind, and would be interested to hear her opinion later.

Alex was nervous for the opposite reason to Beth. He had had several meetings with the man, but always as Alex MacGregor; this would be the first time he had entered these chambers as Sir Anthony Peters, and in doing so he was about to reveal his dual identity to another person. He was not worried about that in itself; this man would not betray him, and if he did, then Alex would have spent his whole life in vain. What worried him was that there might be other people present at this meeting, at least initially; people who had never met Sir Anthony, but who were acquainted with Alex MacGregor, and who must not know that the two were one and the same man.

To that end, he had applied his paint, patches and elaborately curled wig with great care, and was wearing breeches and coat of violet satin, and an ivory waistcoat heavily embroidered with a pattern of stylised leaves and flowers. As the couple arrived at the door they were stopped by the guards, who now stood to sloppy attention.

"You must relinquish your sword, sir," one of them said, looking lasciviously at Beth rather than at the baronet. She sighed inwardly, realising that her attempt to look dowdy had failed at the first hurdle.

Her husband's hands fluttered to his swordbelt, but he seemed incapable of unbuckling it, he was trembling so badly, and in the end, exasperated, Beth reached over and took it off herself, handing it to the guards, who didn't trouble to hide their smiles of contempt.

"Do you have any other weapons, sir?" asked the other guard.

"Of course not. I have not come here to do battle!" squawked Sir Anthony, in a feeble and unsuccessful attempt to recover his dignity. The first guard winked suggestively at Beth, who looked from him to her husband. He was fussing over his appearance, brushing imaginary specks of lint from his coat and seemed not to have registered the fact that this servant dared to openly flirt with Beth in his presence. The guard smiled reassuringly at her, revealing a set of black and yellow teeth, and opened the door for them.

"You may enter," he said.

She was halfway through the door when she felt the hand gently, but unmistakably squeeze her bottom. Outraged, she whirled round, and the sharp crack of her hand as it contacted with the guard's cheek resounded across the room, causing the three men at the desk by the window to look up startled from the papers they were studying. The guard, red-faced with fury and embarrassment, backed out quickly, closing the door with a slam.

It was not the entrance she would have wished for, and the colour rose to her cheeks. She felt the touch of her husband's hand as he took her arm, ostensibly to steady himself, but taking the opportunity to give it a reassuring squeeze, and when she looked up at him, he allowed his merriment to show for a moment, before it was replaced by the apprehensive nervousness he wanted his audience to see. Beth felt a little better knowing that he, at any rate, did not think she had caused any damage by her action.

They moved forward across the luxuriously appointed room towards the three men, who greeted them with a variety of expressions. The man on the left was elderly, thin-featured, pale, dressed in sober shades of brown. He viewed the couple with open curiosity. The second, on the right, who was eyeing them with disdain was much younger, about the same age as Alex, Beth thought, and was heavily-built, stern of feature, striking, although that was mainly because he was wearing the *feileadh mór,* the belted plaid of the Highlander, kilted to the knee, the surplus material draped over his left shoulder and pinned to his jacket by a silver brooch.

Sir Anthony's eyes swept across the two men without recognition and came to rest on the young man standing between them. He made a low and over-elaborate bow.

Following his example Beth curtseyed deeply, and after a moment looked up at the young man, observing him discreetly from between her lashes. His dark blue frock coat and breeches were expensively tailored, and of good material. His bagwig was expertly curled and of the highest quality. But had he been dressed in rags, Beth would have known him to be Charles Edward Stuart, though she had heard no description of the prince. Every inch of him was royal. He was tall, almost as tall as Alex, of athletic build, fair-

159

complexioned, his features regular, mouth sensual, brown eyes smiling as he eyed the unctuous dandy and the volatile young woman who were making their obeisance to him. He stepped forward to greet them and bade them rise, in lightly accented English.

Beth rose smoothly, Sir Anthony stumbled a little and almost fell on his face. The disdain in the eyes of the Highlander deepened to utter contempt, although he did not speak.

"Your Royal Highness!" cried the baronet. "You do myself and my dear lady wife the utmost honour in allowing us to enter into your presence. I am overwhelmed!"

"Sir Anthony Peters, I believe. I am always pleased to make the acquaintance of one of my father's subjects," the prince replied, his voice and smile full of genuine welcome, betraying no sign of the amusement or contempt he must surely feel at the ridiculous sight before him.

"Indeed! And my wife, Lady Elizabeth." Sir Anthony fluttered a hand in Beth's direction. "We are but newly married, Your Highness, and are visiting Rome as part of a tour of Europe."

Prince Charles turned his attention to Beth. He extended his hand to her and she placed hers in his. He grasped it, gently but firmly, and raised it to his lips, and she felt the hardness of the skin of his palms. A swordsman then, or a horseman. Or both.

"Lady Elizabeth. Any lady is most welcome to my house, but such a beautiful one as yourself doubly so." He smiled warmly at her, and she saw that he was neither flirting with her nor flattering her, but merely stating his honest opinion. She returned his smile. "We rarely see such loveliness as yours in Rome," he continued. "The ladies here are of a somewhat darker beauty. That may explain, but does not excuse the behaviour of the guard towards you." He released her hand

160

then and strode to the door, flinging it open. The guards, caught in the act of lounging against the doorpost, shot to attention.

"Giovanni, is it not?" said the prince in Italian to the man with one flaming cheek.

The man muttered something, his head lowered.

"You will apologise to the Lady Elizabeth and Sir Anthony Peters, for your unspeakable insult to them. Immediately."

Colour flooded the man's face, eclipsing the marks of Beth's blow, and his expression was sullen, resentful, but he did not hesitate. Turning to the visitors, he bowed, and spoke a few words in rapid Italian, which Beth assumed was an apology.

The prince turned back to his guests. Beth was as scarlet as her assailant. Sir Anthony stood, mouth open, stunned.

"Are you satisfied, Sir Anthony? Or do you wish to take further action?"

"What? Oh, yes, of course. I am satisfied, I mean, I thought Elizabeth had dealt with the fellow already," he simpered, clearly feeling no embarrassment that his wife should think it necessary to fend off attackers herself when in his presence.

She looked at the prince, catching the momentary twist of his mouth that told her he shared the Highlander's view of the baronet, and then he turned again to the unfortunate Giovanni.

"You are dismissed," he said coldly. "Gather your belongings and leave immediately."

He closed the door in the man's face.

Beth swallowed nervously.

"I am sorry, Your Highness," she said. "I should not have lost my temper."

"On the contrary, my lady," Charles interrupted, the steel gone from his voice. "I seek all the support I can from my father's English subjects, and hardly think it likely that I will

161

make a good impression if my employees insult my guests before they have even entered my presence. I am grateful to you for drawing such unforgivable behaviour to my attention. You are both most welcome. Now, how can I help you?"

"You have done more than enough already, Your Highness, by admitting us to your exalted presence. We never expected such an honour. It has quite eclipsed all the other sights of Rome, even the falls at Tivoli!" Sir Anthony gushed. He was excelling himself today, Beth thought.

The elderly man tutted impatiently, but if Prince Charles resented being classified as a tourist attraction, he was too well bred to show it.

"You have seen the falls at Tivoli, then?" he said pleasantly, seeking to put the baronet at his ease, before finding out what he wanted and getting rid of him. If he wanted anything at all that was, other than merely something to write home to his friends about.

"Well, no, not yet, Your Highness," admitted Sir Anthony. "But I am sure there is no point in troubling to make the journey, as it would only be a disappointment after meeting your exalted person!"

The prince allowed Beth to see his amused look at this outrageous sycophancy. He had already accurately summed up the relationship between Sir Anthony and Elizabeth, she noted.

"We may as well return home immediately, as after today no monument or sight to be seen in the whole of Europe will satisfy my husband." She smiled sweetly at the purple apparition by her side. He beamed down at her, clearly having failed to note the sarcasm in her voice. "You have saved us a small fortune in post-horses and accommodation. We thank you, Your Highness."

Behind them, the Scot coughed politely.

"Your Highness," he said in a soft Scottish burr. "We

really must continue…"

"Oh, quite, quite!" cried Sir Anthony. "We will leave you directly. You have great affairs to deal with, I am sure. But first, I would crave a few words in private, if Your Highness would be so kind." Sir Anthony curved his lips up in an oily smile.

"Allow me to introduce you to my companions," the prince said mildly. He indicated the elderly man. "This is Sir Thomas Sheridan, my tutor and dearest friend. And the other is John Murray of Broughton, another friend. They are utterly trustworthy. You can say anything in front of them without fear that it will reach other ears." His voice was still warm, but a vein of ice ran through it. *I trust my friends, therefore so will you, and I will have no argument about it,* he was saying. Beth's first opinion of him had not yet been shaken.

Sir Anthony looked deeply flustered.

"I intended no insult to your friends, Your Highness," he said. He reached into his pocket. Out of the corner of her eye Beth saw Murray step forward, his hand moving towards his sword. Although Sir Anthony was not facing him, his movements became slow and deliberate, unthreatening.

"I have here a letter," he said, drawing it out of his pocket with his index finger and thumb and handing it to the prince, "which, if you will be so kind as to read, will explain everything."

The prince unfolded it and scanned it politely, clearly having no intention of letting its contents sway him. Then he froze, looking from the letter to Sir Anthony in utter disbelief. His eyes flickered back to the letter again, then he straightened and turned to his friends.

"Thomas, John, you will excuse me for a short while. I find I wish to humour my guests after all." It was not a request, but a command. Sheridan moved forward.

"Charles, is this wise?" he said nervously. "You know

163

nothing of this Sir Anthony fellow."

"I know enough to be sure he poses no danger, Thomas. Go. I am quite capable of defending myself, although I assure you it will not be necessary."

The door had hardly closed on the reluctant men when the prince, to Beth's utter astonishment, leapt at Sir Anthony and gave him a quick but undoubtedly affectionate bear hug, before moving back to hold him at arm's length. Both men's eyes were sparkling.

"My God, Alex, it is genius!" he cried. "Never, never would I have suspected!" He eyed the over-dressed baronet from head to toe. "Remarkable!" he said, shaking his head in disbelief.

"You understand now why I had to see you alone," Alex said in his normal voice, for once breaking his rule of remaining as Sir Anthony while in costume. "No one else must know who I am. It would be too dangerous."

"No, of course, I appreciate that," said Charles, still clearly amazed that he had been so utterly fooled. "But what a shame. It would bring John down a peg to know that he had not recognised one of his friends! He can be a little pompous at times." He turned his warm brown gaze on Beth. "I take it then, that the two of you are in fact man and wife, or are you about to reveal yourself to be another of my dear friends in disguise?" He laughed. Beth found herself laughing with him. His undoubted merriment was infectious. He was not at all disgruntled at having been hoodwinked, as she had thought he might be.

"Aye, she is my wife, or at least the wife of Sir Anthony Peters," Alex said. "But as ye can see, she kens well who I am. She is trustworthy, Your Highness."

"I am the wife of Sir Anthony Peters by law, although I consider myself also to be married to Alex MacGregor," Beth interposed. "I am a loyal supporter of King James, and also of yourself, and although it seems I am trustworthy, I was not informed of the degree of my husband's friendship with Your Highness."

"Ah," said Charles. "You have been playing a trick on your wife as well as on myself. Why did you not tell her we were friends?"

"I wished her to form her own opinion of you, without any influence from me, Your Highness," Alex replied.

"Do not worry, Lady Elizabeth," the prince said, turning to her and taking her hands in his. "I will not embarrass you by asking you what that opinion is – not yet, at any rate. But I will, with your permission, greet you now not just as a loyal subject, but also as a trusted friend."

Without waiting for that permission, he enfolded her in his strong embrace, before kissing her lightly on the lips and rendering her, as he had no doubt intended, his forever.

"Why didn't you tell me you were close friends?" Beth said angrily, when they had reached the security of their lodgings on the Piazza di Spagna, a popular area for English tourists and not far from the Jacobite Court. Angus, told to keep a low profile in Rome, and not to be seen in company with Sir Anthony in case someone known to Alex noted the family resemblance and became suspicious, had gone out. "I thought that you had met once or twice, maybe, as prince and loyal subject. I had no idea you were bosom friends!"

"As I said to Charles," Alex said, scrubbing at the paint on his face with a wet cloth, "I wanted you to form your own impression. If ye'd known we were friends, ye'd have already had a favourable view of the man."

"I already *did* have a favourable view of him," she said. "He's my prince, for God's sake!"

"Aye, that's true. But you're also sensible. Ye ken that being born tae a role doesna always make you fit for it. History's littered wi' inadequate kings. But you love me, Beth, or so ye told me yesterday."

She smiled, in spite of her irritation.

"Yes, I do," she said. "What's that got to do with it?"

"And I love you," he continued as though she hadn't spoken. "And as a consequence, although I've never met them, I'm inclined towards liking Graeme, and Thomas and Jane, and even your wee stable boy John who's away tae the militia, and who I'd normally have nae time for, because you like them, and I trust your judgement."

Beth's anger fizzled out, and she went over to him, placing one hand on his violet silk shoulder, and with the other smoothing his hair, which was dishevelled from removing his wig.

"So, what do you think of him, then?" Alex asked. "Ye had plenty of time to observe him while we were talking."

She certainly had, and had taken full advantage of it, sitting quietly while Alex explained the dual purpose of his visit. Charles shared Alex's delight that the Hanoverian king was paying for his friend to visit him, and it was agreed that Sir Anthony Peters would indeed immediately form a friendly and very public relationship with the prince, which would certainly be reported back to the duke of Newcastle by the various spies who always hung around the Court but were unable to worm their way into the prince's inner circle. In the meantime, in private, they would come up with some usefully misleading information to pass on to Sir Horace Mann.

Charles had then sent for refreshments, and they had talked for a long time about the other reason for Alex's visit.

"Of course I must be at the head of any force Louis sends into England," Charles had cried, after hearing of Angus's experience in the hothouse. He leapt up from his seat and began to pace the room. "This is what we have been praying for, working towards, for years. Why is Louis keeping us in the dark?" He stopped pacing and turned back to Alex. "Do you think my father knows?"

"I doubt it, Your Highness," Alex replied. "Surely he would have told you if he did?"

"I'm not so sure," said Charles, throwing himself down on a chair, before springing immediately up again, unable to be still in his excitement. "He feels I am too impulsive, I think. And sometimes I think he resents that our people are now looking to me to lead them, rather than him. But everything I do, I do to gain the crown for him."

"He knows that." Alex hesitated momentarily, then continued. "He worries only for your welfare. As do all your friends. We dinna ken if the rumours of the invasion are true. And if they are, we dinna ken what's behind them. Louis canna be trusted. You know that, and so does your father."

"We must find out," said Charles determinedly. "And we must find this man Henri, and stop him before he can tell the Elector. Can you do this, Alex?"

"Aye, maybe. But it will no' be easy. Sir Anthony doesna have many connections at the French Court, but I should be able to ingratiate myself. If Henri's there, I'll find him. About the invasion plans, I canna promise anything. If even most of Louis' trusted ministers have no' been informed, I doubt that an English dandy will be entrusted with Louis' machinations."

"Leave that to me," said Charles. "I will find out soon enough what Louis intends, and if it is to invade my country, make no mistake, I will be there, at the head of the troops, to take the throne for my father."

They had gone on to plan how the friendship between Sir Anthony and Prince Charles should develop. It was decided that initially the two men should go out together that evening, first to the theatre, and then on to a club, where they would avidly discuss fashion and the latest intrigues, and generally show to the world that the prince shared many of the interests of his new acquaintance.

Then they had left the twenty-three-year-old prince fizzing with excitement at the prospect of a possible French-led Jacobite invasion, and had returned to their apartment for a short rest.

Beth bent to plant a kiss on Alex's chestnut waves.

"What do I think of him?" she said. "I think he is intelligent and ambitious, and frustrated, and every inch a prince. He exudes energy and enthusiasm, and will stop at nothing to win the throne. He has the youth and determination to do it. He is handsome, too, which helps. Well, no, not handsome exactly, but attractive. Very attractive." She thought for a moment of the boorish, unpopular George, and his fat and arrogant son. "The Hanoverians are right to be worried about Charles. He's dangerous. More dangerous than they know."

"Aye," said Alex. "And if I have my way, they'll no' know it until he's marching on London at the head of an army. Ye havena said if ye like him, though? Do you?"

"Yes," she said, after a pause. "I think it would be almost impossible not to. Yes, I like him. But I'm also afraid of him. He has magnetism, as do you, and the ability to charm people into doing anything he wants, against their better judgement, perhaps. Once he has won a man over, he could lead him willingly into the mouth of Hell, if he wished. He knows he has that power, too, and how to wield it, which makes him even more dangerous. It's only my first impression, of course."

Alex nodded.

"Ye'll have plenty more chances to refine your view of him, I'm thinking," he said. "We canna stay more than a few days, but Prince Charles will be spending most of those wi' his new friends, Sir Anthony Peters and his wife. Then we'll have to go straight off to Florence to report to Mann, then on to France to try and find Henri. Up to now he's behaved exactly as I would have done in his situation, except that I would have checked to make sure the hothouse was empty before discussing secret matters. If he carries on being predictable, he'll take the time to ensure his information is accurate and then go tae London to present it in person to Lord Carteret or the king. With luck, we'll catch him before he does. I'm sorry," he added.

"What for?" asked Beth.

"It's no' been much o' a honeymoon for ye. Ye havena seen any of the tourist sights. We've hardly stopped tae breathe."

"Oh, I don't know," she said. "You promised me travel, adventure and to meet interesting people, and you're certainly giving me that. You didn't promise me time to breathe. I'm not complaining. Most Jacobite ladies would give their right arm to meet the prince, let alone be kissed by him and called a trusted friend."

"Ah, his magic's working on you already," Alex teased, shrugging off his jacket. "I'll have to watch he doesna steal you from me."

"Hmm, let me see," she said. "Queen Elizabeth Stuart. Has a ring to it, doesn't it?"

"Your ears'll have a ring to them, and the Jacobite cause'll be without its leader, an' he tries anything on wi' ye," Alex said placidly, drawing her on to his knee. "So I have magnetism, do I? Ye'd let me lead ye into Hell?" he continued. She thought he'd missed that.

"You know you do," she replied. "And Angus too." She looked forward to meeting Duncan, to discovering if charisma was a general family trait, like blue eyes. "No, I wouldn't let you or Charles lead me into Hell, not if I recognised what you were doing, anyway. But it's not always easy to see where you're going, when you're dazzled."

169

"I can see exactly where I'm going right now," he said, bending his lips to hers. "And it's no tae Hell, that's for certain."

For a while after that neither of them thought of Prince Charles Edward Stuart, or the prospective invasion.

* * *

Three days later, Beth could no longer state that she had not seen the tourist sights, of Rome at least, although she still had had no time to draw breath. Having firmly established his friendship with Sir Anthony during a noisy evening at the theatre, and cemented it with an equally riotous late-night drinking session which sent Alex reeling home to collapse on the bed without removing even his coat, let alone his make-up, the prince now sought to make up for the fact that Beth had seen little of Europe so far, by showing her the whole of Rome in four days. Her arm firmly tucked under his elbow, he whirled her through all the principal attractions, including the Pantheon, the Coliseum, the Castel Sant' Angelo, St. Peter's and the Vatican, Sir Anthony trailing servilely in their wake.

Noting her delight at the many fountains in the Vatican gardens, which she had actually had time to notice, having had to pause to remove a stone from her shoe, Charles dragged her immediately off to the Piazza Navona to see Bernini's elaborate fountain of the four rivers, which was reputed to be the finest in Europe. There at least, they stopped for coffee, and Beth had a little time to contemplate her surroundings while Prince Charles smilingly acknowledged the greetings of the many passers-by who recognised him. Here at least he was treated as the Prince of Wales and heir to the throne of Great Britain, and received the homage of the public with an easy grace, often pausing to exchange a few words, casually

170

scattering his charm far and wide and making no distinction between people of rank, merchants or street vendors.

"Bernini is, of course, also the author of the baldacchino you will have noticed under the dome of St. Peter's," Charles said.

Beth, sipping her coffee as slowly as possible, enjoying the respite, cast her mind back to the immense swirling mass of colour and light which was the impression she had gleaned in her whirlwind tour of St. Peter's. She retained only a vague memory of twisted bronze columns over the tomb of the apostle.

"Yes, of course," she said, praying he would not ask her to describe it, afraid that she would be hauled back to see it again if she was unable to.

"There was a great outcry at the time of its construction, was there not?" Sir Anthony asked, aware that Charles was, as Beth feared, about to ask her opinion of the details.

"Yes," replied the prince, always happy to demonstrate his knowledge. "When they dug the foundations for the monument, they had to disturb a lot of the holy graves beneath the pavement. Quite a few of the workmen died in mysterious circumstances, and a lot of others refused to carry on, thinking the project was cursed by God." He laughed.

"You don't think it was, then?" Beth asked.

"No, of course not. I am a Catholic, of course, but I think the Church brings many of the criticisms against it on itself, with its outmoded superstition and inordinate reverence of holy relics, the vast majority of which are not genuine. Why, if all the fragments of the true cross were brought together, you could build a whole forest of crosses with them! The Church would do well to bring itself up to date a little. We live in enlightened times." He looked at Beth's face. "I am sorry. I have shocked you," he said.

"Yes," she replied. "No. I mean, you have surprised rather

than shocked me, Your Highness."

"You have been reading too many pamphlets published by my enemies." He leaned forward in his chair, his brown eyes earnest. "Neither my father nor myself are the rabid Papists they make us out to be. My father employs many Protestants, and to that end has maintained an Anglican chapel at the palace, in order that his servants may worship as it pleases them. We believe absolutely in toleration. Every Christian should be able to worship as he wishes. I choose to worship in the Roman way; but neither my father nor myself would deny those who choose otherwise the same freedom we will demand for ourselves and all our Catholic subjects, when we come to the throne. Unlike George, we will employ those best suited for the position they are to occupy, regardless of religion."

This was no attempt at cajolery or political propaganda, she realised; he meant what he was saying.

"But we digress," he said, sitting back again and relaxing. "The pope held a similar view to myself on this, and ordered that the baldacchino be completed. He even sanctioned the stripping of the bronze from the Pantheon, which caused another outcry. There was no such controversy over the fountain here, although Bernini was not asked to submit a design for it."

"How did he come to build it, then?" Beth asked. "He was persuaded to submit a model anyway, and a friend of his placed it in a room where the pope could not fail to see it. Good friends are always worth cultivating. And now," he said, leaping up, completely refreshed by the short break, "let us go to see the *fontana de trevi*, which is almost on your way home. It is not yet completed, of course, but is nevertheless worth viewing. And then I shall send a carriage for you, Sir Anthony, at eight o' clock."

***

"Does the man never sleep? Is he always like this?" Beth asked from her supine position on the sofa. She thought she had a zest for life, but the prince positively exuded energy from every pore.

"He does sleep, he just doesn't need much of it, especially when he's enjoying himself. And yes, he is nearly always like this. Are you revising your opinion of him?" He massaged her aching feet with his long fingers as he spoke, and Beth sighed contentedly.

"No," she said. "I think he'll make a wonderful king one day. He's almost too good to be true. He genuinely cares about his people, and no one could deny he has the energy to cope with the burdens of ruling. And if he can convince people that he means what he says about religious tolerance, I don't see how anyone will be able to resist him, once they meet him."

"Yes, but convincing the people and getting him to Britain to meet them in the first place is not going to be easy," Alex replied in the crisp English accent which went with his current appearance. "And he's not perfect, by any means. You've not seen the negative side of him yet. He can be very arrogant and moody, and has a terrible temper when roused. He's used to getting his own way, and when he's set on something it's very difficult to get him to change his mind. And he can drink. My God, can he drink. I thought I could hold my liquor, but Charles could drink me under the table any time. I've had a hangover for three days."

"It's a pity Angus isn't going out with him tonight then, if he's as impervious to alcohol as you say he is."

"He is," affirmed Alex. "But Charles could give him a run for his money, that's for sure."

"It's a shame that Angus can't meet him," Beth said. "I

know he's disappointed, although he won't admit it."

Alex considered for a minute, then shook his head.

"It's too risky," he said. "The similarity between us doesn't matter in normal society, where no one pays close attention to servants, and nobody knows Alex MacGregor anyway. But a lot of Charles's friends know me. They're not looking for anyone resembling Alex now, but if they see Angus, someone's bound to notice his remarkable similarity to me and start making connections. Some of them have even met him before. John Murray has, although Angus was only ten or so at the time. I'm sorry for Angus, but it can't be helped."

After Alex had gone, Beth divested herself of her dusty, constrictive clothes, and donning a loose dressing gown, brushed and loosely braided her hair before settling down with a book, hoping it would be interesting enough to keep her awake until Alex returned in the early hours of the morning.

It wasn't, and an hour later Beth was already nodding over it and contemplating having an early night, when the door opened and Angus entered. He looked as dishevelled as she had earlier, his shoes and stockings red with the dust of the streets, his hair damp with sweat.

"And this is November!" he announced as soon as he'd closed the door. "Christ, I'm glad I wasna here in July!" He tore off his stock, followed quickly by his coat and waistcoat, and walked across to the ewer and basin in the corner of the room, peeling off his shirt as he went.

"The weather's unseasonably warm for the time of year, I've been told," Beth said, raising her voice to be heard above the splashing of water. She was not troubled in the least by her brother-in-law's state of undress; she was accustomed by now to the scant regard for decency her husband and his brother had when in private. As long as the essential parts were covered, that was all that mattered. As Beth too by nature had scant regard for propriety, this suited her very well, and she was as unconcerned as Angus by the indecent amount of leg she was showing as he threw himself onto the sofa opposite her. He had wet his hair, and water dripped from the ends onto his bare chest. He kicked off his shoes and lay back, folding his arms behind his head and sighing blissfully.

"Did ye enjoy being swept round St. Peter's by the prince?" he asked after a moment.

"I'd have enjoyed it a lot more if I'd actually had time to see anything," Beth commented. "You were there, then?"

"Aye, but I ducked away out of sight when I saw ye. Ye're getting on well, then, I take it? You looked like a proper couple, wi' your arm tucked in his an' all. I almost felt sorry for Sir Anthony, trailing along behind, forgotten."

"Yes, well, that's the image we're trying to foster, of the prince as a fop and lady's man, who, if he ever does manage to stir himself enough to make it to England, will spend all his time stealing other men's wives and drinking, rather than fighting for his country."

"He's very handsome, is he no'?" Angus said wistfully. "What's he like?"

"A tornado," Beth said. "I wish you could meet him, Angus. I've asked Alex, but…"

"Aye, I ken it's no' a good idea," he replied resignedly. "At least I've seen him, though. I'm sure I'll get to meet him when he comes to London." That he was in no doubt this would happen, and soon, was clear from his tone.

"Are you staying in tonight?" Beth asked, surprised. "I thought you'd be making the most of your last few days in Rome to capture as many Latin hearts as possible."

Angus turned his head and eyed her suspiciously, but seeing no mockery in her eyes, he relaxed again.

"No, I'm no' in the mood for romance tonight. Or for traipsing the streets either. I'll bide here, unless you want me out of the way."

"Not at all," said Beth. "It'll be nice to have your company." She stood and replaced her discarded book on a shelf before pouring two glasses of wine and placing one on a small table by his elbow.

"Are you missing Katerina?" she asked, resuming her seat.

"No," Angus replied automatically, reaching for the glass and tilting his head forward to take a sip. "Well, aye," he amended. "I am a wee bit. Although I dinna rightly ken why. I couldna understand a word she said."

"Neither could I," said Beth. "But I liked her too. She was beautiful, and full of life."

"Aye, she was, was she no'?" he said regretfully. "That was why I couldna bring myself to do the right thing."

For a moment Beth had no idea what he was talking about. Then the realisation hit her, and the wine turned to vinegar in her mouth. She put her glass down.

"Jesus, Angus, you don't really regret not having killed her, do you?" she said. "I thought you were concerned about her."

"I am," he replied, sitting up. "But that doesna change the fact that if this Henri laddie goes dashing off to the Elector wi' the invasion plans, I'll have destroyed the best chance King James has ever had to reclaim the throne, and all because I was soft on a lassie and couldna hurt her." He drained his glass and reached for the bottle. Beth put her hand out and laid it on his.

"Angus, you can't do this," she said. "You can't torture yourself over something that hasn't happened yet. There's no shame in being human. Even Alex said he couldn't have killed her."

"Alex was lying, to comfort me," Angus replied. "I ken

him well. In the same situation he'd no' have hesitated for a minute. He'd have killed Henri and Katerina too, and dealt wi' the guilt later."

He looked up, saw her stricken face, and folded his hand round hers.

"Did he tell ye otherwise?" he said softly.

She nodded, temporarily speechless.

"Aye, well, maybe I'm wrong," he said. "I'm sorry. I should have gone out after all."

"No, you shouldn't," she said a little huskily. "I need to know these things. I can deal with them. I wish he'd stop trying to protect me."

"He loves ye," Angus said frankly. "He doesna want ye to think ill of him."

"He won't make me think well of him by lying to me," she said sourly.

Angus opened his mouth, hesitated, closed it again. Then he seemed to come to a decision.

"I think he's afraid that if ye learn about the darker side of him, he'll lose ye," he said. "He knows you've been brought up sheltered." She opened her mouth to deny this, and he held his hand up. "Aye, I ken you've no' been sheltered in the way o' your cousins, and all the other silly women I've met since I've been footman to Sir Anthony. I ken you can use a knife, and ye've suffered hardship, and can cope wi' it. But nothing can make ye understand the Highland way of life except living it. I mind that your mother was a MacDonald, and she's tellt ye a good deal about Highland life. But it's no' the same thing as living it every day. It's a hard life, Beth, and to succeed you need to be ruthless at times, man or woman. Ye need to be able to kill to defend what's yours, and sometimes ye need tae kill to take what belongs to someone else with plenty, so you willna starve. I started to learn to fight when I was five, I killed my first man when

I was fifteen. I was sick afterwards, but I got over it. It gets easier the more you do it, easier still in the rage of battle, but I dinna enjoy it, and I never will, and neither does Alex." He picked up the bottle and lifted it to his mouth. Beth watched as he drank, the muscles of his throat working convulsively as he swallowed half the bottle in one go. She had rarely been in Angus's company without Alex being present. She thought of him in many ways as a boy still, carefree and feckless, his main interest the pursuit of pretty girls. She had thought Alex was an ineffectual fop. Wrong, on both counts.

"Am I shocking you?" he said, wiping the neck of the bottle with his hand and replacing it on the table.

"No," she said. "As I said, I need to know these things."

"Aye, I think you do," he agreed. "You're a MacGregor now, after all. It's even harder for Alex than the rest of us, because he's our chieftain, and that's a big responsibility, especially for a fair-minded man like him, who takes it seriously. The clan looks to him to lead them. They'll obey him without question."

"Without question?" Beth said. "I've seen you arguing with him."

"Aye, I'll argue wi' him sometimes, and so will Duncan. We're his brothers, we have that privilege. And he'll listen, because he's fair. But even so, if he orders me to do something, and I dinna agree wi' it, I'll still do it, because he's my chieftain. All his men trust him to look after them and protect them, and in return he trusts us to obey him. It's all about trust and loyalty, Beth. It's a wonderful thing, to know that ye can trust every man and woman around you with your life. That they'll kill or die for ye if they have to, without hesitation. There's nothing better than that feeling. It's worth any hardship to keep it, and it's what the whole clan system's based on. And it's what the Elector George and his cronies are trying tae take from us. Ye'll no understand that rightly, I'm thinking, living as ye do in a society where no one trusts anyone, an' everybody's waiting to stab each other in the back."

"You're wrong, I do understand it," she said quietly. "I've got friends who I feel that way about, in Manchester."

He observed her intently for a moment.

"Aye, so ye have. Ye'll understand, then, that if people start to disobey their leader, look only to their own interests and go their own way, then the trust will be gone and the whole clan will fall apart. The MacGregors have been proscribed for nigh on a hundred and fifty years, and we're fragmented, each group wi' its own chieftain, but when it comes down tae it, we're one clan, and will fight and die for each other against all comers, and that's why we've survived, against all that the law and the Campbells can throw at us." His voice was laced with pride, and Beth smiled.

"Sometimes Alex has to make terrible decisions, decisions I'd no' be able to make," he continued. "That's why he's fit to be chieftain and I'm not. And he can make them, Beth, though it costs him dear, sometimes. Has he told ye about Jeannie MacGregor?"

"No," said Beth.

"Aye, well, it's no' for me to, then. Suffice to say, she broke the trust of the clan and he had to make a hard decision. And he did it without hesitation. The English would say that makes him a savage. I say it makes him a man, and I'm proud to call myself his brother. But I let him down, Beth, and the clan, and Scotland too, though he'll never tell me so. Because Henri and his ilk are threatening our whole way of life. I should have lived up to the trust Alex has in me and killed him. If Henri had known we were there, he'd have killed me and Katerina too without a qualm, to protect himself."

"I still think that makes you the better man, because you couldn't," she said.

"And I think it makes me the weaker one. But we'll agree tae differ." He smiled.

There was a pause while she tried, and failed, to think of something that would comfort him.

"We'll find this Henri, and stop him," she said finally.

"Let's drink to that then," Angus replied with forced joviality. "Or is it the Sasannach way to ration the wine?"

"No, and it's just as well, the amount you get through," she said, draining the last dregs of the bottle into his glass.

There was a knock at the door and Angus shot to his feet. "Relax," she said. "That'll be the ice cream I ordered. There's enough for two, if you want some."

"God, aye, I love the stuff!" he said, licking his lips in anticipation, suddenly a boy again.

He went over and opened the door before Beth could stop him. The maid with the covered dish eyed the young Scot's muscular chest with appreciation, before casting a glance round the room. Seeing Beth also casually attired, she smirked knowingly, before handing the dish to Angus and disappearing.

"Thank you," said Beth crossly, as Angus put the dish on the table before lying back down on the couch, leaving her to share the creamy treat out into two bowls. "Could you not at least have put a shirt on before opening the door? Now it'll be all over Rome that I'm having an affair, and my reputation will be ruined."

"No, it willna," Angus said, unperturbed. "You should be honoured. They'll think I'm your *cicisbeo*. You'll be considered the height of fashion."

"My what?"

"Every fashionable Italian lady has one, and a lot of tourists, too. It's a male companion, usually young, handsome and virile, like mysel', who accompanies a married lady to the theatre and suchlike, when her husband canna be bothered.

He's often her lover, too. It's all above board. He usually receives presents off her, as well." He winked cheekily at her, before replacing his hands behind his head and closing his eyes.

"Young, handsome and virile, eh?" said Beth mildly. She had just come up with something that would take his mind off his troubles, temporarily at least. She carefully smoothed the last of the ice cream into a bowl, before licking the spoon. "Honoured," she added under her breath. "Well, here's your first present, my darling *cicisbeo.*" She neatly tipped the bowl of ice onto his bare stomach, before leaping backwards.

Not fast enough. He gasped, his eyes shot open, and his arm shot out sideways, all in the same moment. His fingers caught the end of her plait, and she was trapped.

"Now that," he said, smiling slowly and ominously, "was a mistake. I think ye owe me an apology."

She reached up to try to pull her hair free, and he twisted his wrist, wrapping the thick blonde braid round his fist once and pulling her closer to him. A trickle of white ran down his side. She contemplated for a moment whether she should break her resolution only to apologise when she was genuinely sorry.

"Would you like a spoon?" she said instead.

"Good God, Elizabeth, I did not think we were so impecunious that we could not afford tableware," trilled a voice from the doorway. Angus turned his head to where Sir Anthony was standing, leaning negligently against the doorpost. Beth tried to turn as well, but was unable to due to her awkward position.

"Your wife, sir, needs to learn to show due respect to her menfolk," said Angus, in a reasonable imitation of Sir Anthony's own falsetto. It was clear that he had no intention of releasing her until she had apologised. His revenge was going to be uncomfortable, probably involving the contents of the ewer and basin and the rest of the ice cream, and she knew from experience that she would get no sympathy or assistance from Alex.

"So, this is Angus, I presume?" came the voice from the corridor behind Sir Anthony. The young man stepped forward over the threshold, surveying the scene before him with a mischievous sparkle in his brown eyes. "I have heard a great deal about you, sir, although I see there is a good deal more still to learn."

"Shit!" cried Angus, releasing Beth's hair and shooting to his feet. The ice cream slid unnoticed down his breeches and landed on the rug at his feet with a wet splat.

"Your Highness," he said, bowing with a commendable degree of finesse and dignity, all things considered. He straightened up, his face burning.

"I am delighted to meet you, sir," said the prince, smiling. "It seems you are well versed in the family tradition of making a memorable first impression. As I remember, your brother was covered in something far more pungent than ice cream when I first made his acquaintance. Indeed, you referred to the substance yourself, only a moment ago."

Angus and Beth turned as one to Alex, who had closed the door and until this moment, had been viewing his brother's discomfort with a mixture of sympathy and amusement.

"Aye, well," he said, turning towards the dressing table to remove his paint. "It's a long story, and ye dinna want to hear it now."

"I do," said Beth and Angus together.

"No," said Alex firmly. "Go and make yourselves decent, for God's sake. The prince is here to meet Angus and to put a proposition to you, Beth."

"Do not worry yourselves on my account, although you may wish to change your trousers, Angus, before the cream soaks through. As for yourself, Elizabeth," Charles said merrily, eyeing the lovely young woman in the thin silk wrap with appreciation, "you look absolutely delightful as you are."

Beth cast a glance over the prince's shoulder at her husband, and was met with a warning glare that sent her off into the bedroom to change. Prince he might be; family he was not, and Alex would not have his wife sitting half naked in the company of any man other than his brothers.

Decently attired, Angus and Beth returned to the sitting room, where Sir Anthony had now effected his nightly transformation into Alex, the ice cream had been removed from the rug, and a fresh bottle of wine had been opened and partially consumed. Clearly Charles intended to stay for some time. Now recovered, Angus was glowing with happiness at finally getting to meet his prince.

"As I was saying," Alex said hurriedly, seeing the continuing curiosity in both his wife's and his brother's eyes. "His Highness has a proposition for you, Beth. But I've told him that if ye dinna want to entertain it, he's no' to try and persuade you, and he's promised he'll not."

"Of course I won't," replied Charles insincerely, draining his glass in one and refilling it. "I won't need to. I am confident that when you hear it, you will agree immediately."

As was often the case at this period of his life, the prince was right. When Beth heard the proposition, she was only too delighted to agree, without any need for persuasion at all.

CHAPTER NINE

Father Antonio Bruno Montefiori smoothed down his black robes and surveyed his domain from the vantage point of the chancel, satisfied that he had made the church look the best he possibly could in the short time he had had to do so. Hidden away in the southern outskirts of the city, this was not a church to be included on the tourist's itinerary, or indeed on any itinerary. Its worshippers were faithful but few. However, this was Rome, and the church, though somewhat dilapidated, did possess a beautiful triptych of the death and resurrection of Christ after, although unfortunately not by, Raphael, an exquisite altar cloth of linen lavishly embroidered with gold thread, and some heavy gold candlesticks, all of which were now on display in honour of the occasion.

Father Antonio sighed and settled himself to wait, a frown lurking on his brow. He had not wanted to undertake this task, but it did not do to refuse the bishop; especially if you were a young and ambitious man who hoped to rise high in the Church.

Nevertheless, he was a man of principle, and was deeply disturbed, in spite of the bishop's reassurances, about performing a ceremony that should rightly be conducted by day in front of family and friends, not secretly and in the dead of night. When the party arrived, he determined, he would have questions to ask and if they were not answered to his satisfaction, he would not proceed, whatever the consequences.

As he pondered how to word his questions, the door

creaked open and four cloaked and hooded figures entered. Three of the figures moved up the stone-floored aisle of the church towards him, removing their cloaks as they came; the fourth remained in shadow by the door. He scrutinised them as they approached.

They made a very handsome trio, he had to admit. The two men were tall and well proportioned, and by their similarity of feature were probably related. The older of the two, presumably the groom, was dressed in the full and impressive garb of the Scottish Highlander. He looked magnificent; his muscular legs were encased in red and black checked hose gartered just below the knee, above which swirled the bright scarlet and black of his kilt. Belted at the waist, the surplus material of the plaid was gathered at the back and drawn over the left shoulder of his black woollen jacket. Lace frothed at his throat and wrist, and his ornate basket-hilted broadsword swung in its scabbard at his hip. He wore the plaid naturally, as though it were his everyday attire rather than a mere ceremonial costume. A Jacobite exile, concluded the priest. But that did not explain the clandestine nature of this occasion. Jacobites had no need to hide in Rome, where the Stuarts were openly accepted as the rightful claimants to the British throne. The Jacobite's face was stern and forbidding and, looking at him, the priest wondered if he would have the courage to ask his questions after all.

And then the ferocious Highlander looked down at the slender young woman by his side, and the harsh planes of his face softened, his eyes became tender. The young woman, dressed in pale green silk, her remarkable hair loose and flowing in heavy silver-blond waves down her back, returned the man's gaze with trusting blue eyes, and Father Antonio saw with relief that one of his questions had already been answered. It was utterly obvious that this woman was not being coerced in any way into marrying the man by her side.

Nevertheless, there were still many reasons why this wedding might not be able to take place, and the young priest now cleared his throat nervously before speaking.

"Good evening, my children," he declared in the tone he used when about to celebrate mass. His voice resounded around the almost empty church. He modulated the volume, then continued. "Before I perform this ceremony, there are some questions I require the answers to." He spoke in French, as he had been told the young lady understood little Italian.

The couple returned their attention to him, and waited politely.

"I assume you are not under any compulsion to marry this man," he said. He would be expected to ask this question; as he had thought, the woman shook her head.

"And do you know of any reason why you should not be married by Holy Mother Church?"

"No, Father," the woman answered. "We are both members of the Church of Rome."

"And are you both free to marry? Neither of you are already committed?"

"We are neither of us married or committed to anyone else," the Scotsman answered. Both he and the woman smiled at this, and the priest frowned.

"Why, then, do you feel it necessary to hold your wedding in secret at two o' clock in the morning? Would you not prefer to celebrate it in the presence of your family?"

The Scot sighed. They had hoped for a priest who would accept the bishop's authority without question. But they had clearly got a man who took his vocation and responsibilities very seriously. Commendable, but devoutly not to be wished for at present. He raised his hand to the other man, who came forward.

"This is my brother," Alex said. "He represents my family,

the rest of whom are not in this country."

"And I have no family living," said Beth. "My parents are dead, and my brother dead to me. My husband's kin are all the family I need or want."

The priest opened his mouth again.

"We have the required witnesses, Father," Alex interposed before the man could speak, "and need no horde of well-wishers to witness our union. The people present, and the Lord himself, are sufficient for us. The reasons we are marrying here, and at this time, do not concern Mother Church." The Scot's voice had a distinct edge to it. But the priest was not comforted. There was some mystery here, and he wanted to get to the bottom of it.

"All things are the concern of Mother Church, my son," he replied haughtily.

There was a muffled expletive from the figure by the door, which now moved to join the others, throwing off his cloak as he came and dropping it carelessly in the aisle.

"I wish to enjoy the nuptials of two of my dearest friends, in private, without the resultant fuss that inevitably attends any official ceremony I am present at," said the man. "I assure you, Father, that every word they have spoken is true. If you wish me to obtain a letter from the Holy Father himself to confirm this, I shall. Although it will take some days and will result in the great displeasure of myself and my friends, one of whom is your bishop. Now do you have any more questions, or can we proceed before dawn breaks and this does become a public affair?"

The priest knew this man. Everybody in Rome knew this man. He had been baptised by the pope himself, and was on extremely friendly terms with the current incumbent. He could indeed obtain a letter if he chose and thus bring Father Antonio's name to the attention of Benedict XIV himself.

On reflection, Father Antonio wisely decided that there

were indeed no more questions. Without further ado he proceeded to join in holy wedlock Alexander Iain MacGregor and Elizabeth Ann Cunningham, which happy event was witnessed by Angus Malcolm Socrates MacGregor and Charles Edward Louis John Sylvester Maria Casimir Stuart, by the grace of God heir to the throne of Great Britain, or upstart Young Pretender, depending on your point of view.

The event was followed by a very quiet and stealthy return to the Palazzo Muti, where the door to the prince's private apartment was firmly locked, the shutters closed, and a merry and very liquid celebration took place. Speculation arose as to whether there was another woman in the world who was bigamously married to the same man, and there was some hilarity over the revelation of Angus's middle name, which that young man took in good part, lamenting that he had unwittingly chosen to make his entrance into the world whilst his father had been deeply engaged with the Platonic dialogues.

Angus did however maintain his credibility, and win twenty *scudi* off his prince, by succeeding, as Alex had predicted, in drinking that royal personage, quite literally, under the table.

* * *

The following day, Sir Anthony Peters, his wife and servant said goodbye to their new friend, leaving him to surreptitiously return the plaid he had 'borrowed' from Murray of Broughton the previous night, and they set off for Florence. Alex's priority now was to get to Paris as quickly as possible, and to that end he hoped to deliver his report on the Stuart prince to the fanatical anti-Jacobite British envoy Sir Horace Mann immediately, before leaving the city at the earliest possible opportunity.

"It's a shame," he said, as they shook out their travel

beds in the somewhat dubious inn they had elected to stay at a few miles south of Florence. A heavy scent of lavender permeated the room. "Florence is a beautiful city. You could stay here for weeks and not see everything. Had we the time, I'd love to show you the sights. But I expect we'll be at Mann's for most of tomorrow, and I'd like to set off the following day if possible."

Beth, due to her concerns over Angus's conscience, which she had not discussed with her husband, instinctively appreciating the confessional nature of the conversation, was imbued with the same sense of urgency as Alex, and raised no objections.

"I think that after the whirlwind tour of Rome I was treated to, the only way I want to see any more sights is either slowly and leisurely, or not at all," she asserted.

In view of their hurry, Sir Anthony and his wife were not a little disappointed on arriving at Sir Horace's palazzo to be effusively greeted by the British envoy in person, who, after inviting them to several receptions to be held over the next week, assured them that they did not need to seek accommodation in Florence for a few days at least, as rooms had been prepared for them in the Palazzo. Angus was quickly recalled from his search for a hotel, and the reluctant couple were shown to their quarters and given an hour to refresh themselves before joining Sir Horace for tea.

The rooms were beautifully furnished in cream and burgundy, the bed spacious and comfortable. Fires burned in every grate and warm water and towels had been provided. All their needs had been catered for. As soon as the door closed on the smiling servant, Alex scowled blackly at the portrait of George of Hanover hanging over the fireplace and let forth a torrent of low-voiced invective in three languages. He could not have felt more trapped had he been accommodated in the darkest dungeon of Newgate Prison.

189

"We cannot stay, Beth," he said urgently. "We must think of a reason to leave, and quickly."

An hour later, washed and brushed but no nearer a solution to their dilemma, they descended the sweeping staircase to the salon, where Sir Horace Mann bustled about pouring tea, and assured his honoured guests of their welcome.

"Really, there is little in Florence to detain the tourist," he said. "Once one has seen the Duomo and the Baptistry, oh, and the treasures of the Uffizi, of course, there is little social life to be had for the English visitor, as, unlike in other parts of the country, the nobility here are remarkably reluctant to extend hospitality to foreigners. In spite of that, you will no doubt have noticed a profusion of English people in the city, and will be wondering why this is."

It was clear from Sir Anthony's expression that this had indeed been his main preoccupation since arriving in Florence.

"If I may be so bold, my dear sir, as to hazard a guess," he said, relaxing back and extending his buttercup-yellow legs to the hearth, over which frowned a plaster bust of the duke of Cumberland, "I would say that it is due to the exceptional hospitality offered by yourself. It is renowned the length and breadth of Europe."

"Really?" said the envoy, colouring with pleasure and curving his full lips in a smile of genuine warmth. "I must confess that no one has ever complained that my modest entertainments are tedious. The Palazzo Masnetti is looked upon as a little England. You will feel at home here, I am sure." He offered his guests a plate of small pastries. "Now, what do you say we dispose of business matters, and then we can devote the rest of your stay to pleasure? Do you have your report on Rome about your person, Sir Anthony?"

Sir Anthony looked deeply flummoxed. "Oh!" he cried. "I did not realise that I was meant to produce a dossier on the Pretender's son. I thought I would merely be expected to answer questions. I am sorry, but as you know, of course, I am new to the exciting business of espionage, and unfamiliar with its routines. If you will provide me with paper, pens and ink, sir, I will set to work immediately." He made a move to stand, clearly upset. Sir Horace waved at him to be seated.

"Did the duke of Newcastle not tell you to submit a report to me of your findings?" the envoy asked a little impatiently. He was a slender man, whose face was nevertheless heavy-featured, the eyes dark, his nose aquiline, his lips thick and fleshy.

"Well, yes, but he did not specify that it should be a *written* report,"

"Do not distress yourself, sir," sighed Sir Horace, ringing a bell by his side. A young man appeared so quickly that Beth surmised he had probably been listening at the door. He took a seat at the escritoire by the window and sat silently.

"Philip here will take notes of all your observations, Sir Anthony. Now I already know that you were successful in cultivating the friendship of the Young Pretender, for which I congratulate you, sir. What did you discover about the boy?"

"Well, I am ashamed to say it, Sir Horace. I am afraid you will be angry with me, and I could not bear to upset such a delightful host as yourself." The baronet smiled ingratiatingly at the man sitting opposite, and Beth raised her eyes to heaven, a gesture which did not go unnoticed by Sir Horace.

"Are you trying to tell me you spent three days in the constant company of Charles and formed no opinion of him?" he said incredulously.

Sir Anthony was shocked.

"No, not at all," he replied. "What I am afraid you will find distasteful is that I found him to be an excellent fellow! A man quite after my own heart! Why, we talked for hours about our tailors, and he recommended me to several good

191

suppliers of silk in France and Italy. He is also a superb dancer, and although I am only moderately accomplished in that art, he was too well-mannered to criticise my performance. We did not attend any formal dances of course, but there was that night in the taverno de, oh, something-or-other. We had imbibed a considerable quantity of brandy. Had I not, I would never have agreed to attempt a balletic performance on the table. Quite an impossible endeavour, I assure you," he tittered. "I truly thought that I had severely injured myself at one point. Really, there are positions the human body is not designed to achieve. Now, what was the name of the tavern? It has quite slipped my mind, but I am sure your observers can supply it later. If you just leave a space for the name, Philip, my dear," he called to the young clerk. "Now, where was I? Oh, yes, he informed me that he plays the cello quite well, although he did not actually honour me with a performance. I assure you though, that he can tell an excellent bawdy tale! He also recommended me to several high-class houses of ill-repute, although of course I would not dream of frequenting them, being as happily married as I am." He seized his wife's hand and pressed it passionately to his breast, a gesture to which she responded by withdrawing her hand as quickly as possible. Philip scribbled away quietly in the corner.

"What did you think of him, Lady Elizabeth? You also spent time in his company, did you not?" Sir Horace asked unexpectedly.

"Yes. He insisted on showing me the sights of Rome, waxing lyrically and at stupefying length about its many attractions. He seems to have made himself entirely at home there. He is very Roman," she said disapprovingly. Sir Horace waited for her to elaborate. "He is very free with his hands," she added after a pause, blushing slightly, and casting a pleading look at the envoy not to insist on details.

"Ah. Yet many ladies find him a handsome man, I believe, with his height and his blue eyes, added to the accomplishments your husband has just outlined."

"Perhaps they do," replied Beth indifferently. "I am not overfond of dancing, myself, or the scraping of a cello. As for Charles himself, it is true that he is tall, but very thin and pale, and I am sure his eyes would be his best feature if they did not lack expression. His face is a little long and sharp for my liking," she said. "And he is quite insufferable in his arrogance, insisting on being called 'Your Highness' all the time, and spouting on about how he has been deprived of his throne, without showing the slightest inclination to do more than grumble endlessly. Which, of course, is a good thing," she added.

Sir Anthony looked at her.

"You did not tell me this, my dear," he said, astounded. "I was under the impression that you liked Charles. He certainly thought you did."

"Well of course he did! The insufferable fool thinks everybody likes him, merely because he is of royal blood," Beth replied, exasperated. "I hardly think we would have been able to deliver any report at all to Sir Horace, had I declared to the Young Pretender that I detested him from the outset!"

"Ah, yes, I see your point, my dear. But you really should have told me if he was making free with your person. I am quite disgusted with the duplicity of the man. I should have called him out, had I known. After all, it is my job to defend you, my dear." Sir Anthony shook his head in astonishment that he could have thought well of such a scoundrel.

The disbelieving expression on Sir Horace's face said clearly that he was fully aware of Beth's altercation with the guard and Sir Anthony's marked lack of interest in defending her on that occasion.

Julia Brannan

"Did he speak to you at all of his plans to invade England, Sir Anthony?" Sir Horace asked hopelessly. This mission had been a waste of time. The lemon-clad idiot had clearly not asked any pertinent questions of the Young Pretender at all.

"Well, no, not at all. We spent most of our time, when not discussing fashion and so on, talking about his prospective marriage to Louis' daughter."

Sir Horace, who had been expecting a lengthy comment on Charles's well-documented love of the opera, or some other triviality of this sort, suddenly froze.

"What?" he said. "Louis? Do you mean the king of France?"

"Yes, of course," replied Sir Anthony, puzzled. "Did you not know? He is hoping to marry the princess, has said he may even travel to France before long to negotiate in person, as things are going very slowly due to the delays in the mail, and he grows impatient. The plague, you know," he added, misinterpreting Sir Horace's stunned expression.

"Yes, I am well acquainted with the problems due to the quarantine, sir. Are you sure of this? Did he speak of it in detail?"

"Oh yes," replied the baronet. "When he had been drinking, anyway. He consumes the most prodigious quantities of alcohol." It was a relief to say something truthful. "And when he does, he becomes very chatty, even more so than normal. We talked in detail about how he could charm the young lady into becoming his wife, on which subject I consider myself particularly well qualified to give advice, having succeeded in obtaining the hand of my own exquisite lady here!" His hand fluttered out, and Beth hurriedly removed hers out of reach before he could inflict another passionate gesture on her. "We discussed the presents he should buy for her and so on and what he should wear on his wedding day. He opted for the blue silk in the end. A wise decision, and I am proud to say I had not a little influence on him in this matter. The colour will complement his eyes magnificently."

The envoy looked about to explode with frustration.

"I think Sir Horace means did he discuss the reasons why he wishes to marry the princess, Anthony," Beth prompted gently. "Political reasons."

"Oh. Well, no. I assumed he was in love. Why else would anyone wish to marry?" he said naively, smiling affectionately at his wife.

"Did Charles mention his impending nuptials to your good self, Lady Elizabeth?" Sir Horace asked somewhat desperately.

Sir Anthony coughed delicately.

"No, he did not," replied Beth. "He was too busy droning endlessly on about Bernini, and the glories of ancient Rome. In fact, this is the first I have heard of it myself."

"Is it really, my dear?" asked her husband. "I thought I had mentioned it to you. I certainly intended to."

"I wish you had," she replied, irritated. "If he had, Sir Horace, I assure you I would have asked some pertinent questions. But my husband has a tendency to be a little forgetful at times, particularly when he is drunk."

"I was not, at any time, drunk!" protested the baronet. "Only a little...ah...tipsy on occasion. I merely attempted to keep up with Charles. A man is expected to be able to hold his liquor, and I couldn't have my manliness called into question by abstaining. You will understand this of course, Sir Horace, being a man of breeding. But I was most certainly not drunk!" He glared at his wife, who returned his look with equanimity.

"If the *tipsy* state of my husband on his return home from drinking sessions with Charles was anything to go by," she said coldly, "and the ability to consume vast quantities of spirits is the measure of a man, then Charles is most certainly a formidable specimen of masculinity."

Philip had stopped writing. Sir Horace stood.

"I thank you both for your endeavours. I will take up no more of your time for the present. You must be tired after your long journey, and in need of rest. I trust I will see you at this evening's reception? Although it goes without saying that you will mention nothing of the conversation we have just had to the company." It was a statement, not a request. "I have been assured by many of my guests that they consider my house to be a home from home. I hope you will feel happy here," he added coolly.

"We already do, Sir Horace," said Beth, standing. Sir Anthony, belatedly comprehending that they were being dismissed, also came slowly to his feet. "Our rooms are delightful. It is a shame that we will only be able to accept your hospitality for one night, or two at the most."

"Why, no, my dear Lady Peters. I expect you to stay here for at least a week. And after that I have reserved rooms for you at the Hotel Margherita. You will of course now be staying in Italy until the spring. Tonight I will introduce you to a number of English people who are also wintering here. You may as well stay in Florence, where you will be amongst friends." Sir Horace smiled at the young lady. She really was adorable. Such a pity that she was wasted on that vacuous idiot. What had possessed the duke of Newcastle to recruit him? True, he had come up with one piece of astounding information, but only by mistake, and having apparently won the Pretender's confidence, had failed utterly to capitalise on it.

The adorable young lady was now looking quite anxious.

"No, Sir Horace, it is quite imperative that we return to Britain at the earliest opportunity. You really are most kind, but it is unthinkable that we can stay in Italy. We must cross to France as soon as possible."

"My dear child, you are surely not entertaining the notion of crossing the Alps in December? It will be a dreadful journey, at the least perilous, if not absolutely impossible."

"Nevertheless," said Beth determinedly. "I mean to try. I will not have my first child born anywhere other than in England, and if I do not leave now, then my condition will certainly render me unable to travel by the spring."

"I had no idea…I congratulate you. Both of you," Sir Horace replied, looking doubtfully at the baronet. "But Sir Anthony, you really cannot contemplate attempting a winter crossing of the Alps, with your wife in such a delicate state."

If Sir Anthony was surprised at the unexpected news that he was soon to be a father, he showed no sign of it.

"Could you deny her anything, if she were your wife, sir? She is the most delightful creature! And as strong as an ox!" He smiled down at the delicate figure of his wife. Anything less ox-like could hardly be imagined. "I think one should indulge one's dearest spouse wherever possible, and especially when she is soon to make me the happiest of men!"

Or especially when it is the line of least resistance, thought Sir Horace as the simpering baronet followed his wife from the room. How the hell such a limp creature had managed to impregnate his wife at all was a mystery. It would be no loss to the Hanoverian world if the man were to be swept away by an avalanche. Shame about the woman though. With a small effort he dismissed them from his mind. If they wished to commit suicide in the Alps, so be it. They were of no further use to him.

Had he been a witness to the whispered scene that took place in the bedroom five minutes later, he would have revised his opinion somewhat. No sooner had the door closed behind them than the limp baronet picked his wife up and swung her round in the air as though she were weightless, with scant regard for her condition.

"That was a stroke of genius!" he whispered ecstatically, crushing her to his chest briefly before releasing her. "I do take it you're not really with child?" He raised his voice. "This room is quite the most beautiful one we have stayed in, do you not think, my dear?"

"Of course not!" she replied in a low voice. "If I was, don't you think I'd have told you first? Would you be disappointed if I was? Yes, it is delightful, although I thought the apartment at Nice just as lovely, if a little more gaudy."

"Perhaps you are right, although I am a great lover of gold work myself," he trilled in reply. "God, no, I'd be delighted," he whispered. "Although it would be a little inconvenient at the moment. But even so…" his voice trailed off wistfully. "We have plenty of time to have children," he continued. "And the making of them is great fun."

He reached for her, and she slapped his hand away.

"Not now," she replied softly. "I think Sir Anthony would be more likely to lie down quietly for an hour than to engage in relations with his wife which will no doubt be overheard by the person listening in the next room." She adopted a bored tone for the next sentence, before lowering her voice again. "You should rest for a while, Anthony, you know how fatigued you become if you do not have a nap in the afternoons. I take it then that it is as likely Charles is to marry the princess as it is that his eyes have become blue overnight."

"How considerate you are, my dear. Yes, I shall lie down directly." He moved towards the bed, taking off his coat and sitting on the edge. She sat next to him. "You're right. But it provides a reason for him going to France, if he chooses to, and will hopefully throw Mann off the scent until after the invasion is launched. I must write to Charles at the earliest opportunity and tell him that he has a spy amongst his guards. Did you see Mann's reaction to my avowal to defend you?"

"Yes," she whispered. "But isn't it most likely that the

guard Charles dismissed has betrayed him?"

"Probably. But we can take no chances."

He kissed her, passionately, once. Then he lay down. For the remainder of their time in Florence both in public and private, Alex made no further appearance, and Beth was made fully aware of how unbearably tedious her life would be if she were indeed the wife only of a superficial, gossipy, frivolous fop, as everyone else thought. It was only three days, but the fact that she missed Alex intensely during that time, told her that she really did now think of him and Anthony as two distinct beings. And *that* told her that, overall, she was probably performing the role of Lady Peters quite well.

By the end of the three days Sir Horace was so desperate to be rid of Sir Anthony, who embroiled him at every opportunity in a lengthy discussion about the quality of silk, or the intricacies of the embroidery on whichever hideous waistcoat he was wearing at the time, that he became positively effusive about the mildness of the weather at the moment, and now considered their chances of crossing the Alps safely to be excellent. When Sir Anthony, seconds before they were due to leave, asked the envoy if he would be so kind as to provide a letter of recommendation to ease their way through the remaining Italian customs posts, Sir Horace agreed without hesitation, and rang the bell for his clerk. When neither Philip nor his underclerk Nathaniel made an appearance, an unprecedented event, the envoy hurriedly penned a letter in his own hand, unwilling to delay Sir Anthony's departure any longer than was necessary.

It was with the greatest relief that he waved the baronet and his wife off, noting with disapproval that Sir Anthony was even too much of a coward or a fool to discipline his own footman, who after having kept his master waiting for a few minutes, strolled casually round the side of the house whistling, and leapt into the coach without receiving any rebuke at all.

That evening, in their local drinking establishment, Philip and Nathaniel greatly increased their popularity amongst the assembled company by performing an extremely indecent song, complete with very explicit actions, concerning a young lady who became curious as to what was to be found beneath a Scotsman's kilt, and was answered by that native of Caledonia in a very direct and hilarious manner. It had taken the Scottish footman some time to teach them the whole thing, which comprised some ten verses and a particularly rousing chorus, but it had been worth it, they felt.

So did the Scottish footman.

CHAPTER TEN

Paris, December 1743

Dear Isabella,

Thank you for your letter, which was waiting for me when we arrived here. It has been a long and sometimes difficult journey from Florence, and I am very relieved to have arrived safely at last.

She was, but not for the reasons given here.

The journey over the Alps was particularly difficult, but had to be attempted if we were not to be stranded in Italy for the winter, which we were most anxious to avoid. We could not make the return journey by sea, as the feluccas rarely put out in the winter, and so we had no choice but to travel over Mont Cenis. One cannot traverse this pass by coach, so our carriage was dismantled and taken by mule.

Sir Anthony and I were taken by chair, carried by two men. At first I must confess that I was very alarmed at the idea of trusting my life to total strangers, and spent some time in trepidation that they would lose their footing and drop me over the side of the mountain, but they are remarkably sure footed. They leap about the rocks like mountain goats and can seemingly walk on sheet ice without slipping at all.

The mountains are spectacular; it is impossible to describe their enormity and grandeur. The sight of the sun rising over the Alps, turning the peaks rose pink and causing the snow to sparkle as if one were travelling over a carpet of diamonds, is one I shall never forget, and certainly took my mind off the fact that for much of the journey I had no feeling at all in my hands and feet, so cold was it. We were most

201

relieved not to encounter any brigands or the Spanish, and we travelled on to Geneva without any incident worth repeating, where Sir Anthony paused briefly to visit some acquaintances.

Beth had been surprised when he had stopped their reassembled carriage outside a small church nestled on the slope of a hill on the outskirts of the town.

"Why are we stopping?" she asked. The Calvinist church was rectangular, stone built and without ornamentation, surrounded by a small, well-maintained graveyard. Nothing that would merit a stop, particularly when they were in such haste.

Angus shrugged his shoulders and shook his head. He had no idea either.

"I wish to make only a brief halt, to visit some people to whom I owe a great debt, my dear," Sir Anthony said, climbing down from the carriage and holding out his hand to assist his wife to descend. The postillion sat resigned to waiting in the bitter cold, hunching his body deep into his heavy cape.

Instead of going to the church itself, as both Angus and Beth expected, he took the small path around the side of the building, and came to a stop in front of a large, recently-erected stone, its edges as yet unweathered, the lettering crisp and clear.

"He has done it, then," Sir Anthony murmured mysteriously.

Beth moved round to his side, partly to use him as a shelter from the biting wind, which he seemed not to notice, and partly so that she could read the lettering.

Erected In Loving Memory of
Anna Clarissa

widow of Sir John Anthony Peters
who departed this life on 7th February 1740
in the 45th year of her life.
Also in memory of their three daughters
Anna Mary
3rd June 1715 – 10th February 1740
Caroline Anne
12th December 1716 – 6th February 1740
Beatrice Elizabeth
25th March 1719 – 25th February 1740
May they rest in the eternal peace of our Lord Jesus Christ.

Sir Anthony knelt down by the side of the grave, leaving Beth exposed to the wind. She gasped, but not because of that. After a moment she crouched down next to him. Angus remained discreetly in the background.

"They were real?" she asked. She had always thought the Peters family to be a fabrication of Alex's sponsor, whoever he or she was. She had never imagined for one moment that they had really existed.

"Yes," her husband replied simply. "My sponsor erected the stone last year at my request, but they were real. It wouldn't have been practical to wholly invent a family. If we had done that, even the most cursory investigation of my background would have revealed that Sir Anthony didn't exist. As I said, after my father died I returned to Scotland to lead the clan, not really having any intention of continuing with the idea of espionage. In the April of 1740 I received a letter from my sponsor to say that he had found a possible identity for me, if I was still interested."

"And you were," she said.

"Yes. There wasn't much going on in Scotland at the time, nothing Duncan couldn't deal with. So I made a trip down to…my sponsor's house, and the rest is history, so to speak."

She looked again at the gravestone.

"They all died within days of each other," Beth commented. She shivered, and not wholly because of the wind. "What did they die of?"

He turned to her, his painted face blank.

"Smallpox," he replied. "Which is why their son wears so much paint, as the sole survivor of the family, although horribly scarred, of course."

She considered for a moment, laying aside the sympathy she felt for this tragic family, and dwelling on more practical matters.

"But in spite of the fact that there is a real Peters family, would it not still be easy to prove you don't exist?" she said. "Anyone going to Cheshire would soon discover from the registers that Sir John and Lady Peters had no son."

"No, they wouldn't," he replied. He plucked absently at a small weed struggling to grow in the shelter of the costly marble stone. "They did have a son. Anthony was born in Cheshire, in 1713. Sir John died six years later, and the family left the country soon after."

"You mean Sir Anthony really exists?" she cried. She thought for a moment. "What happened to him? Is he dead?" she asked, and her husband smiled, having followed her thought patterns and been satisfied with the conclusion she had come to.

"He died in France in 1720, weeks after they arrived, which can't have done Anna's state of mind any good. He's buried in a small church near Blois." He reached down and ran his fingers across the four inches of smooth marble that separated Beatrice's date of death from the wishes for their souls. "I owe him a debt," he said earnestly. "Which is why, one day, when it no longer matters, I will add his name and date and place of death to the stone, so that anyone who cares to investigate will know that Sir Anthony Peters, court fop and Jacobite spy, was no relation whatsoever to this poor, tragic family. I will not sully their name. They deserve that, at least."

He straightened, brushing the dirt from his gloves.

"Shall we go?" he said. There was a pale green stain on the fingers of his right glove, from where he had uprooted the small weed, which now lay wilting on the ground, its tiny roots exposed to the icy wind.

We stayed for a night in Geneva before travelling on to France. Really, the customs men are nothing short of robbers, and in spite of the numerous letters of safe conduct that my husband had obtained before leaving England (you, of course, dear cousins, know how numerous and influential are his acquaintance),

It would do no harm to remind them of this. Although the letter was addressed to Isabella, all of the cousins and probably Richard too, would read it.

we were not allowed through until a substantial sum of money had changed hands, after which we continued on to Lyons, where we stayed for two nights to recover from the rigours of travel. Although one is sitting in a coach for most of the day, it is still incredibly tiring. The jolting on badly-maintained roads, the tedious halts at post-houses while the horses are changed, and the dubious nature of some of the accommodations, are quite exhausting. At this time of the year there is also the weather to deal with, and in spite of my furs and the bags of heated semolina that Sir Anthony was kind enough to procure for me to warm my hands and feet, the cold does take its toll.

Shortly before Lyons, it started to snow heavily, so we cut short our journey and put up at a small inn for the night. It was, thankfully, warm, due to a large log fire in the main room, which was consequently crowded. Unfortunately a small pony, who had been left untied outside, kept expressing his desire for shelter by butting open the door of the inn with his nose, letting in flurries of snow and a howling wind. The sensible thing would have been to go and stable him, but the landlord, not wishing to venture out into the snow, contented himself with closing the badly-latched door in the face of the unfortunate animal, which after a few minutes would repeat its performance. After several repetitions we moved from our seat near the door into the interior of the room.

It was as well that they had moved into the shadows. Five minutes later the door had opened again to a general groan from the company, but instead of the chestnut nose and soft pleading eyes of the pony, in had come a heavily cloaked and hooded man, brushing the snow off his shoulders and stamping his booted feet before entering the room.

Sir Anthony observed the traveller, who threw back his hood as the landlord approached him. The baronet started visibly, then leaned over to Angus and hurriedly whispered at some length into his ear, relying on the chatter and general noise to cover up what he was saying. Angus stood, and taking an extremely circuitous route round the room, finally approached the stocky red-headed stranger from the other side. Beth leaned forward to get a better look at the man, who now greeted her brother-in-law with recognition, although not affection. A sharp tug on her arm pulled her back into the shadows.

"Really, my dear, the noise and the smoke in this room are giving me the most dreadful headache. Why don't we retire to our chamber? Jim will ask the landlord if he will be so kind as to provide us with a hot meal of some sort. I really feel quite unwell."

Unwilling as she was to forsake the warmth of the common room, which was just starting to dislodge the cold from her bones, she knew an intrigue when she saw one. The landlord was now talking to the newcomer, who was shaking his head and moving across to a table, his face pale and lined with exhaustion. Angus took up the conversation on the stranger's behalf, and that was all she saw before Sir Anthony led her up the wooden staircase to their small, but at least clean, bedroom. There he had explained, his breath forming small clouds in the frosty room, that the man was William MacGregor, or Drummond, of Balhaldie, chief by election of the MacGregor clan, although in Alex's view not fully worthy of the title, and that he knew both Alex and Angus well enough for it to be inadvisable that he meet the former in his present disguise.

"I thought you were supposed to show complete obedience and loyalty to your chief," Beth observed.

Sir Anthony, as he still was, looked at her wryly. He would not take off his paint until full dark tonight. Whilst no one would be eavesdropping on their conversation from the next room, as at Mann's, it was highly likely that someone could barge in at any moment. Not least the landlord, with the much wished-for hot meal.

"Angus has been talking to you, I see," he said. "That's true, but it's a two way relationship. The Balhaldies were elected chief just before the '15, although there were disputes at the time about their right and seniority and many of the clansmen, myself included, don't acknowledge him as chief. And it was not the Balhaldie of the time, but Rob Roy MacGregor who took the leadership in the rising." He stood up and paced around the small room in an attempt to warm himself. Beth huddled deeper into her fur-lined cloak. "We just don't see eye to eye, that's all," he said. "I think that James and Charles should know the truth about the level of support they have in France and Britain, and that without strong French support, the English Jacobites, and many of the Scots too, will absolutely not rise. I also think they should know that Louis is a devious bastard who will always look to his own interests first and will only invade England if it's to his personal advantage to do so."

"Which it is, at the moment, because he wants revenge for the British victory at Dettingen," Beth said.

"Possibly," her husband acknowledged. "But I still don't trust Louis, and won't believe he's sincere until James is sitting in London with the crown on his head."

The conversation was interrupted by the appearance of the somewhat harried landlord, who was carrying two bowls of steaming onion soup and a long loaf of bread. A few sticks of firewood were tucked under his arm, which he proceeded to stack in the bare grate haphazardly, before lighting them and disappearing. The couple took their bowls and sat on the wooden floor by the hearth, to take full advantage of the meagre heat.

"So how does Balhaldie's view differ from yours, then?" she asked. The soup was good.

"He's very eager for a fight. So eager, that I strongly suspect he's been greatly exaggerating the level of support James can expect, hoping to incite him to action. Which in my view, and that of many others I might add, is not a good thing. I'd rather wait another ten years for a successful invasion, than have an immediate failure. If James, or more likely Charles, attempts to take the throne without French help, the country will not support him in sufficient numbers. I tell him that, every time I see him."

"Surely that's all right, then? Charles certainly trusts you."

"Yes, he does. But Balhaldie gets to see him more often than I do. And he tells the prince what he wants to hear, that his subjects are loyal and oppressed, and only waiting for him to land on British soil to sweep away the hated German tyrant and restore the Stuarts to their proper place." His voice was heavy with sarcasm.

"You really don't like your disputed chief much, do you?"

Beth commented.

"His loyalty's not in doubt, which is more than can be said for many a chief. Lovat, the Fraser chief, for one. But he's dangerous, and no, I don't like him that much. Murray of Broughton hates him, and it certainly doesn't help the cause to have its chief protagonists constantly bickering with each other."

Angus entered at this point, his cheeks rosy with warmth from the fire below. He eyed Beth's pinched face and red-tipped nose with some sympathy.

"He's no' staying," he explained, to his brother's relief. "Ye can go back down an ye want. Christ, it's cold enough in here tae freeze your…ah…"

"Balls off?" Beth suggested. She smiled at the expression on Angus's face. "One day, I hope, you'll get to meet Graeme," she said. "And when you do, you'll understand why there's little you can say of that nature that will shock me."

"What did you find out?" Alex asked.

"No' as much as I'd hoped," Angus admitted. "He was awfu' close-mouthed. But he was verra cold, and the brandy here is surprisingly fine. You owe me…"

"Yes, I'll pay you later," said Alex impatiently, retaining his crisp English accent, but not the flouncing manner. "What did he tell you?"

"No' a great deal in words. But he's tired, verra tired. He's travelled hard, without stopping more than necessary, and he's heading over the Alps to Italy, then south. I mentioned that I'd just come that way myself, and he was particularly interested in the state of the passes, and the number and nature of the people I'd met. He also wanted to know about the quarantine regulations, how strict they were. He's hurrying. He didna even ask me what I was doing travelling through Italy, which I was grateful for, as I couldna think of a good reason myself. What he couldna resist saying was that

209

he's got an important message for King James and the prince from a great ally of his, and he tellt me to hold myself in good readiness."

"Louis," said Alex immediately. "But why would Louis tell Charles what he was planning, if he wants to keep it secret? He might tell James, because if he intends to invade without the prince, he would need documentation from James supporting the invasion to convince the British supporters to rise."

"Would King James not tell his son?" Beth asked.

"Not if Louis told him not to. James is far more cautious than his son. He does everything by the book. He will see the sense in Charles staying in Rome until the invasion is launched and there's no more need for secrecy. But he knows Charles will not. So he won't tell him."

"Why do you look so worried then?" Beth asked, looking at the two brothers, who wore identical frowns.

"Because if James won't tell his son that the invasion is a reality, and imminent, Balhaldie certainly will. And a lot more besides, I shouldna wonder," Angus had said.

Concentrate. She would never finish her letter if she let her mind wander after every sentence.

Although the rooms were clean, they were not heated. That was the coldest night I have ever spent. But now we are in Paris, and our lodgings are very comfortable and warm. It would have been a great surprise to encounter Lord and Lady Winter and Miss Maynard, had you not advised me in your letter that they were also travelling in France. We met with them yesterday, and will travel to Versailles together tomorrow, making a very merry party, I am sure.

She sighed. Might as well get all the lies over with at once.

I am very pleased to hear that Richard has received his Cornet's commission, and looks to be promoted to Lieutenant in the very near future. Of course, as I am sure you know, Sir Anthony had provided the funds for the Lieutenant's commission, but I did not expect he would achieve this rank so soon.

Commissions only became available when the previous holder died, retired, or bought himself a higher commission, leaving all those below him to move up, if they had the requisite funds. Maybe Richard had quietly done away with his superior. He was certainly capable of it. She would put nothing past him.

I am sorry to have missed him, but find it interesting that he has seen fit to return to our old home during the winter period, when there is no fighting to be done. I am certain he will find everything in order, as the servants are excellent, and that he will take the time to make a few improvements to the building, which is in urgent need of a new roof. I am sure he will be busy once the spring comes, with the war in Europe showing no signs of concluding soon.

She certainly hoped he would be busy, losing against the French in England.

I am sure that Lady Winter will inform you of the wonders of Versailles, and whether the Court is really as corrupt as we have heard. I will also of course write to you again, and Sir Anthony and I will certainly pay you a visit upon our return. It goes without saying that I would not be now enjoying the wonders of Europe had you not launched me into society in the first place, enabling me to attract the attention of a man such as Sir Anthony. You cannot know how grateful I am.

Or how horrified they would be if they truly knew why she was so grateful.

I remain,

Your loving cousin, Elizabeth.

* * *

"I must say," sniffed Lord Winter. "If one wished to put forward a case against an absolutist Catholic monarchy, one could not do better than to conduct one's argument here." He scowled around the beautifully sculptured gardens of the Versailles orangery with their neat paths and central fountain, rainbow-hued in the winter sunshine, as if he expected at any moment to be accosted by a flock of priests brandishing crucifixes, heaven-bent on converting the heathen. The palms and oleanders together with the pomegranate, Eugenia and orange trees, placed in the gardens in the summer, were now housed in great vaulted galleries which ran round three sides of the garden. "The ridiculous waste of countless millions of livres in order to house a corrupt family in tasteless splendour is insanity itself," he complained.

They had just completed a perfunctory tour of the Palace of Versailles. A lengthy tour would take weeks, Beth thought. The stables alone, Sir Anthony had pointed out in twittering ecstasy, could accommodate twelve thousand horses.

"Really, my dear, one could spend days just enjoying the gardens, without even entering the chateau at all!" he had said.

Nevertheless, they had entered it and wandered around the public rooms, which were full of tourists, who seemed to be allowed to go anywhere at will, clattering across the parquet floors, commenting on the innumerable marble statues and exquisite wall paintings, and surreptitiously stealing silk tassels and gold braid from the curtains and tapestries as souvenirs. Although the royal family themselves were not in evidence at the moment, Lord and Lady Winter assured the company that when they were, the tourists treated them as just another attraction, crowding round to watch them eat, or dress. Or so they had heard.

Beth sighed. She seemed to be sighing a lot this morning. Probably because she was by now aware that of the three of them, she had by far the worst task, although it had not seemed to be the case yesterday, when they had sat in their Parisian accommodation and hatched their plan for today.

"We must remember at all times that our ultimate aim is to find this Henri," Alex had reminded his wife and brother. "Because we dinna ken what the man looks like, we must listen for anyone wi' a sibilant 's', and then find a way of asking his name. Our best chance is to get intae the palace, but it'll no' be easy, as I havena the contacts."

"I thought anyone could get into the palace," Beth said. "Isn't the place constantly full of tourists?"

He shot her a disparaging look.

"Aye," he said. "But I dinna think we're likely to encounter a trusted employee of the king's wandering around chatting to the tourists. It's possible, but I doubt it. No, we have a far better chance if we can get intae the palace as guests. We need to get ourselves invited to a function of some sort, where we can chat to the courtiers, and find out more."

"I should be able tae get into the servant's quarters, without too much trouble," Angus said confidently. There was no doubt his confidence was well placed. Any servant girl he exercised his charm on whilst waiting for his master and mistress to finish their lengthy tour would be sure to invite him somewhere before too long. Alex nodded.

"I need to talk to any courtiers I see around when we're touring tomorrow, see if I can procure an invitation of some sort. It'd be a damn sight easier if we were no' with the Winters and that limpet Maynard lassie."

"What do you want me to do?" Beth asked.

"You might try chatting to any female courtiers you see.

Maybe ye'll get yourself an invitation to the Queen's rooms," Angus suggested.

"No, that would be nae good at all," Alex said. "She never attends any functions. The king and queen dinna get along. Ye'd be better trying tae make the acquaintance of one of his many mistresses. They have far more influence wi' Louis than his wife does."

Beth frowned.

"I don't think I'd have much success with women of that sort," she said. "Society women don't seem to like me very much. No matter how hard I try, I think they realise that I'm not that interested in the things they like."

The two men looked at her. Slender, curved in all the right places. Perfect face. And the hair… It was all too clear why women disliked her.

"Ye really have no idea of just how beautiful you are, do ye?" Alex said.

"Oh, that." The fine brows drew together over the cornflower blue eyes in a frown. Not the normal reaction from a woman who's just been told she's beautiful. "Yes, of course I do. It's a damn nuisance. Everyone judges me by the way I look. I often wish I were ugly. At least I might be taken seriously, then."

Instead she was taken in an impulsive bear hug by Alex, and then soundly kissed, which drove all the breath from her lungs, and nearly all thought from her mind. That he would have followed through on his affectionate impulse was clear from his dilated pupils and the darkening of the irises to a deep, smoky blue. But Angus was there watching, approving, amused.

"I do love you," Alex contented himself with saying instead. "But aye, you're right. Maybe ye can occupy Lord and Lady Winter then, and prise Anne off me if I see someone, gie me the chance to have a wee blether with them."

And so she had. And had indeed had to link her arm forcibly through Anne's in a firm gesture of friendliness to stop her following the baronet as he coo'eed his way across the orangery and round the circular pond towards a startled courtier dressed in sumptuous blue velvet.

"There are so many practical uses to which such an enormous sum of money could have been better put." Lord Winter continued his criticism of the French king's extravagance.

Anne, deprived of her baronet, now turned her simpering attentions on the only other male present.

"Indeed you are right, my lord," she said. "There are so many fine art works decaying in damp buildings, and classical monuments in need of maintenance. You would think the king would spend his money on far more tasteful things."

I will not say anything provocative, Beth determined. She agreed with her acquaintance to some extent, although having travelled through the poverty ridden villages of France, restoring monuments was not top of her list of more worthwhile royal expenditure.

"Like waging war on Britain?" She could not resist it. Pompous men like Edward and Lord Winter brought out the worst in her.

Lord Winter favoured her with a scathing look.

"I hardly think waging war on us would be tasteful, do you, Lady Elizabeth?" he replied condescendingly.

"No, but it would certainly be a more practical use for the money, would it not?" Beth pointed out. "From Louis' point of view, of course."

Lord Winter glanced across the grass at Sir Anthony, who had now engaged the courtier in a spirited conversation. Another man dressed in long black clerical robes was approaching the pair. The lord sniffed again. It was his genteel way of showing disapproval. He sniffed a lot in the presence of Sir Anthony.

"Only if he considered throwing his money into the sea a worthwhile use for it," he said. "For our navy would of course vanquish any invasion attempt. The British navy is the best in the world."

"Maybe," she replied. "But then, of course, King Louis may consider the money well spent on Versailles. Although the palace may not be to your taste, or mine for that matter, it undoubtedly proclaims to the world that France is a prosperous and powerful nation, which was surely the intention of the king's grandfather when he built it."

"Fine clothes do not a gentleman make," the lord replied haughtily.

No, but they could certainly make a good impression. Sir Anthony was now returning across the ruthlessly trimmed grass, almost skipping in his glee. He deftly circled Miss Maynard and gripped his wife's hands rapturously. When she kept herself at arm's length, he pulled her towards him, planting a wet kiss on her nose before releasing her.

"You will never guess why I am so excited!" he chirruped to the company, not noticing Beth take out her kerchief and wipe his kiss from her nose. Lady Winter certainly noticed, though. It would be all over London in a week that the marriage of Sir Anthony and his wife was already foundering.

The baronet gave the company no time to make any suggestions as to the reasons for his ecstasy. "I have been talking to Count…ah…er….anyway, he has most kindly invited us to observe the service at one o' clock today! Isn't it exciting? The king himself will certainly be present." He laughed and clapped his hands joyfully.

Anne smiled happily at Sir Anthony, moving forward to congratulate him.

"The service at one o' clock?" Lord Winter spluttered. "Do you mean the mass, sir?"

"Well, yes, I suppose I do. It will be in the royal chapel, Elizabeth, which I have been told is the most remarkable building, decorated in the style of Bernini. You remember Bernini's work, of course, from Rome. Quite glorious."

She did.

"Sir Anthony, are you insane?" the lord cried. Anne hesitated. It seemed a smile was not appropriate after all, but as she was as yet unsure of a suitable expression with which to replace it, it remained in place, drooping a little at the corners.

Sir Anthony looked at the other man, perplexed.

"I hardly think a man can be called insane for admiring the style of Bernini, my lord," he said coolly. "I am amongst exalted company in doing so. Why, even…"

"No, no," Lord Winter just stopped himself from adding 'you fool'. "I mean to consider going to a Papist mass, of course. Why it is unthinkable, even if you were the most devoted aficionado of Bernini. What would your countrymen think?"

"I am sure they would think I was extremely lucky in having the chance to view the Chapel Royal. The count assures me that he can procure us seats within a few feet of the royal family themselves, and many other prominent courtiers, of course. I had no idea you felt so strongly, my lord. I did not realise you were so weak in the Protestant faith as to feel your soul to be in danger from a single mass. However," Sir Anthony continued, oblivious to the gathering clouds on the Winters' faces, which was duplicated, after a hurried glance at them, on Anne's, "if you are so adamant that you will not join us, I shall go and tell the count immediately. He will be disappointed, although I am sure he will have no difficulty in finding others to take your places." He made a move towards the blue nobleman, and Beth found herself thrust aside almost rudely by Lady Winter, who took Sir Anthony's arm to prevent him leaving.

"Let us not be so hasty. I must admit to a passion for the Italian style myself, although I have seen little of it, as Bartholomew has not yet seen fit to escort me to the Italian states in person. You say you have seen Bernini's works in Rome?"

"Yes, we have," replied Beth, her eyes sparkling, keeping her expression neutral with some effort. "They are remarkable. The Baldacchino in St. Peter's is…"

"How fascinating," interrupted Lady Winter crisply. "Well, I think we should see this style for ourselves. By attending this idolatrous service, we are only showing the strength of our own faith, unafraid to walk into the Devil's snare, knowing ourselves invulnerable to his machinations."

Lord Winter subsided as always in the face of his wife's determination. Sir Anthony beamed.

"I could not have put it better myself, my dear Wilhelmina," he said.

"You test my composure to the limits, sometimes," Beth whispered in his ear as they waited in the crowd to be admitted to the chapel, having mastered her impulse to laugh at the transparency of Lady Winter, who would rather die than be excluded from anything worth gossiping about. "How on earth did you procure us an invitation to mass?"

"I expressed a great interest in the Roman faith. They hope to convert us. Do not cross yourself or genuflect to the altar. We are Anglicans."

It was hard not to do so automatically on entering the remarkable building. Beth had expected stained glass, a jewelled dimness within, and was pleasantly surprised by the cool red, green and white marble floor and the clear glassed windows which, coupled with the white walls and pillars, drenched the chapel in light, sparkling on the gilded highlights of the altar and the organ case, and drawing attention to the spectacular painted ceiling, which showed representations of the three parts of the Trinity. They were shown to their seats, where Beth immediately resumed her examination of the ceiling, head tilted back. The paintings were remarkable, beautifully executed.

She ignored her husband's tug on her arm and turned round to look down the church; and straight into the dark eyes of King Louis XV, who had just entered and was making his way down the aisle with his entourage, and of whose entrance her husband had been trying to warn her.

The king's eyes swept over and past her, then back. He smiled, briefly, then moved on before she could curtsey in acknowledgement of his notice, and took his place ahead of her in the front pews.

Anne was still clinging to Sir Anthony's left arm, and next to her was Lady Winter, who became respectfully silent when the priest and his attendants entered. Beth's right hand fluttered automatically upwards until her husband nudged her, after which it remained determinedly at her side throughout the service.

After a few moments, it being obvious that the general chatter, albeit subdued, was not going to cease in spite of the fact that a religious service was taking place, Lady Winter and Anne continued their whispered discussion of the handsomeness of the king and the ugliness of the overpainted hussy at his left, who was certainly one of his mistresses. Or was it the one on the right? Whichever it was, they were all hussies, and therefore ugly.

The service was short, irreverent, punctuated by bursts of wonderful music, and ribald laughter, which Beth had not expected, and of which she did not approve. Religious feasts and festivals should be joyous occasions; communion itself was serious, in her view. Not a time to chat and make obvious intrigues with your neighbours, as much of the French Court had been doing.

They had hardly exited the building before Lord Winter exploded in a froth of indignation at the lack of respect and licentiousness of the French papists towards the Almighty.

For once, Beth agreed with him.

"Well, that doesn't seem to have done us a lot of good," Beth commented, once they were safely back at the hotel. "Although I thought Lord Winter was going to have an apoplexy at one point. You'd think he'd be pleased that Catholics don't take themselves seriously. He'll be there at the pearly gates, sniffing merrily away, waiting for God to cast the whole congregation down into the pit for daring to chatter and laugh in His house."

"You were no' exactly approving yourself," Alex said.

"No, I wasn't. Were you?"

"No, I must admit, when I go to mass, it's generally to think about our Lord and the sacrifice he made for us, rather than to arrange to bed the lusty wench in the next pew. But it did give us a chance to listen for men wi' speech impediments."

"Did you hear any?" Beth asked.

"No, although I'd thought we had a chance. Let's hope Angus has had better luck."

He'd stayed below on their return to wash himself under the pump in the yard, and now made a smiling appearance, complete with a tray of tea and three cups. He surveyed their faces.

"No luck, then?" he said.

"How about yourself?" asked Alex.

"Well, I got myself into the kitchens, thanks to a young lady by the name of Francoise, who took pity on me after I'd been stamping my feet and blowing on my hands and suchlike for twenty minutes. Oh, and I also got myself a promise of an evening wi' Jeanne, who's a chambermaid. She isna likely to have a deal of information, but…"

"It'll be fun finding out," Beth interrupted. "Won't Francoise be jealous?"

"Ah, weel, now she was by far the bonniest o' the two," Angus replied sadly. "But she also has a husband who looks to be rather handy wi' his fists."

"Tae hell wi' your love life," Alex cut in impatiently, teapot in hand. "Did ye discover anything of import?"

"Aye, I was coming to that. There are either four or six thousand people working at the palace, depending on who you talk to. Of those, Louis has a couple of hundred who seem likely to be of our friend's ilk. Clerks, servants of the bedchamber and suchlike. And around ten or so of those are called Henri. We should be glad he's no' called Pierre or Jean. It seems around a thousand of the servants are. Must get awfu' confusing."

"How did you find all this out? Wasn't anyone suspicious?" Beth asked.

"Not at all," Angus replied. "I tellt them I was a Catholic, you see, though of course my employer, the idiot Sir Anthony doesna ken that. They thought that was quite amusing, and it got them on my side. And my auntie's husband's sister upped and married a Frenchman, Henri something or other, I canna quite recall the surname, as she was no' inclined to wed a Protestant, ye ken. And her son is also called Henri. She's awfu' proud, because he got himself a good job at the palace, and although I've never met my cousin, I thought I'd look him up, maybe, while I was here. The servants were verra helpful."

Beth looked from Angus to his approving brother.

"God, you're a devious pair," she said. "How can I believe anything you tell me?"

"Because we only lie when there's reason to," Alex pointed out. "And with family, there isna reason to. That's narrowed it down, at least. Did ye mention his 's'?"

"No. I had to admit I didna ken what my cousin looks like. They might have thought it strange I ken about the way he speaks, but no' about the colour of his hair and suchlike."

Alex sighed.

"Ye did well, man," he said. "But it looks like Sir Anthony'll have tae go and toady to another courtier tomorrow. D'ye think we can avoid the Winters altogether for a day? And the Maynard woman?"

They were just debating whether it would be possible to do that when they were all staying in the same hotel, when a message arrived. The man, being in the royal livery, was shown up to the room immediately, where Lady Elizabeth listened to his message, her husband being temporarily indisposed.

Inexplicably, it seemed that the king requested the pleasure of the company of Sir Anthony Peters and Lady Elizabeth his wife, of whom, as far as they knew, he had never heard, at a small dance to be held at the palace on Saturday. Four days from now.

CHAPTER ELEVEN

"No," said Beth, subsiding ungracefully to the floor in a heap of blue velvet. "No more, not today." She looked belligerently up at her torturer, who stood over her, feet planted apart, arms folded, face equally determined.

"We have at least two hours before the Winters expect us for dinner," he said. "And you've no' got the turns right yet."

"I don't care," she replied sulkily. "I've had enough. There is a limit to human endurance, you know." It was clear that she felt she had reached that limit long ago. It was equally as clear that Alex did not.

"Just be thankful that the prince isna here," remarked Angus from his prone position near the fire. He had hardly moved all afternoon, and Beth glared across at him. "He's an expert at the menuet, I'm tellt, and ye ken how energetic he is. He'd have had you practising in your sleep."

"I *have* been practising in my sleep," Beth moaned.

Since the invitation had arrived and Alex had discovered that Beth, whilst having learned several country dances in her childhood, did not know the first thing about the menuet, the favourite Court dance, he had driven her ruthlessly, first talking her through the steps and then practising, repeating the same step over and over again until she got it right, or dropped. Last night she had indeed dreamt that she was dancing alone in front of the French Court, her husband shouting disparaging remarks at her across the ballroom, Louis watching her amateur stumblings, his dark brows drawn low in a disapproving frown.

Of course in reality Alex, or rather Sir Anthony, would be on the floor with her tomorrow, and expected a graceful, accomplished performance, which was why he was driving her so hard now.

"No one will notice us anyway. There'll be hundreds of people there," she reasoned, attempting a pitiful look upwards.

"They will," he said, unmoved. "I've already tellt ye, in the menuet, the couples get up one at a time, starting wi' the king and his latest mistress, and moving down the aristocracy from there. Your performance is all important. Everyone will be watching and criticising. Our future reception at Court could depend on you *getting the turns right.*"

He leaned down and placing his hands under her armpits, lifted her off the floor as though she were a child, in spite of her attempts to make herself heavy.

"Have some mercy, Alex," she begged. "We'll be at the bottom of the pecking order. I'll wager we never even get to perform one step." He retained his hold on her arms, as though he expected her to run away if he released her. She doubted that she was capable of crawling away at the moment, let alone running. "And even if we do, I can't believe that the whole future of the Stuart dynasty depends on whether I can perform a demi-coupé correctly or not."

At last. His face relaxed a little, the corners of his mouth turning upwards.

"No, that's true," he conceded. "It may depend on us finding Henri, though. And we have a much better chance of doing that if we're invited back to the palace. And our best chance of being invited back is…"

"To impress them with our dexterity and grace in the menuet," she said tiredly.

"Exactly. And in spite of being low in the pecking order, we *will* be asked to demonstrate our skill, because we're new to the Court, and because it seems King Louis has invited us personally." That still puzzled him. But the important thing was that they were in. Now they had to stay in. "So," he said, planting a kiss on her forehead before releasing her and moving back into the starting position, arms forward and down, hands out, palms facing the floor. "Let's try it one more time."

Defeated, she stood, hands folded, heels together and took her weight on her left foot, preparing to step forward onto her right. She felt the sharp stab under her little toe as the blister burst. He had got his way, again. He always got his way. It was one of the things she loved about him. It was one of the things she hated about him.

* * *

To Beth's great relief, they practised the now detested menuet for only an hour the following morning, as she had finally mastered the dreaded turns. The final rehearsal was conducted in front of Lord and Lady Winter, Miss Maynard, and half a dozen other assorted guests staying at the hotel, one of whom helpfully produced a violin and proceeded to play a menuet for the couple, which was a great improvement on Angus humming and beating the rhythm out on the arm of the chair. Their performance was greeted with applause, and a few very minor improvements to hand position, elevation of leg etc were suggested.

Lady Winter also informed Beth of the best way to cure a blister, and to that young lady's surprise, called for water, a cloth, and needle and thread, and personally cleaned and dried Beth's foot, before running a thread through the blister.

"I have worn enough beautiful but impractical shoes in my time to know how to deal with such things," she said, replacing her needle in its little embroidered case. "The trick is to leave the thread protruding a little from each side. That way the blister cannot keep refilling, as the water will drain out along the thread."

To Beth's amazement, the trick worked, and although the toe was still a little sore in the evening, the blister had not swollen again. In return, she promised to give the envious ladies a blow-by-blow account of the evening when she returned.

Sir Anthony was resplendent in burgundy and gold-embroidered velvet. Beth, complementing him, wore a dress of the same wine-red colour, cut almost indecently low at the neckline, but relieved by a fichu of gold lace, which partially hid her cleavage. She had rarely looked more beautiful. Or more nervous.

"Relax," he whispered as they carefully ascended the stairway which led to the king's apartments. Beth hardly noticed the coloured marbles and wall paintings; she was too busy trying to stop her legs, which were trembling violently, from giving way beneath her. It was not the thought of meeting the king that bothered her; he meant nothing to her. She had been more nervous about meeting Prince Charles, but had not shaken like this. It was not even the thought of dancing in front of the French Court that terrified her, although it was a little unnerving.

No, it was the thought that she might fall on her face, become an object of derision, and be rejected from the Court. Then they would never find Henri, who would be free to speed off to London with the invasion plans, and Angus would spend the rest of his life thinking himself personally responsible for the death of the Jacobite cause. It did not bear thinking about.

"Try not to think about it," her husband said, unconsciously echoing her thoughts. "If this fails, there are other ways to achieve our aims. Don't worry."

He did not say what the other ways were, but he would find one. He always did. She felt a little better, but even so, at the top of the stairs she halted, allowing the following couples to pass her before stamping her feet hard on the marble floor.

"What on earth are you doing, my dear?" Sir Anthony asked, puzzled.

"If it worked for the girl at Tyburn, it might work for me, too," she said.

It did, a little, and the couple were smiling as they entered the Salon of Apollo, where the dance was to take place, which made an impression immediately on the man who had been intermittently keeping an eye out for them.

Both Sir Anthony and Beth were surprised on entering the salon. They had expected an enormous, luxuriously appointed room. Luxurious it certainly was, but it was not large, by Versailles standards, and there were no more than fifty couples standing in groups chatting. It *was* a small dance then, as the messenger had said. Even more strange that they had been invited.

One end of the room was dominated by a carpeted dais, at the top of which was an elaborate gilt and burgundy damask throne under a canopy of cloth of gold. The throne was currently unoccupied. Beth gave it no more than a cursory glance, relieved that the king was not yet present, and that she would have a little time to familiarise herself with her surroundings before he put in an appearance.

She stayed at her husband's side as he reacquainted himself with the courtier in blue, today in green, who he had so successfully accosted earlier in the week. She allowed the conversation to flow around her for a time without listening or taking part, absorbed the admiring glances of the men and the envious darts of the women, and started to relax a little.

The courtier introduced the baronet to others of his

acquaintance, and a conversation took place in which the fact that Britain was in all but name at war with France was courteously avoided. There would be no controversy tonight. Beth nodded and murmured polite responses, a cipher at her husband's side, but listening now, and observing the courtiers. She would take a lesson from Anne Maynard, and echo the expressions and mannerisms of the company.

Sir Anthony was far more unobtrusive at the French Court than he was in England, she noticed. More than one man wore paint and rouge, was dressed in brightly coloured clothes and adopted affected gestures. He was at home here, chattering merrily, insinuating himself into the company.

After a time the musicians entered and took their places at the opposite end of the room from the dais. The throne was still empty. The conversation continued. Everyone was very friendly. It would not be onerous to dance in front of these people, Beth told herself. She thought that perhaps the king had changed his mind and would not make an appearance after all.

Then a man who had been lounging casually on some cushions on the steps of the dais, and whom Beth had only seen glimpses of through the mass of courtiers, and to whom she had paid no attention, stood, and the hubbub quietened. The throng moved to the sides of the room, bowing and curtseying, and the man took the hand of the beautiful slender lady in green silk who had already risen beside him.

King Louis XV of France moved down to take his place on the parquet floor, clapped his hands, and the music started.

It was as Alex had told her. The king and his partner performed their elaborate sequence of steps to much applause before leaving the floor to the next couple, and so on, down the social ladder.

Beth watched, memorising foot positions, hand movements, the carriage of the body. They were all very accomplished. She realised now what a good teacher Alex was. If she could perform the steps exactly as he had taught her, she would not be greeted with derision.

Then her husband was taking her hand, squeezing it reassuringly, smiling, and leading her to her place on the floor. She felt as though a million eyes were watching her, ready to find fault. She felt the colour drain from her face. She turned her head, looked into Sir Anthony's eyes, Alex's eyes, and saw there only love, and the confidence that she could do this, reassure their place at Court. And give them the chance to find Henri. Oh God.

Her gaze roamed panicked over his shoulder and met that of the woman standing by the king. She had noted Beth's sudden pallor and was scornful, mocking, uncertain. It was the gaze of a woman who had thought her beauty unsurpassable, and who had just discovered she was wrong. The challenge was given, and accepted. It was what Beth had needed. She raised her head, and smiled. If she could only remember which foot to start with, she would be fine.

"Wait three counts, right foot," Sir Anthony whispered as the music started. She moved forward into the reverence and the million eyes melted into the background, leaving only herself and Alex, dancing for Angus in their room. She did not stumble, or look at her feet, or mess up the turns.

"That was wonderful, my dear," Sir Anthony said as they left the floor to applause a few minutes later.

"The other couples performed much more complex moves," she pointed out. She felt exhilarated, drunk. They would not be laughed out of the palace. The beautiful woman no longer looked mocking, but sour. Beth reminded herself that she was not supposed to be making enemies, but friends. She would make amends later. She could afford to be magnanimous in victory.

"Their moves were more complex, but not as well

executed," her husband pointed out. "You have a natural grace. I am proud of you. Now, for God's sake relax and enjoy yourself. I doubt we will find the one we seek tonight, but I am sure we will have other opportunities."

The evening progressed. Beth drank one glass of wine, then two. The king returned to his cushions, chatting amiably with his companions, watching the dancing. People talked and talked. Her faced ached with smiling, and she was weary. She had become separated from her husband now, and during a pause in the conversation, looked round for him in vain.

A man approached, dressed in dark blue silk, and because of the noise of music and laughter had to repeat himself twice before she understood what he was saying. Then he took her arm and led her to the bronze-clad figure lounging on the steps, who rose to his feet. She curtseyed, deeply. The courtier moved back a few paces.

"You dance very well, Lady Elizabeth," King Louis said, smiling. The woman had also risen.

"I had an excellent tutor, your majesty," Beth replied.

"Ah," he said. "The best tutors of dancing, as of many other things, are French. What is his name? Perhaps I am acquainted with the man."

"I think not, Your Majesty, although I hope you soon will be. My husband taught me the steps of the menuet only this week."

"Only this week?" The king's eyes widened. "But you must certainly be adept in other dances. No one could learn the menuet so quickly otherwise."

"I am familiar with some of our English country dances, Your Majesty."

"Then I look forward to partnering you in one at our next meeting," he said. Was he flirting with her? Surely not. Although the beautiful woman seemed to think so. She moved forward now, eyes flashing.

"And where is your husband?" she asked. "I would like to meet such an accomplished man. You must treasure him." Her eyes scanned the room.

"Indeed I do. He is a most unique individual," Beth replied. She did not give the woman a title. If rebuked, she could claim, rightly, that she did not know it.

Louis' eyes were occupied with Beth's fichu. The woman's gaze passed from him to her enemy.

"I must compliment you on your dress, Lady Elizabeth," she said. "I was unaware that the remnants from the wall hangings had been put on sale to the general public."

The Peters' outfits did indeed match the colour of the burgundy and gold-embroidered wall hangings. It was a coincidence. Sir Anthony had found it amusing. So had Beth, until now.

Louis raised his eyes from Beth's bodice and smiled. He had a strong, rather than a handsome face, she thought. Regal, certainly, and the eyes were shrewd, but there was something petulant about the mouth.

"For myself, I take it as a compliment to my good taste that you should see fit to attire yourselves in a colour I favour so much. Red becomes you, *ma chere*. As green becomes Marguerite."

Beth's mind raced. Green was the colour of envy. Had the girl Marguerite noticed? Yes. She was astute, then. And probably knew the king well. He must often utter *double entendres*. Red was the colour of passion. Take care. Take it at face value.

"Thank you, Your Majesty." Her smile was innocent, pleased at the compliment to her attire, no more. Louis raised her hand to his lips, then changed his mind, drew her towards him and kissed her lightly on the mouth. He nodded at the servant who took his place at her side.

"I look forward to furthering our acquaintance in the

near future," the king smiled, before turning away. She was dismissed

It seemed to be the servant's job to escort her back to her husband, or if he could not be found, to keep her occupied with light conversation until he returned or some other company could be found to amuse her.

The man was of medium height, slender, handsome, polished, a little effete, perhaps. His eyes were green and reminded her of Thomas's. His nose was snubbed slightly at the end. He had a small white scar over one of his eyebrows, the left one. They were black, which meant his hair must be too, although it was concealed beneath a powdered wig at the moment. She noted everything about him, committed it to memory. His words flowed over her, polite enquiries about how she was finding France. He was a courtier. She was wasting her opportunity. The evening was coming to an end and the king had left. Taking their cue from him, everyone else was preparing to leave. In a moment Sir Anthony would come looking for her.

"Do you live in Versailles, my lord, or are you also merely visiting?" she asked her companion.

He did not correct her use of title. A lord, then.

"I do indeed live in the palace, my lady," he replied. "I have the great honour to be a member of the king's staff."

"Really?" she replied, with genuine interest. "How exciting! In what capacity are you employed?"

"I have the honour to be a gentleman of the bedchamber, my lady."

"That is a most privileged position, is it not, Lord... ah...?"

"Not a lord, I regret." Ah. He did regret it. He hoped to be one, then, one day. He bowed, introduced his lowly self, a mere Monsieur, and then Sir Anthony appeared, with her cloak, and a languid, pleasant expression on his painted face, beneath which was a coldness she had not expected. The Monsieur melted away into the background and disappeared, and then Beth's arm was taken by her husband and she was led away to their carriage.

She was ecstatic, relieved beyond measure that the evening had been such a success, could not wait to discuss it. But when she leaned forward to whisper in Sir Anthony's ear, he shook his head and jerked his hand at the roof of the coach. She sat back. It would have to wait, then, until they were safely in their room and could not be overheard. What was wrong with him? Now they were not being observed, the languid expression had vanished, but the cold rage had not. Something had happened. What was it?

She found out as soon as the door of the room closed and was locked, and Sir Anthony exploded into Alex before he had even taken off his wig, which was the first thing he always did, hating it. He tore it off now and hurled it into the corner of the room with a blast of Gaelic invective which Beth was glad she did not understand. Angus obviously did. He remained by the door, silent, wary.

"The bloody, lascivious, fornicating bastard!" Alex raged.

"What? Who are you talking about?" Beth asked, confused. Her mind was so full of her chat with the courtier, all that had happened before it had faded from her mind.

"Who the hell d'ye think I mean?" he said, his eyes blazing. "The king. Louis. So that's why we were invited to the palace. I had wondered. He saw ye in the chapel. He thinks he can ogle your breasts, kiss you in public, and get his panderer to butter you up for his bed. Well, if he thinks I'll stand by while he fucks my wife, he can think again. I'll see him in hell first!"

Beth stared at him.

"Don't you think I might have some say in all this?" she said coldly. "I hardly think Louis is likely to drag me off to his bed by force, do you?"

"No," Alex replied. "He's more subtle than that. He'll woo ye, probably buy ye expensive presents, arrange for us both to be invited to a very private function, and then make sure we're separated, so he can take ye off somewhere and seduce you."

"And you really think I'm going to let him do that?" she said, her voice rising to match his.

"No, Ye're not. I'm no' going tae let him get the opportunity. I'll…"

He broke off as Beth's open palm cracked hard against his cheek. She swung again and he ducked back adroitly, grabbing her hand as it flashed past his nose. She pulled against him, and his grip tightened.

"What the hell's wrong wi' ye, woman?" he shouted.

"What's wrong with me? Do you think so little of me, that you think I'll be persuaded into committing adultery with a man, king or not, by a few words of flattery and some presents? Well, I have respect for myself, even if you don't!" she cried, close to tears. She blinked them back, angrily. "And if you think that Louis has the slightest chance of fucking me, as you so delicately put it, no matter what he or his panderer does, then it's you that's the bastard, not him. And it's you that can go to hell!"

With a supreme effort she detached herself from his grip and stormed towards the door. Angus moved quickly out of the way. She had her fingers on the handle when Alex's voice halted her.

"I'm sorry," he said quietly. It was not the words, but the tone that made her turn round. The rage had vanished, replaced by remorse. And pain. She moved back into the room. Angus stood forgotten, in the corner now.

"Alex," she began, and hesitated, searching for the right words. "I married you because I love you. Surely you know that?"

"You married me tae get away from your brother," he replied.

"No. I married Sir Anthony to get away from my brother. I married you, in Rome, because I love you. I do not love lightly, Alex. I haven't told you that, because I thought you already knew it." She looked at him, her eyes intense.

"I do know it," he said, averting his gaze. "But I couldna stand tae see him make eyes at you like that in front of the whole Court. Christ, I was on the other side of the room and I could tell what he was doing, it was that obvious. He even looked at me and smiled before he kissed you! He made a fool of me, an' a whore of you, in front of everyone!"

"You're wrong," she replied. "He made a fool of Sir Anthony. Sir Anthony wants to be made a fool of, to be underestimated. You should be pleased by your success. He showed me that he finds me attractive. He can only make a whore of me if I let him, which I assure you I do not intend to." She moved closer, took his hand in both of hers. "If you get this jealous of every man who finds me desirable, Alex, you're never going to have a moment's peace," she said softly. "I'm beautiful, you said so only yesterday. It's a weapon. We can use it to our advantage. Men want me. But you are the only man who has had me, and I don't want any other. If you trust me you will accept that and learn to deal with men admiring me, knowing I'll not let it go further than that."

He looked at her, his eyes dark, unfathomable. But the pain had diminished, at least.

"I trust you," he said after a moment. Some of the tension left his face.

"Good," she replied. She took a deep breath. "Then relax, for God's sake. And tell me what a panderer is."

Angus took Beth's advice, although it had not been addressed to him, and relaxed. He came forward out of the shadows.

"A panderer is a man who helps to procure women for another man, for sexual purposes," he said. "Not something I have need of myself. I wouldna think a king would, either. Is Louis deformed, or something?"

"No," Alex said. He went to the dressing table, began the nightly ritual of removing his paint. "But not every king wants to be bothered wi' the chasing himself, particularly if he might be publicly rejected when he does. So he employs someone like yon laddie who was blethering wi' ye to pave the way for him, find out the woman's interests, see if she's amenable."

Beth was stunned. She still had a lot to learn about royalty, that was obvious.

"So you mean...? But he didn't ask me anything about myself. He was talking about Paris."

"Aye, tonight he was. But we'll be invited again, soon, ye can depend on it. And next time he'll get ye to one side and find out what you like, your favourite colour, if you're partial tae jewels, or flowers, and what ye think of your husband. He'll be very subtle about it, and charming too. I saw ye hanging on his every word tonight, and, well, I thought he was winning ye round. I can see now I was wrong."

She laughed, unexpectedly, joyously. He looked round at her, puzzled. Now the paint was removed, he had a faint pink mark on one cheek where she had hit him.

"You're right," she grinned. "I *was* hanging on his every word. He was fascinating. Far more interesting than the king. I can't wait to meet him again and have a much more detailed conversation. I intend to find out everything there is to know about him. In fact, nothing will make me happier than going to the palace and seeing the king's panderer there. If he's not there, I'll be desolate."

"Christ, was he that good?" said Angus. "I must meet the

man, get some tips."

"No, Angus, you're a damn sight better than he'll ever be," she said, "as I've already told you. But you don't hold the same fascination for me. Because you don't speak with a sibilant 's', and your name is not Henri Monselle."

CHAPTER TWELVE

The young man and woman were sitting on an ornate wooden bench in the *Bosquet des Dômes*, one of the numerous groves which comprised part of the gardens of Versailles. Sheltered by the latticed trellis which arched over them, fracturing the afternoon sun into small squares of gold, they were engaged in lively debate, unaware of the other couples strolling by on the gravel paths taking advantage of the unseasonal warmth. They made a pretty picture and one might have taken them for lovers had it not been for the fact that they were not touching, and were not debating with passion, but with intellect. A book lay open on the bench between them.

"So, you hold your ancestress Eve in contempt, then?" Henri Monselle was saying.

"No, I only disagree with Milton's interpretation of her," Beth replied. "He maligns her from the very beginning. He makes her first action on waking from her creation to be seduced by her own beauty in a pool. It is up to Adam to show her that her purpose on earth is to be utterly subservient to him."

"You don't agree then, that many women are obsessed with their own beauty?" he replied, looking up and catching by chance the eye of Marguerite, who was walking on an adjacent path. She frowned, knowing what Monsieur Monselle's task was, and hoping he would not succeed. Beth followed Henri's gaze and smiled.

"Yes," she said. "But it is not only women who take an hour to walk the length of the hall of mirrors."

No, it wasn't, thought Henri. Lady Elizabeth's own husband was a case in point, preening in every glass, whilst his wife stood impatiently waiting for him at the other end of the gallery. Henri had never known a woman so careless of her beauty. It was enchanting.

"But in *Paradise Lost*, Eve is representative of all women," Beth continued. "From the beginning Milton states that Adam was created for valour and contemplation, for absolute rule, and she to be subject to him, her only purpose to be soft and attractive, and, how does he put it," she lifted up the book and leafed briskly through it. "Ah, yes, 'nothing lovelier can be found In woman than to study household good, And good works in her husband to promote!' Huh! No wonder Milton's wife left him! And yet it takes all the wiles of Satan, an immortal spirit and powerful enough to corrupt one third of the angels, to tempt the frivolous Eve to eat of the fruit. Whereas in spite of all his great contemplative powers, Adam is tempted only by Eve, who he knows is inferior to him. Who then is the weaker?"

"Adam, no doubt," Henri replied. "For all men are weak in the face of woman's beauty." Except himself. He was not seduced by feminine wiles. His tastes lay elsewhere. Which was one of the reasons Louis trusted him to find beautiful mistresses for him. "And, although you are indeed as beautiful as Eve, you are also intelligent and independent. Do you think, then, that you could have resisted the serpent?"

"Have I not proved that this week, Monsieur Monselle?" Beth asked.

Both knew what she was referring to. After a week of intense persuasion and returned presents, Henri had finally accepted that Beth's virtue was unassailable, and had told Louis so the previous evening. Totally mismatched as she and her peacock of a husband were, still she seemed unwilling to betray him. Even for the love of a king. The king in question, though highly sexed, was indolent. That was why he employed Henri to do his courting for him. He trusted Henri's judgement where women were concerned.

"Indeed you have, Lady Elizabeth. Your husband is a lucky man," he said without thinking.

"Why?" Beth asked. "Because I will not make a cuckold of him? Every man should expect that of his wife. And vice versa."

"Yet the love of a king is not lightly renounced."

"I do not have the love of the king," she replied tartly. "I have the lust of the king. That is quite another matter. But even if His Majesty did love me, as he claimed in the poem I received last night, which you wrote for him, I would still not betray Anthony."

Henri laughed. He had indeed written the poem, as he did many of Louis' declarations of love, but she was the first woman who had recognised it.

"I would that everyone were as honourable as yourself, my lady. Yet you are a rarity, I think. Ambition drives many to betray their friends. Power and wealth are very attractive, are they not?" His tone matched hers, and she turned and looked at him. He found the directness of her gaze disconcerting and after a moment he averted his eyes.

"Satan is very seductive," Beth replied, "as Milton demonstrates so beautifully. But wealth? Not for its own sake, no. 'Let none admire that riches grow in Hell; that soil may best deserve the precious bane'."

"So you agree with Milton in some respects, then? You despise wealth?"

"No, I despise what men, and women, will stoop to to attain it, and the uses they put it to," she said. "Too often they spend it on frivolous displays, thinking thus that others will be too dazzled to see the corruption that lies beneath."

Too late she became aware of the shadow that had fallen

across them.

"Do you have any particular man or display in mind, Lady Elizabeth?" The voice was amused, but there was an edge of ice beneath it.

She rose, as did Henri, and curtseyed.

"Your Majesty," she said, her face flaming.

"Please, be seated," he said, joining them. Henri felt a sharp pang of sympathy for this forthright girl, and realised that he liked her far more than he should. In his profession it was essential to remain detached. Nevertheless...

"We were just discussing Milton, Your Majesty," he said.

"No," Louis replied. "You were discussing frivolous displays of wealth." He was not going to be deflected. The thin ice creaked around Beth's feet.

"I was not speaking of any particular man, Your Majesty," she replied. "Sometimes displays of wealth are necessary to show the great power of a nation, and thus ensure that others will think twice before attacking it. Such a display may be wise, if it results in peace for the people. I was explaining this only recently to an acquaintance of mine."

"Would this acquaintance be your husband, by any chance?" Louis replied.

"No. My husband enjoys displays of wealth for their own sake, as I am sure you have noticed, Sire."

"He is much taken with Versailles, is he not? He loses no opportunity to say so."

"He does indeed find the palace extremely beautiful."

Henri wondered how she would deflect the next comment – *but you, who despise wealth, do not.*

"He is rare among his countrymen, from what I have heard. They think nothing of royal display and find their boorish king worthy of loyalty, who stumps about his ragged palace like a peasant, disdaining beauty and learning." The king's remark took Henri by surprise. Looking at the woman,

241

he saw she too had been taken aback. He saw her select and reject a number of responses to Louis' unexpected comment.

"I cannot speak for my husband, Your Majesty," she replied carefully after a moment. "But as for my fellow Britons, I think that if you were to visit our country, you would find that learning is held in high regard, and that many would welcome a visit from a king who possessed intellect and knowledge."

"Ah. You think then that I would be welcome, if I were to pay a call on St. James's?" Louis' tone was casual, amused.

"Indeed, Your Majesty, I think you would meet with a positive reception in London, if you came for the right reasons." So was Beth's.

"Are you then loyal to your king, Lady Elizabeth?"

"Loyalty must be earned, Your Majesty. It cannot be bought," came the evasive reply.

Henri looked away and half rose as if to leave. Louis waved him back into his seat, without taking his eyes off Beth.

"There are many who would disagree with you on that. You are loyal to your husband, Henri tells me."

"Yes, I am," Beth replied.

"You are from a noble, but impoverished family, I believe. And he is a man of some wealth, is he not?"

"Yes, but that is not why I married him, or why I am loyal to him,"

Louis nodded.

"If I may be so bold as to ask, why are you then loyal to him?"

"Because he delivered me from evil, Your Majesty, and I owe him a great deal," she answered, meeting his dark brown scrutiny unwaveringly.

The king smiled. He was handsome when he smiled. The ice remained firm under her feet.

"I see you will not be led into temptation, no matter how I try. You were right, Henri. I will leave you to your discussion of Milton." He rose, and they with him. They made their obeisance and he moved on. Beth sank down on to her seat. She looked tired, as well she might. Henri decided to steer the conversation into smoother waters.

"What did he mean, you were right?" she asked before he could find a trivial topic.

"I told him last night that I did not think you would betray your husband for him. I advised him to seek another to replace Marguerite, of whom he is tiring."

"Poor Marguerite," said Beth.

"Do not feel sorry for her. She has brought it on herself. She has forgotten to be grateful that the king has raised her, and thinks she can maintain her position without any effort." He dismissed Marguerite with a shrug. "Do you really believe the king would receive a positive reception from your countrymen if he were to visit London?" he said. His tone, like Louis', was casual. His scrutiny was not.

"I do not think it likely that he will get the chance to find out," she said lightly. "King George will hardly invite him to St. James's. France and England are on opposing sides over the Austrian succession. They are enemies."

On the other side of the disturbing fountain of Enceladus, which showed an agonised gilded giant half crushed beneath rocks, she saw her husband, a splash of orange, enter the grove. She stood.

"I must thank you, Monsieur Monselle," she said. "Life at Court will be easier for me, now that the king has given up his pursuit. Or will we no longer be invited?"

"You will still be invited. The king likes you, as do I, and is amused by Sir Anthony, as am I. I look forward to our next conversation. You do not need to thank me. It is refreshing to meet a virtuous woman. Your worth is indeed above rubies."

He meant it. It was a delight to converse with her, and he thought she also enjoyed their conversations. She must be starved for intellectual debate, being married to such a man as Sir Anthony. Henri, seeing the man approach, pausing to exchange pleasantries with his many new acquaintances as he came, stood as well, and bowing to her, walked away, a graceful, athletic figure. She watched him go, her face momentarily troubled, then pasting a tolerant expression on her face turned to greet her husband, who was mincing up the path towards her.

* * *

Although they entered the hotel foyer together, by the time Beth managed to escape the clutches of Lady Winter and gain the safety of the room, Sir Anthony, who Beth had last seen as a flash of tangerine scampering gleefully up the stairs, had effected the transformation into Alex, and was sitting at the escritoire writing a letter. He was dressed only in breeches and shirt, his unbound hair falling forward over his face as he worked.

"Thanks," said Beth crossly, throwing her cloak at the nearest chair, and missing. "Next time you need my help to get away from Wilhelmina or Anne, or anyone else that bores you silly, before I dive in to help you, I'll bear in mind that you threw me to the lions tonight."

"You did well enough without me," he replied mildly without looking up from his task. "Ye've only been an hour. Be thankful I didna tell them I've managed to get them an invitation to the concert on Monday. Ye'd have been there discussing appropriate Court wear till the morning."

"No, I wouldn't," she said. "Court dress codes are Sir Anthony's department, not mine. Why have you done that then?" She kicked off her shoes.

He stopped writing for a minute.

"I'm doing it for Anne, mainly, to give her a wee bit of excitement," he said. "I feel sorry for the lassie. All she wants is to be married. It wouldna greatly matter who the man was. Just knowing she was capable of attracting a man would do wonders for her self confidence. She's nae personality of her own, and takes her cue from whichever man she's with. It's awfu' confusing for her. If she had a husband, she'd be able to devote herself just to him. But she's no chance, and she minds it well, though she tries not to show it. That's why she's so unhappy. Her family willna let her marry beneath herself, and she hasna the looks, brains or money to marry otherwise."

Beth considered for a moment.

"Yes, I suppose you're right. I must confess, I hadn't really thought about her beyond finding her a pest." She felt guilty now, in the face of Alex's perception and altruism. "It's very kind of you to think of her. She'll enjoy the evening. Louis is hiring a full orchestra, I believe."

"Aye," he said, smiling. "It'll give her life a wee bit of colour, give her something to talk about when she gets home. And I warn you now, so ye dinna take it amiss on the night; I mean to pay her a lot of attention on Monday, give her an evening to remember."

Beth's eyes narrowed suspiciously as she looked at her husband.

"Are ye jealous?" he asked smilingly, misinterpreting her look.

"No," she said. "I know Anne's not trying to make a serious play for you. She craves attention, that's all. It's not that. You had me there for a minute. I really thought you'd invited her and the Winters for purely unselfish reasons. What are you up to?"

The dark blue eyes were round, innocent.

"Me?" he said. "Maybe I'm just trying to make ye a wee bit jealous. After all, it's no' easy, seeing a handsome man fawning over your wife and being unable tae do anything about it."

"Oh, that," she said, coming over to where he was sitting, and presenting her back to him. She allowed him to evade the question, temporarily. "I can put your mind at rest on that. Louis isn't interested in me any more. Henri told him I was not to be won round, and he's accepted it. He told me so himself, today."

Alex reached up and unhooked the back of her dress, before untying the laces of her stays. She expanded her ribs and drew in a great breath of air, blissfully.

"It's no' Louis I'm talking about. You seem to be on very friendly terms with Monsieur Monselle. He's verra handsome, is he no'?"

Before his recent jealous outburst she would have teased him for a while before laying his fears to rest. She searched his face for clues. His expression was neutral. She had no way of knowing whether he was really concerned about Henri's attentions or not.

"You did ask me to get friendly with him," she pointed out. "To try to find out as much as I could about him. You can hardly complain now that I have. And anyway, he's not interested in me at all, I can assure you of that. Or any woman, for that matter. He spent a good half hour today trying to get information out of me about your handsome manservant. It seems Angus has made another conquest."

"Have I?" said the handsome manservant, who had chosen that moment to enter. He was clearly very pleased with himself about something, if the ear to ear grin was anything to go by.

"Did ye manage it?" asked Alex.

"Aye, nae problem at all. What's this conquest I've made,

then? Is she beautiful?"

"If you like your conquests tall and slender with bright green eyes and thick black wavy hair, then this could be the one for you," Beth said. Alex dipped his head, allowing his hair to fall over his face, hiding his smile. Angus's grin expanded.

"Lead me to her," he said eagerly. "What's her name, then?"

"Monselle," Beth replied. "Henri Monselle."

"What?" The grin disappeared abruptly. Beth and Alex both burst out laughing.

"It seems he's seen you several times in the courtyard, and once hanging around the servant's quarters, looking for your fictitious cousin," Beth explained. "He's quite taken with you. I told him I'd bring the subject up and see if you were interested." Another giggle escaped. Angus glared at her.

"Ugh," he said expressively, shuddering. "I mean, it's nice to be irresistible an' all, but…ugh, no. Ye didna tell him I *would* be interested, did ye?"

"You surely don't think I'd do that?" Beth asked.

"I wouldna put anything past you, if you thought it would cause me embarrassment, no," Angus replied. His look was dark, threatening dire consequences if she had.

"Relax, *mo bhrathair*," Alex interposed. "She hasna forgotten Henri's no' a matter for jest, even if you have. She was reassuring me that in spite of all the time they're spending together, our marriage isna in danger."

"Is he really a molly, then, or were ye just jestin' wi' me?" Angus asked.

"No," said Beth, serious now. "He is. But he's discreet. That's why Louis employs him to procure mistresses for him, I think. He knows there's no danger Henri will want to sample the wares first."

"No, molly or no, friend Henri's too busy helping himself

247

to Louis' private correspondence to be interested in his mistresses. Let's have a look, then," Alex said.

Angus delved into his coat pocket, producing a small wooden box. He opened it. Inside was a block of wax. Beth moved closer to the two men to see. Indented in the soft yellow tallow was the perfect outline of a key.

"Henri's room key," Angus said proudly.

"How did you manage that?" Beth asked, impressed.

"Jeanne cleans the rooms of the gentlemen of the bedchamber. I managed to persuade her to let me accompany her this morning. Henri's bed is awfu' soft," he said, nostalgically.

Alex thrust his fingers through his hair.

"Christ, man, will ye never learn? Ye were supposed to get in and out as fast as ye could, no' tumble the wench in his bed! What if the man had come back for something?"

"Aye well, ye didna specify what I was to get in and out of." Angus grinned. "I was following your instructions, in a manner of speaking. And I had tae give her a wee reward for letting me into his room."

Alex inhaled sharply through his nose.

"Did ye manage to see anything other than the bed while ye were wasting this golden opportunity?" he asked, rubbing his hand through his hair again.

"Oh, aye, what d'ye take me for?" Seeing that Alex was about to say exactly what he did take him for, Angus hurried on. "Jeanne canna read, ye see. Which is why Henri sees no reason tae hide all his personal correspondence when he goes out of a morning. Have ye a pen and paper to hand?"

Alex's expression changed. He turned hurriedly back to the desk, laid his letter aside and took up a fresh sheet. He dipped his pen and waited.

"'Dearest Aunt Mary,'" Angus began, eyes closed, hands behind his back like a schoolboy reciting a poem to the class.

"I am very well at present, and am greatly enjoying my stay in France. It came as a great surprise to me to learn that Cornelius is to be married to Annabelle. Indeed I think it a most unsuitable match, and feel the lady's father will reconsider when in possession of all the facts regarding the suitor. If indeed it is not merely a figment of his imagination. He is a most fanciful young man, and I will try to find out the facts of the case. I did think myself settled for the winter in Paris, but find myself homesick for England. I have it in mind to bring you a surprise present and will stay until it is ready. Of course, you know nothing of this, but I am sure you will be delighted, and will appreciate its exquisite workmanship. I will say no more, but remain, your loving nephew, Martin.'"

Alex, who had been scribbling away, now put the pen down. He turned from the paper to his now serious-faced brother and puzzled wife.

"We can waste no more time," he said. "We must act quickly. I was already hoping to act on Monday, if we could, but now we *have* to."

Angus nodded.

"It shouldna be a problem," he said. "I can get the key cut tomorrow."

"Will someone tell me what's going on?" Beth said. "Why does a letter from someone called Martin to his Aunt Mary mean we have to act quickly? And if you're hoping to do something at the musical evening, don't I need to know about it?"

Alex picked up the paper and handed it to Beth.

"Read it," he said. "And while you're reading it, bear in mind that Martin is Henri, Aunt Mary is Horace Mann, Cornelius is Prince Charles and Annabelle is Louis' daughter. I'll leave it to you to work out what the surprise present is."

Beth read. After a while she looked up.

"The invasion plans," she said softly.

"Aye. Of course, this is the first draft of his letter to Mann. He'll put it in code before he sends it. But there's nae doubt now that he intends to go to England, very soon. He has the information he wants and is just waiting for the details."

"How do we know he hasn't already written to Mann, giving an outline of the plans?" Beth said.

"Because he said it's a surprise present. Ye said ye think his motivation for spying is financial?"

"Yes. I'm certain of it after today, although of course I couldn't ask him directly."

"Aye, well, the letter bears out your suspicions," said Alex. "He's building up the anticipation with Mann in the hope of obtaining an even greater reward. If he was a patriot, he'd already have revealed his suspicions, giving George time to prepare, and would send the other information on as he received it. But he isna. He'll get a much bigger reward if he waits until he's in possession of all the facts before he goes tae England and drops it on them like a bolt from the blue. By keeping it to himself he reduces the risk of someone pre-empting him and taking a share of the cash. That's to our advantage. If we can take him out now, we can be sure he's no' shared his prize wi' anyone. The other thing we've learned from this is that he is, as I'd hoped, in regular contact with Mann. Which will make the letter I'm writing more believable."

Beth went across to the writing desk. The half-finished letter, which appeared innocent and gossipy, not unlike the missive Angus had just recited, was not in Alex's normal clear writing, but in a flowing, flowery hand, embellished with many curlicues. To one side was another letter in the same script, recommending that Sir Anthony and his wife be granted hospitality and safe passage in all the Italian states. It was the letter Sir Anthony had requested on the last minute in Florence, written and signed by Sir Horace Mann himself, his clerks being otherwise engaged learning a bawdy song.

"So if I'm right, you intend to plant this forgery in Henri's room on Thursday while he's at the concert," Beth said. "And then what? Make sure King Louis learns of it?"

"Something like that," Alex said. "Actually, that's the other reason I've invited Anne on Monday. If I'm occupied wi' her, it'll give you reason to be a wee bit disgruntled and seek out Henri's company. I'm relying on you to keep him with you until Angus has had time to plant the letter."

She ran her hand lightly over the elaborate script.

"What will happen to Henri when Louis finds out he's a spy?" Beth asked. Her tone caused the two men beside her to exchange a worried look over her head, which she missed, her attention still on the note.

"Does it matter?" Alex said carefully.

"Yes. No, I suppose not," she answered, her head still bent over the letter.

Alex moved between her and the desk. She stepped back, looked at his chest.

"Beth, he's the enemy," her husband said softly.

"I know that," she replied.

"But you like him." It was a statement, not a question, although she treated it as such.

"Yes. Yes, I do. I didn't want to, and I know what he is, but he's intelligent and interesting, and caring as well. He's risen from nothing to get to where he is, and he gave his sister a dowry and looked after his mother until she died."

"Look at me," Alex said, his voice still gentle. When her lashes remained downcast, he placed his hands on her shoulders. "Look at me, Beth."

She looked at him.

"The man's a murderer, *a ghràidh*. He garrotted a man, and would have killed Angus and Katerina as well if he'd kent they were there."

"Wouldn't you have done the same, if you'd been him?" she asked.

He stared at her for a moment, his eyes darkening. His fingers curled, cupping the narrow shoulders.

"No. You're wrong," he said, not answering the question she'd asked, but the one she hadn't dared to. "I'm no' like him, Beth. We may both be charming when we want, and we may both kill when necessary. I dinna ken whether he takes pleasure from the killing or no'. Maybe not. I know I dinna. But I'm doing what I'm doing for the cause I believe in, Beth, as are you. If Henri was a committed Hanoverian, I could at least respect him, though it'd no' prevent me acting against him. We're on opposite sides. But this man ye compare tae me is willing to put the lives of thousands of people in danger for money. No' for a cause, or his faith, but just tae line his own pockets. He's greedy. And your intelligent, interesting and caring wee man will no' shed a tear for those who die so he can live in a fine house and drive a fancy carriage. Dinna compare me wi' a man who earns his living by procuring young girls for his over-sexed master. Christ! D'ye think he cares what happens to them after Louis tires of them? That he's condemning them for life to being prostitutes, or courtesans if they're lucky? I'd die before I'd do that to any young lassie! He's paid by Louis to be charming, Beth. That's why he's good at it. Dinna let that blind ye to what's beneath."

His voice and his hands on her shoulders were gentle, but he was very angry, and disappointed too, she thought.

"You're right," she said, moving back and breaking his hold. He was, but she couldn't help liking Henri on one level, even while she deplored what he was. He *was* paid to charm, but she suspected he liked her anyway, for herself. "So, what will happen to him then?"

Alex's shake of the head was so minuscule she didn't see it, as was intended. Angus did, as was intended.

"He'll be thrown in the Bastille, I should think," said Alex. "He'll be kept there until Louis tires of finding his own mistresses. By then James should be on the throne, and Henri will be no more danger to us."

"Don't you think Louis will do more than just imprison Henri, if he knows he intends to leak the invasion plans?" Beth said.

"Aye. But we canna let Louis discover that. Because if he has the slightest suspicion that anyone other than those he's told ken about his scheme, he'll call the whole thing off. This letter," he waved at the desk, "deals with far more mundane matters. But when Louis finds it, he'll ken Henri has been contacted by Horace Mann and that he's attempting to recruit him as a spy. Louis will lock him up until Henri's convinced him that he hadna any intention of accepting Mann's offer, that's all."

Beth tried to hide her relief.

"Good," she said. "So, I think I can manage to stop him going back to his room on Monday evening. He probably won't want to anyway. He's looking forward to the concert as well."

"I wouldna mind having a wee chat wi' him, though," Alex said. "Just to try tae find out a bit more about the man. I've hardly exchanged a word wi' him. I'd like to get an idea of what he's like myself. D'ye think ye can get him by himself for a wee while, so I can come upon ye by accident, as it were, and engage him in conversation?" His tone was casual. He clearly didn't think it important whether she could do this or not.

"I can try," Beth said, smiling. "Although I think Angus would be likely to have more success, being as Henri is already so well disposed towards him."

"I'd love to," Angus replied lightly. "Such a shame I'll be otherwise occupied planting evidence."

"Did you really memorise that whole letter, word for word?" Beth said, impressed.

"Aye, I did," he answered matter-of-factly. "I can hold short pieces of writing in my mind, if I read them through a few times. When I close my eyes, I can see the page as if it was in front of me. But that's nothing. Alex can mind everything everyone's ever said tae him, and recite whole books if he needs to."

"Can you?" Beth said, amazed. She had been married to this man for nearly six months, and learned something new about him every day.

"No' whole books, no," said Alex, settling down to finish his letter. "But I've an awfu' good memory, aye. Ye need it, in this business."

* * *

If Beth, not being possessed of the formidable recollective powers of her spouse, had forgotten what a crashing bore Lord Bartholomew Winter could be, she was reminded forcefully of it on Monday evening.

Against all his principles and indeed his avowed declarations, he had been railroaded into accompanying his wife and Miss Maynard to the Catholic devil King Louis' concert, and both Sir Anthony and his wife noticed what a fine semblance he made of enjoying himself immensely from the moment he entered the salon. He could have rivalled Garrick in his acting abilities, Sir Anthony noted wryly in a whispered aside to Beth before he disappeared into the crowd with Anne.

Unlike Lord Winter, Miss Maynard felt no need to feign a pretence of being happy. From the moment Sir Anthony handed her into the carriage he gave her his full attention, and Beth was under no illusion that regardless of his other motives for engineering her presence at the concert this evening, he was going to make sure she had a night to remember. As Anne blossomed under his outrageous compliments, Beth wilted under the interrogation of the Winter family, who wanted to know all she had learned in her previous visits to the palace, although she had already told them everything that was relevant.

"So how would one attract the notice of the king?" asked Lady Winter, having examined and commented with a creditable semblance of knowledge on Bernini's bust of Louis XIV, the painting of *The Sacrifice of Iphigenia* over the marble fireplace, and the ceiling paintings of Diana, after whom the salon was named.

"We have no wish to attract the notice of such a man, Wilhelmina," sniffed Lord Winter. They were speaking in English, Lord Winter being of the firm conviction that the French would not have troubled to learn the language of the enemy, and that therefore anything they said would not be understood by the Court.

"No, of course not," she said hastily. "I was merely curious." Nevertheless, she tilted her head towards Beth, waiting for an answer.

"His Majesty has only spoken to me twice, Lady Wilhelmina," she pointed out. The room was crowded, but there was no sign of Henri as yet. Sir Anthony was clearly visible in the distance due to the combination of his height and vivid magenta costume. He was waving his hands over a huge display of unseasonal forced roses. Anne Maynard, dressed in drab brown, clung to his arm, her plain face upturned to his, enraptured. Beth tried to be pleased for her.

"Nevertheless, dear child, you must have some idea of what would induce him to pause and converse with one for a few moments. What manner of man is he?"

"He appears very regal, as I'm sure you noticed in

the chapel." Wilhelmina probably knew how many eyelashes he had, she had scrutinised him so closely. This was not what she wanted to know. "He is intelligent, and of course inspires awe, as a monarch should," Beth continued, aware, as her companions were not, that many of the courtiers did in fact speak excellent English, "but he was very friendly and charming towards myself. More than that I could not ascertain, in two meetings."

"Three," came a familiar voice at her shoulder, and she started violently, to Louis' obvious amusement. When she raised herself from her hasty curtsey, his eyes were sparkling. Marguerite was nowhere to be seen.

"Your Majesty," Beth said in French. "Allow me to present my friends, Lord and Lady Winter. They have looked forward to meeting you."

"So I heard," he said, making Beth wonder how long he had been hovering unnoticed nearby.

"Your Majesty does us too much honour to invite us here tonight," Lady Winter gushed in execrable French.

"Indeed, perhaps we do," Louis replied coolly. Quite some time, then. It was the first time Beth had heard him use the royal pronoun. He turned to her again. "I am delighted that you have decided to stay on for a few more days, although I hear you will be returning to England before too long." He smiled and managed to be instantly amiable to Beth whilst remaining hostile to her companions.

"Yes, Your Majesty, as soon as Christmas is over. We have already been away for longer than we intended, and my husband is anxious to see to his business affairs."

"I will wish you a safe voyage home, then. I hope we will meet again, before too long."

"So do I, Your Majesty." *In London.* Her fervency was intended, and did not go unnoticed. He raised her hand to his lips, and did not change his mind this time, to Beth's relief. Then he nodded to her companions and vanished into the throng. Lady Winter watched his progress raptly. Lord Winter sniffed.

A bell was rung and the guests proceeded to the much larger salon, dedicated to Mars, where the concert was to take place. The orchestra had settled themselves in the musicians' galleries, which were supported by columns and which flanked a central fireplace in which a huge fire burned merrily, warming the room. Three enormous crystal chandeliers blazed with candles, adding considerably to the warmth of the room. Rows of chairs had been laid out for the audience, who were now taking their seats.

She still could not see Henri, which was starting to concern her, and had no choice but to sit next to Lord Winter. His wife sat on his left. Sir Anthony held back so he would not have to sit by Beth, and was pointing out the décor of the coving, which showed chubby naked children training for war. He intercepted his wife's anxious gaze, and smiled quickly, nodding his head to the left. She followed his gesture and saw the man she had been looking for. Catching her eye, Henri smiled with genuine warmth and made his way over, taking the seat in front of her. Introductions were made, another bell was rung. The audience quietened, and the performance began.

Beth had heard of Bach, but had never heard any of his music. The orchestra were to play the first three of the six concertos that were to become known as the Brandenburg concertos.

The musicians stood, bowed to the king, to the audience, sat. The music began. Lord Winter leaned across.

"Do you play an instrument, Lady Elizabeth?" he asked in a stage whisper.

"No," she lied, not wishing to encourage him.

Sniff.

"Ah, then if you are not familiar with the instruments of the orchestra, you will perhaps not realise what a remarkable instrument the bassoon is. That is the one you can hear now. The gentleman on the left. Listen."

"I am trying to, my lord," she said.

Pause.

"It is of course the bass instrument of the wind section. To achieve the lower registers the instrument is actually folded back along itself. If it were not, it would be some five feet in length - far too unwieldy. You will certainly not believe that it is known as the clown of the orchestra, as it is used to produce comic effects at times."

She did not reply.

"Of course, I now recall you were present at the Fortesques' little musical affair, were you not?"

She nodded, curtly.

"Ah, then you will remember the instrument from Vivaldi's bassoon concerto."

"Yes, I do remember actually being able to listen to that concerto," Beth replied pointedly.

"Yes, ah, well, we are in France now, and if you have taken the time to visit the dreadful warbling that passes for opera in this country, you will certainly have realised that the French have no respect for good music." Sniff.

In front of her, Henri's ears turned a delicate shade of pink.

"I have never heard such noise from an audience," the stage whisper continued, "although at least it masked the screeching of the singers. The scenery and dancing were quite exquisite though, I must admit."

The music ended, the musicians stood, and Lord Winter stopped speaking to applaud. Beth unclenched her fists and smashed her palms together. The orchestra resumed their seats. Beth's palms stung but she had succeeded in releasing a little of her anger. The second concerto began. Lord Winter did not. Beth listened. The music washed over her. It was beautiful.

"You will have noticed that the bassoon does not feature in this piece."

Oh, for God's sake.

"The trumpet, however, plays an important role. Do you see the bag at the side of the trumpeter's chair? In it are a series of crooks, which the player uses to change the key of the instrument. To do so he must…"

"Lord Winter," said Beth softly, but fiercely. "This is very interesting, but I find this movement particularly moving and would be obliged if you would allow me to give it my undivided attention."

"Ah." Sniff. "Of course."

Bliss. The haunting notes of the oboe and flute wrapped themselves around her heart. She began to relax. The second movement finished, and the third began.

"Ah, now you hear what a rousing instrument the trumpet is!"

Henri's shoulders shook. Beth grimaced. She was glad someone was finding it amusing. She concentrated single-mindedly on the music.

"Of course, it enhances the pleasure of the music greatly if one can follow the score. Do you read music, Lady Elizabeth?"

"No, I prefer to listen to it, *when I am allowed to.*"

For a moment she actually thought he'd finally got the message. Then he leaned forward and tapped the elderly man in front of him on the shoulder. The man's head had been bent over a paper, but he now looked round, somewhat red-faced but polite.

"Er…*Avez vous un*…ah…" the lord hesitated. "What is the word for score, Lady Elizabeth? It has temporarily slipped my mind."

"*Couteau*," she replied fervently. There was a snort from the seat in front, quickly smothered.

Using Beth's helpful suggestion, Lord Winter completed his request.

"*Je regrette, non*," replied the elderly gentleman. "But I assure you, if I did, I would certainly make good use of it forthwith," he finished in English. He turned forward.

Lord Winter sat back, rebuffed. Three bars of music passed uninterrupted.

"Well really," said the peer huffily. "His answer was quite incomprehensible. One should not attempt to speak English unless one is quite sure of one's command of the language. It is perfectly clear that he has the score. If he did not wish to let me look at it, he had only to say so. I am quite capable of understanding that much French."

Beth leaned forward to the red ears and the shaking shoulders.

"*Au secours*," she whispered desperately.

"Really, Lady Elizabeth, I must say, it is very rude to use a man's ignorance of a language against him," Henri admonished insincerely as they strolled down a nearby gallery five minutes later. He had responded to her cry for help by extricating her from the room the moment the interval began, with the excuse that he had a private message from the king for her. Lady Winter's ears had been out on stalks, but she could hardly follow them from the room uninvited. "What would you have done had M. Feuillet provided him with a knife, as he unknowingly requested?"

"Snatched it from him and cut my throat, I think. Or his. He's unbearable. I would rather sit next to Cousin Edward. He's as pompous as that idiot, but at least he would sulk silently through the concert. I didn't hear a thing."

"When we return I shall endeavour to seat us in another part of the room. I think there were a few empty chairs at the back," Henri said.

"You will have my undying gratitude if you do," said Beth. "I take it that the important message from the king was a fabrication? If it was I will have to think of something to satisfy Lady Wilhelmina's curiosity later."

"It was, but I must admit I had hoped to get a chance to speak to you alone." He had led her back through the Diana salon and out onto the gallery. At the moment they were its only occupants, but it was eminently possible that other courtiers would take the opportunity to stretch their legs during the interval. Beth wondered if this was private enough for Alex to have his 'wee chat', and thought it probably was.

It was clearly not private enough for Henri, though. Taking her arm, he led her to the end of the corridor, through the *Salon de L'Ovale,* which was, unlike many of the more elaborately frescoed public rooms, painted white, the plaster mouldings etched in gold. Beth looked around with interest as Henri led her to a door, also white, at the end of the room.

"The king prefers to hang pictures on the walls of his more private rooms than to have permanent paintings as his predecessor did," Henri explained.

Before Beth could ask whether or not they should be walking in the king's apartments, Henri had opened the door and led her into Louis' *Cabinet des Livres,* which was, as the name suggested, completely lined with white and gold cabinets filled with books. And the inevitable marble busts, of Aristotle, Plato, Socrates.

Beth smiled, thinking of Angus and wondering whether he had managed to plant the incriminating letter yet. Her smile faded, and a wave of guilt washed over her. Would Alex find them in here? Maybe not, but he had not seemed too bothered whether he spoke privately with Henri or not. The main thing was to stop Henri returning to his room. Beth sent up a silent prayer that Louis would be lenient with his employee and tried to dismiss the matter from her mind.

Henri had left the door open for propriety's sake. If they were disturbed, people would be unlikely to think they had any improper intentions. He turned to her now, smiling, his green eyes warm.

"You told me that you are leaving for England in a few days," he said. "I hope you will not think me too familiar when I say that I shall miss your company greatly. I have enjoyed our talks enormously. I only hope your husband appreciates what an exceptional wife he has."

"I am sure he does," Beth murmured. *He is the enemy*, she reminded herself.

"We must return to the salon soon if we are to find seats away from your tormentor," Henri continued. "I wanted to see you alone to give you a small parting gift."

Before she could protest he took a slim volume from his pocket and held it out to her. She took it automatically. The book was beautifully bound in soft red leather, tooled in gold. She looked at the title, and then up at him.

"Please, do not refuse it. I put you under no obligation. I have another copy of *Paradise Regained*, and it will give me the greatest pleasure to share this with you. You said you have not read it?"

"No," she said. She looked back at the book, and the gold shimmered mistily. She blinked several times. *He is the enemy.* "Thank you," she said, running her fingers reverently over the cover.

Henri smiled broadly.

"If I may be so bold, may I request that you write to me with your opinion, once you have read it?"

She succumbed.

"Yes," she said, smiling up at him. His eyes were very

green. "Of course I will. I do not think Anthony would object." She tried to imagine how angry Alex would be when she told him she was going to write to an enemy. She would not ask his permission, nor would she conceal her intention from him, which would be easier. They kept no secrets from each other.

"You have made me very happy," said Henri. "Now, I think we should return to the salon before the concert resumes."

"It has already resumed," came the cold reply from the doorway. "You have been absent for longer than you thought. But time flies so quickly when one is in thrall to Venus, does it not?"

Beth and Henri turned to the door. Henri was clearly surprised, but not worried, in spite of Sir Anthony's comment. He had not been caught in a compromising position, after all. Beth and he had not been touching, and he would hardly engage in a clandestine romantic liaison and leave the door open.

Beth, who had been half expecting her husband to make an appearance, was nevertheless as surprised as Henri, by his attitude and his eyes, which were ice cold. He moved into the room, and to Beth's further surprise, she saw Angus behind him. What was he doing here? As a servant, he should be waiting with the coach, or hanging around in the courtyard with the other menials.

"I have suspected something was amiss for some days," the baronet continued, his voice high-pitched and indignant. "And now I see what it is."

"I do assure you, Sir Anthony," Henri began earnestly, "that your wife is the most virtuous..."

"Do not tell me what my wife is, sir!" shrilled Sir Anthony. "I think I should know her better than you. Although perhaps I do not."

Beth moved forward, puzzled. She had expected her

husband to engage Henri in friendly conversation. Not this.

"Jim," her husband said to his servant, before she could speak. "Would you be so kind as to escort my wife to our hotel? I wish to have a word with Monselle in private."

Angus moved to Beth's side, his expression neutral, obedient. He took her arm. She pulled away from him. This was not what she had expected Alex to do. As Angus was here, he had presumably planted the letter. Now it seemed Alex wanted her to leave him and Henri alone to talk. She didn't think this was the best way of going about it, but she would fall in with him, be indignant, return to the concert as he no doubt intended she should.

"I have no intention of returning to the hotel!" she cried. "I wish to listen to the rest of the concert. I assure you that nothing untoward has taken place between myself and Monsieur Monselle. You are being quite ridiculous. I will return to the salon."

She made a move to leave, but to her surprise Angus took her arm again, and this time when she tried to pull away he did not release her. Sir Anthony stepped towards her, glared down at her, his eyes chips of blue ice.

"Madam," he hissed. "You are unwell. You will go home voluntarily. If you do not, I assure you my man will carry you bodily from the palace, and you will make a spectacle of yourself. Go. Now."

She stared at him for a moment, utterly confounded. The blood roared in her veins. Then she obeyed, tearing her arm once again from her brother-in-law's grip as they left the room, and storming from the palace, obviously far from unwell. Angus followed behind, face closed, ready to intercept her if she changed her mind and decided to return to the concert, or the library. She did not. She was so angry she knew she was in danger of losing her temper, letting something slip, perhaps.

She managed, barely, to wait until she was in the coach

"Angus," she said, the moment they were under way. "What the hell's going on?"

He put his finger to his lips by way of reply.

"Jim," she amended hotly. "What the hell's..."

He lunged across the coach and put his hand over her mouth, stifling the rest of the sentence.

"*Isd!*" he whispered. "Ye ken the rules."

Yes, she did. Don't speak when you might be overheard. Maintain the pretence until you were sure of privacy. Let the left hand know what the right hand's doing. Damn him. What was he up to? And why hadn't he told her?

She stormed through the foyer of the hotel much as she had through the palace, taking the stairs two at a time in spite of her cumbersome dress. They entered the room, she hurled the key at the table, slammed the door and rounded on Angus.

"What are you up to?" she said, her eyes blazing. "And why wasn't I told? Is it a sudden change of plan? Has something gone wrong?"

Angus looked deeply uncomfortable, and remained uncharacteristically silent. She observed him intently for a moment. It was not a sudden change of plan, then.

"Did you manage to secrete the letter in his room?" she asked. "Can you tell me that much, at least?"

"Aye," he replied. "Aye, I did."

"Right. Good. So what is Alex doing that he thinks I won't approve of?"

Angus looked away.

"I have to get back to the palace," he muttered after a moment.

She moved out of arm's reach before she lost control and struck him, and threw herself down in a chair. It was not

Angus who deserved to be hit. "Sit down," she commanded. "You're not going anywhere until you've told me what's going on."

He remained standing.

"I canna," he said helplessly after a moment. "He tellt me not to. He'll explain it to ye himself later. I have to get back. I'm sorry."

He moved to the table, picked up the key, went to the door.

"Angus," she said coldly. He stopped. "If you lock that door, I swear by Christ that I will scream the place down until someone comes to let me out, and then I will go straight back to the palace and cause such a scene it will be the talk of Versailles for years to come."

He looked at her. She meant it.

"He…"

"Tellt ye to," she finished for him. "And he's your chieftain, so you do as he says. Well, he's my chieftain too, I suppose, but if I haven't earned his trust, then he's not earned my loyalty. You do as you're told, then. You'll see me back at the palace later. Or hear me, anyway."

He swore, in Gaelic, at who she wasn't sure. He stood for a full minute by the door, torn.

"He doesna want ye to go back to the palace," he said finally. "He'll be angry if I dinna lock the door."

"And I'll be angry if you do. Which puts you in an impossible position. If it's any help to you, I'll tell you this. I have no intention of going back to the palace tonight, Angus. Unless you shut me in like a naughty child. Then I'll behave like one, and we'll all be sorry."

He came to a decision, threw the key back down on the table and opened the door. Behind him she inhaled sharply, as though in pain. He turned back again. The fact that he trusted her, when his brother clearly did not, had dissolved her anger, making space for something else. She was sitting in the chair, face turned up to his, lovely, delicate, blue eyes brimming.

"Why, Angus?" she cried in sudden anguish. "What cause have I given him to distrust me?"

At that moment he hated his brother with a vehemence that shocked him. He clenched his fists instinctively, then forced them to relax in case she should notice, should think he intended to do her violence. The comforting platitude he had half-thought to utter remained unspoken.

"None," he said instead. "I'm sorry. For what it's worth, I dinna agree wi' him."

He went out, closing the door quietly behind him. Free to leave, she did not do so. Instead she sat for a time staring into space, unseeing. Then she stood, took off her shoes, turned up the lamp, replenished the fire, poured herself a glass of wine, drank it in one, poured another, then sat down again and settled herself to wait for her husband to come home.

CHAPTER THIRTEEN

At one a.m. there was a light knock on the door. Beth, still in the chair, still wide awake, nevertheless started. No doubt he knew Angus had not locked her in, and thought she had locked the door from the inside.

"It's open," she said. "Come in."

The door duly opened and a head popped round it.

"Are we intruding?" Lady Winter asked. Her voice had the trembling eager tone she adopted when she had great news to impart. Her eyes sparkled.

Yes.

"No," said Beth. "I wasn't sleeping. Come in." She did not stand up to greet them, as propriety demanded.

The rest of Lady Winter appeared, followed closely by Anne, whose eyes were not sparkling, but deeply anxious. If the two women noticed Beth's lapse in manners, they did not comment on it.

"We have just returned from the palace and saw the light burning under the door. We thought we would see if you were feeling any better," Lady Winter said. "Your servant told us you had left the concert early as you were unwell."

"Yes. I am much better now," Beth said calmly. *Tell me what he's done; you are dying to,* a voice in her head screamed. "I am waiting for Anthony to come home."

"Oh, is he not here?" cried the lady, looking round as though expecting the baronet to emerge from behind the curtain or under the chair. "He left before us. I thought he would have been home by now."

But she had hoped he wouldn't, that was clear. She wanted to be the first to impart the news, whatever it was.

"Oh, Lady Elizabeth, it's terrible!" cried Anne unexpectedly. "Sir Anthony has challenged Monsieur Monselle to a duel! What can he be thinking of?"

Lady Winter scowled blackly at her companion, thereby missing Beth's initial reaction to the news. The colour drained from her face and she jerked forward in her seat, almost tumbling to the floor. White flashes sparkled in front of her eyes. *I am going to faint,* she thought remotely.

Capable hands took her by the shoulders, eased her back into the chair. The strong smell of ammonia assailed her nostrils and she jerked her head away, grimacing. Then her vision cleared and her senses returned to her, in a fashion.

"Really, Anne!" Lady Winter was saying crossly. "Such catastrophic news needs to be broken more gently than that!"

"I'm sorry," said Anne, her brown eyes full of tears. She was kneeling at the side of the chair, holding one of Beth's hands between hers. She was, at least, genuinely concerned.

"It's all right, Anne," Beth reassured the young woman. "I am fine now. It was a little unexpected, that's all." She looked up at the older woman, who was replacing the smelling salts bottle in her reticule. "So Anthony has challenged Monsieur Monselle to a duel. How utterly ridiculous. Did he say why?" She was amazed at how unconcerned she was managing to sound. In a moment she would have her mask back in place.

"He was somewhat excited, but it seems he suspects the Frenchman of attempting to assail your virtue, against your will. Is that why Monsieur Monselle contrived to get you out of the room during the interval, my dear?" She obviously had images of Sir Anthony interrupting the attempted rape of his wife by a dissolute foreigner. Was that what Alex wanted everyone to think? *To hell with him,* thought Beth. He could not expect her to read his mind. If he wanted her to play a part, he should have told her what that part was to be.

"No, of course not. He had a message for me from the king, as he said." She did not elaborate on what it was, to Lady Winter's obvious disappointment. "We merely went for a short stroll. The door was open when Anthony found us talking. He is over reacting, as usual. Monsieur Monselle has not the slightest interest in me, nor I in him, as Anthony will realise when he recovers from his hysteria. I am sure he will not risk his life for what is clearly a misunderstanding. Did Monsieur Monselle agree to this charade?"

"It would appear so. He would have to, or be branded a coward. Although I can reassure you that I doubt your husband's life is at risk. Sir Anthony has agreed that he will be satisfied when first blood is drawn. I am sure a flesh wound is the worst that will result from the encounter."

"I see. And do you know when and where this duel is to take place?" Beth asked disinterestedly.

"At dawn, of course, as is traditional. There is a small clearing in the trees to the south of the palace. Bartholomew tells me that is the normal venue for duels, although of course duelling is frowned upon, and so the meeting places are not made public."

"Well, then," said Beth, gently freeing her hand from Anne's grip and getting to her feet. "I had better prepare."

"Oh my dear child!" exclaimed Lady Winter, eyes dancing. "You are surely not thinking of intervening to stop the fight, are you?"

"Of course not," replied Beth coolly. "If my husband wishes to spend the morning making a fool of himself, I will not prevent him. I merely intend to assemble needle and thread, and bandages, for when he returns."

* * *

In the clearing, sheltered by overgrown shrubs, brambles and saplings, frost lay heavy on the ground, as yet untouched by the weak rays of the winter sun, which had risen only a few minutes before. The grass was crisp underfoot, the frost melting when stepped upon, and the men's green footprints showed clearly as they moved quietly about the clearing. A few birds sang intermittently in the bare branches of the trees. The air was cold, clean, bracing. It was Christmas Eve. Today all over France, people would decorate their houses with evergreens, and later would go to confession in order to celebrate the mass of the Lord's birth at midnight with a clean conscience.

Henri, who was not generally troubled by matters of conscience, had fought two duels when young and hot-headed, one to the death, and had never thought to fight a third. He made his preparations quickly and efficiently. He had dressed practically for the occasion, in dark woollen hose and breeches, and plain linen shirt unadorned with lace, which could snag a weapon. His shoes were of stout leather, his sword sharp, functional, and sheathed in a plain scabbard. He wore no wig, which could fall over his eyes and blind him, and his thick black hair was tied back and clubbed to ensure it would not come loose during the fight. He took off his coat, rolled up his sleeves and performed a series of stretching exercises designed to loosen the muscles, while he waited for his opponent to ready himself.

The baronet had clearly never fought a duel in his life. He entered the clearing as though for a ball; sporting full make-up and neatly curled wig, he still wore the magenta satin breeches and silk shirt of the previous evening, embellished with costly Brussels lace. His shoes were ridiculous smooth-soled pink satin confections. By the darkening of the material, Henri could see they were already soaked; the fool would skid about on the slippery grass as though on ice. Sir Anthony took off his coat and handed it to his servant, then arranged the lace at his wrists carefully over his cream leather-gloved hands. The young blond man who Henri found so attractive stepped forward, murmuring something in his master's ear. The baronet smiled, foolishly.

"Ah. Of course," he said. He rolled up his sleeve, no more than a couple of inches; his forearms were still covered. Henri had hoped to see his adversary's bare arm; one could ascertain whether a man was a swordsman or not from the over-developed muscles of the right arm. Beth, had she been present, and Angus, if he'd had a mind to, could have told him that both of the baronet's forearms, as well as his biceps and shoulders, were knotted with heavy muscle due to years of practice, not just with sword, but with dirk and targe, axe, and any other weapon that came to hand in an emergency. But Beth was not present in the clearing, Angus kept silence, and Henri had no reason to suspect that the baronet was other than he appeared to be. He felt no apprehension regarding this contest. The clumsy way he drew his ornate jewelled sword with difficulty from the scabbard told Henri that Sir Anthony carried it as decoration, no more.

Henri felt a mixture of pity and derision for the pathetic fool. What had prompted the Englishman to issue a challenge was beyond him. Maybe he felt his lack of manhood, and was hoping by this ridiculous display of misguided chivalry to gain his wife's respect. All he would gain was a ruined and bloody silk shirt, Henri thought contemptuously. The right arm, perhaps, just below the shoulder. That would satisfy honour and prevent Sir Anthony from issuing any more hasty challenges until it had healed, by which time he would be safely back in England. It was a shame that the fight was not to the death. It would be a pleasure to release the lovely Elizabeth from her bondage to this moron.

The two men moved forward into the middle of the

clearing and presented their swords to the scrutiny of their opponent's seconds, who declared them to be acceptable. It was reiterated that they would fight only until first blood was drawn, after which the duel would be over. There would be no retaliation. The men agreed, and took their positions.

Sir Anthony was visibly nervous, and made no move at first to engage his adversary's weapon. It was left to Henri to move forward and make the first thrust, forcing the baronet to parry. To Henri's surprise the fop then suddenly sprang into action, charging forward, flailing wildly with his sword and causing the Frenchman to jump back in surprise. He fended off the other man's panicked swings with insulting ease, although this was not any technique he recognised. It was not any technique at all. Henri continued to parry, allowing the baronet to tire himself. Then he would wound him and retreat to a very welcome breakfast in a warm room.

After perhaps a minute of this frenzy, Sir Anthony drew back, breathing heavily. Henri contemplated for a moment whether to allow the man to continue for a while longer, enabling him to boast to his lovely wife that although he had lost, it had been a close thing. No. End the tiresome affair now. It was cold and he had more important and interesting things to do with his day.

The point of the baronet's blade was drooping downwards as he fought to regain his breath. Henri moved in to finish the duel.

He was within an inch of his target when the Englishman's sword shot up with remarkable speed, screeching along the other man's blade and wrenching it from his hand, sending it curving through the air. It had been a lucky blow, and Henri cursed himself for his carelessness. Sir Anthony smiled gleefully, danced forward, eager to deliver the winning blow, aiming for his opponent's upper arm.

At least it was the left arm, Henri thought gratefully as

he resigned himself to losing, against all the odds. This would take some living down. He smiled ruefully, watched the baronet skid at the last minute, slip and sprawl on the grass, throwing his arm out as if to save himself and missing the shoulder, the blade instead moving forward and down as he fell, driving into the Frenchman's chest with all the force of Sir Anthony's falling weight behind it. Henri staggered backwards, keeping his balance with difficulty.

A look of utter horror disfigured the painted face, and Sir Anthony, scrambling to his feet, pulled back his arm in panic, as if by removing the sword he could somehow turn back time, undo the terrible wound he had accidentally, certainly accidentally, for there could be no doubt of the man's incompetence, inflicted.

A red flower blossomed on Henri Monselle's shirt, unfolding its scarlet petals with alarming speed. He sank to his knees, stared into the eyes of his enemy, saw the satisfaction momentarily flicker in the sapphire depths and knew his mistake. Then his green eyes glazed and rolled back in his head, and he toppled sideways onto the grass.

The small figure dressed in drab brown, who had watched the scene unfold from the nearby shrubbery where she had concealed herself an hour earlier, waited until her husband, sobbing hysterically, had his back to her, before she carefully backed her frozen body out of the bushes and made her silent way to the hotel, passing the four men dressed in the king's livery making their way along the road without registering them, or what they might signify.

Silently she made her way up to the room, responding with only a distracted nod to the sleepy greeting of the chambermaid she met on the stairs. Silently she packed, selecting only the essential items for a journey which could be carried in one bag, and left the building, locking the door behind her and leaving the key at the desk with no explanation.

An hour later she was on the stage coach, along with eight other people bound for Calais, and home, wherever that might be.

She responded to the attempts of her fellow passengers to engage her in conversation with polite monosyllabic answers, at first because she was numbed and incapable of more, and later, as she recovered her wits, because she wished to be left alone to think.

She thought.

Until the moment she had seen Henri drop to his knees, fatally wounded, Beth had been prepared to give Alex the benefit of the doubt. She thought he had maybe challenged the Frenchman to a duel as a delaying tactic, to prevent him returning to his bedchamber until the incriminating letter could be discovered. Maybe he had insisted she return to the hotel so that she would not be implicated in his actions in any way.

After witnessing the outcome of the duel however, she could no longer believe that. Henri's death was deliberate; Beth was in no doubt about that. Alex was brilliant, devious and manipulative. He had never intended that Henri be imprisoned. He had wanted him out of the way permanently, and could not take the time to find a way of disposing of him privately, so had instead contrived a way to do it publicly without being accused of murder. If Henri had been arrested, there was still a chance that he would somehow get a letter to England, or that Louis would release him early enough for him to get to England before the invasion force was ready. The only way to be sure Henri posed no threat was to kill him. She understood that now, and realised that she had been naïve to think that Alex would settle for anything less.

What she could not understand was why he had not entrusted her with his plans. But then, he had not trusted her with the information that plague was raging in the Mediterranean, nor with the situation regarding Jeannie MacGregor, whatever that was. She was certain now that Angus was right. Alex would have killed both Henri and Katerina had he been in the hothouse, and had not trusted her enough to admit that, either. He had not trusted her to resist King Louis' advances, initially.

He did not trust her.

How could you love someone and not trust them? What had Angus said? It was all about trust and loyalty. The whole clan system was based on it. Whatever Jeannie MacGregor had done, she'd broken the trust of the clan, and Alex had acted. Now, knowing him better, she could make a fair guess as to what the hard decision had been. She did not expect to meet Jeannie if she ever went to Scotland.

She had loved him and trusted him, and now no longer knew what the words meant.

She racked her memory all the way across France, across the English Channel, across south-east England, trying to think of what she had done to betray his trust. Nothing. She had done nothing to endanger him. But still he did not trust her. He was her husband, her chieftain. His distrust put her outside the clan, made a mockery of her marriage.

Because she was grieving, although she did not know it, the death of Henri and the possible death of her marriage, and had no one with whom she could share her troubles, her exhausted, overwrought mind ran wild. Why hadn't he killed her, if he didn't trust her? She knew enough to send him and half the MacGregor clan to the gallows. Maybe he had intended to, after the duel. Maybe he was even now galloping across the countryside to intercept her before she could get to the authorities and denounce him. Had he written to Iain and Maggie to warn them she might be coming home, that she was no longer to be trusted? Would they be waiting for her when she knocked on the door, dirks at the ready?

By the time she got to the door in question, ten gruelling days later, she no longer cared what reception she received. She had used the last of her ready money to pay for the carriage from Dover, had not even had sufficient funds to pay for a hackney from the terminus in Fleet Street and had walked over a mile to the house, changing her bag from hand to hand with increasing frequency as her tired muscles protested.

She dropped her bag on the step, knocked on the door and waited, swaying with exhaustion, for Iain to open it, his face set in the superior footman's expression.

After a short time the door opened. A man appeared. It was not Iain, and he was not wearing a superior expression. Beth found herself looking into the face of the man she had last seen when she had been trying to murder him, over a year ago in Manchester. On Christmas Eve.

She knew immediately who he was, although he did not have the exceptional height of his brothers, or the beautiful slate blue eyes. But he did have the athletic, muscular build, and the sensual mouth that turned up at the corners, threatening always to break into a smile. And he also had the impossibly long sweeping lashes, framing eyes of a clear grey, which now flickered over her shoulder, scanning the square before returning to her.

Alex had not written then, to warn them of her coming.

"Duncan, I presume," she said, before he could introduce himself. In that second, as the familiar mouth curved upwards in a smile, she could see in her mind's eye the way it should have been, Alex and Angus standing behind her grinning at her mortification as she discovered that the brother she had been so eager to meet was the man she had almost killed.

Now she knew why they had refused to describe him. In other circumstances she would have felt embarrassed, blushed, apologised, then rounded on her laughing husband and his brother, threatening dire revenge. Now she was too tired to feel anything.

Duncan MacGregor moved forward onto the step and took her hands in his.

"*Fàilte, mo phiuthar,*" he said.

Welcome, sister.

She looked into his eyes, saw only welcome, acceptance, trust. Trust. She opened her mouth to respond, uttered instead an inarticulate moan of despair, and was drawn quickly into the hall, into the strong, comforting embrace of her brother-in-law, where she broke down, completely and utterly.

She found that she was not too tired to feel anything, after all.

It was to Duncan's credit that he let her cry, helplessly and noisily like a child, clinging to him until the wails had given way to sobs and the sobs to hiccups, and did not press her to tell him the reason for her distress, although he had expected his brothers to accompany her, and they were not here, and he did not know why.

When she finally calmed down enough to become aware of her surroundings, she was in the kitchen sitting on Duncan's lap, her face buried in his shoulder, which was very wet. One hand stroked her hair, the other was warm on her back. Over her head his troubled grey eyes met those of Iain, who was sitting opposite, his thin face pinched with anxiety. Maggie, ever practical, poured a large measure of whisky into a glass, then sat with it in her hand, waiting for Beth to recover sufficiently to drink it.

"Oh God, I'm sorry," Beth faltered as soon as she could

speak, her voice muffled by Duncan's shirt. She looked round sheepishly, saw Iain's expression, understood, felt the glass thrust into her hand.

"They're all right," she said, and swallowed the contents of the glass in one gulp, coughing and grimacing, then feeling the warm glow begin to spread downwards to her stomach. "At least they were all right the last time I saw them."

Iain closed his eyes and let the breath he had been holding out in a rush.

"When was that?" Duncan asked quietly. He had stopped stroking her hair, but his hand was still splayed across her back. She needed the physical contact badly, but he was a stranger, and must be mortified at having this lunatic throw herself at him. She made a move to get up, and his arm wrapped round her shoulders, restraining her gently. "It's all right, *a ghràidh*, bide a while," he said. His voice was deep, soothing and warm, like the whisky. He didn't seem embarrassed. She stayed where she was, resisted the urge to snuggle into him, felt her eyes start to close and opened them with an effort.

"Ten days ago," she answered his question. "I'm sorry I frightened you. I'm tired, that's all. There's nothing wrong. With them. They should be on their way back by now." The whisky, taken on an empty stomach, was starting to make its presence felt already. "I'm sorry," she said again, looking up at her brother-in-law. "What you must think of me, I have no idea. The first time I meet you I try to stab you, and the second time I try to drown you."

"I'll be ready for ye the third time," he said, smiling. "Dinna fash yourself, lassie, I'm no' so easily got rid of."

She sniffed, and smiled weakly. The whisky was rendering her pleasantly fuzzy. Her eyes started to close again. It was warm in the kitchen. There were bunches of festive greenery hung around the fireplace. She remembered sitting on another knee, in another kitchen, worried voices murmuring around her as Thomas, Jane and Graeme tried to ascertain how she had been injured. There were no voices around her now, but the atmosphere held the same tension. She struggled awake again, opened her eyes.

"I came home ahead of him, that's all," she said, her voice slurring slightly. "We had an argument."

"Now that I find awfu' hard to believe," said Duncan. "Alex being so docile and even tempered an' all, and you looking to be the same."

She laughed, and let her eyes close again, relaxing. It was good to be home.

Over the next few days her relationship with Duncan continued as it had begun, relaxed and friendly. He did not press her at breakfast the following morning to reveal the details of what had gone on in France, although it was clear that he was worried. When Beth saw her face in the dining room mirror she understood why. Her eyes were so shadowed by fatigue they appeared bruised, and her skin had the pallor of deep grief or sickness. She looked like someone who had just suffered a bereavement, as, in a manner of speaking, she had.

While they were eating, a letter arrived from Sir Anthony Peters, dated the twenty-sixth of December. Duncan read it aloud. It was short, and stated only that he had been arrested for duelling, that he did not expect to be incarcerated for long, and that he would return home as soon as possible. He had obviously been supervised while writing the letter, and whilst it told them that he was alive and well, it did nothing to reassure the three Scots that he would remain so. Beth then explained what had happened, about Angus's adventures in the hothouse, the trip to Rome, France, and the finding and dispatching of Henri. She did not tell them that she had not been privy to Alex's plans, merely that they had argued about a silly personal matter and she had left for home ahead of him.

If Duncan did not have the blue eyes of his brothers, they certainly held the same intensity, and she was uncomfortably aware from his scrutiny of her face as she finished her tale that he did not believe she had told him the whole story.

She was right. Duncan did not know his sister-in-law well, but the erratic letters he had received from Angus from various locations in Europe had sung the praises of this fragile-seeming English rose. She was strong, adventurous, courageous, hot-tempered, good-humoured, stubborn, wonderful. Reckless as he could be, Angus was not stupid, and was a good judge of character. Duncan could well imagine how a woman possessing many of the qualities her husband also possessed, would clash violently with him on occasion, on many occasions, probably. He could *not* imagine such a woman walking out on her husband in a childish sulk because of a trivial personal argument, leaving him to deal alone with the consequences of killing the king's servant.

Nothing he saw over the next two days changed his opinion, as Beth wandered wraithlike around the house waiting as they all were for Alex and Angus to return, although she would not admit it. Whatever the argument had been about, it was not trivial. Something was very wrong with his brother's marriage, but Duncan had to trust that whatever it was, she would have told him if Alex had been put in danger because of it. He let it be known, subtly, that he was there for her if she needed to confide in someone, and left it at that.

She *was* tempted to confide in him. If he did not possess the dynamic fiery charisma of his brothers, he had a quality she needed far more at the moment; a rocklike dependability and calmness that soothed her. She knew the welcome she had received from Duncan, Iain and Maggie had been genuine, for which she was more grateful than they would ever know. It meant she could stay in the bosom of what she now considered to be her family, at least until Alex returned or sent a letter telling them she could not be trusted. By that time, she thought, she would be strong enough to cope with that.

On her second day in London, already tired of passively waiting, she wrote two short letters to Manchester, then, whilst waiting for the replies, she busied herself as best she could, helping Maggie with the household chores, taking down the festive greenery on Twelfth Night, and discussing with Iain and Duncan the problems of smuggling goods direct to Leith now that the weather was so treacherous, and the alternative problems of landing the goods on the south coast of England and then transporting them north by land.

"I was hoping Alex would be home by now," Duncan admitted on the fourth day after Beth's return. "Gabriel Foley has said he can provide a trustworthy crew to take the next lot of merchandise up to Scotland. It'll cost a wee bit more than if we do it ourselves, but Alex seems to set store by Foley, so it could be a lot less risky. I really want to discuss it with Alex before I make a decision, though. He kens Foley far better than I do."

There was a short silence while everyone pondered on the possible reasons for Alex's continued non-appearance. What if King Louis did not accept that Henri's death had been an accident?

"I'm sure he will," Beth said, when Iain voiced his concern. "If I didn't know Alex better, I'd have sworn it was an accident myself. Louis will probably hold him for a few days, then let him go. I did come home by stage coach, which means I left him the carriage. They'll have to travel as Sir Anthony and footman, which means they can't hire horses and gallop hell-for-leather across country, and with the weather and French postillions being what they are, they'll be lucky to make it home by the end of the month."

That was true, but it did not stop everyone worrying.

Time went on and Alex did not appear, nor send further word. Duncan finally rode to Hastings himself, returning five days later half-frozen and frustrated, with the news that Gabriel Foley was in Calais and would possibly be there for some time.

"Maybe it's for the best," he said, shivering, sitting so close to the hearth that he was in considerable danger of setting himself on fire. "Alex is sure to be home any day, and the weapons are in a safe house in Calais. They'll come to nae harm if they stay there a wee while longer."

Nevertheless, Beth went out early every morning to the post, muffled up in layers of clothing, ostensibly against the cold, but also rendering her unidentifiable. She did not wish to be recognised by anyone; while the coach was absent, society would assume Sir Anthony and his wife to be still in France, and that suited her fine. Every day she returned empty-handed, and the household would settle to the business of passing another day.

On the twentieth of January Duncan declared that if there had been no word from his brothers by the end of the month, he would go to Paris himself and try to find out what had happened to them.

On the twenty-third there was, finally, a letter waiting at the post, although it was not from France, but from Manchester, and was addressed to Beth. She read it straight away, then took a hackney to the Swan Inn on Snow Hill and booked a place on the stage coach for the next day. Then she went home and packed, before going downstairs to tell the others that she was leaving. It was gratifying that their sadness at her imminent departure was not feigned. It was less gratifying that they could clearly not understand how she could go off merrily visiting friends in Manchester when there had been no word of Alex for nearly a month.

"He knew I wanted to go to Manchester as soon as we returned from Europe," she said, when Maggie protested that she should wait until they knew Alex and Angus were safe. "He agreed I could. I need to sort out some business matters, and find out what damage Richard caused when he went home in November. It's driving me mad, hanging around here waiting day after day. I'd rather be doing something useful."

Duncan took Beth's side, and agreed that she should go. He had seen that she was not a woman to sit and mope for long. She needed to have her mind, and her body too, engaged in activity. He did not find it difficult to understand this woman. After all, he had lived all his life with a brother who was startlingly like her, in so many ways.

He insisted on accompanying her to the coaching inn, and waited with her while the horses were made ready. They ordered a drink, then sat in companionable silence at the table for a short while, as only people at ease with each other can. It was one of the things she liked about him, that he didn't feel the need to fill every silent moment with conversation. She observed him surreptitiously, committing him to memory, the pleasant face, like and yet unlike his brothers', the dark hair, darker than Alex's but with the same red highlights. He radiated serenity and self-containment, not at all like Alex. He was her newest friend, and could have been a good one, she thought. But she did not know if she would ever see him again.

He looked up now, and smiled. She realised that he had been aware of what she was doing and had allowed her the time to do it. She bit her lip.

"Write to me the moment you hear from them," she said. "I won't rest until I know they're safe."

"I will," he promised. "Do you want to tell me where you're

staying, or shall I just send a letter to the post? Manchester's no' a wee village. Ye'll maybe not receive it."

"Send it to the post at Didsbury," she said. "Didsbury's a small place. I'll get it there."

The bell rang. The coach was leaving in five minutes. They finished their drinks and went outside. She reached out her hand to him to shake, and ignoring it he pulled her into his arms and hugged her tightly, kissing her on the forehead before letting her go.

"Have ye any message for him?" he said at the last moment. Beth hesitated on the steps of the carriage, causing the woman waiting to ascend behind her to click her tongue impatiently.

"Yes," she said, turning back and looking down at him. "If he asks, tell him I've gone to those I trust, and who trust me. He'll know what I mean."

When Duncan arrived home there was a letter waiting for him, together with an extremely impatient Iain and Maggie, who had balked at opening anything addressed to someone else, but were fast overcoming their reluctance, in view of Duncan's tardy return.

"It came by courier, so it must be urgent," Iain explained as Duncan unfolded the letter and scanned its coded contents, running his eyes down the page, searching for the problem contained in it. Then he looked up.

"It's all right," he said. "He's safe. They're both safe. He's on his way home. Angus is on his way to Rome."

Then he sat down and read the letter to them slowly, deciphering the familiar code as he went. The contents confirmed everything Beth had told them, and added some things she didn't know, having left so precipitately; that Louis, irked by the loss of such a useful employee but unable to proceed against Sir Anthony as even Henri's second had

Julia Brannan

stated the death to be an accident, had decided instead to let the baronet kick his heels in prison for a while whilst the paperwork to secure his release was sorted out. He had not been allowed to write, apart from the brief missive he hoped they had received. Angus, being only a servant, had been released two weeks previously and due to circumstances Alex would explain on his return, had ridden post-haste for Rome.

The demand in the postscript, which was why Alex had gone to the expense of a courier, Duncan could do nothing about. He was very glad he could do nothing about it.

* * *

Alex had spent his first days in prison in a state of permanent frustration. He had known there was a possibility that he would be arrested; after all, he had just killed the king's employee; but he had not expected it to happen quite so quickly. He had thought he would have time to return to the hotel, explain to Beth and get Angus on his way to Rome before facing the consequences of his actions. Instead they had been apprehended whilst still in the clearing, and both the sobbing Sir Anthony and his footman had been politely but firmly ensconced in the Bastille.

Sir Anthony had, predictably, spent some time bemoaning his fate and complaining about the state of his cell, which was actually far better than he had expected. The well-fortified mediaeval fortress of the Bastille was the most dreaded prison in France, but the room he was taken to, though sparsely furnished with a pallet and straw mattress, chair and table, was nevertheless clean. He rapidly discovered that many privileges were available to those with the necessary funds to pay for them. He had then immediately demanded, and been refused, pen and paper, permission to speak to a notary, and the release of his innocent servant. The warden was not at present available; when he was, he would visit the baronet to discuss his situation.

Alex had known what that meant. The warden was finding out how wealthy Sir Anthony was, and what instructions the king had left regarding his incarceration. Then he would visit and the bartering would begin.

He had two main priorities at the moment; one was to get a message to Beth to tell her what had happened; the other was to procure Angus's release. After Alex had read through the secret papers in Henri's room the previous night, he had realised that Prince Charles Edward Stuart must at all costs be discouraged from coming to Paris until expressly invited to do so by Louis. The whole invasion plan would be compromised if it was discovered by the British that Charles was going to France, which they certainly would the moment he left Rome, if not before; he was constantly monitored by spies. And the ever-cautious Louis would probably call off his planned invasion altogether if he thought the British suspected what he was up to. Balhaldie would be in Rome by now, telling the eager prince that the restoration of his family was imminent; it was imperative that Angus follow hot on his heels and deter him from any rash move.

It did not escape Alex's notice that before escorting Beth home the previous night Angus had been very reluctant to ride straight off to Rome after the duel, leaving his brother to face the music alone; but that after returning from the hotel he had raised no more objections and in fact seemed eager to get out of Alex's presence as quickly as possible.

The warden had finally put in an appearance the following day. He regretted that Sir Anthony was dissatisfied with his accommodation and for a consideration could provide better quarters, and excellent food and wine. He could also permit the baronet to write a short letter to his friends in England who were awaiting his return, and a note to his wife at the hotel. He regretted he could not permit the release of the servant Jim, although he would be escorted to the hotel to collect any necessary personal items the baronet might require to make his stay comfortable.

Sir Anthony Peters had accepted this somewhat hysterically, with protestations of innocence, repentance and sobs; Alex had calmly accepted that although Louis was not angry enough with him to cast him into one of the notorious dungeons this prison boasted, neither did he intend to release him imminently. Angus had therefore been despatched with a written note for Beth, verbal instructions to collect clothes, make-up and other essentials, and unspoken instructions to give his escort the slip if possible and ride for Rome, regardless of the consequences.

Angus had returned two hours later with assorted gaudy costumes stuffed unceremoniously into a bag, the required make-up and spare wigs, and the tersely delivered news that Beth had left the hotel without leaving any message. He had been unable to escape his escort, who were well-armed and vigilant.

The next eleven days had been the longest of Alex's life. Under constant surveillance and therefore permanently trapped in the guise of Sir Anthony, he had been unable to discuss the situation with his unusually tight-lipped brother. It was quite obvious that Angus thought Alex to be in the wrong regarding Beth, and wanted to discuss the matter in time-honoured Highland fashion, but this was not the place. After a day or so the naturally good-humoured and loquacious Angus had returned to his normal behaviour, within the limits of his role as servant to Sir Anthony; but they both knew that the matter between them was merely postponed, not forgotten.

On Twelfth Night the king had celebrated the end of the Christmas period by issuing the good news, delivered by the warden, that there would be no charges brought against Sir Anthony in the matter of the unfortunate death of Henri Monselle. No doubt, Alex thought, Louis had found the letter planted in Henri's room and had, as intended, decided that the nincompoop of an Englishman had unwittingly done him a favour in ridding him of a spy. The warden smilingly added that James Campbell, Sir Anthony's servant, was now free to leave, although the paperwork to secure the baronet's release was somewhat more complex, sir would understand, and there would be a short delay before it was completed. However, the warden would now be pleased to allow visits from friends to be made and to provide Sir Anthony with pen, paper, reading materials and anything else he required apart from the key to the prison. Sir Anthony hurriedly wrote the scribbled note Duncan was to receive some two weeks later, gave it to Angus to post, and waved his servant off tearfully.

He had finally been released from the Bastille on the twenty-first of January. He had set off for home the following day, making his leisurely way to Calais, hindered, as Beth had predicted, a little by the weather and a lot by the postillions. He was not now too worried about arriving home speedily. Beth must surely have gone back to London. She had definitely taken the stage to Calais, that much a young guard had found out for him, for the bargain price of a guinea. She would not go to Lord Edward's, Alex thought, and she had formed a good relationship with Maggie and Iain, so it was almost certain that she would go there. Duncan would have received his letter by now, and would act on it. Alex decided he would worry about how he was going to deal with her when he arrived home. He did not anticipate it with relish.

Consequently he didn't rush, and at Calais he temporarily became Abernathy, and kept his flexible appointment with the bull-like smuggler Gabriel Foley, which resulted in the successful transport to Hastings of various goods of a martial nature, together with a dismantled carriage, and Messrs Abernathy and Foley themselves, who, together with most of the crew, once safely arrived at their destination, repaired to a somewhat disreputable inn. There they made short work of several bottles of brandy, and rather longer work of attempting to fleece each other at Loo, which resulted in a good-natured brawl. Mr Abernathy participated in this with great enthusiasm, needing a release for his pent-up emotions, emerging smiling, with a black eye, bruised ribs, and the respect of all who had come in contact with his fists. He gained the respect of the remaining occupants of the inn and the landlord when he offered to pay for the damage and treated everyone to a drink immediately afterwards. The following morning, the goods had set off on their way to Manchester accompanied by Foley's men, where they would be temporarily stored before continuing on their way to Scotland when the passes were open. His relationship with Foley and his men was now on an excellent footing. It had been a good few days' work; the goodwill of men with boats, Jacobite leanings and few scruples was always worth cultivating.

Abernathy, refreshed if somewhat hungover, sat down with Gabriel Foley for a hair of the dog and a private talk the following morning. He expected the talk to be about the next consignment of arms, and at first it seemed that he was right.

"I need to tell you that after this shipment, I doubt I will be able to give you my personal attention for a while, as I expect to be occupied with other matters," Gabriel commenced.

He had never shown any inclination to explain his movements before. That, and his apparently relaxed attitude whilst at the same time closely observing his companion over his wine, put Alex on full alert.

"Are these matters in which I might have an interest?" he

replied casually. He sipped the wine. His stomach threatened to rebel, violently, and then subsided.

"I think it very likely, yes. I am going to tell you something. If you think you might not wish to hear that something, tell me now. Because if do I tell you, and you take any action other than what I approve of, your future might become somewhat...unfortunate."

Alex thought for a minute, then nodded for Foley to continue. After a few minutes the smuggler stopped talking and refilled their glasses. He eased his bulk carefully back into the chair, taking care not to move his head more than necessary, and regarded his companion with bloodshot sea-grey eyes. They had drunk an awful lot the previous night.

"Why are you telling me this?" Alex said. "I'm no' familiar with the sea routes from Dunkirk to Blackwall. I canna act as a pilot."

"I don't expect you to. That's my job. There will be two lots of pilots. One set will go to Dunkirk. The moment that Admiral Roquefeuil has decoyed Norris and his fleet away from the invasion area, the Comte de Saxe will set sail with ten thousand French troops. I, along with my colleagues, will be waiting at the Hope to bring them up the Thames to Blackwall. The date is not yet known, but I thought you might be inclined, at that time, to pay a visit to your ailing aunt in Blackwall, should her condition suddenly deteriorate. Perhaps you might like to bring a group of friends with you, for company."

"I havena got an aunt, as is well known in all the circles I move in," Alex said. "But I do have a dear friend, who lives in that very same place. We were friends at university. His name is...John. Phillips. Aye, John Phillips. I would be awfu' upset to hear he was ill, and would probably need the consolation of...maybe thirty people or so, perhaps? It's no' many, but I find the English, yourself excepted, remarkably unwilling to do more than drink toasts to absent kings and vow undying loyalty. If I had time to gather friends from my native land…but I take it the element of surprise will render that impossible."

"You're right. It's imperative that the Government do not become aware of the invasion until the last possible minute. I will send a courier to…?"

Alex hesitated. "To the White Horse coffee house," he said after a moment. "I will send someone there every day, if I dinna go myself. Address your message to Mr Jonson. Benjamin Jonson." This man could almost certainly be trusted, but it did not pay to take unnecessary chances.

Gabriel raised his glass in his beefy fist.

"Then, Mr Benjamin Abernathy Jonson, let me propose a toast to the King over the Water. May he soon cross it."

"And to those who are prepared to do more than propose toasts. May they multiply a thousandfold, as I'm sure they will once the French have taken London for the Stuarts." The two men drank deeply.

Having taken his leave of his sea-faring friends, Mr Abernathy reluctantly became Sir Anthony once more, and set off on the final leg of his journey home, realising that he had been away too long, although his trip had not been unproductive. But now he needed to pick up the threads. And sort out the situation with Beth. He was both dreading the imminent meeting with his wife and looking forward to having it over with. It had been on his mind almost continuously, in spite of his resolution not to dwell on it, and he still wasn't sure how he was going to resolve matters between them, or even if he could. Maybe she had mellowed with the passage of time. Maybe. He doubted it, particularly if Duncan had had to carry out his instructions.

Sir Anthony Peters finally returned home from his lengthy honeymoon in Europe on the thirtieth of January 1744, alighting from his carriage outside the house and being waylaid before he could mount the steps and slip through his front door to safety.

Duncan opened the door and stood calmly waiting as the baronet replied to the polite enquiries of the extremely beautiful young woman who had come flying across the street in a most unladylike manner on seeing his carriage.

Word was already all over town, thanks to Lady Winter, that Sir Anthony had fought a duel in defence of his wife's honour, and that she had taken exception to his behaviour and had left him. It was most exciting, and the first person to hear the details from the horse's mouth would be able to dine out on it for weeks. That Lydia Fortesque was not to be that person was obvious from her petulant expression as Sir Anthony made his excuses, holding his left hand to his forehead whilst clinging to the railings with his right, migraine and exhaustion written in every line of his turquoise-clad body.

While he was waiting for his brother to get rid of the troublesome wee besom, Duncan ran through the news that Alex would be anxious to hear, news of the welfare of the clan. It was always the first thing he asked about when returning home after an absence. He would be pleased to know that Janet MacDonald, after keeping Simon MacGregor waiting for two years, had finally agreed to marry him. The couple had celebrated their impending nuptials with such enthusiasm that the priest had been called in more speedily than expected, to avoid embarrassment. The baby was due in March. Alasdair's wife Peigi had given birth to twin boys, who had both survived. Alex would also be very pleased to know that the cattle raid led by Duncan and in which the whole clan had taken part, had been spectacularly successful, and had cost only four lives, all of them Campbells, which was cause for further rejoicing. The resultant funds had ensured that the MacGregors would not starve this year.

Alex would be less pleased to hear about Kenneth MacGregor, wife of the unfortunate Jeannie. When Duncan had told Kenneth that her brothers and Alex had agreed to him dealing with her treachery himself, he had merely nodded wordlessly. Then to everyone's surprise, he had turned and marched straight into his house, knocked his wife out with one blow to her jaw, and had immediately smothered her with a pillow, holding it over her face until long after she was dead. She had not suffered. The same could not be said of Kenneth, who, once sure that Jeannie had stopped breathing, had uttered an unearthly cry that sent shivers down the spines of everyone within earshot, and had drawn his dirk.

It had taken six of them to stop him cutting his own throat and to disarm him, and another two weeks of constant supervision before they were certain that he would no longer try to take his own life. He had by then accepted that no one doubted his own loyalty to the clan, in spite of his wife's treachery.

The baronet had succeeded in shaking off his interrogator. Holding his head and looking unutterably weary, he climbed the steps and walked into the hall. The door closed behind him. He straightened, called Lydia several rather cruel, but reasonably apt things in Gaelic and looked at the brother he had not seen for over six months. Duncan waited for the greeting, for the inevitable question. He would tell him about the cattle raid first.

"Where is she?" said Alex.

CHAPTER FOURTEEN

"She isna here," said Duncan. "She left a few days ago."

"Christ, man, did ye no' get my letter? I asked ye to hold her here, by force if ye had to!" Alex said irritably, reaching up automatically to scrub his fingers through his hair and instead dislodging his wig, which landed on the floor of the hall. A small cloud of scented white powder puffed out of it. Duncan eyed it with distaste. He looked back at his brother. His expression didn't change.

"Aye, I got your letter," he said. "It was waiting for me when I got back from waving her off to Manchester."

"Hell, Duncan, could ye no' have gone after her? Ye could easily have caught up wi' her, and…"

"No, I couldna," Duncan interrupted firmly. This was not at all how he had envisaged the reunion with his beloved brother to go. "I dinna ken what's between you, Alex, but whatever it is, I hardly think it'd have helped matters if I'd abducted her from a public coach and locked her up here against her will for a week, do you? Unless you think she's about to betray us. D'ye think that?"

Alex wiped a hand across his face, smearing his heavy make-up. His eyes were bloodshot. The fatigue he had shown to Lydia Fortesque had not all been an act to get rid of her; he really was very tired.

"No," he said wearily. "No, I dinna think that."

"Well, then," said Duncan. "Go and wash that disgusting stuff off your face, and lie down for a wee while. Then we'll talk."

He watched his brother slowly climb the stairs, then shook his head and made his way to the kitchen to give Iain and Maggie the news that Alex was home, and warn them of the possible range of moods he might be in when he came back down.

Alex reappeared three hours later, washed, changed and, albeit briefly, rested. As he walked into the cosy warmth of the kitchen with its appetising smells of roasting meat and whisky, the three occupants looked up at him, their faces welcoming but wary. He had no desire to be either confrontational or confiding and was aware that they would take their cue from him.

"So," he said brightly, grabbing a plate from the dresser and helping himself to a slice of beef, putting on the face they would be most relieved to see. "What's been happening in Scotland while I've been away off gallivanting in Europe?"

If Iain and Maggie were relieved that Alex had reverted to his more predictable self, Duncan was not. That Alex was genuinely pleased at the news of the successful cattle raid, the wedding of Janet and Simon, and the tiny additions to the clan, and was deeply concerned about Kenneth MacGregor's mental health following the death of his wife was obvious. That he was also very unhappy under the bright exterior was also apparent, although only to Duncan. Alex was a consummate actor, after all, and not only when wearing white paint and gaudy clothes. But Duncan, who was the only person in whom Alex normally confided, was not easily fooled. They were too close for that.

The fact that after two days Alex had made no mention whatsoever of Beth, and had shown no signs of confiding in him, left Duncan in no doubt that his brother had noticed his initial look of distaste, and assumed from that that Duncan was on Beth's side. Erroneously, as it happened. He was not in the business of taking sides. But this assumption told Duncan that Alex felt himself to be in the wrong and was in a defensive, and therefore volatile mood. Duncan played along with his brother's façade of cheerfulness, and waited for the dam to burst. He did not mention Beth's parting words, deciding to wait until Alex asked about her.

Alex made only one visit dressed as Sir Anthony, then instructed Iain to tell all callers that the baronet was away on business. On his return from Edwin and Caroline's he informed the others that whatever Angus was doing, he had not succeeded in stopping Prince Charles from leaving Rome.

"It's known that Charles left Rome on the ninth," he said. "Apparently he tellt everyone he was going to Cisterna to hunt, and as soon as he was out of Rome, he disguised himself as a courier and went in the opposite direction. The latest information is that he's embarked for Antibes, and he's in a hell of a rush to get to France."

The company were silent for a minute while they absorbed this news.

"Do the Whigs suspect that Louis is about tae invade, d'ye think?" Duncan asked.

"Christ, I hope not," Alex said, tearing his fingers through his hair. "I tellt Edwin about my spying venture in Rome, and that Charles is hoping to marry Louis' daughter. Hopefully it'll get back to Carteret and the Elector, and they'll think that it's love rather than war that's inspiring Charles' headlong dash for France. I'd imagine Mann's already written to Newcastle wi' the news, anyway. He was certainly eager when I tellt him about the betrothal in Florence. I canna do any more."

The following evening, after Maggie and Iain had gone to bed, Duncan shared a bottle of wine with Alex, reluctant to leave him alone. He was not eating properly, Duncan noticed, and had dark shadows under his eyes. He seemed even more distracted since he'd returned from the Harlows, and Duncan thought it was due to more than just the news about Charles, bad as it was. He could not force his brother to confide in him about Beth, but he could at least give him an opening.

"Did Mr Harlow tell ye something else yesterday?" he ventured.

Alex looked up from his gloomy perusal of the fire.

"No. Nothing relevant, anyway. Caroline's had a laddie. He's a bonnie wee thing. Why d'ye ask?"

"Ye seem more distracted since ye've seen them, that's all," Duncan said. He sipped his wine and waited. There was silence for a minute or two, after which Alex sighed and put his glass down on the table.

"Aye, well, I tellt Edwin a lie yesterday, and I dinna feel good about it, that's all."

"Ye had to, man," Duncan pointed out. "Surely it's worth it, if it puts George off the scent?"

"Aye, I ken that, and I'd tell worse lies than that, if I had to." He frowned. "When I started all this Anthony stuff, I didna think it possible that I'd ever come to like a Hanoverian, Duncan. But Edwin and Caroline have become good friends. They're honest, good people, and they genuinely care for me and B...for us." He paused for a moment, clearly debating whether or not to say more. Duncan remained silent.

"Caroline asked me to be godfather to the bairn," he said after a while. "She wanted to call him Anthony, after me."

This was not what Duncan had hoped Alex was going to confide, although he was obviously upset about it. Having a child named after you was a great honour. He did not ask whether his brother had agreed to Caroline's proposal. It was out of the question.

"What excuse did ye give them?" he asked.

"I tellt them a whole lot of nonsense about being superstitious. I said I'd been godfather tae three bairns before, who'd all died young. Caroline was awfu' hurt at first, but I managed to persuade her that I was truly terrified the baby would die. I couldna let her name the laddie Anthony. If I'm ever discovered, the poor thing would have to carry the stigma of being named after a traitor for the rest of his life."

"Ye did the right thing, Alex," Duncan said. "Although if the invasion succeeds, he'd be named after one of the greatest heroes of the Stuart restoration."

Alex smiled grimly. "Aye. Though I doubt Edwin and Caroline would see it that way. But it doesna make me feel any better that I lied to them. To both of them. And used Edwin too. I feel guilty, that's all. It'll pass." Alex stood suddenly.

"I'm no' in the mood for drinking tonight," he said. "I'm away to my bed."

He knows, thought Duncan, as the door closed behind Alex. *He knows that I was about to ask him whether the Harlows had broached the subject of Beth, and what he was going to do about her.* He sighed, and drained his glass before turning down the lamp and making his own way to bed.

The situation would not get better with time. But there was no point in pressing him to talk about his feelings, Duncan knew that. When Alex was ready, he would talk, or act. Until then, there was nothing any of the MacGregors could do, except be there for him.

* * *

On the thirteenth of February, at the inconvenient hour of four a.m., the third and final instalment of the MacGregor family returned, at last, from Europe. Alex, who had only been asleep for an hour before being roused by Duncan with the news, stumbled downstairs into the dining room, dressed only in hastily-donned breeches, bare-chested and barefoot. Duncan, looking equally sleepy, was coaxing the embers into a blaze, while Angus, who should have been tired after the events he had just experienced, was instead bursting with energy and brimming with wakefulness.

"......so hard in my life," he was saying as Alex came in. "God, he's amazing. Hello, Alex, I'm back. D'ye ken, he rode from Rome to Genoa in five days? *Five days!* He had almost no sleep, hadna changed his clothes and lived on nothing but eggs, so he tellt me, and I've nae cause to disbelieve him. He couldna get anyone tae take him in a boat frae there, so he carried on to Savona. That's where I caught up wi' him. I was still recovering from the trip in." He grimaced, remembering the state he'd been in when he'd staggered off the felucca at Savona, sick and faint, only to discover within a day not only that his ordeal had been in vain, but that he was about to have to make the return trip through even rougher seas, if the prince got his way.

"I'm sorry, Alex," Angus said from his chair near the fire, looking at his brother, who had taken a seat adjacent to him. Duncan, having stoked the fire to the best of his ability, sat down opposite. "I said what ye tellt me to, and I really tried to persuade him to turn back, but no one short of God himself could ha' stopped him then. I thought the best thing was tae head back to France wi' him, to protect him."

"Aye, I ken that, man. Ye did the right thing," Alex said. "It's known, though, that he's on his way. He did well, all the same. The British didna suspect a thing until the twenty-first."

"We were in Monaco by then," Angus said, pausing to take a bannock from the plate Duncan had thoughtfully brought up from the kitchen. He took an enormous bite. "It'll be a cold day in Hell before I cross the sea again, I can tell ye that. It doesna get easier with practice," he said indistinctly. He swallowed. "Anyway," he continued in a clearer voice, "when we arrived in Antibes it got really interesting, because the

English had sent a pinnace tae intercept us, and it was so close tae us when we were in port that it nearly scraped the stern." He laughed delightedly, and his two brothers, relieved beyond measure that he was home safe, laughed with him, and entered for a time into his exhilaration, putting to one side all the issues that might arise from the prince's unwise journey.

The heat from the fire started to penetrate the room, casting a rosy glow over the animated features of the three brothers as the youngest continued his tale.

"The governor had been told to expel any vessel that landed from Monaco or Italy, because of the plague, but Charlie sent a message to say that a great secret'd be revealed tae him, if he'd only be rid of the English boat. So the governor, being of a curious disposition, said both boats had tae go, but the English one first, and as soon as it was out of port, the prince went and revealed himself to the man, Villeneuve, his name is."

"I bet that pleased him," Duncan said dryly.

"I dinna ken, but he took our side, and that's what matters," Angus continued. "He had us transferred to another ship, which was just as well, as Matthews, that's the admiral of the British fleet, ye ken, sent in a wee boat on the pretext of obtaining supplies, but really just tae take a look round. Villeneuve was brilliant. He gave the captain of the felucca that brought us in a real dressing down, and tellt him tae leave immediately, which he did, closely followed by the British ship. But of course we werena on the felucca, but in Antibes, enjoying the hospitality of the governor. And very hospitable he was. There are some awfu' bonny lassies in Antibes, as well," he said happily.

"Christ, man, ye'll be dead of the pox before you're twenty," Alex said disgustedly.

"No, I willna. I've got they sheepskin condom thingies

ye can buy. They're no' so bad when ye get used to them. I'll come to my wife pure as a virgin."

Alex and Duncan snorted in unison, but Angus only half heard them, he was so fired up, reliving the events of the last days.

"We were stuck there for six days, wi' Charles climbing the walls, but he had to wait until he heard from Villeneuve's superior, some Marquis of something."

"Mirepoix," suggested Alex.

"That's the laddie. Anyway, the message came in that we had to be kept in quarantine for eight days and then we could go, but the governor had sent another courier to the Foreign Minister in Paris wi' a bit more information. I think he knew there was something important going on, and that when Louis knew about it he might want to stop Charles going on to Paris. Charles kent that an' all, and as soon as the first message came in from Mirepoix, saying we could leave, Charles acted on it, persuaded Villeneuve to let us leave, and we all rode out the next morning, without waiting for the reply from Paris."

"What date was that?" Alex asked, considering. He had spoken to Edwin yesterday, and it still wasn't known exactly where the prince was, although the duke of Newcastle had received a coded letter from someone in Paris, which was in the process of being decoded, and which the duke was apparently very excited about. The contents were not yet known. Sir Anthony had shown only a mild interest in what they might prove to be. Alex was somewhat worried. Had he known the letter to be from Francois de Bussy, French diplomat and King Louis' trusted representative in London, he would have been very worried. Had he known that de Bussy was also known as 'Agent 101', had been recruited by Walpole a few years earlier, and was now, after all this time, about to prove his worth to the British government, he would have been desperate. But of course he did not know that. Edwin, his main informant at the moment, did not know that. King George, who would tell him a great deal more later, also did not know that.

Angus was thinking. "Oh, hell, I dinna ken the date, wait, it was a Wednesday, I think, and we got to Avignon three days later, on the first. The twenty-ninth, then? Aye. We were dead on our feet. And the roads were dreadful, as bad as any I've seen. But we didna stop there, we set off again the next morning. That's what I was saying when ye came in, Alex. I've never seen anything like him. He rode like the devil all the way to Paris, eating in the saddle, not changing his clothes, none o' that fancy palaver ye'd expect from a prince of the blood. And cheerful! He was laughing and jesting all the way. He means to take the throne, and it'll take a better man than that German shite George to stop him!" Angus's eyes shone with fervour and adulation. Charles at his best had that effect on people. Alex had seen him work the same magic on Beth. He said nothing. He didn't want to burst his younger brother's bubble now, but he knew that however worthy Charles Stuart was, he could not take the throne alone, and his sudden appearance in Paris was not likely to endear him to the French king..

"How did Louis take it?" Alex asked the question uppermost in his mind. A thin grey light was starting to seep through the closed curtains. In an hour or so Maggie and Iain would get up, and then Angus would have the pleasure of telling his story again. If he wasn't fast asleep by then.

Angus sat back and stretched his legs out. The strain he had put his body through in the last weeks was starting to make itself felt; his muscles were stiffening. He rotated his shoulders and flexed his arms. The whisky bottle had also been liberally passed around between the three men, and he could feel its effects, a little. But he was not sleepy yet.

303

"I dinna ken," he replied. "I didna think it wise to go there, with everything that had happened before. I didna think ye'd be wanting Sir Anthony's manservant to be seen to be openly associating wi' the Stuarts. I parted company wi' Charles at the gates, then made some enquiries, found out ye'd been released days before and figured ye'd come home, so I followed ye. Did I do wrong?" he said, looking at his brother, whose forehead was creased with worry.

"No," Alex reassured the youth, leaning over in his chair and squeezing his shoulder. "Ye did right. Ye couldna have found out much, anyway, and it could have caused problems here, for all of us. What's done is done. We just have to pray Louis doesna take exception to it, and call off his invasion."

"Ye should get yourself off to bed, man," Duncan suggested, thinking to do the same thing. "Ye look dead on your feet."

Angus looked at the window, at the strengthening light, and made a reasonably accurate estimate of the time.

"No," he said, "I'll wait a wee while, till Beth gets up. I dinna want you telling her my adventures while I'm sleeping, and I canna trust ye not to." He smiled, then the smile faded as he looked at Duncan's face. "What's wrong?"

"She's no' here," Alex supplied before Duncan could speak. "She's in Manchester, visiting wi' friends."

"Ah," said Angus, clearly disappointed. "But ye've sorted out what's between ye, right? She'll be back in a day or so?"

There was a taut silence. Seeing that Alex was not about to reply, Duncan did it for him.

"She left before Alex got home. He didna get back until the end of January."

The atmosphere in the room changed subtly. Duncan shot a warning look at his younger brother, who ignored it.

"Ye mean to tell me you've been home for nigh on two weeks, and ye ken where she is, and ye havena been to see her…"

"Leave it, Angus," Alex growled.

"…to beg her forgiveness for the way ye treated her?" Angus continued as though his brother had not spoken. "She loves ye, d'ye ken that, even though you dinna deserve her. D'ye no' care at all for her?"

"Angus," Duncan began.

"Have you met her, Duncan? She's wonderful. Christ, if she was my wife, I'd no' be treating her like shi…"

Duncan watched with weary resignation as Alex's fist ploughed into his brother's face, sending him tumbling sideways out of his chair into the hearth. The last time Alex had hit Angus with intention to hurt had also been in this room. Then the circumstances had been quite different, and Angus had not retaliated. He had no such restrictions on him now, and he leapt up from the hearth, shook his head once to clear it, then launched himself at his brother who had just started to rise from his seat, the force sending the chair and its occupants tumbling over backwards in a flurry of limbs. The two men landed in a heap on the floor, Angus, initially at least, on top.

Duncan continued to observe with some interest as his brothers proceeded to attempt to do each other serious harm, with considerable success on both sides. Angus had filled out a little since he had last seen him, Duncan noticed. He was still slender compared to his eldest brother, but was starting to lose his coltishness. He had put on muscle, on his shoulders and back especially, as was clearly visible through the rent in his shirt, which left his right shoulder and upper arm exposed. As he watched, Angus, who had achieved a little respite from the battle, having just run his brother's head into the door, tore at the flapping material, stripping the remnants of the travel-stained garment off, dropping it to the floor and then joining it as Alex, recovering, took him by the knees. The battle continued.

Yes, give him another year or so, and they would probably be equals in strength, although the older man would still have experience on his side. Alex for instance would not have wasted his advantage by taking the time to remove his shirt while his brother was stunned, as Angus had, but would have followed through immediately and brought the fight to an abrupt end. Duncan picked up the whisky bottle and slowly drained the last inch of its contents. Then he yawned, stretched, stood and left the room, carefully stepping over the small puddle of blood by the door. He was not sure whose it was; both his brothers were bleeding freely from the nose.

By the pump in the yard stood two buckets that Iain had filled the evening before, then having been distracted by something, had forgotten to bring in. Duncan rolled up his sleeve, smashed his elbow through the ice that had formed on top of the water, then picked the buckets up and carried them into the house. He smiled at Maggie, who was making her sleepy way down the stairs, woken no doubt by the muffled noises from below.

"Madainn mhath, a Mhairead," he greeted her amiably. "Angus is home," he continued, as though that explained everything, before continuing into the dining room, a pail in each hand. There was a crash as the door opened, as of breaking pottery, and Maggie winced. She took a couple more steps down, then stopped. Duncan did not seem particularly bothered. She sat down on the stairs, yawning, to await the outcome. There would no doubt be a mess, which she would have to clean up.

When Duncan entered the room he paused for a moment to survey the damage. The table had been overturned, breaking the plate, although the empty bottle had rolled harmlessly into the corner. This confrontation had clearly been brewing for some considerable time, which was why

Duncan had allowed it to continue for a while. If he had intervened immediately he would have only succeeded, at best, in postponing the conflict for an hour or two. Hopefully they would now have released enough of their anger to be able to talk it through later without coming to blows again. It had gone on long enough, though. Both men were still conscious, just, and on the floor, Alex straddling Angus, who had his hands round the older man's throat, and was doing his best to strangle him. As Duncan lifted the first bucket, Alex gripped his brother by the ears and lifting his head, smashed it back into the floor with enough force to render a lesser foe unconscious. Angus's grip relaxed slightly, before tightening again. They were oblivious to Duncan's presence, to anything except killing each other. Alex lifted his brother's head again. His face was scarlet.

Duncan threw the freezing contents of the first bucket over his two siblings, followed closely by the second, then went and sat back down. The grunts and dull thuds of the previous minutes were transformed into splutters and Gaelic oaths. A few moments later, the two brothers stood, and approached the chair where Duncan was sitting. Four dark blue eyes, or more correctly three, the fourth being swollen shut, regarded him balefully. Duncan returned their look calmly. Water dripped from the tangled ends of Alex's hair. Angus's face was smeared with watery gore.

"It seems to me," Duncan said conversationally, undisturbed by their apparent hostility towards him. He knew his brothers, and they knew him, "that we all agree Beth is a fine woman. And it's also clear that ye still love her, Alex. So, it strikes me that ye've the two options. Either ye trust her, in which case you really should go and talk tae her and sort out the misunderstanding between you, because she thinks ye dinna. That's why she's left, to go to those who trust her, and who she trusts. She tellt me to tell ye that, if you asked.

Ye havena asked, but I think it's time ye knew it anyway. She said ye'd ken what she meant."

Angus sneezed and moved closer to the fire, shivering. His face was almost unrecognisable as that of the handsome young man who had entered the room a few hours earlier. Alex did not move, but his hands slowly relaxed by his sides. His face had not suffered as badly, but his nose was bleeding, the skin over his ribs was darkening, and there were distinct finger marks on his neck.

"What's the second option?" he said, his voice rasping painfully.

"That ye dinna trust her, in which case she poses a danger to all of us," Duncan said, eyeing his brother carefully. The hands remained relaxed. The violence was over. Hopefully. "Now, ye both ken her well, better than I do, having spent a lot more time wi' her, and are obviously very taken wi' her, in your different ways. So, if the second option is what it's to be, I'll volunteer to go up to Manchester and kill her for ye. I'm no' so close to her as you both seem tae be."

"What?" Angus gasped from his position by the fire. Alex's eyes darkened. Duncan held his gaze, his grey eyes calm, measuring, his body tensed in readiness.

"If ye dinna trust her, Alex, then she canna be allowed to live, with what she knows. Ye ken that well, man. Ye canna have one rule for yourself, and another for the rest of the clan. If any MacGregor proves themselves to be untrustworthy, they must be got rid of."

"She's no' proved herself untrustworthy," Alex said, reluctantly.

"Has she no'?" He held his brother's eyes, saw the hostility, the wish to avoid the issue, to avoid the pain. To avoid the pain, at all costs. By sheer force of will he refused to let Alex look away, pushed through the reluctance, willing him to face it, to recognise that he had to deal with it one way or another, because he could not continue like this. Angus, aware of what was happening, remained wisely silent.

"No," Alex murmured, after thirty interminable, exhausting seconds. "She hasna proved herself untrustworthy."

Duncan relaxed and passed his hand over his eyes, breaking his hold on Alex.

"Then for Christ's sake, man, stop torturing yourself, and her, and go and tell her ye trust her, and bring her back," he said wearily.

"I'm no' sure that she'll come back, if I do," Alex whispered. His eyes were very dark. Duncan hadn't realised until then just how much he loved her, how afraid he was.

"She'll definitely no' come back, an' ye dinna," he pointed out gently. "But she wants to, I can tell ye that much. An' ye leave it too long, she'll likely change her mind, though. It's up to you." He stood, feeling exhausted. What his brothers must feel like, he had no idea. "I'm away to my bed," he said. "I'd suggest ye do the same."

They did. Duncan slept for five hours, Angus for fourteen. When he surfaced, swollen, stiff and sore, and limped downstairs to eat everything in the house and tell Maggie and Iain of his exciting adventures in Europe, his eldest brother was gone. How long he had slept, no one knew. The household settled down to wait, again.

CHAPTER FIFTEEN

The letter from Duncan advising Beth that Alex was all right and was on his way home arrived in Didsbury the day after she did. It was brief and to the point, but annoyingly devoid of any detail. She assumed from it that her husband had not sent any personal message to her, as Duncan would surely have sent it on if he had, and she decided to try to forget about him. That was not too difficult in the first few days, as she had plenty to occupy her mind.

First of all there was the long and very difficult interview with her solicitor, financial adviser and friend Edward Cox, regarding the remaining amount of her dowry, which Sir Anthony had signed over to her, and which was considerable. She had written to Mr Cox to advise him of what she wanted to do, but did not expect him to accept it without a fight. She was right; he did, very courteously, but also lengthily and firmly try to dissuade her from the course of action she was set on, which he finally said in exasperation, his courtesy sliding, was insane.

He was right, it was insane, if you were not in possession of all the facts. As much as Beth liked him, she could not apprise him of them. Finally she had no choice but to override his protests by advising him that it was her money and she could do whatever she wanted with it, and this was what she was set on doing.

Secondly there was the reunion with her friends, which was far more pleasant than the interview with Edward Cox, but not without its own emotional trauma. They had known she was coming. The second letter she had written from London had been to ask them if she could. She had sent it to her old house, and Jane had replied with their new address and a standing invitation.

The house was larger than she had expected and was painted white, with small-paned sash windows and a tiled roof. It boasted three bedrooms, two reception rooms, a decent-sized but overgrown garden which Graeme had already made some headway in taming, and a warm and cosy kitchen, to which Beth was taken by an excited and considerably taller Mary. Graeme was sitting at the table in solitary splendour. He had not changed at all, Beth was gratified to see. He still wore the same homespun breeches and leather waistcoat, and his face was still tanned and seamed from years of work in the open air. Maybe there was a little more grey in his hair, that was all.

He looked up as she came in, and considered her from under bushy eyebrows.

"So," he said, "are you here just for a visit, or have you spent the present we gave you?"

The six sovereigns were still tied up in a cloth in her bag, but she knew what he was asking.

"I don't know, yet," she replied. "Can I stay until I do?"

"If you need me to answer that question before you sit down, no, you can't," he said. He stood up, went to the back door, bellowed something incomprehensible across the yard which made her jump, and came back. She had shed her cloak, and was still standing looking round the room. She was sure she would soon feel at home here.

"Ah, lass, it's good to see you, I'll not deny it," Graeme said, taking her hands and bestowing one of his rare smiles on her. She tried not to think of Duncan, who had done just the same thing. And then Thomas and Jane appeared, Mary re-entered from having taken the bag Beth had dropped carelessly in the hall up to what was to be her room, the threatened tears were washed away in a sea of questions and laughter, and she realised that she did feel at home already.

An hour later she had been fed, watered, taken on a whirlwind tour of the house by Jane and Mary, and delivered back to the kitchen, where Thomas opened a precious bottle of brandy.

"Perhaps we should go up to the drawing-room to drink this," he suggested. "It is a special occasion, after all."

"You'll be sitting on your own, if you do," Graeme said. "It's bloody freezing in there. I'd rather drink water in the kitchen than perch shivering on the edge of a chair in a fancy salon with my finger in the air, discussing the weather or whatever the hell the aristocracy find interesting."

"Who's sleeping with whose husband or wife, mainly," Beth supplied.

"Well, then, I'm not sleeping with anybody's husband or wife, so there's the gossip done with," Graeme said. "Now, are you going to admire that stuff all night, or drink it, as the good Lord intended?"

They drank it.

"It's just like home," Beth said happily after a while. "Although it's strange not to have Grace sitting by the fire, darning socks."

"She felt guilty, leaving so soon after the money came through," Jane said. "But she's much happier with her family, and we all knew it was only a matter of time before we all left Richard's anyway. We should have gone earlier than we did, but it was home to us, and we were reluctant to let go, I suppose. Maybe we hoped Richard would change once he got the commission he wanted."

"Was he really terrible, when he came back?" Beth asked.

"Not at first, no. He was quite reserved. He complained a bit that the house wasn't warm enough, but he seemed to accept it when I said that we hadn't kept fires in unused rooms for economy's sake. It was when his officer friends came to stay that things went wrong." Jane blushed, and stopped, and Thomas took up the story.

"In fairness to them, they were all polite enough when they were sober. And in the evening, when they'd been drinking, we kept out of their way, and just cleared up the mess in the morning. But then something happened, and we all left the next day," he finished abruptly.

"So here we all are!" Jane said brightly. She smiled warmly at her husband. Graeme finished his brandy and refilled his glass, topping up Beth's as well.

"Wait a minute," she said. "I know I've been drinking, but either I'm a lot more drunk than I thought, or you've missed something out. What happened to make you all leave so abruptly?"

It was the eleven-year-old Mary who answered. In honour of the occasion, she and Ben had been allowed a small glass of very well-watered brandy. She sipped at it now, and then looked at Beth.

"One of the soldiers tried to get me to do it with him," she said bluntly. "And when I said I didn't want to, he pushed me up against the wall and tried to do it anyway."

"And then I hit him, and knocked him out!" Ben put in proudly. "And then we ran away before anyone else came."

Beth looked at the skinny figure of the twelve-year-old boy incredulously.

"Ben hit the soldier with the butt of his own musket, which he'd left in the hall. He was very brave," Thomas said, looking at the boy, who grinned.

"Please tell me it wasn't Richard," Beth said. She felt sick.

"It wasn't Richard," Graeme answered. "But before you feel relieved about that, when Thomas and I confronted him the next day he told us that as far as he was concerned the girl had asked for it, and he'd a good mind to haul Ben up before the authorities for assault. It was the officer who'd tried it on with Mary who told Richard he'd do no such thing, and apologised for his drunken behaviour. Then we all left. I haven't seen him since, and I hope I never do," he finished grimly.

Beth took rather too large a gulp of brandy, then looked at Mary, who was still sipping hers, clearly not enjoying it but determined not to pass up this illicit treat. Her colour was rather higher than normal, but otherwise she seemed unperturbed.

"I'm sorry, Mary," Beth said inadequately.

"It's not your fault, Miss," Mary responded. "I didn't encourage him, whatever your brother said. I'm not ashamed."

"Nor should you be, lass. It wasn't your fault," said Graeme. "And as for you, Beth, if it hadn't been for the money you gave us, we'd not be here now. Don't you ever apologise for him. He's nothing to do with you any more."

No, he wasn't. And he no longer had any hold over her. Or those she loved. Thanks to Alex. Or Sir Anthony. No, she was not going to think of him.

"Are you planning to stay long?" Thomas asked, changing the subject to what he thought was safer territory. "You can stay as long as you like, of course. I just wondered."

"I don't know, Thomas," Beth answered. "I'd intended to visit you anyway, when I got back from Europe. I've got some business to do, and I wanted to see you and visit Mary Williamson as well, but I might stay on for a while." She reached for the bottle again, and Thomas moved it out of reach.

"Slow down a bit, Beth," he advised. "You've certainly got a taste for brandy since you've been living in London. Your husband's been teaching you bad habits."

"Whisky," she said without thinking. "It's usually whisky

we drink at home."

Thomas, Jane and Graeme exchanged surprised glances.

"I must admit, I can't imagine the purple popinjay knocking back whisky," Graeme said, amazed. "It's pretty raw stuff. I'd have thought a fine claret or champagne more his style."

"Ah. Well," Beth stuttered. "Em...he's got a couple of Scottish servants, from Edinburgh, and I think they've given him the taste for it. It's quite nice, when you get used to it. Very warming."

"Hmm," Thomas said. "Well, I think you've had enough of this warming stuff for tonight."

She did not demur. She had. Otherwise she never would have made a slip like that. And being tipsy wasn't helping her to forget Alex at all. Quite the contrary. She did not drink strong spirits again for the duration of her stay. Being with people you trusted implicitly and not being able to confide in them was difficult enough when sober; impossible when drunk.

* * *

A few nights later, Graeme was in bed, and was just about to snuff out his candle when there came a light knock at the door. He bade Thomas, as he thought it must be, enter, and swung his legs out of bed, reaching worriedly for his shirt. There must be something wrong.

The door opened and a figure slipped furtively in, shutting the door quickly. Graeme leapt back into bed, drawing his knees up and pulling the sheet up to his neck.

"What the hell are you doing here?" he said rudely. "Get out!"

Instead of explaining, or leaving, Beth laughed.

"You look like an old maid in mortal fear of being

ravished," she said. "I need to talk to you, Graeme."

"Fine," he replied curtly. "In the morning. Out."

She came and sat on the edge of the bed, and looked at him.

"Your virginity is safe with me," she giggled. He moved, threateningly, and she held up her hands in mock surrender. "All right, I'm sorry. But I do need to talk to you privately, Graeme."

"It's not seemly," he said primly, "for you to be coming to a man's room in the middle of the night."

"Oh for God's sake," said Beth, exasperated. "I often used to go to my father's room in the night, and I'm as safe with you as I was with him, and we both know it. And so for that matter do Thomas and Jane, and there's no one else in the house tonight."

Graeme relaxed his legs a little.

"All right," he said. "Talk. But it had better be important."

She talked. It was important. By the time she had finished he had forgotten all about the proprieties. The sheet had slipped down to his waist, revealing his still hard-muscled torso, which was white, although his sinewy arms, face and neck were brown. As she finished outlining her proposal he became aware of his state of undress and reached a hand out to grab his shirt from the stool at his bedside, slipping it over his head.

"Can you do it?" she said.

"Yes, of course I can do it," he answered. "Whether I'm going to or not is another matter."

"You have to," she said simply. "There's no one else I can trust. Not with this."

"I need to know more before I decide, one way or the other," he said.

There was a silence. It became clear that she was not going to volunteer any information.

"If you can't trust me with the reasons why you want to do such a thing," Graeme said finally, "then I won't help you. It's as simple as that." His words were uncompromising, but his tone was gentle, and she raised her head and looked at him intently. She was clearly battling with herself over something, and he didn't move, just held her gaze with his clear light grey eyes. He realised that what he had said was wrong. She was impetuous, or had been, but this act was not. She had thought it through.

Finally she looked away.

"I can't," she said. "It's not a matter of trusting you, Graeme. I'd trust you with my life, you know that. But this involves someone else, and I can't betray their trust. All I can say is this, and it's more than I should; one day it might be discovered that I have no right to that money, and that will probably be the day I need it most. If that happens, Richard will claim it, and I will not let him have it, Graeme. This is the only way I can stop him, if that day comes."

He reached over suddenly and seized her hand.

"What the hell have you got yourself into, lass?" he said earnestly.

"Nothing I don't want to be in," she said.

"Has your husband put you in danger? Is that why you're here?"

She squeezed his hand. The knuckles were swollen and gnarled, but his grip was still strong, secure, safe. When she spoke she did not answer his question.

"You are the only friend I have who has followed your heart, regardless of the cost, Graeme," she said. "I'm taking precautions, that's all. Help me. Please."

Two days later Graeme received a letter, he said, although he didn't show it to anyone, from a friend he had not seen for many years, and who was in Liverpool awaiting passage to the colonies, where he hoped to start a new life. He would like to see his friend before he sailed. Accordingly, the next morning Graeme set off for Liverpool, he said, returning after three days, tired and unaccountably stiff. Thomas and Jane later remarked that they couldn't have got on well, as Graeme had been remarkably tight-lipped on his return home and had volunteered no information about his reunion, saying only that everything had gone as it should, and his friend had been seen on his way.

Beth had been in Manchester for nearly three weeks and had received no further news from London, from either Duncan or anyone else. She had to face up to the fact that Alex must have been home for some time, but had sent no word. Maybe it was time to cut her losses, and try to move on.

She tried. She visited her friend Mary Williamson, who was full of gratitude to Beth for buying Joseph a share in Mr Thwaite's tailoring firm, which meant they could get married next year, and Beth and Sir Anthony would be guests of honour at the wedding, of course. Mary rambled on excitedly about the wedding plans, while Beth smiled and tried not to think of her own marriage, and how short-lived it had been.

On the way home she popped into the Ring o' Bells, to see if there was any news of her servant Martha, of whom there had been no word since she had left the house with her small daughter abruptly, over a year ago. No one had any news of her, but the landlord came striding out to congratulate her on her marriage to Sir Andrew, was it? The landlord remembered him well. An unforgettable fellow, very aristocratic, slightly odd in his dress, but not too high and mighty to comment favourably on the excellent food the inn served.

She had travelled nearly two hundred miles to get away from any reminders of her husband, and it seemed that at every turn there was someone lying in wait to remind her about him.

So when the next morning there was a knock on the door and she opened it, being in the hall at the time, to see Sir Anthony Peters in all his powdered and perfumed glory standing on the step, she thought for a moment that she was hallucinating. Then he spoke, and the illusion was shattered.

"Beth," he said simply, and stopped.

She had not prepared for this, although she realised now she should have. She bit her lip, looked down, then up at him again, not wanting him to think she was afraid of him. Or wanted him.

"Can we talk?" he said, his voice soft. "We have to, I think." He was dressed as Sir Anthony, although his royal blue outfit was unadorned with silver or gold embroidery, and his accent was unmistakably English. But he had none of the flamboyant mannerisms of the baronet. She realised that he had affected only the briefest sketch of Sir Anthony. He wanted her to see Alex, and she did.

A hand descended on her shoulder, and she jumped. Sir Anthony's gaze drifted away from Beth to the man standing behind her.

"Graeme, I believe," he said.

"Mr Elliott," Graeme, who never stood on ceremony, corrected.

"Mr Elliott. That's a Scottish name, is it not?" Sir Anthony said conversationally. Another man had come into the hall now. A handsome man with fair hair. Sir Anthony registered his presence, but did not take his eyes from Graeme.

"Yes," said Graeme. "My ancestors were border Scots."

Beth looked up in surprise. She had not known that. Graeme had never mentioned it before. He didn't look at her. His gaze remained on the baronet. She realised that the two men were assessing each other, as adversaries do.

"They were very fierce fighters, I believe," Sir Anthony said after a moment.

"They still are." It was a challenge.

The baronet nodded slightly, respectfully. Then he looked back at Beth.

"Will you talk with me for a moment, in private?" he asked.

Beth opened her mouth to answer.

"Anything you've got to say, you can say in front of us. I don't trust you alone with her." Beth remembered now that she had not answered Graeme's question as to whether her husband had put her in danger, and he had not forgotten it. His hand was heavy on her shoulder. Thomas had moved closer as well.

"Please, Beth, you know I can't," her husband said.

She looked at him. His eyes were soft, heather-blue, lovely, pleading. Every line of his body radiated uncertainty. She had seen many aspects of Alex in the time she had known him, but she had never seen him unsure of himself. Not like this. Was it an act, to lull her? He was a master of dissimulation. She had no idea what his intentions were. Graeme had a point.

"We'll talk in the garden," she said, breaking her silence. "We'll be out of earshot there, but Graeme and Thomas will be able to watch from the window."

It was a compromise, but the implication was clear. She did not trust him not to lay violent hands on her. Why should she? He had done in the past. She did not know what his motives for coming to Manchester were.

Sir Anthony followed her round the side of the house and across the yard, until she came to a halt by the small ramshackle wooden shed that was serving as a henhouse until a better one could be constructed. He looked back at the house. The faces of Graeme and Thomas could be seen at the kitchen window.

"Right," she said, turning to face him. "No one can

overhear us here. You can speak freely." Her voice was cool. She had used the walk to compose herself. She was ready for anything.

"Have ye tellt him?" He blurted suddenly.

She was mildly surprised by his sudden lapse into Scottish, but supposed it was to be expected. He was telling her that he had come as Alex, and that he trusted her when she said they would not be overheard. It was a start, anyway.

"Have I told who what?" she asked.

"Yon man, Elliott. Have ye tellt him who I am? He suspects something." He was agitated.

She froze in the act of sitting down on a log set in the ground for that purpose. She was not ready for anything, after all. She straightened again.

"Is that why you've come?" she said, her voice icy. "To find out whether I've told anyone about you? To see whether you can limit the damage by just getting rid of me, or whether a wholesale massacre of the household is needed?"

"No, I…"

"Let me reassure you," she interrupted. "I haven't told anybody anything. If Graeme suspects something, it's that you've come here to hurt me in some way, nothing more. Now," she continued, looking down at the ground, and sliding her foot along it experimentally. He followed her movement with his eyes, puzzled. "I'm afraid the ground isn't very slippery here. You can try stumbling on the cobbles and accidentally skewering me if you want, but let me warn you that I doubt Thomas and Graeme will be as easily taken in as Louis was, so you'd better be ready to kill them, too."

"You saw it," he said, aghast. She looked at him, her face set. He had never seen her so cold. His heart sank.

"Yes, I saw it," she affirmed. "And if you kill Thomas, you might as well kill Jane too, because she couldn't live without her husband. She loves him, you see. They trust each other.

So, it looks like you're in for a busy morning. On the other hand, you could, for once, believe me when I say that I have not, and am not going to tell anyone anything about you, now or at any other time. In which case you can go home, because I have nothing more to say to you. I'll leave you in peace to make your decision."

She turned briskly and started to walk away. He realised with crystal clarity that if he let her go now their marriage was over. He reached out his arm to block her way and when she swerved round it, he stepped forward, gripping her elbow and pulling her round to face him.

The transformation was instantaneous, and took him by surprise.

"Let me go!" she screamed, pulling backwards and reaching her free arm up to tear at his fingers in an attempt to free herself. Her fragile control had shattered the moment he touched her and she began to fight him in earnest, to his utter, utter relief. She was not indifferent after all. He could cope with her fear, her hatred, even. As long as she felt emotion of some kind for him, there was hope. He pulled her into his chest, wrapped his arms around her to restrain her. The faces at the window disappeared, and a moment later the kitchen door opened.

"For Christ's sake, Beth, listen to me!" he said urgently into her ear. "I'm sorry. I didna come here to kill anyone. I want to talk to you, that's all. Let me talk. I swear to God, I'll no' lay a finger on you, no matter what happens. Please. Please."

He took a chance, let her go. Graeme and Thomas were walking down the path. Graeme had a sword, Alex noted, and looked as though he knew how to use it. Thomas carried a stout wooden stave. If she ran to them now, it was over. He would not fight for her if she didn't want him. He raised his hands palms out to the two men in a gesture of surrender.

They continued to advance on him.

She did not run. She stood, flushed, her chest heaving, glaring at him. There was no comparison between the ice statue of a moment before and the woman standing in front of him now, fingers clawed ready for defence, or attack. He far preferred the latter. She took a deep breath, steadied herself with an effort and turned to her friends.

"It's all right," she said shakily. "Really. He won't touch me again. We need to talk. Go back. I'm fine."

Thomas showed every sign of overriding her, but to Alex's astonishment Graeme merely looked from Beth to him and then nodded.

"Come on, Thomas," he said. "Leave them."

They remained silent until they were alone again. Beth sat down on the log. Her face was still flushed, but her fingers had relaxed. She folded them on her lap. They were trembling slightly.

"So, talk to me then," she said.

He sat down carefully beside her, keeping a measured distance between them.

"I havena prepared a speech or anything," he said. "I didna realise ye'd seen the duel."

"Anne Maynard told me you'd challenged Henri," Beth replied. "I thought you'd done it as a ploy to keep him from his room while the palace officials searched it. I didn't realise you meant to kill him. I was naïve."

"I had to, Beth," he said. "I ken ye were fond of the man, but I couldna let him live, and take the risk that…"

"I know," she interrupted. "I understand now. I would have done then, if you'd trusted me enough to explain it to me."

He nodded.

"Aye, I should have. I'm sorry. I thought ye'd try to stop me."

"It's ironic, really, isn't it, that it was all for nothing. George knows about the invasion anyway, doesn't he? Is it because Charles went to Paris?"

This was good. They were having a normal conversation.

"No. Well, aye, maybe partly. But it's no' just that. I'm pretty sure there was another informer. Edwin told me that Newcastle had received an important letter. It was still being decoded when I left. I dinna think George would revive the Act suppressing Catholics and declare openly in the newspapers that France is preparing to invade unless he'd received definite confirmation. Someone's given him the invasion plans. But we didna ken that. At least I bought us some time by killing Monselle. And stopped him passing any other information on."

"You shouldn't be here," she said.

"Why not?"

"Aren't Catholics supposed to stay within five miles of their houses?"

"Aye, but we're also supposed to all leave London. George canna have it both ways. It's all a waste of time anyway. There are more Protestant Jacobites than Catholics, but the Whigs are too stupit to see it. Anyway, Sir Anthony's no' a Catholic, he's an Anglican, if he's anything. Anyone'll tell ye that." He looked at her. She was smiling. His heart soared.

"I sent Angus off to try to stop Charles," he said.

"Did you? He didn't have much success, then."

"No, but he's got some wonderful stories to tell ye. He canna wait for ye to get back. He rode from Savona to Paris wi' the prince, but I canna tell ye more than that or he'll kill me. You are coming back?" he finished hopefully.

The smile vanished.

"I don't see the point, Alex," she said.

"We love each other," he said softly. "Is that not point enough? Or I love you at any rate. Ye tellt me ye loved me too. Have you changed your mind?"

No, no, please say no.

"No. But it's not about that," she said, sadly. "It's about trust. Maybe you do love me. But you don't trust me."

"I do!" he protested. "I realise now that I underestimated you with Henri. It wasna about trust, I thought ye wouldna understand. I should have tellt ye, I see that now. I will in future."

"No," she insisted. "I wouldn't have left if it had just been Henri. But you've hidden things from me all along, Alex. And you've lied to me, too. You told me you couldn't have killed Katerina, but you could, and you knew it. You didn't tell me about Jeannie MacGregor and…"

"Did Angus tell ye about her?" Alex interrupted hotly.

"No," Beth said. "He mentioned her in passing. He thought you'd told me about her. When he knew you hadn't, he shut up. I still don't know what happened. I don't want to. That's not the point. You didn't trust me enough to tell me yourself. You didn't trust me not to jump into bed with Louis, either. You thought I'd come here to tell Graeme all about you. You didn't even trust me not to run home from Italy because of the plague, for heaven's sake! You don't trust me, Alex, and I've racked my brains to discover what cause I've given you not to. I can't think of any."

She looked at him. He was still sitting next to her, staring down, apparently engrossed in his shoes. The long lashes shadowed his eyes. The make-up covered his face. She had no way of knowing what he was thinking. It started to drizzle.

"Angus once talked to me about the clan," she said. "He told me how wonderful it is to know that everyone around you is absolutely trustworthy, that they'd die for you, and kill for you too. 'It's all about trust and loyalty', those were his words. I haven't forgotten them, or what his face looked like when he said them." Alex hadn't moved, was still looking down. The rain became heavier.

"So, what use is it if the chieftain, on whom the whole clan depends, is married to a woman he doesn't trust? It renders the relationship meaningless, no matter how much they love each other, and it puts her outside the clan. I can't live like that, Alex, and I don't think you can, either. Whatever I've done to make you mistrust me, I'm sorry. I swear to you I will never betray what I know to anyone. I don't know how to convince you of that, but it's true. It's raining," she said unnecessarily. "I'm going in. If you want to come in, I'm sure Jane will give you something to eat before you leave." She stood up. He remained seated. His eyelashes were wet, because of the rain. He didn't speak. She looked at him sadly, then turned and walked away, one step, two, three. He reached out his arm, remembered his promise, lowered it.

"I was afraid," he said, so softly she hardly heard him. In fact, although she caught the words, she knew she could not have heard them correctly. Alexander MacGregor was not afraid of anything. She turned back. He was still sitting, his hands loosely folded over his knees, but he was no longer looking at his shoes, but at her. His lashes were wet, and not because of the rain. He blinked, took a deep breath.

"I was afraid," he repeated. "I am afraid."

She came back, sat down, looked at him. There was no mockery, no triumph in her eyes. Only concern, and confusion.

"I'm afraid that if ye learn what I'm really like, ye'll no' love me any more," he said. It sounded childish, even to his ears, but if she thought it so, she showed no sign of it. She reached over, took his hand, carefully took off Sir Anthony's calfskin glove, and enfolded the strong brown hand of her husband in both of hers. The scar stood out, ridged and white.

"Tell me what you're really like," she said softly. "And I'll tell you if there's anything I didn't already know, or suspect. And I'll tell you if I don't love you any more."

His hand lay passively in hers, the palm broad, the fingers long, immensely powerful, utterly helpless.

"I've killed, many times, ye ken that. But I've killed no' just in the heat of battle, but in cold blood, too. And once, in pure temper, when there was no need. I was young, then, younger than Angus. You're right, I would have killed Katerina, aye, without hesitation, and I ordered the death of Jeannie, and would have carried out the sentence myself, but her husband asked to dae it instead. I'm protective of those I love, and I'm jealous, too. I dinna always see reason, and I've an awfu' bad temper. I can be violent without good cause, at times." He couldn't bring himself to look at her, afraid of what he might see in her eyes.

"I've a pretty bad temper, myself," she said.

"Aye, ye have," he confirmed absently. "I love danger and adventure. I hate being Sir Anthony at times, but I love it, too. I like to think that I'm forthright and honest, but I'm no'. I prefer to fight face to face, wi' sword and dirk, that's true, and I'll no' be sorry to see the back of Sir Anthony when the time comes, but I also love the acting and the deception, and the risks. I enjoy making fools of George and Cumberland and all the others. And I've dragged my brothers, and the clan, and you as well now, into it, and I'm playing with your lives, and I'm ashamed of that."

"But not enough to stop," she said.

"No, not enough to stop, which makes it worse. And I've nae right to do that. I'm no' God, I shouldna be acting as though I am. I could get you all killed."

"We could get you killed, as well," she said.

"Aye, but that's a risk I'm willing tae take."

"Has it not occurred to you that maybe it's a risk we're willing to take, as well?" she replied. "It seems to me that the

MacGregors relish danger, to a man, or woman. I know I do. I don't think you're leading them, or me, anywhere we don't want to go."

There was a silence. The rain had softened back to a thick drizzle, silvering his ridiculous powdered wig, darkening his horrible velvet suit. In a minute his paint would start to run. He didn't care. He was concentrating fiercely on the slender white hands holding his.

"Look at me, Alex," she said firmly. He hesitated, then looked at her. "You haven't told me anything I didn't know or suspect before I married you in Rome. Your clan loves you, and so do I. I might not always like what you do, and I might question your judgement, belligerently at times, but I still love you, and as long as you're honest with me, I always will. In fact I'll still love you if you're not honest with me. I think I'll always love you, God help me. I'm a lost cause." She smiled at him, and he returned the smile, tentatively. "But I won't come back with you, and stay with you, unless you stop hiding things from me, and learn to trust me, like you trust Angus and Duncan. They know all the horrible, dark, evil things about you, and still love you. Why should I be any different?"

"You're not," he admitted. "Well, you are, I dinna want tae ravish my brothers every time I see them, but ye ken what I mean." His lips curved upwards, then he was serious again. "I love you, Beth. I love you so much it's made me blind, I think. Angus kens you better than I do. He said you could be trusted, he said ye wouldna be scared away so easily. But I couldna see how you could possibly still love me, if you really knew me. Christ, I'm sorry, Beth. It's no' too late to mend, is it?"

"You underestimate yourself, and me," she said. "No, it's not too late."

When Thomas, watching from the window, saw Sir

Anthony leap to his feet and lunge at his wife, dragging her roughly from the log she was sitting on and crushing her to him, he grabbed his stave and moved to the door.

"Wait," Graeme, who hadn't moved, said. "I think that's what you'd call a reconciliation."

Thomas maintained his grip on the stave, but went back to the window. It was without doubt a reconciliation, even though Beth was clearly unable to move, her arms trapped and her feet several inches off the ground.

"What the hell does she see in him?" Thomas asked, watching in amazement as the baronet finally replaced her on her feet and released her arms, which immediately wound themselves round his neck. They appeared to be crying, or laughing, or both.

"Christ knows," Graeme said. "And I think we'll get to know too, in good time. When they're ready to tell us. She's happy, that's the main thing. And I'm willing to make allowances for any man who makes her happy. He's not what he seems."

"What do you think he is?" Thomas asked.

"I don't know what he is. But he's the man she's chosen, and she loves him, and that's enough for me. For now," he said.

* * *

They lay together in bed, she with her head pillowed on his shoulder, one hand lightly resting on his chest, which was damp with sweat from their lovemaking. His arm was wrapped loosely round her, as much to stop her falling out of the bed as anything. The narrow bed, whilst more than big enough for one person, was not designed for two, particularly when one of those people was half as broad again as an average man. But the couple were not complaining, and had taken full

advantage of the necessary intimacy such cramped quarters
had forced on them. They lay in companionable silence for
a while until their breathing returned to normal, revelling in
the small familiar things that they had both missed so much
about each other, and had thought never again to enjoy. The
sweet smell of her hair, and the delicate touch of her fingers
as she gently ruffled the light dusting of hair on his chest;
the feel of his bicep flexing against her shoulder as he shifted
position slightly, and the gentle strength of his long fingers
curled possessively round her hip.

After a while she sighed, and in the dim light felt rather
than saw his head turn to look at her.

"Are ye sore?" he asked softly. "It's been a while. I didna
mean to hurt ye."

Her heart lifted as she heard the soft Scottish burr of
Alex, rather than the clipped English tones of Anthony.
Partly because it was Alex and not the baronet she had
missed so dreadfully. But mainly because by accepting her
assertion that it was safe to speak in his normal voice, as
none of the household would dream of listening at the door,
he was showing that he had, at last, begun to trust her. As
long as they trusted each other completely, nothing could
ever come between them again, she was sure of that.

"No," she said, planting a kiss on his shoulder. "I am a bit
sore, but it's wonderful. No, I was just thinking how nice it
would be if we could just stay like this forever and not have
to…you know."

He did know, exactly, and sighed himself.

"Aye, I must admit, I miss Scotland sorely. I've often
thought myself how it would be if I gave it all up, this Sir
Anthony business, and just went back to being the chieftain
o' the MacGregors again."

"And how would it be?" she asked.

"Wonderful," he said. "To smell the clean air again, to

work wi' my muscles instead of my head, and wash the sweat off in the loch at the end of the day before coming home to a good honest meal. To face my enemy wi' a sword and dirk, openly, instead of a flurry o' lies and deceit. And to wear the feileadh mór and the plaid, instead of these horrible tight satin breeches. I'm terrified that I'll castrate myself every time I sit down."

Beth giggled.

"I don't think there's any danger of that," she said. Indeed, he had just proved beyond doubt that three years of wearing skin-tight trousers had done nothing whatsoever to hinder his performance in bed.

He smiled and settled her closer to him.

"It sounds wonderful, though," she said wistfully. "Running around in the heather all day and swimming naked in the loch."

"Ye'd no' be swimming naked in the loch or such frivolities," he growled. "Ye'd be in the house, lassie, waiting for me to come home from toiling in the fields, providing me wi' a hearty meal before I ravished ye."

It still sounded wonderful.

"From what Maggie's told me, it's the women who do all the toiling in the fields, while the men sit around telling tall tales of their prowess on the battlefield. And in bed."

He made a non-committal sound in the back of his throat.

"Aye, well, we've got our own toiling to do, in London," he said resignedly. "If Louis doesna use Charles's appearance in Paris as an excuse to call the invasion off, they'll be landing in a few weeks. And Charles wi' them, I shouldna wonder. We've a lot to do, if we're to succeed. We'll be more use in London than in Scotland right now."

"I know," she said miserably. "But I'm sick of it. I can stand the boredom and the pointlessness of the society life, now I've got you. But it's the lying to friends I hate." Alex

331

had told Beth earlier about Caroline's request that he be her son's godfather, and the lie he'd told Edwin. "I hate lying to Graeme, Jane and Thomas, as well. It's horrible. And I've never been to Scotland. I'd love to see it, the mountains and the glens, the heather and the lochs, and to meet all the clansmen you've talked about."

"It isna so romantic as I've maybe painted it, Beth," he said. "I'm missing home, ye ken, and that makes ye think only of the good things. It's a verra hard life, and a dangerous one. Ye often have to go hungry, in the winter. And it rains a lot, and is damn cold a lot of the time, too."

"Even so," she said, the yearning in her voice for the land she'd never seen matching that in his heart for his home.

He sat up suddenly, pulling her with him, and turning her to face him.

"Is that really what ye want?" he said.

She blinked at him, surprised by his vehemence.

"Well, yes, of course it is," she said. "Isn't it what you want, too?"

"Aye, though I'd thought tae wait until James Stuart was on the throne."

She stared at him, stunned.

"Are you telling me you intend to give everything up that you've worked for and go home?" she gasped.

He took her by the shoulders, gently, and looked into her eyes.

"Aye, if it's truly what ye want," he said.

He was serious. He'd dedicated his whole life to restoring the Stuarts to the throne of Britain, and for the last three years had walked the tightrope of being Sir Anthony, knowing the terrible fate that awaited him if he fell, and thinking the freedom his clan would earn if the Stuarts succeeded worth the risk. And now he was willing to give it all up.

A great surge of love welled up in her, bringing a lump

to her throat and rendering her incapable of speech. Tears pricked in her eyes. That he would do this, abandon his prince, sacrifice everything, for her. She closed her eyes, swallowed hard, then swallowed again.

"No," she said, her voice trembling. "No. I can't ask you to do that for me. And, in truth, we've come so far, I'd never forgive myself if we stopped now. We'd regret it for the rest of our lives."

"I wouldna regret it, if I had you," he said simply.

"You have me, anyway, whatever happens," she said, the tears overflowing. "No, I want to see James ride into London, and see him crowned, with you by my side, holding my hand. And then we can go home."

"Ye could end up by my side on the gallows, if it doesna go according to plan," he reminded her.

"True." She smiled, and leaned forward to kiss him. "But I won't regret it, if I have you."

About the Author

Julia has been a voracious reader since childhood, using books to escape the miseries of a turbulent adolescence. After leaving university with a degree in English Language and Literature, she spent her twenties trying to be a sensible and responsible person, even going so far as to work for the Civil Service. The book escape came in very useful there too.

And then she gave up trying to conform and resolved to spend the rest of her life living as she wanted to, not as others would like her to. She has since had a variety of jobs, including telesales, teaching and gilding and is currently a transcriber, copy editor and proofreader. In her spare time she is still a voracious reader, and enjoys keeping fit and travelling the world. Life hasn't always been good, but it has rarely been boring. She lives in rural Wales with her cat Constantine, and her wonderful partner sensibly lives four miles away in the next village.

Now she has decided that rather than just escape into other people's books, she would actually quite like to create some of her own, in the hopes that people will enjoy reading them as much as she does writing them.

Follow her on:
Facebook:
www.facebook.com/pages/Julia-Brannan/727743920650760

Twitter:
twitter.com/BrannanJulia

Pinterest: www.pinterest.com/juliabrannan

Made in the USA
Columbia, SC
20 May 2018